On
Borrowed
Time

Jacklin Kimkris

DEDICATION

To Jack, my son and best friend,
and to Tuk and Doc
wherever you two are raisin' hell

ACKNOWLEDGMENTS

Thank you to all friends old and newly acquired over the course of this writing adventure. To those who encouraged, prodded, inspired, reviewed, edited, and aided in research and publishing, I owe a huge debt of gratitude. You have helped make a dream come true.

FORWARD

After thirty-seven years in the insurance business, the American frontier history has become a second life career. It has brought about performances of Wyatt Earp and Doc Holliday bio-dramas and the writing of a one-man show on Will Rogers.

Yet Jacklin Kimkris has, with her historically based fiction, <u>On Borrowed Time</u>, given me an experience as entertaining and adventuresome as any I have known. This will be a page-turner for both the "baby boomers" and the present day generation.

Her use of a "time portal" permits a valid story of two eras. The vivid description takes you there and yet the pace is crisp enough to appeal to the "sound bite" generation. She has true history and present day intrigue that excite the reader side by side.

Wyatt Earp
Actor-Writer &
Blood Relative of Wyatt
Earp

PREFACE

Many a yarn has been spun about the legendary Dr. John Henry Holliday. Friends, enemies, historians, and novelists have depicted this complex man as intensely loyal, murderous, a gentleman, a rogue, a gambler of questionable ethics; anything but boring. The often-contradictory portrayals caught my attention and generated a need to find the truth, the real Doc Holliday. I have often felt that I was born a century too late. The more I uncovered, the more I regretted not having been privileged to know the man. This inspired the story you are about to read.

CHAPTER 1

I had imagined the room to be smaller and the population confined within the wall of steel drawers. Instead, I find myself confronted with several rows of occupied tables, though mercifully draped in white shrouds. It is considerably cooler than I had anticipated, and I mentally rebuke my lack of forethought to bring a jacket. Outside, typical California weather is defying the calendar with a morning temperature of eighty-three degrees. The interior chill is coupling with escalating panic making it impossible to control my shivering. I cringe. The odor reminiscent of freshman biology dissection sessions augments the morbid atmosphere. An attempt to breathe shallowly is making me light-headed as my heartbeat thunders inside my head. I taste the bile in the back of my throat. It takes all my effort to swallow. My legs threaten to wobble. One by one, my senses are deserting me and the self-discipline I am famous for is slipping away. I let my head drop to my chest, bend at the waist, palms on knees, and will back control.

The apprehension that has been building since the officer appeared at my door this morning is evolving into physical distress. He and the coroner on duty stand silently on either side obviously respecting a familiar need they sense in most visitors to this parlor of death. I search for a positive thought to crowd out the anxiety. The mind, more often than not, I tell myself, conjures up far worse than actual reality. Still, someone they think I know is dead.

I have no doubt as to the identity of the victim. Stephanie Deluca, a fellow employee and my neighbor of four years, has been missing for several weeks now. Along with others in our apartment complex, I had been questioned regarding her routine and visitors prior to her disappearance. The Friday before she went missing was our usual movie/pizza night, my turn to host. She went back to her unit just after eleven. I had plans with my mother on the next day. Steph had a weekend date. Hence, she was not missed until she failed to report for work on Monday. She had not called in nor was she answering her phone. Knowing we were close and had exchanged keys, our supervisor suggested I go home to check on her. When Steph failed to respond to my knock, I cautiously opened the door and was immediately confronted with physical chaos that reeked of foul play. Without venturing further, I dialed 911. It was immediately determined that Steph was not in the apartment and, in the six weeks since, there has been no word.

After a minute or two, my name is spoken with concern in the tone. I strain to refocus, mentally "buck up."

"Yes." I clear my throat, and swallow again. "Go ahead." Arms clenched stiffly around my body; knees locked in place; I inhale deeply and close my eyes as the coroner begins to roll out the drawer. Recalling the condition of Steph's apartment, I brace myself for the condition of the body and say a silent prayer that my friend did not suffer.

"Miss?" I feel the slightest contact at my left elbow, and slowly open my eyes. One squinted glimpse triggers my gag reflex. I whirl away slamming into the detective who had positioned himself behind me with such force he has to take a step back to keep both of us upright. Strong hands grip my shoulders. I feel myself being rotated, then a chair seat at the back of my knees. The two men have become shadowy figures floating away and shuffling back again; their voices muffled and echoing. I hear the muted sound of the drawer rolling back into place. An odor far worse than formaldehyde assaults my nasal passages. My head snaps back. I am vaguely aware of the slightest pressure on my face and warmth draping my shoulders. My vision slowly clears, and garbled mutterings become distinguishable words.

"Are you alright, Miss Blakely?" I look up into the kindly face and nod. The detective is in his shirtsleeves. It is his suit coat that is easing my trembling.

"I'm okay . . . really," I lie as I hold up one hand and put the other to my chest. Nothing will ever be right again. My arms become jelly.

"I can assure you that your reaction is quite in harmony with the circumstances; hence our generous supply of smelling salts," says the coroner tossing the expended capsule into a nearby trash receptacle. This must be routine procedure for this man, witnessing the shock and grief of survivors; yet his demeanor is one of genuine empathy.

Likewise, for Detective Paulson, now kneeling at my side, his hand is resting on my shoulder. "Do you need another . . ."

"No!" Panic rules my response, and my hands automatically fly to protect my eyes. My immediacy forestalls the coroner's motion toward the drawer handle. Another look would only permanently imbed the gruesome image in my memory bank. In spite of the discoloration and distortion of swelling, the mop of blond curls, the distinctive mouth, and mole on the left side of the chin leave no doubt.

"It's my mother?" I whisper as a question while my mind grapples with the incredulity of the words. Both men remain silent for the next several minutes, no doubt to allow me time to assimilate the awful truth. I finally nod my willingness to continue.

"Before we go into the details, I need to beg your indulgence one last time, Miss Blakely . . . if you think you are up to it." I look up at him. All inner resources have dissipated. The detective winces. "This is beyond insufferable, I know, but imperative, and for you, I believe, best gotten out of the way as quickly as possible.

Knowing that the worst is behind me, a strange calm settles. A sliver of optimism emerges. The police have killed Mother's assailant and need to know if I can identify him. The chances are nil. My mother has no enemies save for the desperate criminals common to the population as a whole. It will not bring her back, but it will satisfy my need for swift justice.

Grasping the sides of the chair, I let out an "okay, I'm ready" sigh as I nod. Legs aquiver, I am appreciative of the arm behind my back and the hand supporting my elbow as I rise. This time, I raise my head and keep my eyes on the drawer as it rolls toward me. Dr. Calabreze gently pulls back the sheet. I thought I was primed, but nothing could have prepared me for the gruesome display before me. Instantly, I feel reinforced tension of my supporter. If not for the jagged scar on the left shoulder, I would not have recognized the man. Half his face is gone and the rest so mutilated it is unidentifiable. My hand flies to my mouth and I am guided as I stumble back into the chair. I drop my head, completely defeated and, without warning, give in to the first truly unrestrained sob-fest of my life. I have commenced mourning, I know, not only for this present horror, but for every unvented sorrow of my life. My father's death has somehow released me from stoicism he had imposed. I feel a wad of tissue being stuffed between my fingers and sense Detective Paulson again squatting at my side. If not for the arm firmly around my shoulders, I would fall into a limp heap on the floor. He remains silent; making no attempt to quiet me. When the tears are spent, it takes deliberate effort to raise my hand to wipe them away and blow my nose. I take several deep breaths in an effort to regain physical control. My heart rate begins to slow. I am so tired, so cold. Contrary to all reason, I find a sort of peace, then wonder if I am slipping into some form of psychosis. Time becomes meaningless.

"Miss Blakely?"

Mechanically I confirm what the detective already has discerned. "The man is my father, James Martin Blakely. I'm sorry; I really need to get some fresh air."

"Thank you, Michael," the detective directs to the coroner. He squeezes my shoulder, and I sense the encouragement and assistance to stand. I am forced to rely on him for support as we make our way out of the building and into the reviving warmth of the sun and what passes for fresh air in Los Angeles. A second detective standing outside the unmarked sedan opens the door, gently ushers me into the back seat, and places my purse in my lap. The three of us ride in silence for the ten minutes it takes to get to Parker Center. After ushering me to a straight-backed chair across from the desk in his glassed-in office, Detective Paulson motions to his partner who promptly leaves the room. He returns a minute later with a much-appreciated mug of coffee. I cup it in both hands, praying that it will quell the lingering chills. Patience is the detective's forte. He shuffles papers for several minutes. Without thought, I sip heartily. The liquid sears my tongue. I jerk my hand and manage to slosh more over my fingers. The second detective, as if anticipating the mishap, rescues the mug and towels my hands with a handkerchief. I am too numb to be embarrassed. I thank the detective who wipes the mug and hands it back. I blow ripples over the coffee before taking a tentative sip. After a few more, I cradle the mug in my lap. Warmth is returning and I make an effort to relax in the chair.

"I am truly sorry for your loss, Miss Blakely. Contrary to your personal assessment, I can assure you that you are holding up quite well under the dire circumstances." He sighs and pauses. "Regrettably, there are a few questions I must ask as quickly as possible." I nod my cooperation.

"First of all, can you tell us where you were last evening around seven?"

It is taking a concerted effort to recall; seems odd to have to search my memory for yesterday's agenda. Finally, "I was having dinner with a co-worker."

"Did you visit your parents at any time yesterday?"

I scoff at the absurd notion. The detective's brow creases deeply and I panic. "No!" What I had accepted as a routine inquiry, now smacks of an interrogation. Am I being considered a suspect? Alarmed at the thought, I spew out the details of my alibi. "I was at work from eight a. m. to five in the afternoon. We work an occasional Saturday. Jen, a fellow employee, and I went to The Galleria, had dinner in the food court, and then went off to take advantage of the after-Christmas sales. We left around 8:30. I went directly home. Surely, you don't think . . . You can call Jen . . ." I fumble in my purse for my cell phone.

"That won't be necessary," he says gesturing across the table. "I am sorry if I gave you the wrong impression. We know you didn't kill your parents," he says leaning forward. "But tell me; when *was* the last time you saw either of them?"

Relief quickly dissipates with the stab of regret that shoots through me at the all too vivid memory. It was my eighteenth birthday, the day my father evicted me from the family home, the consequence for rejecting his continued monitoring of my every move. I hesitate, toying with the idea of omitting this conceivably incriminating detail but decide to "come clean". If it were to come out later that our parting had been far from amicable, I might just wind up back on the suspect list. "I last saw my father eight years ago on March seventeenth." Again, raised brows tell me that the response is unexpected, and I explain forthwith rather than wait for the detective to ask. "My father is . . . was extremely old school, as they say, and inflexible." I swallow mixed emotions. "He had expectations for me that included an arranged marriage to his protégé." My hand reflexively goes to the left side of my face. "You must think me foolish not to have jumped at the opportunity." The man cocks his head in a question. "Oh come now, Detective, how many men do you know who would give me a second look, let alone want to spend the rest of their life with me, great personality or not."

"Really, it's not that bad and there's . . ."

"Never been an option. Anyway, when I refused to comply, that was it; I was out and on my own . . . immediately . . . with just the clothes on my back . . . literally. Later I learned that he had been caught unawares by my willingness to give up the standard of living to which I was accustomed." I could hear the resentment echoing in my tone. It has been a long time since I have thought about the heart-wrenching confrontation. The memories of living under my father's uncompromising rule, devoid of his affection, had been carefully tucked away in the recesses of my mind where they would not be allowed to interfere with my life. For all practical purposes, henceforth, I was dead to my father and sadly, him to me. The old bitterness rises in my throat, and I quickly take another sip of coffee to dilute it.

"I see," said the detective, as if pondering the weight of this information. "And your mother; were you estranged from her, as well?"

"Not at all. I saw my mother a week and half ago. We met, without my father's knowledge of course, every month or so, to catch up."

"How did *she* feel about the estrangement from your father?"

"My mother is . . . was a truly good woman, kind, loving, a dutiful wife and wonderful mother. Outwardly, she conformed to my father's chauvinism, but inside, she knew he was wrong or rather, as she insisted, temporarily misled." I shake my head. "Whenever I brought up separation, she countered with her marriage vows; that she would love and obey till death did them part. She did, didn't she?" An involuntary shudder escapes. "My mother was resolutely convinced that something in my father's past was responsible for his controlling nature and his lack of warmth; that if she could just find the key . . . that if she loved him enough . . ." I release an exasperated sigh. "I hated to leave her, but . . ." Tears begin again. I retrieve the tissues I had earlier jammed into my purse, wipe my eyes, sniff, and dab at my nose. "I don't know how she did it, with Father in total control of the finances, but she helped me with tuition. My salary still barely pays the rent, and she wanted me to . . ." Without warning, the recent vision of my mother's mutilated face overwhelms me. I reach to absorb a fresh onslaught of tears. At the same time, I realize that I may very well have handed them motive, at least for my father's murder.

Detective Paulson remains silent, but I can feel his eyes monitoring, as if my actions will betray some sort of clue as to my possible guilt. Suddenly, it is too much. I know I am in shock; I am scared, confused, and oh-so tired; and finally, offended at being thought of as a suspect. "*I did not have anything to do with the death of my parents. My father disowned me years ago. I assure you, I will not benefit

7

financially from his death. If murder for inheritance had crossed my mind, I would have killed him that night before he had a chance to officially follow through on his intentions to cut me out of the will. But my Mother, I would never . . . Now, if you will just tell me what *you* know . . ." My tone is as demanding as my waning stamina will allow. "What happened? Was it a robbery? Do you have *any* idea who killed my parents?" As I ask the questions, possibilities dance in my mind. My father's self-appropriated dominion reached beyond our household to include the members of his congregation. Both, from the pulpit and privately, he sought to direct the lives of his flock; and if his ideology was disregarded, he made it plain that *his* church was a place for the obedient. Those who chose a different course were encouraged to attend elsewhere, where, in his opinion, the words of God were "watered down" to be more palatable; all the while warning of the "wide road leading to the fires of hell." I remember how angry Jennifer Power's brother was when my father rebuked her publically one Sunday after he found out she was pregnant without the benefit of marriage. Such was not uncommon for the Reverend Blakley. Could an offended parishioner become outraged to the point . . .

Detective Paulson takes a deep breath and a long pause before answering. "Again, I apologize. We know what happened, but thought you might be able to provide some insight into the circumstances, and you did. I am afraid that the facts are quite disturbing, but, I assure you, leave no room for speculation. It was a murder/suicide."

A wave of guilt crashes over me. "My father . . . I knew I should have . . . Oh my God." Suddenly, I am outraged at everyone and everything. Life is so cruel, like a puzzle we are expected to put together right the first time; and if we do not, we pay the consequences. I want to pound the desk in front of me, but find it physically impossible. Again, the forgotten mug is rescued just in time, as I slump back in the chair. I look across the desk but avoid eye contact. I am not open to any more sympathetic expression. "No!" I aver. "My father was not a nice man. He could be unspeakably cruel, but he never lifted a hand to my mother or me. Words were his weapons. Besides, she would never have given him cause."

"I'm sure she wouldn't," Detective Paulson says softly. He pauses and I know he is choosing his next words with great care. "You see, your father died first, shot in the back of the head while sitting at his desk."

I close my eyes as if that will erase the mental picture and take another deep breath. "It's obvious," I say slowly, "that someone broke in. No, that would have been impossible. It must have been someone they knew and let in."

"We considered that, but had to rule it out. The security system was uncompromised and the log showed no entries the entire day."

"What are you saying?"

"Your mother was found lying on her bed with the gun in her hand. The only set of prints on it was hers. The powder burns on her hands and the side of her head are consistent with suicide."

I feel my eyes swell as this unacceptable deduction takes root in my mind. A new surge of fury erupts. I pull from the last reserves of strength and leap out of the chair towards the desk. "That's absurd. My mother would never . . ."

Detective Paulson does not react to my outburst, but my peripheral vision picks up concerned movements on the other side of the glass, and I feel the detective behind me gently but firmly take hold of my shoulders and guide me back to my seat. Without taking his eyes off me, Detective Paulson raises a hand to quell his colleagues' response, while extending a paper encased in a protective vinyl sleeve across the desk. I sink back into the chair as I recognize the stationery and the handwriting.

To whom it may concern:

I, Elizabeth Jane Blakely, shot my husband, and am taking my own life. The reasons are irrelevant. I ask that you spare my daughter, who had no knowledge of my intentions, any unnecessary grief. Regretfully, Elizabeth J. Blakely

Before my hand involuntarily crumples the document,

a second detective grabs my wrist and snatches it from my grasp. "Again, I am so sorry." The words barely register as a wave of debilitating shock engulfs me. All sensation fades.

When it begins to return, my wrist is still being held, but by another and less firmly. "Welcome back, Cassie." With effort, I flutter my eyes open and see a bearded man of about fifty in a white coat. "Don't be alarmed. You're okay," says the doctor before I can ask. "Had a nasty shock, from what I hear." His smile is calming. He explains that I fainted in the police station. The detectives became concerned and had me transported to the hospital. When I look at the needle in in my arm, he adds, "The IV is to combat dehydration and includes a vitamin cocktail for your nerves and a mild sedative." I acknowledge the second smaller bag of clear liquid above and to the side. The clock on the wall reads 4:20 and below it through the window, I see the sun setting. "What happened here?" he asks running a finger down the jagged scar usually camouflaged by carefully arranged hair.

"Reaching for something I shouldn't." I want to leave it at that but his expression presses for details. "I was nine. The chair I was tiptoeing on slid sideways and I fell; took out a priceless antique on the way down. My arm was repairable; the vase and my face, not so much."

"Pretty sloppy repair job. Who did it?" he asks brushing aside the hair.

"How would I know? I was a kid." I wince at my rudeness, and while not in the mood to apologize, amend my tone. "I suppose they did what they could."

I reach to pull my hair over my cheek, but the doctor takes my hand in his. "I don't agree. It makes no sense. This is fixable. It would have been easier at the time of the injury, but, even now, there is no reason for you to continue to live with this. I can't imagine why your parents . . . that's neither here nor there," he says waving his other hand. "The point is," he says reaching a pocket and putting a card into my palm, "Dr. Benton is a friend of mine. David is a first rate plastic surgeon. Call him. You won't be disappointed." I smile at the nice idea, but my medical plan does not cover elective procedures, and my income barely allows for the hair stylist that makes the imperfection less noticeable.

_____#_____

In a matter of days, my life has taken a U-turn. A lengthy letter Mother had mailed the day before her death, answers all my questions and those generated by the answers to them. While I have yet to make peace with her actions, I now understand the profound agony that drove her to them, and admit that I would be hard-pressed to come up with an alternative that would assure her the outcome she sought.

"Believe me," Mr. Devonshire, the family attorney, says apologetically, "I had no idea what your mother had in mind when she came to me with this." He leans across the massive mahogany desk as I examine the document before me. "As you can see, she saw to it that all necessary details have been decided and are being executed as we speak."

Much to my astonishment, Mother, with Mr. Devonshire's guidance, and of course, her fatal actions, had been able to circumvent my disinheritance. Overnight, I have become the sole heir of an obscenely vast estate that is in liquidation, with the exception of personal mementos Mother knew I would treasure. Mr. Devonshire pauses to let me assimilate. "There is however, a codicil in your mother's will that contains one of those unusual stipulations . . .

CHAPTER 2

Firelight dances off highly waxed pine walls erected over a century ago. The antiquity cradles me in a heretofore-unfamiliar sense of pleasantness. It has been seven months since the death of my parents. In that brief interval, I have gone from a "paycheck-to-paycheck-hope-the-car-doesn't-break-down" existence, to never again having to concern myself with finances; thanks to the skill of Dr. Benton, from ugly duckling to semi-swan, and per Mother's "stipulation", from Californian to Coloradan. She made my inheritance contingent on moving to and residing in her family home outside the small town of Florissant. After living here for a full year, I will be free to dispose of the property as I see fit and live where I choose. So here I sit, in the spacious log home where my mother was born and lived until she ran off to marry my father some thirty years ago.

Tucked away against a hillside in the Rockies the two-story structure was the effort of one man, Jefferson Fielding, in 1875 in preparation for marriage to thirteen-year-old Sarah Higgins the following year. According to the family Bible, they were my great, great, great grandparents. The impressive structure has been carefully maintained and upgraded through successive generations and occupied continuously until the passing of the grandmother I was never privileged to meet. Miriam Collins had been preceded in death by Mother's father, Jackson, in 2003. These facts I learned in another lengthy letter that mother had made sure was waiting for me upon my arrival.

Previously, I had known little of either of my parents' background. Father professed, almost too adamantly, as I think back, that he was an orphan, a self-made man. The only thing I knew about Mother's family was the story my father seemed never to tire of relating to his congregations and us; using it to illustrate the need for strict adherence to God's Word. Wifely submission and the obedience of children were favorite topics for his Sunday sermons. Mother's family was "over the top" on record-keeping and family history. The females, at least, keep personal diaries, all leather bound and engraved, which I discovered on an early exploration of the study just off the living room. Per the family Bible, Jefferson Fielding, the original owner of the property died in 1895, leaving all to his only child, a daughter, Mary. According to the records, the home continued to be passed down to the only child, all daughters, born to each generation thereafter; Emma Bartlett, Miriam DeLong, my mother, who abandoned her home without taking up residence as the owner, and finally, to me.

In spite of the tragic road here, and my apprehension at adapting to life at 9000 feet, I am beginning to feel like a princess in a fairytale. I had never thought of a life outside of Los Angeles, but Mother knew me better than I knew myself. Upon arrival, I fell in love with the family home and knew immediately that the move to Colorado would be permanent. With my newfound wealth, I threw myself into further renovation, careful to preserve the home's rustic charm. Previous generations had kept up with the times. Electricity, propane, premium insulation and a large generator for power outages during storms were already in place, and I had added solar panels.

Not unexpected, a few of the older residents in the area remember my mother and the mini-scandal stirred when she eloped with "the preacher" who breezed through town scorching sinners with his hellfire and damnation revivals. When asked, I simply say that my parents died in an accident. People kindly offer their sympathy and press no further.

A few months shy of twenty-seven, I find myself in the midst of intoxicating beauty that I had previously experienced only through film and the printed page. Florissant, Colorado is nestled in the shadow of Pike's Peak, the view from which I quickly learned, inspired one of our nation's most stirring patriotic songs. I do not miss the rat race of Los Angeles, and since I am free to do whatever I choose, I am toying with doing some writing of my own, instead of editing the work of others. For now, though, I am reveling in my new surroundings, eager to soak up mountain living in all its glory, the quiet, and the unique experiences it has to offer. Freed from the constant bombardment of the outside world, I am getting acquainted with me, sans the baggage of my childhood.

As for life in the mountains, I am discovering that while it can afford all the comforts of modern technology, it compels those who want to enjoy a long, healthy existence, to adapt to a slower pace of life in several ways. Windy mountain roads, many unpaved, are at the mercy of snow, eroding rain, and the ever-treacherous ice, especially the black variety. Wildlife roams freely and bids a driver exercise caution. Ironically, the freeway traffic of LA moves at a much slower pace and requires much more vigilance. I get along just fine without pizza delivery and am adapting to thinking ahead, as it is highly impractical to run out to the market for a forgotten item. Woodland Park does boast a twenty-four-hour Walmart, but it is some twenty-five miles down the pass. Consequently, for the most part people here are different from stereotypical Californians. While I had few, what I would term genuine friends in my native state, here I am finding solid relationships easy to build. I doubt that it is the upgrade in my physical appearance that accounts for my expanded social circle. These rural folk seem to base their assessments on character rather than looks. Honesty and helpfulness abound among the neighboring ranchers who have given generously of their time and effort to help a female tenderfoot prepare for her first winter on the Front Range. There is a standing joke here; the Front Range has only two seasons; winter and the Fourth of July. All kidding aside, there is a sincere warning in the jest. Cal Jenkin, a local logger, has filled my shed with enough wood to last through the harshest of winters. Bill Moss has put me on a regular delivery schedule for propane and will monitor the gasoline supply for the emergency generator. Thanks to David Babcock, my chest freezer teems with a variety of meats, fish, and poultry. The pantry is generously stocked with canned goods and staples recommended by several of the neighbor women. Unexpected treasures line the shelves atop the kitchen cupboards, cookbooks dating back to Sarah Fielding's day, among them, a binder containing her handwritten recipes, which I immediately preserved via scanner before the pencil printing fades beyond deciphering. In the interim years since leaving my parent's home, my diet has been at the mercy of coffee shops, fast food, and microwave fare. Resurrecting and adding to my mother's culinary instruction is on my growing bucket list.

Not one to tiptoe into things, I have acquired three horses, two pigmy goats, a dozen laying hens, and a very vocal rooster who doubles as an alarm clock sans the snooze button. Among *my* contributions to modernization; insulating the barn, installing heaters, and automatic watering. Each of the animals came with on-going tutoring in care and feeding. Paul, who sold me the two mares and the handsome buckskin gelding, helped me with the selection of saddles and tack. His daily riding lessons for several weeks have turned me into what he terms a respectable equestrian. This leap across lifestyles has me vacillating between "Oh my God, what have I done?" and "I can't believe how wonderful this is. What's next?"

CHAPTER 3

"I can't thank you enough for inviting me to share in the festivities with your family. This is delightful." I am with Jim and Nancy Pruitt and their six-year-old twins Jimmy and Janet in Heritage Park, the center of activity today in Woodland Park. It reminds me of the Fourth of July depiction in Sleeping with the Enemy, red, white, and blue accenting a sea of adults, children, and dogs enjoying the food, music, and craft booths; patriots united in celebration of their country's birth. Hot dogs, popcorn, and cotton candy satisfy like fine cuisine. Life is simple here, good at the very core, and have I mentioned the air is fresh?

I make several new acquaintances, many of whom are long-standing friends of the Pruitt's. James and Nellie Masters, a delightful couple in their seventies are here with their grandson, Dr. Jack Johnson. A brief conversation brings me up to date. Jack, who appears to be thirtyish, was raised by his grandparents after their daughter and son-in-law died in a small plane crash when he was just five. Until a few years ago, the three lived on a ranch in Florissant. Jack's demanding schedule and the encroaching restrictions of the elder Masters' age made it advisable for the family to move into Woodland Park. It is here that Jack has his practice. "Grampa and Grandma" bought a lot with two houses a couple of miles from downtown; they live in one and Jack occupies the second. I feel comfortable with them immediately. All are refreshingly honest and share a good sense of humor. Meeting them has saved me the trouble of searching out a local doctor. I make a point of getting the necessary information to have my records transferred from my physician in Los Angeles.

"How are you getting along up in the woods?" I turn to see Deputy Robert Anderson and his wife, Kim, who runs a small gift shop in Divide. "No more prowlers, I trust?" he adds with a chuckle.

"Don't tease her, Bob," Kim chides with a playful fist to his shoulder. "It takes a while to distinguish sounds in the mountains. You'd be hard-pressed to keep your cool in the middle of L. A." Bob nods in concession. "Besides, it's better to be safe than sorry," she says in defense of my nine-one-one prowler call during my first month in residence. I mistook a noise at the side of the house for a break-in. The offending tree branch was promptly taken into custody by Deputy Bob.

I laugh along with them. "Things are great. I promise the next time I call it will be a genuine emergency."

"Let's hope there is no next time," he says. "How do you like Fourth of July in the mountains?"

"I love it," I say enthusiastically. We chat for a while longer before parting ways.

"We're so glad you could come with us." Nancy's hug swells my heart. The fireworks display we are watching, while dwarfed by those in venues I have attended in the past, stirs the emotions no less. On the drive back to the ranch, I meditate on our great nation and the principles on which she was founded; values that are still held dear in Teller County. The day has gone much too quickly, I think as the five of us stand before my front door. Nancy and I exchange another warm embrace. The twins, who have taken to calling me Aunt Cassie, are just as free with their affection, and Jim kisses my cheek before they climb back into the king-cab and depart along the driveway. I make my way out to the barn for one last check on the stock. Another neighbor volunteered for the evening feed in my absence so I could enjoy the holiday with the Pruitts.

Back in the house, I decide to continue my perusal of the

study bookshelves. If I were to be snowed in for a year, I would not be able to put a dent in the reading material stored here for more than a century. Like the cookbook collection, the volumes filling the floor-to-ceiling shelves date from the Civil War Era forward into the latter years of my grandparents. A whole section is devoted to diaries kept by the female members of the family. I noted earlier that Sarah's, if she had penned any, were absent. Below the shelves are cupboards I have yet to explore in any depth. I am drawn to the one on the far left that I recall from my initial probing to be full of old papers and periodicals. I lift them one by one giving full consideration to the fragileness of age and set them gently on the huge oak table that dominates the room before settling in one of twelve matching chairs. One April issue of a Denver paper in 1912 announces the sinking of the Titanic; and lists one of Denver's prominent citizens as a survivor, Margaret Brown, since "Hollywoodized" as the "unsinkable Molly." I make a mental note to scrutinize my miniature morgue at a future time and consider seriously, how I might preserve the treasures therein. I envision many of these frayed yellow scraps framed under glass on the entry wall; others laminated and filed in albums. I knew Teller County was rich with history, but I never expected to find a private museum in the family home. Several Life, Look, and National Geographics are interspersed in the stack. With due care, I return this trove of treasure to its cupboard and turn my attention to the over-sized tome on the right. The leather is intricately tooled around the cover's edges and Fielding – 1875 is embossed in large elegant script in the center. There is a tarnished silver latch holding the four-inch thick volume together. I have found my reading material for the evening. With one arm barely encompassing the album, I rise. I detour to the kitchen and pour myself a generous glass of merlot, before making my way upstairs. After donning the men's heavy tee that reaches below my knees, I plop down on the bed, gingerly undo the clasp, and open the volume in reverence for the antiquity it represents. Centered on the first black page is a grainy tintype of a couple in wedding attire. The neat printing below it identifies them as Jefferson Davis and Sarah Jane Fielding on July 21. Reaching across to the nightstand drawer, I retrieve the large magnifying glass that I have found annoyingly helpful the last several months. I have been putting off an eye exam, opting, instead, for cheap readers from the drug store; but the poor quality of the photographs and faded notations require added magnification. Jefferson looks to be in his fifties, and might be rather handsome underneath all the facial hair and the pronounced deadpan countenance that was popular in photographs of those days. His bride is as short as he is tall, and considerably younger. His suit does nothing to disguise the muscular build typical of men engaged in demanding ranch work. I move the glass over the petite woman with the equally dour expression. There is something familiar . . . Oh my God! I grapple clumsily for the small table lamp and manage, in the process, to topple the half-full goblet onto the hardwood floor. Miraculously the crystal does not break but the crimson splatter is widespread. Torn between the immediate satisfaction of my curiosity and cleaning up what might otherwise become permanent staining to the floor, walls, and drapes, I set aside the volume; then replace the lamp, and scramble to the bathroom where I retrieve the appropriate cleaning product for each surface. I have to discipline myself to take the time to repair the damage thoroughly, all the while impatient to get back to the captivating photo. This time Mohammad goes to the mountain; I place the album under the lamp. Hunching over the ancient photograph, I hold the glass directly over the face of my ancestor. I strain my weary eyes and when they focus, the original suggestion takes on reality. Looking across to the mirror above the bureau, I pull back my hair and mimic my ancestor's lack of expression. If my great, great, great grandmother was a shade under five foot two, I am her clone. I laugh at my original shock. Why not? Drained from the unexpected excitement on top of a physical day, and caressed in the wash of wine, I close the album and set it on the cedar chest at the foot of the bed. Tomorrow is another day. Oblivion takes me quickly and for a restful eight hours.

CHAPTER 4

There is something profoundly satisfying in waking up to the smell of coffee wafting up the stairs from the kitchen, amid this rustic setting. I wonder if our computerized appliances would have changed things for Sarah. The blend of sturdy antique furnishings and décor with ultra-modern appliances affords me the best of the old and the new. I love the rich warmth of the aged wood, but favor the option to push a few buttons to accomplish tasks that would have taken hours of toil and vigilant oversight on the part of the home's first occupants. As I make my way downstairs and across the living room clutching the old album, I am glad that I chose to conceal my prized collection of electronic entertainment within the reconfigured insides of an antique armoire and original cupboards. Even my desktop computer setup has been cleverly disguised within the confines of the enormous roll top desk in one of the spare bedrooms upstairs. The inviting kitchen is the only area that "outs" its owner as technologically spoiled. The fridge, range, oven, and microwave are the most innovative to be had. The high-capacity dishwasher seems to be overkill but allows me the option to entertain and clean up with ease. I also added a spacious island. The computerized washer and dryer in the cellar are encased in an old cabinet, as is the enormous freezer. The prospect of being marooned up here, while not a constant threat, is a very real one that behooves preparation. Loss of electricity is a possibility both in the winter and during summer thunderstorms. A large generator housed in its own building just west of the house will ensure that lights and appliances are kept running during power-outages. I am probably one of the few residents that have ever looked forward to the isolation of a blizzard.

Designer java in hand, I reopen the album before me on the oak dining table, morning sunlight streaming through the large kitchen window does wonders for my vision. I am pleased with having let myself sleep on the initial discovery. With rested mind and eyes, it is easy to confirm my strong resemblance to my ancestor. This appears to be the only photograph of the wedding. On the next several pages, there are faded photographs of the house as it was originally structured and furnished, both exterior and interior shots. I knew it was common in those days for people to take and develop their own photographs and I am grateful that the Fieldings seemed to be so thorough in pictorially recording the family history. Some shots lay loose, the mountain dryness having weakened the fixative that once held them in place on the black construction paper pages. Although faded and grainy, it is easy to see that the basic structure of the house, barn, pump house, and other out buildings have changed little since Jefferson erected them. Even the original outhouse has been maintained and it serves for answering nature's call when I am tending to outside chores; and, God forbid, if the indoor plumbing should back up. I have been warned that gardening at this altitude is a thankless venture and best left to nature's whims. My newly reinforced rebellion is nagging at me to challenge this restriction with plans for a sizeable greenhouse where I can control temperature and lighting. My great, great, great grandfather must have been a man of vision. Rather than starting with a small house for just himself and his bride, he had evidently seen a large family in his future, a home that would serve large families for generations to come and acreage large enough for continuing expansion of herds. The second bedroom was huge and originally designed for six, with built-in triple bunks. There was a large closet and several dressers on the wall across from the door. It is ironic that only one child had been borne into each generation. If these walls could speak . . .

Under the skillful hands of neighbors and local craftsmen, the room has been reconfigured into an office and two private bedrooms. The logs used in the original construction had been preserved and maintained regularly to prevent any compromise of structural integrity. The best of hardwoods had been used on walls, flooring, and built-in furnishings and shelves. They, too, retain their original beauty from hours of polishing by a succession of excellent housekeepers. The workers have been meticulous in preserving, reusing, and matching the woods and patterns that it was hard to tell new structure from original.

After briefly reviewing these photographs, I decide to compare them, in detail, with the interior I have not altered, starting at the top. Armed with the album, I pull the ladder down from the second floor hallway ceiling. The rungs creak as I make my way up to the space I have visited only once to store the few possessions of my parents that I opted to keep. The opening is centered a few feet this side of the back of the house. The room is enormous as it encompasses the entire floor space of the house itself. Its height at the peak must be over a dozen feet, sloping down to about four on the sides. I gently set the album on a stack of boxes and open it to the page where the first of the attic photos begin. They are of a room with few wooden trunks accented with leather straps and metal hinges. Those old trunks are still here, but the straps are weathered; the hinges tarnished. They now share the room with several other less aged coffers lining the walls. Everything is covered in a thick layer of dust. The floorboards groan slightly under my footfalls as I walk over to the antique crib under the window on one far wall. Modern regulations would have a field day with its lethal construction. A closer examination of the old rocker next to it confirms that with a little lemon oil and elbow grease, the chair would fit perfectly in that vacant corner in the living room. It is a shame, though, that the handmade cushions are beyond restoration. The faded calico fabric is shredding and the filler crumbles under my touch. That is another skill I am determined to master, sewing. How hard can it be?

A stream of light from the eastern window illuminates an antique hobbyhorse. As I approach the timeless toy, I am mesmerized by the intricacy and suspect that a proud father must have designed and constructed it himself. The detailed wooden body is accented with a mane, tail, and long lashes that appear to be real horsehair. A leather saddle, complete with tiny stirrups straddles the steed's back. The miniature tack is the work of a skilled artisan; in a time when people took pride in their work, and its ability to remain viable for generations. When and why did the world take a turn for the disposable? Today's technology produces toys molded of cold plastic that falls easy prey to the younger set, yet defies the powers of nature to degrade and recycle. Go figure. Next to the horse is a small cradle complete with quilt and handmade cloth doll. The doll even has a doll. I imagine my female ancestors in their youth, perfectly content, sans what are now deemed *necessary* amusements for modern children. I reach for the chest I have chosen to explore next and nearly drop the lid as the hinges moan in protest. Balls, stuffed animals, and other dated playthings comprise its contents. It will take numerous visits to complete an inventory of three generations. My mind quickly assesses the possibilities. If I carefully catalogue the contents of the house and compare the items with photos, perhaps I will be able to match up ancestors to their personal items, get to know each ancestor, based on their clothing, the books they read, their skills; whatever might be revealed through the relics left behind. Could this unearthing of the past form the outline for an honest-to-goodness salable book? The idea intrigues me and I decide to proceed with that end in view. My next trip to the attic will be with cameras and notepad. It crosses my mind that I am living in a museum, and find the idea quite acceptable. While the spring ladder I descend could use some lubrication, it is sturdy and fully functional.

The room I have chosen for my personal quarters needs no further examination. I poked into every nook and cranny before resting my head on the intricately carved four-poster bed. It is as sound as the day it was constructed. The dressers and armoire match the wood and design of the bed, while the nightstands and lamps added in a later generation are only slightly dissimilar. The bathroom upstairs is quite large, and although the plumbing has been modernized; the original porcelain sink has been encased in a beautifully carved wooden cabinet topped with a marble slab. I adore the clawed-foot bathtub. The bath downstairs was added later and is outfitted with more modern fixtures designed to mimic the old.

The study off the living room measures twelve by twenty-four feet, and is lined, floor to ceiling, with shelves and cupboards, save for one window on the side facing the barn. A long oak table claims the center of the room. Its legs and border are beautifully carved, as are the heavy chairs that sit around it. The room is illuminated by three modest chandeliers hanging above the table. A scan of the shelves suggests the family has focused on education throughout its generations. Historic texts, Shakespeare, and other classics are in abundance, along with the leather-bound personal journals. Then there are the cupboards. This collection will require hours of sorting and classification, and, I am anticipating, will provide stories behind the artifacts upstairs; thus opening the door to getting to know each of my ancestors personally. I imagine holding the doll upstairs, discovering that it had once been cherished in the arms of one or more of my grandmothers. Being snowbound will be an opportunity, not a hindrance.

The kitchen has revealed all its secrets, as has the spacious living room; so I head down to the cellar via the door tucked under the staircase that leads to the upper floor. The subterranean room is divided by the stairway into two rooms. The area off to the right is now a den, complete with a second fireplace. Two sofas that look to be convertible and three overstuffed chairs surround a large coffee table, and lamps, once oil burning, converted to electric adorn end tables The photograph reveals that this room was a root cellar, where apples, carrots, and potatoes were nestled in huge barrels of sand for preservation through the rest of the year. Despite the fading, I can make out strings of onions and garlic hanging from the ceiling along with strips of jerky. These pics confirm that Jefferson Fielding finished the cellar with its current wood floor and oak-paneled walls, save the one against the hillside, of course. How clever of him to use that hillside as one entire side of not only his house, but the barn, as well. I have been downstairs regularly since taking up residence, but only to the left of the stairs, doing laundry, retrieving food from the freezer and pantry, and of course, raiding the wine cellar. To my surprise and delight, it is well stocked with vintage wines, many of the bottles encrusted with decades of dust. I can attest firsthand that the extended aging has not affected the contents, at least, not in a negative way. I try to imagine my ancestors first placing these bottles in their niches, anticipating future celebrations.

The space under the stairs houses the cabinets that now conceal the freezer and laundry appliances. The south wall is devoted almost entirely to the pantry that I have stocked with food enough to supply a formidable army for months; again, excessive; but I will rarely eat out in my new environment. I am not antisocial, but, in the aftermath of the several foregoing months, it will not bother me to be sequestered on the ranch with some time to deliberate on life in general, and mine in particular. The stable cool temperature makes the cellar excellent for food storage. At the end of that wall are steps leading up to typical double doors that flap open upward to the outside. A huge rough-hewn worktable claims the center of the room. A dozen sturdy matching chairs surround it. I imagine my female ancestors and neighbor women working on one of the many quilts that I keep discovering in cupboards throughout the house. Centered above is a wagon wheel chandelier whose lamps were also converted from kerosene to electric at some point. I close my eyes and envision another scene, this time a group of men playing cards under its flickering glow, or perhaps discussing the politics of the day.

I set the album on the table. There are no windows in this underground chamber, but the chandelier is outfitted with five high wattage bulbs that illuminate the entire space quite adequately. In addition, there are fixtures above the appliances and pantry. Although I have frequented the room, I am, for the first time, surveying it from a historic perspective. The entire north is the mountainside. The rocky projections and niches have been artfully claimed by lanterns and other objects from days gone by. Someone in the family seems to have evolved into an accomplished woodcarver over the years. Whittlings of crude animals progress to intricately carved scenes combining images of people, animals, and structures. I lift a horse and its rider to find the bottom signed J. D. F., my great, great, great grandfather. A crude but recognizable rooster bears the initials M. A. F. I will have to check the family Bible for that one. Several seem to be images of the same person, one a bust, others, full figures standing, sitting, and on horseback.

The opposite wall sports parchment maps, so weathered by time I doubt they could survive even a delicate touch. There is one of the States circa 1900; another of Colorado dated 1884; a third of Teller County in 1936. I make a mental note to contact someone in the field of preservation of museum pieces about these specimens.

Referring back to the album, I study the photograph of the west wall that contains the door leading to the wine cellar. The wall is roughly thirty-five feet in length. The wine cellar's width takes up roughly a third of that. A large gun safe stands against the wall midway from the wine cellar entrance to the steps leading up to the outside entrance.

The photo is dark, but upon closer scrutiny, my suspicions are verified. I can just make out a second door where the gun safe now stands. I search, but do not find a corresponding room among the photographs. The safe is a good six feet tall and almost a yard in width and depth. It was locked when I arrived, but the combination was among the detailed data that came with the property. The extensive array of firearms inside required no cataloguing. Each shotgun, rifle, and revolver has its own handwritten label, identifying it, appropriate ammo, and its original owner. My museum and its value rose considerably with this discovery. Sizing it up, I cannot guess how much this beast must weigh, but I am the proud owner of a crowbar and large furniture movers. Dare I? Curiosity outweighs the anticipated enormity of the task.

It takes less than ten minutes for me to return with the needed tools and the determination to move a mountain. I position the first disk next to one corner, the outside of my foot posed ready to nudge it under the safe if I am able to pry the base of the massive chest off the floor. I bless the discoverer of leverage, as my slight, but toned frame is able to accomplish the seemingly impossible. Three successive attempts complete the mission. The safe is now on a magic carpet, and I am able, though, with considerable effort, to budge it a few inches at a time. My determination is solidified when the antique knob comes into view and the door in the old photo is exposed. I continue only enough for me to squeeze between the safe and the doorframe. A true romantic at heart, I allow myself a few minutes to wallow in the adventure of it all. When and why was the door obscured? What is behind it? I stave off my inquisitiveness and run upstairs to get my camcorder, sensing that I must surely be on the verge of a significant discovery. Standing before the door, I take a deep breath and turn the ancient knob. The hinges whine as if in agony as I force them to rotate for the first time in what might be decades. It is pitch black inside the exposed room. A foul mustiness invades my sinuses, obliging me to step back and reclose the door. I breathe deeply several times to purge the disagreeable odor before heading upstairs.

I search the toolshed for a nose mask, stop in the bathroom for a dab of eucalyptus salve. I know from editing crime novels, that application of a dab at the base of my nostrils can mask even the most offensive of stenches. Re-outfitted, I return for a second attempt and wave away the thought that the room is home to some dangerous toxin. This time the odor is bearable, strangely ancient; what I imagine it must smell like when archaeologists first enter tombs of the Pharaohs. It is pitch black in this subterranean room. I reach around for a light switch in vain. Is it possible that the area had been sealed before electricity was installed? In any event, I am compelled, once again, to delay the expedition to retrieve the flashlight I keep perched on the post at the base of the stairs. Flashlight first, I turn sideways and suck in my gut to squeeze between the safe and the door frame, taking care as I pull the camcorder behind me. Once in, I secure its strap around my neck. The narrow but powerful beam of my flashlight cuts through the darkness. The first thing I see is a small wooden table with a solitary chair in the middle of the room. Upon closer examination, I see the small, leather-bound book and what appears to be an inkwell and an ancient pen. Directly overhead is a kerosene lantern suspended on a chain from the ceiling. It appears to have been the room's only source of light. Excitement takes hold and I juggle flashlight and camcorder to start recording my adventure. With each change of scene, I record my vocal reactions. I abandon the flashlight altogether lest I break the spell that is enveloping me. I do not want my initial thoughts edited by interruptions. Instead, I follow the less powerful beam of the camcorder down to one corner, and as smoothly as I am able, begin to peruse the room. It appears, at first glance to be a sort of utility room. A large lidded crock rests in one far corner. A little farther down the wall is a chest of drawers. Abutting the next corner, and extending down the adjoining wall, is a protrusion that appears to be a built-in bunk, lumpy with dusty bedclothes. Beyond the makeshift bed, is a succession of tall, narrow cupboards. With one hand, I stretch to open the nearest door while maintaining the aim of camcorder, wishing my arms were a few inches longer. Through the thick layer of dust, I can see several pieces of women's clothing from a bygone era. Curious. Who would have lived down here, perhaps live-in help? Everything is entwined in dust-laden webs of long-deceased, I pray, arachnids. The thought sends the sensation of a million tiny legs running around my neck, causing me to jerk and shiver. When I return with better light, it will be a treat to explore the wardrobe in depth. I retrace my steps to the bunk. Even through the barrier of the mask and ointment, I sense that this is the main source of the odor that assailed me earlier. Wishing I had thought to don gloves, but too impatient to pause now, I, with the tips of forefinger and thumb, pick up the edge of the fragile quilt and pull it back an inch at a time so as not to tear the rotting fabric. The revulsion engendered more than rivals that of the glimpse of my mother in that morgue drawer several months earlier. The camera slips from my grasp; the strap tugging sharply at my neck as it aborts its crash to the floor. Fear of awakening in this room and the eucalyptus under my nose prevent me from passing out. I stagger back through the door, the camcorder strap getting hung up on the door handle as I force my hasty retreat. I am yanked back, and in the process, my head bounces between the door jam and the safe. Thankfully, the strap is freed in the process. I slam the door shut with such fury I fear it will splinter, as if that could dispel the horror behind it. Once satisfied that it is secure, I slump against the safe for support just as my legs dissolve into jelly and pull the rest of me to the floor with them. I rip the mask from my face. My accelerated heartbeat and respiration are competing for dominance. I grab at my arms in an attempt to control the shaking. It takes several minutes for rational thinking to return. A quick check reveals the camcorder no worse for its collisions. Still unsteady, I pull myself up with help of the ancient doorknob, brush myself off, and slowly shuffle across the room, before hurriedly stumbling up the stairs.

CHAPTER 5

Again breathless when I reach the top, I shut the door and fumble with the lock, as if the corpse below has animated and is shuffling up the stairs. I turn and brace my back against the door. Physically spent, I slowly slide to the floor. It takes several minutes for my breathing and pulse to return to normal. The hysterical laughter I hear is my own. I find myself powerless to stop it; then, just as spontaneously, convulse into racking sobs. The upheaval of my recent past is stirred, no, whipped into frenzy. The images of my mutilated parents that I had successfully repressed play in front of me like scenes in a horror movie. I had left that world behind, yet death is staring me in the face again, uglier than before. I shudder to think that I have been sharing my cozy domicile with a cadaver. I cannot stop the shouting inside my head. Who? How? When? Why? I attempt a scream of outrage, but it refuses to come. The last drop of strength drains and I am too tired even to get up and move to the couch a few feet away. My eyes close and I give in to sleep right there.

I have no clue to how long I have been napping. I take in a deep breath and find I now have the strength to rise; though it is on shaky limbs that I make my way to the kitchen, lunging toward sink board and grabbing for support. I force myself to breathe slowly and purposefully fix my gaze on the Peak so perfectly framed by the window. I wonder if

Zebulon Pike's first sight of this majestic mountain was similar to mine upon arrival, a sense of power and protection for those in its shadow. After several minutes of wallowing in its reassurance, I push away from the counter and very deliberately reach for the teakettle, fill it with water, and light the burner. Still shaken, I find I must think about every determination. I retrieve a mug from the cupboard, a tea bag from its canister and take them to the table. Gripping the chair back with both hands, I turn back toward the window. I love it here, I tell myself. I have made a new life, a good life with heretofore-unfathomed promise. The thought of retreating from my "Shangri La" unacceptable. I dig my mental heels in. Logically, I have nothing to fear from the remains downstairs. Whatever transpired in the family basement is long in the past, of no tangible concern to *me*; has nothing to do with *my* life. Still, I am hopeless to wrest the wandering misgivings from my mind. The shrill whistle of the kettle jars me back to the present.

The Earl Grey warms and calms; a few bites of oatmeal cookie restore strength. Lucid thinking is returning, and with it, a burning curiosity that supersedes the earlier panic and revulsion. Objectivity kicks in and I determine I must solve the mystery downstairs or forever wallow in speculations of the horror. The mummified corpse has been deceased for several decades, at the very least. It cannot hurt me. If foul play was involved, the perpetrator presents no danger to me in the twenty-first century. With that resolve of logic, I don more salve, a new mask, and a pair of latex gloves before making my way back to the cellar armed with a renewed spirit and a powerful camping lamp. Despite the return to rational thinking, I fall short of trusting myself not to falter, and concentrate on my descent as if I were traversing a rickety rope bridge swaying in a strong wind. Once at the base of the stairs, I take in several fresh lungsful of air. Ignoring the bombardment of morbid thoughts and a conscience nagging me to call the local authorities, I slither my way back into the tomb, lamp first. I set the lamp on the table in the center of the room now bathed in bright, but less forbidding light. Barring all thought, I walk directly to the small bed, and with gloved hand, slowly pull the disintegrating coverlet from the mummified body. From the size and dress, the body is of a small woman or girl. The legs are drawn up to her chest in a fetal position; spindly arms wrapped around her petite frame. I shiver as I imagine the cold and loneliness that she must have felt so long ago. I bite my lip and manage to suspend my emotions, to take in the scene impassively and concentrate on whatever facts might be discernable. After several minutes of deliberation, I reverently replace the blanket. It is only then that I miss my camcorder. Somehow, the idea of recording the scene strikes me as sacrilegious invasion of the victim's dignity. Making that decision seems to reinforce my composure. I scan the room before I turn my attention to the closet. Illumination and deduction confirm that the wardrobe most likely belongs to the deceased, and the style suggests an adult, though, like myself, petite in stature. Emboldened by curiosity, I dust off one high button shoe below the dresses. It compares favorably to my own size five sneakers. Gently I push between the calico dresses, so fragile with age. On the far end is a yellowed mass of satin and lace. In spite of the cloud of age, I recognize it is the gown worn by the woman in the wedding photo in the Fielding album. The unspeakable conclusion elicits questions that spin inside my head, demanding but fearing the answers. This woman had not been accidently trapped in this room. She had been purposely locked inside, left to die. Was it lack of oxygen? If it was the winter season, she had she frozen to death; or did starvation or thirst claim her? I feel tears on my cheeks as I contemplate how she must have suffered, whatever fate had taken her. In any event, she knew what was coming and more than likely, the identity of her warden. It is then I call to mind the story my father had so often related about the wife and mother who had deserted her family. Could Sarah have been . . . but it has to be . . . the clothes, her . . . Oh no. The tragic inference engulfs me. Sarah lost her life along with her reputation. I scrape together the details of Father's narration of the young woman who had allegedly tired of a dreary life and sought to spice things up by running off with another man. Father never put names to the tale and mother never spoke of it. I sensed pressing her for details was unwise. Surely, there must be a record of what happened somewhere, if not in print, maybe in the memories of some of the older families in the vicinity. One thing I knew for sure; Sarah Fielding had not run away from her family. She had been murdered in an especially cruel fashion. Who was the coward who tore her from her family; the man with whom she had supposedly left? My mind runs with the theory. I think of my great, great, great grandfather and how devastated he must have been; how heartbroken to have been deserted by his wife; and how he must have hated the man. But wait; how could the lover have locked Sarah up in the cellar without her husband discovering the blocked doorway sooner or later and . . . I retrace my steps and stand before Sarah's resting place. No, it could not have happened that way. A chill threatens to turn me to stone as the sole alternative becomes apparent. Perhaps the account of Sarah's unfaithfulness is true. Still, even if she had succumbed to the advances of another man . . . it was not right that she . . . that my great, great, grandfather should . . . Reflexively I search for another explanation, one that doesn't include my ancestor being a cold-blooded murderer. I remind myself that speculation with limited knowledge is often erroneous; yet any fool could see that a grave injustice has occurred. My religious background has left me confused as to the hereafter. I would prefer to think that any wrong has long since been righted, that the innocents are looking down without malice. What about the tales of lost souls who wander in some "limbo" until they are put to rest by a resolution of their fate and a Christian burial? A shudder ripples through me and with it, a resolve. "I swear to you, Sarah Fielding, I will not rest until I find out what really happened to you and why," I whisper. The self-assigned undertaking immediately brings a measure of comfort.

As I make my way across the room, my eyes settle on the table in the center, and on the book that rests thereon. Closer examination reveals that it is a journal much like the others in the study. It is so old, so fragile, and I employ due diligence in taking possession of it. A flitter of conscience questions the legality of my action. Technically, I suppose, I am tampering with evidence. On the other hand, this evidence, if it is such, has long ceased to have any value. Besides, I have probably broken a dozen laws already. I am in no mood to be dictated to by the powers that be or self-imposed ethics. I dismiss my qualms. After all, the house and all its contents belong to me, although I am more than willing to part with my houseguest. I can always plead shock or ignorance of the law. I clutch the small book to my chest and go upstairs with the intent of calling the sheriff's department forthwith.

CHAPTER 6

I chicken out and end the call before the first ring, then opt for a less intimidating contact.

"Hello, Kim; it's Cassie Collins." I am shaking as I relate the grisly discovery. My friend volunteers to call the sheriff's office and is already sitting with me in the kitchen when Bob and a fellow deputy arrive. She directs them to the basement; then sets about making us some tea. "When you said your next call would be a genuine emergency, you weren't kidding," she quips attempting to lighten the atmosphere. "Of course, if the body is as old as you think it might be . . ."

"Trust me," I assure her, "It resembles something out of Tales from the Crypt."

"Gosh," she says, "that door was behind that safe all those years. It's funny your grandparents never . . ." I nod. "What made you decide to move the thing?" I point to the faded image of the room. "I don't know that I would have noticed it," she says. "Do you know who might have moved it in front of the door in the first place and when; any idea who it is down there?"

"I'll take it from here, Honey," says Bob when he appears in the kitchen doorway. Kim's presence has had a calming effect and the fact that Bob is the one taking my statement is a relief. I start by telling him about the day's quest and show him the photograph of the cellar as it was originally, pointing out the faint outline of the door; then relive for him, the discovery.

"So, *do* you have any idea whose body that might be?" Bob gives his wife a look. Kim shrinks back in mock fear. "Sorry."

I turn back to the first page of the album. "That dress," I explain, "is hanging in the closet along with other clothing of the same size. The people in the photograph are identified as my great, great, great grandparents," I say pointing to the faded caption below. From what I could see, the body is in a dress and looks to be about my size."

"I see," says Bob, scribbling away on his note pad. After making his notes, he pulls out a small camera and snaps pertinent shots of the album.

"There's something else. I can't vouch for the accuracy, but . . ." Distasteful as it is, I relate my father's story. "No identity was attached to the characters, only that they were members of my mother's family in the past." Kim is shaking her head, but having been reminded of her civilian status, doesn't comment or question.

Bob sighs. "So you think this is your great, great, great grandmother, Sarah Fielding". I nod. "We've put in a call to the El Paso County Coroner. We're in luck; they have a wagon available and will pick up the remains immediately. I'm no expert, but I'm guessing the body is quite old; so old, in fact, that it may be impossible to determine the cause of death; and since the perpetrator would be long deceased, the coroner might very well deem it unworthy of an investigation."

"If my father's story is accurate, and if Sarah Fielding is the woman he was talking about, it could be that my great, great, great grandfather found out about the affair and locked her in that room in lieu of doing away with her by a more hands-on method. Still, it's . . ."

"A horrible way to die, alone, no food or water, the air being depleted with her every breath. One thing is for sure," Bob adds, "the woman didn't lock *herself* in that room."

We sip our tea. Kim's attempt at small talk is welcome and I force myself to concentrate on her endless supply of cheerful updates. Forty minutes later, Bob looks up. "That must be the coroner, now. Excuse me."

Kim reaches for my hand. "How are you holding up?" she asks as her husband goes out to meet the coroner's bus.

"I'm okay . . . I mean . . . it is a shock, finding the body; but it isn't as if I knew the person, relation or not. I can't help but think about what Bob said; that it must have been horrible for her. Oh, Kim, I can feel her hunger, her thirst, her fear. How long did she pummel the door, begging to be released, before she resigned herself to her fate? Did she gasp for air? How long did she suffer before she lost consciousness? I never knew her; never even knew of her until I found the album, but . . ." My heart wrenches in empathy for the young woman, who over a century ago, died alone, no doubt grief-stricken; her young child on the other side of a door that would never again open. I take a deep breath to maintain control, but the sadness is too much and I cannot hold back the tears. Kim rises and goes from handholding to a full embrace, rubbing my back in consolation.

"It's okay, Cassie. Let's not think about it anymore. She's not suffering anymore, hasn't for a very long time. And soon, she'll be resting in a proper grave." Kim squeezes my hand. "On second thought, bawl your eyes out." I can't help but laugh through the tears that soon dissipate. I nod and wipe my face with a napkin.

"This is so wonderful," she says diverting attention to the album. "I wish my family would have documented our history like this." Carefully, she begins to turn the pages in the album and through a fresh set of eyes, I learn a little more about my Colorado heritage. It provides the needed distraction from the coroner's men who are passing through the mudroom toward the cellar entrance, gurney in tow. Kim gasps. "Oh my God, Cassie, this woman, she could be you!" She takes a moment as if she is trying to take it in." Who's this?" Her finger rests on the picture of the baby.

"Mary Fielding," I say reading the tag below the photograph of Sarah seated with what looks to be a child in its first year. "My great, great grandmother. I wonder how old she was when . . ." Fresh tears flow as I think of the young child left motherless.

"Let's leave the timing for the forensic team," says Kim. "Look, here's another of Mary at three, with her mother." I force a smile and inwardly applaud her endeavor to lead my mind toward more pleasant thoughts, and make an effort to cooperate.

"That hobby horse in the attic," I say. "You should see the detail. And that doll she's holding is up there, too, and the cradle." With that, I proceed to relate my earlier expedition in the attic along with my plans to catalogue and refurbish. As we talk, I feel my spirits lifting.

Bob reappears. "They're just about finished down there. I'm pretty sure I've got everything I need, but don't rule out another Q & A session."

"No problem, but . . ."

"Yes?"

"Cassie was worried about publicity, Bob. Is there any way . . ."

"I don't know why anyone has to know about this. I'll pass it on to my guys and the forensic team. It's not like there's going to be a murder investigation."

"What *will* they do?" I ask. "I'd like to know . . ."

"Well, they will try to determine the time and cause of death. We have the evidence you provided about the identity. Other than that . . ."

"I understand and thank you so much. Can I clean up the room? I'm not really comfortable with it the way it is."

"I don't see why not. We have everything we need."

"Just let me know when you're ready and I'll help," offers Kim. I smile in acceptance.

Just then, we hear the footfalls on the cellar stairs accompanied by muffled warnings not to falter. A few seconds later the first of the men emerges, his hands behind him gripping the handles of the gurney. I rise to watch the procession as if a newly deceased were being escorted out. The men pause as I act on the urge to touch the drape over the body in reverence of my ancestor.

Kim stays behind when Bob follows them out. "Call me if

you need anything," she says firmly. A few minutes later, I am alone in my home; at least I'm fairly certain I am.

CHAPTER 7

It has been several weeks since I uncovered, literally, Sarah Fielding's body. I have yet to hear, but then again, know it is not realistic to expect the authorities to expend much time or effort on ancient crime. Sarah's murderer is dead and gone, as well. I am in the midst of organizing old correspondence and the diaries when I run across the small book I had lifted and tucked in among them before calling Kim. I cannot believe I forgot about it and immediately abandon the task at hand. To my delight, I find that it is Sarah's journal from 1879. It makes sense. I wonder . . . but won't for long. I feel compelled to read it downstairs where the final words were penned. The authorities had disturbed little in the room. My only attempt at the clean-up, I had thought so urgent, has been to leave the door open to the main cellar and to light a few odor-absorbing candles whenever I am doing laundry. They had done their job. The rancid stench of death is finally gone but I am grateful for the faint mustiness still in the air, as if it will engender the atmosphere in this room in 1879. I turn on the lamp I had set on the table that fateful day I first entered the room. If I had kerosene and knew how to operate the old lantern above, I think I would light that instead. In spite of the modern illumination, eeriness engulfs me as I sit in the chair where Sarah had sat. I open the journal and begin to read the thoughts of my condemned ancestor over a century ago.

January 01. In her own words, 1879 starts out full of promise. I visualize her words. The family and the ranch are flourishing. Cattle and horses are growing in number and Sarah is full of praise for her husband's accomplishments. Contrary to my father's editorial, marriage and motherhood seem to agree with the young woman. Little Mary is her pride and joy. Several weeks of entries reveal a content housewife, who, while at times, found her duties a challenge in her isolated mountain home, enjoyed her role as the wife of a successful rancher and looked forward to a long and happy future. She describes the moderate growth of Florissant and a few new neighbors in the area. The age difference is never mentioned.

It is early spring when things begin to sour. Some sort of flu afflicts many of the area residents. Jefferson is one of the first to be stricken, upon returning from a trip to Denver. Shortly thereafter, Little Mary takes sick and nearly dies. Sarah expresses her fear that she will lose one or both of them. Abruptly, Mary takes a turn for the better and recovers quickly with no lingering effects. Jefferson's case is different. Sarah thanks God for Mary's recovery but continues to agonize over her husband's fate. As his fever rages, with no letup in sight, Sarah hires a hand to keep the ranch going. She refers to twenty year-old Frank Brady as a godsend, strong, knowledgeable, and willing to work for room and board. He also assists with Jefferson, who drifts in and out of feverish dementia and is too much for petite Sarah to handle physically. I feel the anguish in her words over the next several weeks. I rejoice with her when the fever breaks and her husband begins his recovery, am disturbed as I read on. Sarah is having serious misgivings, concern that her still bed-ridden husband is becoming suspicious of their benefactor. She is torn between her reliance on the hired hand and Jefferson's growing dislike for him. Sarah says nothing to Frank. By the time Jefferson is back on his feet, his unfounded distrust is reaching distressing proportions. As her husband is still unable to handle the full load of work, the increasingly uncomfortable arrangement continues and his jealousy is festering to the point that it becomes obvious to

Frank, who does his work and otherwise makes himself scarce. Sarah is grateful for Frank's forbearance, and, at the same time tries to reassure her husband of her unwavering devotion.

I feel the toll this stress is taking on the young wife. Frank takes his meals out in the barn now, but Jefferson remains sullen and silent at the kitchen table save for complaints; barely responding, even to his daughter, who has quite naturally taken a shine to the nice young man who would stop, play, and answer her never-ending list of questions.

Sarah wrote her last entry on the afternoon of September first. Some of it is smeared and hard to decipher.

Jefferson woke up a new man today. I was so relieved when he announced at breakfast that he was feeling strong enough to let Frank go. He has not regained his full strength, but thanks to Frank, the ranch is in good shape for the approaching winter.

Sarah goes on to describe her preparation of Jefferson's favorite meal and her plans to reveal that she is halfway through her second pregnancy, news she had been holding back until she thought that the added responsibility would be welcomed.

Jefferson worked inside all morning; said he was working on a surprise for me, and not to question him further. He was up and down the stairs a dozen times or more. When he came into the kitchen, he smiled as he caught the aroma of roast pork and apple pie. Then he kissed me for the first time since he took ill.

She then describes taking Mary with her to get water from the well. Her account of what transpires next is inexplicable and heartbreaking.

When we returned, Jefferson instructed Mary to play upstairs. He asked me to close my eyes, took my hand, and led me downstairs to the cellar and across the room. I heard the door to the spare room open. My anticipation was high as I tried to imagine what kind of surprise Jefferson was about to reveal.

I can almost feel my ancestor's strong hands on my shoulders as Sarah describes being shoved though the opening with such force that she skids on her hands and knees across the rough wood floor. I flinch as I hear the door slamming shut, the click of the lock, and the slow grating of the safe being tediously pushed into place. I suffer with Sarah as her recently renewed hopes are dashed and she feels her world crumbling. I experience her angst for little Mary left in the hands of a father that has lost his mental balance; the horror of dying alone. I imagine rising to my feet and hopelessly scanning the room for a possible escape from the underground chamber, coming to realize there is none; that even the loudest of screams will go unheard. Is she reeling in panic at the thought that there is no renewable source of oxygen? My tears join her dried ones on the brittle page as I read her final words.

I know it is the sickness that has robbed Jefferson of his right mind. I pray that God will forgive my husband, and will heal him so that he can take care of our Mary properly.

As if it were playing before my eyes, I watch her close the journal and lay down the pen. She is not ranting, raving, or beating on the door. Is she holding out hope that Jefferson will come to his senses in time to save her? I see her walk over to the small bed, lie down, and cover herself with the quilt, calmly awaiting her fate. Clasping Sarah's diary to my chest, I sob until there are no more tears. I would like to think that she breathed her last in peaceful sleep. I visualize her curled up in the bunk; the lantern flickering as the flame claims the last of the oxygen.

I make myself come to terms with this revelation, welcoming the amendment to the family history, bittersweet as it is. My great, great, great grandmother had not been an unfaithful wife and unfit mother. On the contrary, Sarah was a saint of a woman who, in the face of ultimate betrayal and cruelty, had forgiven and wished well to her executioner. Jefferson Fielding, sadly, was not the husband wronged while incapacitated, left a single parent to raise a small daughter. He was, at best, guilty of murder, though, probably, by reason of insanity. I think back over history and the countless times injustice claimed the lives of innocents . . . If only the living had the power to undo the wrongs of the past . . . but alas . . .

Armed with this new knowledge, I retreat upstairs. As I replace Sarah's diary, I resolve to thoroughly clean that cellar room the next day. For now, curiosity demands that I see what else I might learn about this incident from other members of the family. I scan the reorganized library and browse the shelves I had designated for the journals. It seems that all my female ancestry have recorded their personal histories. I reach for the one that bears Mary Fielding's name. She begins her story on the first day of January in the year 1882. Based on her mother's account, this was a little over two years since Sarah's death. Mary was five years old, and per her introduction, is writing under the guidance of her father, alerting me to proceed with caution. I decide to set this journal aside for the time being. Instead, I pull my laptop front and center, open a new document, and begin to type what I have learned thus far before the details fade. So many questions linger. Are their answers to be found among the contents of this study? It might take months to read the contents of the scores of diaries, but when satisfied I have the "truth, the whole truth, and nothing but the truth", the result could prove the basis for an intriguing book. Completely engrossed, I type for three hours and realize that I am late for feeding the animals.

Eyes weary, I turn off the computer and make my way to the barn, dispensing apologies in response to the snorts and pawing along with the alfalfa at each stall. The goats and chickens are equally vocal about my lapse, but as with the horses, all is forgiven and forgotten the minute it is remedied. Locking up, I am off to the kitchen for a light supper.

Outside, the wind picks up, a signal that the monsoon season is resuming its onslaught, a welcome one, though, as the region is in dire need of moisture after several years of drought. The latest is the second storm to pass through today. During my meal, the lightning moves from dim flashes in the distance to huge jagged strikes that illuminate the entire sky; the thunder from distant rumbles to deafening explosions. The time interval between the two shortens as the volume increases, until lightning and thunder crash in unison. The inevitability of the next detonation does not prevent the sudden jangling of one's nerves. The initial sprinkle is now a torrent of rain accented by hail of increasing size. I open the cupboard near the entry door where I have an intercom connected to the hen house, goat shed, and barn. I know it is overkill, but it eases my mind to be able to monitor the animals from the house. If the truth be told, the contented sounds alleviate my own uneasiness during these storms. "Good night kids." Satisfied that all is well, I pour a glass of wine and take my weary self up the stairs.

CHAPTER 8

I am being shocked by a defibrillator is my first thought. My heart is pounding, my ears ringing. Short-term memory connects with the present and I realize that I have awakened to the loudest clap of thunder I have ever experienced, formidable enough to jolt the house and leave it quivering in its wake. At first, I think it is my bed that is still shaking, but realize that I alone am trembling. Several deep breaths restore my calm to my vacillating vitals. The lamp switch fails to respond. Momentary concern passes when it flickers to life a minute later. This latest strike must have taken out a transformer, and I am pleased to note that the expensive generator has come to the rescue as programmed. I pick up the extension on the wall above my nightstand. I don't expect to hear a dial tone and am only slightly unnerved at the thought of being cut off from the rest of the world for the first time since the move. No cell service up here and, depending on the severity of the weather and the damage inflicted, the internet may be down as well. Quickly, though, I remind myself that I have planned for this and am better off than most. The house and peripheral buildings are fortressed beyond reason. The pantry and freezers overflow; hay and grain stores are at optimum levels. It is almost three and I know a return to slumber will elude me. Donning robe and slippers, I tiptoe downstairs bracing myself for more fireworks. I am at the kitchen window filling the coffeepot with water when the next flash and simultaneous deafening clap threaten my composure. Instantly I recall warnings to stay away from windows during these storms. California, this is not. Subsequent explosions lessen in intensity and frequency, a signal that the tempest is moving on.

I turn on the radio and learn that Teller County streams are flooding, dirt roads are washing out, and some paved streets may be impassable. Power is out throughout much of the county and parts of El Paso and Douglas, as well. Well, I think, this is it, my initiation into the wild weather of the Front Range. A cup of coffee in hand, I walk to the intercom and listen in on the "kids". All sounds calm and I conclude that they take nature in stride.

Heading for the living room, I ease into my recliner and tune the TV to the weather channel. The map is full of yellow and red and the forecaster is predicting brief breaks between a series of strong storms to pound the area over the next week or ten days; at least that is what I am able to piece together in between digital disruption. O . . . kay.

At five, I head for the shower. By six, I am ready to start the day, grateful for the enclosed causeway I had added between the house and the barn. Note to self: add branches to the hen house and goat shed. The rain is abating so I take advantage of the weather window to tend to them first. While the pens stand in two inches of water, their shelters are dry and cozy. I add to my to-do list; drainage for these areas. The Papa, Momma, and baby goat surround the feeder and start to chomp their breakfast hay. The hens abandon their nests as I enter their abode and distribute the grain, leaving me access to gather the eggs.

Back in the barn, I am greeted in impatient grunts. I feed the mares, then Buck, and check to see that the automatic watering system is functioning properly. It is when I pause to commune with Buck who is snatching greedily at the alfalfa, that I hear unexpected noise from the stall at the far end. A handsome bay pokes his head over the half door, startling me as I approach. Flabbergasted, I shake my head. "Where in the world did you come from?" I ask as I open the door to the stall to check out my surprise guest. He shakes his head up and down as I stroke his white blaze. I note that he has been ridden hard recently and is slightly lame in his right front leg. Confusion reigns. The barn is secured with heavy-duty deadbolts. Only the Pruitts have a spare key in case of emergencies. That has to be the explanation. For some reason between the evening feeding yesterday and this morning, Jim must have dropped off the animal. Either I didn't hear his knock or the acceleration of the storm forced him to head back home without stopping to chat. Phones are down, so he couldn't call. Still, I would think he would leave a note, knowing there is paper and pen in the office. Then again, time and weather must have generated urgency. No worries; I am pleased to know Jim trusts me to see to the horse's care until he can retrieve him. I shrug and toss the handsome gelding a flake of alfalfa before making my way to the cupboard where I keep a sundry of veterinary supplies.

When I return with the appropriate balm and wrap I notice the halter hanging outside the stall. It is unfamiliar and seems of a passé style, though in excellent condition. The horse is a fine specimen and responds with minimal fuss to my efforts to tend his leg. "See you got some company, Guys," I say as I pass the other stalls. I am about to make my way up the ladder to the loft, when I see the saddle and other tack neatly posed on a sawhorse just outside the office. Although in good shape, it, too, is unfamiliar. Of course, I am fairly new to all this. I quickly decide it makes sense and continue on my way to fill the grain bucket. After distributing the grain, I open the door to the room that sits behind the stalls. It had once served as a bunkhouse and is no doubt the room where Frank Brady stayed during his stint at the ranch. Today, it houses a well-worn swivel chair and an old roll top desk where I keep hard copies of records pertaining to the animals, per Jim's suggestion. "If you have a problem that requires a vet," he had told me, "it's good to have a record of the diet and any medication or action you might have taken." Two shelves hold the books on animal care that he recommended. At the far end, behind a drape of burlap, one bunk remains in case one of the horses needs monitoring throughout the night. Leaning over the chair back and desk, I make a notation in the daily log of our guest, his food and treatment. I hear what sounds like a muffled cough. I pass it off as coming through the wall from the stalls. The second, however, belies an equine source and draws my attention to the curtained bunk. "Jim?" I whisper thinking he must have decided to stay the night. Why on earth didn't he come to the house? I tiptoe across the floor. My reach to pull aside the curtain is aborted by the unmistakable sound of the cocking of a revolver. As I drop my hand, another adorned with a diamond pinky ring parts the curtain. The man to whom it is attached is righting himself while maintaining his aim of what looks to be a forty-five. I swallow, instinctively raise my hands, and stumble back.

"Forgive me," the man coughs out. "Ah was not expectin' a female." He stands, albeit a bit shakily, and returns the revolver into the shoulder holster. Too stunned to speak, I fumble for the chair in front of the desk. If not for the gun, I would pass this off as some sort of joke being played by Jim Pruitt. On the other hand, he does not seem the type to pull something so extreme on a newcomer. If he did, I am dead sure Nancy would nix the idea . . . if she knew. The man plops back down on the bunk, as soon as I am seated. His already precariously perched hat tumbles down beside him. Holding up a hand, he coughs again, and clears his throat, before rifling through the coat that is sliding off his bent shoulders. He comes up with a metal flask and takes a swig, letting the liquid sit against the back of his throat before swallowing, then wiping his mouth with the back of his hand. When he sighs, his face takes on an expression of relief. "Again, Ah apologize for the excessive response," he slurs in a southern drawl. Still unprepared to join the conversation, I wait for further explanation. "Excuse my trespassin' an' availin' myself of yor hospitality without first securin' the ownah's permission. Ah am not . . ."

"No . . . that's okay," I say when I find my voice. He is a trespasser but his pallor assuages any fear of harm from him. I feel justified in demanding an explanation, but decide to question him gently. "It's just . . . I mean . . . who are you . . . why are you dressed like that . . . and *how* did you get into my barn?"

"Ah beg yor indulgence, Ma'am? Yah see, I have been on the back roads from Denvah for hours through this God-awful storm an' must present quite a pitchah. Ah may have a layah or two of trail dust, but Ah assure yah Ah am a gentleman an' take pride in mah appearance." My non-plussed expression prompts him further. "Might Ah ask where yah got *yor* attire?"

"*My* attire? Are you for real?" I peg this guy for a western re-enactor who takes his gig a little too seriously. Not only does he dress the part, he has adopted the chauvinism of the nineteenth century. "I respect your right to play whatever part you want; but you can't expect women today to parade around in the restrictive and painful dress of bygone days. What? Oh, you don't approve of women in pants? Those of us who work as hard as men these days opt for a wardrobe that befits the job." I feel my dander rising. How dare this intruder question how I dress. I direct the discussion back to the real issue at hand. "And why would anyone in their right mind ride a horse all the way from Denver in this day and age?"

A slight smile begins to spread into the confusion on his face and the chuckle that accompanies it evokes another coughing spasm. He tips the flask again then shakes his head as if searching for a plausible explanation. "Look," I say, "I have no problem offering shelter to you and your horse, but I could use some clarification here. How do I know you're not a fugitive? I mean, this is a free carry state, and I'm all for the right to bear arms, but . . ." I do not know quite where to go from here.

"I assure yah . . . Miss . . ."

"Collins," I offer a bit unwillingly, "And you are?"

He hesitates before answering. "McKey, Tom McKey, and Ah assure yah that yah have nothin' tah fear from me. Ah am jus' passin' through on the way tah Coloradah Springs where Ah will board the rails south. Ah am not guilty of any crime, nor do I plan tah be."

When talking sets off another spasm, I study him. He is nice looking with stunning blue eyes that suggest their color is enhanced by contacts. Overnight wear could account for the redness. Dirty blonde locks generously streaked with gray caress the collar of his coat and he sports a full mustache muddied by a couple of days' surrounding growth. I would estimate his age around fifty, but then again, he could be a dissipated thirty something. There is a spark of recognition but it fades quickly when I conclude that men of his type are a dime a dozen in western films and TV. Over his pale blue shirt, he wears a smartly patterned vest, and the holstered gun. His jacket matches the gray of the ulster coat that lies rumpled on the bunk. His boots are quality leather and accented with spurs. Wherever he shops, they carry quality authentic western wear.

"Ah am prepared to pay yah handsomely for mah and mah horse's room an' board. If Ah might presume upon yah for a hot meal, Ah will take mah leave directly. Ah can wash up in the trough and Ah can eat out . . ."

"You'll do no such thing!" My tone is more indignant than meant and it triggers the quickest draw I've ever seen. "Whoa . . . I just meant . . . Geez . . . I'm just trying to be hospitable. I don't entertain guests in the barn. You'll eat at a table in the kitchen like a civilized man, and if I were you, I'd think about being a little more appreciative before I change my mind and toss you out of here, which I have every right to do." Instantly, I regret the rash words and let out a sigh of exasperation. "Look, I don't know why I believe you, but I do. So put that thing away and follow me." Whether it is those blue eyes or the determined set of his jaw, my gut tells me this guy is legitimate.

More slowly this time, Tom McKey holsters the weapon, and with some difficulty, rises to what appears to be around six feet; thin, no more than a hundred and thirty or forty pounds, I would guess, and clearly suffering from a dissipated existence of late. He leaves his coat and the saddlebags he has been using as a pillow where they lay. I look back as he follows, steadying himself on anything that presents itself along the path. I wonder whether he is legitimately ill or just impeded by the liquor. He seems surprised as I open the door into the enclosed causeway to the house. "I had this built for a safe passage to and from the barn during storms. I might add, it was my *own* idea, albeit the invention of the inferior female brain." I immediately chide myself for trying to impress. Then, again, *he* started the battle of the sexes.

"It's jus' that Ah don't recall seein' it when Ah rode in last night." In spite of using the sills of the windows along the causeway for support, the man falters and stops, racked with yet another series of choking coughs.

"Maybe you shouldn't drink and ride," I say hoping a touch of humor will lessen the tension. But it seems to be lost on him and he merely nods. When he rests his hand heavily on my shoulder, I realize that he is weaker than I had first assessed. I alter my pace for fear he will collapse before we make it to the house. My strength has gradually increased with all the ranch work, but I would trust it to support him all the way to the house. When we step inside the mudroom, he immediately lowers himself onto the bench and begins the struggle to remove his boots. Exhausted, he leans back against the wall and protests weakly before allowing me to take over. The man is educated, well mannered, and from the charming accent, I'm guessing a *southern* gentleman. "Ready," I ask as I offer my arm.

We make it safely to the living room, where he collapses into the recliner. "Thank yah, kindly, Miss Collins."

"It's Cassie," I say. "May I call you Tom?" He nods but jolts upright as I adjust the chair. When he again relaxes, I reach for the afghan on the sofa and spread it over him. "You rest for a bit while I make us some breakfast." He nods, thanks me again, and closes his eyes. I am torn. Either he is quite ill and deserves whatever I can provide, is very drunk, or he is a great actor, and he and whoever put him up to this deserve . . . will have to think about that.

CHAPTER 9

I pour myself a cup of coffee and take a sip as I open the fridge. From the looks of him, my guest is in need of hearty fare and plenty of it. Setting the cup down on the counter, I reach for the carton of eggs, milk, the plastic container in which I store bacon, and the loaf of bread I baked yesterday. After scrambling the eggs and milk, I stir in a bit of cinnamon/sugar and some vanilla, and pour it into a glass baking dish. I cut three thick slices from the loaf of sourdough and gently slide them into the mixture.

A sudden rapid pitting on the window gets my attention. The wind is driving the rain sideways into the front of the house. Well, well, if it isn't Jim Pruitt. He exits his vehicle and with some difficulty, makes his way through the gusts toward the front door. "Come on in, Jim." I beckon him to enter, anxious to give him the business. "What brings you out in this weather?" I ask, with feigned innocence stifling the grin that threatens and covering it with a determined look of concern. He will pay for this little joke.

"Sorry, Cassie; no time. Nancy insisted that I stop by and check on you; you know, make sure you haven't found any more dead bodies." He grins. Jim and Nancy are, at the moment, and, hopefully for all time, the only friends other than Bob and Kim who know about Sarah.

"No, Jim, no more *dead* bodies." My facetiousness seems lost on Jim who just continues with his news.

"Listen, the phones are down and likely to be for a while. The twins are down with colds; at least Nancy and I hope that is all it is; and to top things off, we have the Carter's two beasts as he refers to the couple's Saint Bernards, at our house. Barry was afraid Marcie would go into labor and they wouldn't be able to get down to the hospital during the storms, so they left yesterday to stay with friends in Woodland Park. The weather service is predicting one storm on top of another for at least another week, and Marcie's due any day now, you know. No tellin' when they'll get the power back up and running. Good thing you installed that generator. Anyway, I'm making a quick run down to Florissant. You need anything?"

"No, Jim, I've got more than I need; more than you know." I pause and look out to the storm. "It's raining cats and dogs out there. Wouldn't be surprised if *people* don't start dropping out of the sky." Jim's quizzical expression is accompanied by the cocking of a gun somewhere off to the side and behind me. I flinch in fear. Thankfully, the pounding rain has muffled the sound from Jim's earshot and he assumes I am reacting to the cold.

"Well, if you're sure you're okay. I won't keep you at the door."

"Yeah, don't need to catch pneumonia. You'd best get going while the road is still passable. Tell Nancy hello and that I'm perfectly fine. Oh Gosh, I've got breakfast on the stove," I say, hoping to wind up the conversation before Tom decides to take another hostage; for that is how I'm beginning to feel.

"Okay, I know you can take care of yourself, Little Lady, and hopefully this weather will give us a break soon. We just feel sort of responsible for you, you know, being our friends' grandchild and all."

"And you're doing a fine job, Jim," I lean to kiss his cheek before he bolts away through the torrent to his truck.

Closing the door, I swing around to face my houseguest. "What do you think you are doing?" I demand with as much attitude as I can muster. I fully expect to see the muzzle of the forty-five pointed at me. But no; the weapon is back in its holster and the man's arms hang limply at his sides. "I don't appreciate being spied on in my own house or threatened." From his demeanor, I sense my attempt at bravado is working.

"Yah were about tah tell him."

"Up to the minute you pulled that gun again, I was thinking that you were part of a joke he was playing on me," I quip back in annoyance. I push briskly past him into the kitchen. He falters at the contact and reaches for the wall to steady himself. "I'm sorry, I didn't mean to . . ."

"Why would yor friend . . ."

"Obviously he didn't. I guess that's settled. So, you're here of your own accord." Where to go from here? "Okay . . . but if you're innocent, as you claim, why were you concerned about Jim?" When he doesn't answer, I add, "After I've fed you, Tom McKey, I'll want some answers, the truth this time."

Feebly he shuffles to one of the kitchen chairs and plops down. I move a large cast iron skillet from the storage compartment under the stove onto the largest burner. I turn to see him scanning the room. He shakes his head and blinks as if trying to focus, looks around again and rubs the back of his neck with one hand. He remains mute, struggles to rise, and comes to stand next to me as the flame erupts under the burner. He stumbles back and stares at the pan as if this is the first time he has watched butter melt. I ignore the odd behavior, chalking it up to a hangover, and proceed to add the fully engorged bread slices into the pan. He is back looking over my shoulder as I pull away from the slab several thick slices of bacon, straddling them over the wonderful little plastic thingy that allows the bacon to cook perfectly in the microwave without the mess of spattered grease on the stovetop. He knits his brow as I turn the dial. He examines it more closely as I move to the refrigerator, and I almost knock my shadow down as I back up with the bottle of pure maple syrup in my hand. He extends his hand and prevents me from closing the door as he studies the inside of the appliance. I can't imagine what is so interesting. "I'm not a gourmet but I am perfectly capable of cooking a decent meal."

"Ah can see that," he says, but remains standing.

After several minutes, I flip the toast and push the start button on the microwave. "What *is* it you find so damned fascinating?" I step aside when he leans in to watch the carousel turn. Within a few seconds, the bacon begins its transformation from raw, limp slices of pork to crispy rashers. He watches the process to the finish, then turns and glances around the room again. His gaze rests on the sports calendar hanging on the far wall next to the swinging doors leading to the living room. He moves in for a closer look, touches the glossy photo of a player sliding into second base. He lifts a few pages and shakes his head again.

"You a Rockies' fan?" He does not answer; some gentleman.

"It's ready," I say as I finish loading the plates. The microwave pings again and I retrieve the glass pitcher of pure maple syrup. Still speechless, he comes to sit at the table. I pour juice and coffee before seating myself.

I lift a forkful but hesitate just short of my mouth. "It's better when it's hot," I say.

"Yes, an' thank yah, kindly," he says. He is still perusing the room when he takes his first bite. I am pleased to see that it claims his full attention. "This is exceptional," he adds with a nod.

"Glad you like it," I say. I let him eat in peace for several minutes. "Okay now, Mr. McKey, where did you *really* come from, why did you stop *here*, and where are you going?" I throw in quickly, "Well, where you're going is your own business, I guess."

He dabs the napkin to his mouth and swallows. "Ah, too, feel that Ah am the victim of some sortah hoax. . . only . . ."

"I'm all ears."

He clears his throat. "I know there are advancements in the world that Ah have yet tah experience owin' tah my life on the frontier, but this . . ." His brows are raised.

"This what?" My patience is approaching its limit.

He points to the wall. "The calendah for instance. . ."

"It's a calendar; it's Wednesday, August, 21st. What's the mystery? Oh, I see. Did you lose a few days on your drunken jaunt from Denver, was it?"

"Ah beg tah diffah, Miss Collins. By mah reckonin' it's Tuesday, the 20th of June," he pauses before adding, "1882." His tone is matter-of-fact as he re-inspects the environment.

I grab for my napkin just in time to keep my gulp of coffee from spewing across the table. My subsequent laughter triggers my own choking spasm. In spite of his infirmity, the man jumps from his chair, seeming to come to my rescue, but settles back when I signal I am okay. By the time I recover, my eyes are damp. "Oh, pleeeeease! You are good, I'll give you that."

He sits blank-faced. I push on.

"I'm done with this farce." I rise and toss my napkin in my plate. "If you don't tell me right now who you really are and who put you up to this, I'm calling the sheriff," my hand inches from the phone.

Tom McKey does not move. "Ah do believe Ah heard yor friend say that the phone lines were down," he says calmly. "Now suppose yah tell *me* what's goin' on here. What kindah place is this?"

"Seriously?" I throw up my hands in frustration. "I suppose you're going to tell me that you fell asleep last night in 1882 and woke up in 2013?" If this jerk thinks I am going to fall for this Rip Van Winkle act, he has another thing coming.

What his smile lacks in humor, it makes up for in sarcasm. "Ah, Ah see yor a student of literature. Ah am sorrah, but Mr. Irving's character slept for only twenty years an' had a luxurious growth tah show for it," he says stroking his mustache and whiskey drip. "If Ah undahstand yah correctly, Ah stirred after some hundred an' thirty years, but as yah can see, my dear lady," he says rubbing the stubble on his cheek, "mah last shave was quite recent, a couplah days ago."

"Now, we're getting somewhere," I say, letting out the buildup of frustration.

"Yah have an explanation?"

"I can't believe you're holding on to this absurdity!"

He dabs at his mouth; then sets the napkin aside. "Thank

yah again for yor kindness. Ah believe it is time I take my leave. Ah'll just retrieve mah animal an' be on mah way,"

"Whatever!" It is not a word I like to hear or use, but it's the only one that fits in this instance.

He seems duly refreshed by the rest and nourishment. I accompany him but let him fend for himself on the walk along the causeway into the barn. I flip on the overhead fluorescent lighting. Planting my feet apart, I cross my arms rigidly against my chest and watch him take some time to scrutinize the barn as he had the kitchen. We are standing a few feet from our entry point. The rain has taken a sabbatical and I move toward the large door ahead unlatching Buck's, and the mares' stall doors as I do. They snort and whinny their joy at being turned out and charge out into the pasture as soon as the door is open wide enough for one to gallop through. The trio will be muddy messes when they return, but need the exercise. Tom enters his horse's stall and checks the leg that still appears a bit swollen. "You can't ride him that way," I say in spite of my need to have this unnerving intruder gone. "He'll need another day or so." I see him grimace ever so slightly. "I'm not thrilled either," I respond, "but I will not see an animal abused. Let's get your things and—"

"Ah'll bunk out here—"

"My house, my rules," I insist. "Look let's call a truce." I read concession in his expression.

"You're not worried Ah'll—"

"You're not in any condition to do any harm," I say. My gut feeling, despite the situation, is that he is innocuous, at least as far as a woman is concerned.

I let out a sigh. "At least tell me how you got in here last night?" I plead. "Everything is locked from the inside and Jim is the only one with a spare key. That's why I figured this was his idea. Obviously, I have missed something."

"Ah entahed through the door in the back—"

"Knock it off!" His horse throws his head back at my animated outburst.

"Yah asked me . . . Ah'm tryin' to tell—"

"There is no *back* door," I say deliberately. "There's that

59

door," I say pointing to the exit the horses just used, this side door, and there's the door we came through from the walkway to the house." I jam my hands on my hips and follow him as he retreats and turns the corner to the back of the barn. He stops and stares at the solid rock that forms the rear wall. He looks to the right through the door into the room in which he spent the night; then looks back again, turns, and repeats the actions as if tryin' to get his bearings. "Ah couldah sworn . . ." He points to the wall. My patience run out, I throw myself to the wall, slamming my fists against the rock. I immediately regret the action, but am determined to hide the self-inflicted pain.

"You were drunk," I say flatly. "See, no door; only a wall of solid rock that has been here long before the barn was built. Now, I am asking you for the last time; how did you get in here?" My shouting evokes another equine snort of disapproval.

Tom moves his hand to the back of his neck and rubs it. His hands go to his hips and he stares at the barrier for several seconds. I give up trying to force an answer, having decided that, due to illness and/or the whiskey, his mind has scrambled the events of the last twenty-four hours. I will have to find the breach on my own. "Look," I say, in a sympathetic tone now, "maybe . . ." He reaches forward and as his fingers brush the stone surface. . .

My thoughts arrest midstream. My mind refuses to process the data being sent from my eyes. Tom grabs at my shoulder to prevent falling forward as the wall splits and gives way as if it were a pair of swinging bar doors. My own legs weaken and I stumble backwards. This time, it is Tom that keeps us upright. I turn back to the windows on the side wall. The sky is overcast as opposed to the utter darkness beyond the mysterious opening. Tom releases my shoulder and signals that I remain where I am as he ventures forward, keeping a hand on one side of the new doorway as he crosses the threshold into the seeming void. He is scanning his surroundings. In the shadows, I can see his shoulders relax. He looks upward; then motions me to come to him.

I shake my head, unable to speak.

"It's awright," he says, continuing to wave me outside. "Yah gotta see this." I am frozen where I stand. "Yor missin' out, Dahlin'," he says with teasing raise of his brow. My curiosity wins out, but I temper it with caution. I reach down and pick up the large pry bar resting against the wall to my left, and wedge it firmly in the opening to prevent being trapped outside the barn. Why I imagine that this ounce of prevention cannot be overridden by whatever force has taken control of my world, I cannot explain. It just seems the prudent thing to do, and somehow allays my trepidation. Satisfied, I venture toward Tom's outstretched hand, all the while thinking I am in the throes of one of those outlandish dreams one thinks is real at the time, only to awake in a cold sweat, heart pounding like a sledgehammer. Tom takes a firm grip on my hand and leads me into what should be the solid mass of rock that forms the north of this barn and the house fifty or so feet to the west. He points to the sky, still faintly littered with diamonds and we take a few steps; then turn to the left. In the shadows of dawn is my house standing as it should in relation to the barn. But where is the hill that abuts it and the barn? To the north, I can make out what I know to be the next rise. Looking east, I can just make out the faint glow of the sunrise. Closing and opening my eyes, shaking my head, do nothing to reorder the terrain. It appears that my guest can move mountains. I look back to see the pry bar still in place before I respond to the tug. A rooster's crow pierces the quiet accompanied by twitters and tweets of wild fowl in the trees. My mind is doing flip-flops; so much normal in the face of the impossible, the stuff realistic nightmares are made of. I follow in tiptoe forward beyond the hillside along the side of the barn. With the increasing light, I begin to see that more is not as it should be. My causeway is gone and I feel that something is not quite right about . . . I turn back and see the wall of rock, just as it should be; both buildings solidly abutting it. I wrestle from Tom's grip, run back toward the hillside, stopping just short of it, and reach out. To my horror, it is solid; so much for the pry bar in opening. Tom follows immediately, passes by me right through and into the rock; all but his outstretched arm disappearing before he stops. "Well," his voice echoes from within the mass. I grab his hand and, miraculously the stone disappears. Two steps and I am by Tom's side a few feet from the opening to the back of the barn, which from this vantage point, indeed, appears to be opened doors into the structure. I turn back and in the dawn light, see smoke rising from the chimneys of the house. My fright is just dissipating when my escort into this other dimension pulls me forward. We retrace our steps along the barn and beyond. I can now see the front of the house, very much the same as it is now. Through the kitchen window, I can see lantern light and shadows of movement. I am unprepared when I hear the latch on the front door. Tom breaks into a clumsy run yanking me along and pulling me down behind an old wagon twenty or thirty feet from the barn.

"Come along, Mary," says the owner of a gruff voice. The man who appears in the doorway is followed by a young child, maybe six or seven, carrying a wicker basket. Both are dressed for another time. "Oh my God," I whisper in disbelief.

"Yah know these people?" Tom whispers.

"That's imposs . . ." but then, to my utter amazement, I know I am looking at . . . "The man is my great, great, great grandfather, Jefferson Fielding." The words leave my lips of their own accord as if I have been plied with truth serum, and I listen as if they are spoken by someone else, before I add, "The little girl is . . ."

"Yor great, great grandmothah?" he finishes for me, as we watch her skip to keep up with her father's long strides. When Father and Daughter reach the barn, the man heads inside while she continues on to the familiar hen house. "Yah sure?" whispers Tom.

"Family photographs," I manage to get out in spite of my astonishment. I rub my forehead, tempted to pinch myself.

Several minutes later, the child reappears, at a more cautious gait this time, the basket brimming with eggs. The sky is considerably lighter, now. When she reenters the house, Tom takes me by the upper arm and leads me toward the edge of the forest beyond the road in front of the house which is a mere trail, wide enough for only a wagon to pass. From our new vantage point, we can see both the house and the barn. Horses burst from the barn and we watch my ancestor as he distributes feed, then pumps water. It takes several bucketsful to fill the trough. He heads back into the barn and reappears with a saddled mount that he leads to the hitching post in front of the house that still stands in *my* world. I shake my head in rejection of the idea. "You do realize that this whole nonsense is a dream; and sooner or later I will wake up; and you and this ridiculous scenario will evaporate from my imagination. I probably won't even recall it."

"An' yah from mine, Dahlin'. Ah can assure yah, we are together in willin' tah awaken; the soonah, the bettah. Those gorgeous blue eyes frolic wickedly. "Well," he says. "In the remote prospect, howevah, that this isn't a product of nocturnal imaginin's, Ah suggest that we make it back tah the barn before yor ancestor reappears. I don't know why, but he strikes me as a less than hospitable type. Yah mustah inherited yor mannahs from the maternal side." This *is* a dream, I assure myself enough to test the theory. Without warning, I start skipping, singing as I go in the direction of the mountain ahead. Tom rushes from behind, grabbing my hand as he passes by and nearly pulling my arm from its socket as he drags me to the hillside. A second later, we hear the gruff voice again accompanied by the blast of a shotgun as we melt into the mountain. I am panting and Tom is being racked by a coughing spasm by the time we stop just inside the wall of rock. I turn around to see Jefferson Fielding walking briskly in our direction, pumping the shotgun for another blast. He stops a foot or two shy of the barrier and looks left and right; then up and down. He lifts his hat and scratches his temple. Eyes glued to the hillside, he sets the butt of the weapon on the ground and rests barrel against stone. He runs a gloved hand over the jagged depression left by the shotgun blast and I get a close-up of my great, great, great grandfather. His face is swarthy and etched with time, neither handsome nor homely. Creases around his mouth suggest Tom's suspicions. This man expresses disapproval far more than joy. His jaw is set hard and there is coldness in those dark brown eyes, a visage that evokes dread. He reaches down, eyes never wavering, and pulls a large knife from its sheath on his belt. He starts first to pick at the hole; then stabs at it aggressively. I jerk back. Tom and I exchange another "What the" look, before he embarks on another choking fit. Jefferson drops the knife and grabs for the gun. We are not seen, but very much heard. From his expression, I can see that Jefferson is more than baffled by the source of the sound; he is angry at what he must think is some kind of practical joke. I know the feeling. He removes his right glove and continues to scrutinize the rock. I can see the flat of his calloused hand as if it was pressed against a pane of glass in front of me. Tom is bent over, a handkerchief to his mouth in an effort to stifle another cough. Jefferson walks a few feet to his left where there is a steep path to the top of the hill. I am curious, but this is too much and I opt to help a distressed Tom back into the barn. Once inside, I yank the pry bar from its position and, in a state of utter disbelief, watch as the doors swing toward me, unite, and turn to stone, leaving no trace that anything out of the ordinary has taken place. I stare at the wall of rock for a minute or two before asking, "What time did you get in last night," I ask as if it is a normal query.

He swallows after the spasm relaxes. "About four in the mornin', if Ah recall." He pulls out the pocket watch tucked in his colorful vest. "Huh, my watch mustah stopped about an hour laytah." He shrugs and proceeds to wind it. "Damn," he adds. He shakes it, looks at it again, and shrugs. "The dang thing has quit workin' altogethah; an', Ah paid a pretty penny for it. Ah am sorrah, if yah could indulge me once more, I believe Ah must lie down," he says. I notice he is sweating, is paler than before, and now shaking from the cold. We hadn't planned an outside excursion.

Back in the house, I lead him to the downstairs bath. He sits on the toilet lid, head drooping, as I add some musk bubble bath to the water as the tub fills. "I'll be right back," I say. "Turn this off before it overflows." He looks at me oddly, but nods. I knock before entering. To my surprise, Tom is already sunken in the tub, his clothes neatly folded on the small stool between the sink and the toilet. I grab up the dusty clothes and replace them with a pair of striped flannel pajamas, slippers, and a fleece robe topped off with a super-sized fluffy towel. One of my recent accomplishments has been to go through the more recent boxes in the attic. I found them filled with the neatly folded wardrobes of my grandparents. I had laundered and repacked them, intending to donate them to the local Goodwill on my next trip down the pass. I open the mirrored chest above the sink where I keep spare toiletries for the guests that until this morning I had yet to accommodate. I set out on the sinkboard a new toothbrush and paste, a brush, comb, and deodorant, hoping I don't have to explain it. I add to them the bottle of cough syrup I usually keep on hand with aspirin and other first aid items. The steam seems to have quieted his coughing. I leave him, arms resting along the top of the tub, knees bent above the bubbles, breathing more easily. "Don't fall asleep. It would be a pity if you drowned . . . I mean with what we've just survived," I say a bit sarcastically. How would I explain another dead body in the house?

I close the door behind me and pause to lean against it. Inhaling deeply. I decide to proceed as if the uncanny is perfectly normal. Relax, I think, still half expecting to wake up sans my houseguest. I set Tom's clothes down and head for the bunk in the barn where I pick up the overcoat, hat, and saddlebags, forgotten in the excitement of the side venture. In his condition, it is clear that Tom needs several days rest to be able to continue his journey. Exiting the bunkhouse, I again look over at the hillside wall. I cannot help but reach out, but, as expected, there is no response; Tom, alone has the power to open the portal.

Hearing the rain pounding the roof again, I set my burden on the floor and go out to corral the horses. Once I have them inside and the rest of the stock safely out of the storm, I retrieve Tom's items and head back into the house, where I slough the bags off my shoulders onto the floor next to the sofa. Grabbing up the rest of the clothing I head down to the cellar. I feel awkward going through the man's pockets; but have no alternative if I am to launder them. No longer capable of surprise, I deposit the contents into the basket I keep for just such a purpose. I fill it with the old bills and silver coins, and a substantial wad of large paper money that I do not recognize, a couple of envelopes, and of course, the metal flask. A slight jostle tells me it is about empty. I toss the appropriate clothing into the washer. The coat, pants, and vest, I put into a dry-cleaning bag with the packet of solvent and set the bundle in the dryer.

When I return upstairs, I remove its cushions and pull out the sleeper/sofa; after which I gather fresh linens from the hall cupboard and make up the bed. I plug in the electric blanket and set it on high. I am glad for all the diversion, as I am not ready to sort out the events of the day. It is all sci-fi and contradiction; but somewhere along the line, I find I am compelled to acknowledge the unacceptable. My mind searches for a substitute hypothesis, but none will come; and at this point, I have decided that the dream thing is not flying either.

I forget my manners and enter the bathroom without knocking. "Sorry," I say covering my eyes and swiftly backing out of the room, when I realize I have caught him mid-exit out of the tub reaching for the towel. I hear muffled laughter that is immediately accented by that disturbing cough.

Tom emerges a few minutes later, my grandfather's nightclothes hanging on his too thin frame. There is heightened color in his cheeks and he is breathing evenly. He seems taken aback by the waiting bed. "Ah am mighty obliged for the hospitality." His voice echoes with exhaustion; obviously no threat to me.

Still not ready to explore the experience, I thank him and instruct him to get into the bed. He needs his rest, and I am tired as well. It has already been a long day. We can talk later. He offers no resistance and falls asleep almost immediately. It is a little after noon and raining hard. Exhausted, I wrap the afghan around me, sit, and adjust the recliner to full tilt, but find I am too wired to sleep. Throwing back the afghan, I right the chair and head for the kitchen.

CHAPTER 10

In the kitchen, I turn on the TV that is suspended high in one corner before retrieving two steaks from the freezer. What man doesn't like a good steak dinner? This one looks like he could use a month of them. I study the cookbooks on the shelf and grab the one that contains the apple pie recipe I have been anxious to try. Concentrating on the directions, with one ear taking in the talk show conversation, assures that my mind is fully occupied, diverted from the disquieting affairs of the foregoing hours. I have yet to rule out the idea that I am in the throes of a captivating dream. Rolling out the crust and preparing the filling is therapeutic. Once the pie is in the oven, I turn my attention to the rest of the dinner menu. I prepare the marinade per Nancy Pruitt's recipe and set the steaks aside before vigorously scrubbing two hefty russets. I slather them with olive oil and wrap them in foil; ready for oven baking. I don't care what anyone claims, microwaved spuds just don't cut it. Coming away from the fridge with an array of salad vegetables, I begin tearing, chopping, and dicing, a little tension releasing with each motion. At three, I decide the meal will not be complete without bread and throw myself into kneading the dough for dinner rolls. That done, it is still early and I have exhausted the menu possibilities. The pie is cooling, the rolls rising, meat marinating. The potatoes await their turn in the oven and the salad sits in the fridge, ready for tossing. I look up. Dr. Phil is shaking his head in the wake of some disgusting admission by today's guest, while the audience gasps in disbelief. You ain't heard nothin' yet, I think; and with that, decide a generous glass of hearty burgundy is in order, as well as a change in channels. It's five o'clock somewhere, I rationalize. Aiming the remote at the TV I flip channels until I hear the Jeopardy theme. I check on the plumping rolls, then on my boarder. He remains in the position I left him; resting peacefully, it appears. I make a trip to the cellar to take care of the laundry, hangin the fresh dry cleaning and tossing the contents of the washer into the dryer. Then I trudge up the stairs. Another benefit to my relocation is all the exercise I get in and out of the house. In California, I drove from my single level apartment to a job where I sat for most of the day.

Back in the kitchen, I pop the rolls into the oven, and begin to match wits with the contestants in "double jeopardy". The leading contender blows it all in the final round. The winner walks away with very little money, but gets to play another day. An early edition of the news follows. No surprises there. The local lead story is the weather and the inevitable related complications; flooding, mudslides, and road closures. Multiple accidents are reported, mostly along the interstate, mostly minor. Why don't people heed the warnings to stay off the roads? I remind myself how fortunate I am; that most others have no choice but to be out there making a living.

Amidst this thought, the timer goes off. The rolls are a perfect golden brown. Immediately, the aroma of fresh baked bread overpowers that of the cooling pie. I adjust the temperature and insert the potatoes before pastry-brushing the rolls with melted butter.

On the national front, murder and assorted mayhem, mostly political, fill the airways. I have little patience for the tired rhetoric and click to a sitcom rerun. Seeing a horse in a commercial reminds me of my animal family. I make haste to the barn and in added haste, feed and check the automatic waterers. Satisfied that all is as it should be, I secure barn and other buildings before returning to the house.

I am refilling my goblet. "Ah could use a spot of that." Under the cover of the anchor's laughter, Tom has entered the kitchen. As I turn to respond, I see he is gawking upward, reminding me of our time warp. This is for real; the man has never seen television. My own discombobulation is one thing, but I would be hard-pressed to put myself in his place. I reach for a second goblet and fill it for him. My evolving acceptance continues to wrestle with known reality.

"I thought your beverage of choice was made of grain," I say extending the glass and acting as if nothing is out of the ordinary.

He stares for a minute longer at the talking box, looks blankly at me. "Ah am sorrah; yah were sayin'?"

I repeat my comment.

He clears his throat. "Ah have an extensive palate for fine food an' drink," he says swirling the liquid and inhaling. He takes a sip and allows it to rest on his tongue before swallowing and emitting a contented sigh. On the screen, a provocative woman is assuring the male audience that touching up their gray will greatly enhance their sex appeal. Tom watches as I point the remote vanishing picture and sound. He lets out another sigh, this one of resignation. "An' just like that, she was gone from our lives forevah," he says. The statement is vaguely familiar, but I can't place it. Clearly, I have the advantage in this phenomenon, but he is taking it better than I, sense of humor intact. Hindsight is twenty-twenty they say. Earlier today, when I stepped with him into the past, I had history to fall back on. Things were definitely out of sync, but not totally alien. I sense he is not a man comfortable with this kind of unfamiliarity. He is wandering in the uncharted future; no doubt on the alert for the next disruption of his realm of understanding; yet somehow, he tolerates it as if he is awaiting a logical explanation. The devilish idea of how much fun I might have with this, floats along in my thoughts . . . I suppress blossoming laughter. Of course, it will have to wait until he is up to it. For the moment, he joins me in ignoring the obvious. "Speakin' of food, the aroma in this room is delightful."

69

"I am a novice in the kitchen, but learning," I admit. "I've stuck to the basics for tonight.

"Ah beg tah diffah, Dahlin'," he says gesturing to the pie and pan of rolls cooling on the countertop to his right.

"Better to reserve judgment until you taste it. How are you feeling?"

"Much improved, thanks tah yah; an' soon to be back on the top of mah game," he says with a graceful wave of his glass.

More than a tad buzzed, I nearly misstep as I move to open the oven. My squeeze of the potatoes tells me they need another few minutes. He feigns disregard as I prepare to put the steaks into the broiler. I imagine the questions that must be whirling inside his brain. He is a man of patience. I will grant him that.

By some unspoken mutual consent, we continue to ignore the hundred and thirty years between us, pretending all is normal for the duration of the meal. Tom reminds me of a restaurant critic as he carefully savors each bite, refusing to swallow until he has wrested the last bit of flavor from each morsel.

He directs the discussion to our earlier visitor. "That neighbor this mornin' . . ."

"Jim Pruitt."

"What did he mean about findin' dead bodies?"

I'm taken off guard. "Oh that." What should I say? What does it matter? I decide. I feels good to shelve the current issue.

I start the narration with inheriting the house and bring him up to date, as if he were an old friend home after a long sabbatical. Tom listens with interest as I reveal the alternate story that had been handed down; how the incident relates to the people we saw during the morning's excursion into the past. The wine has loosened my tongue and I disclose my own determination to clear the name of my ancestor.

"When did this all happen?" he asks after a thoughtful pause.

"1879. It was all in her diary." My eyes begin to sting with the threat of tears as I relate Sarah's words of forgiveness. I quickly dab my eyes and leave Tom to his thoughts as I clear the table and load the dishwasher. I pour more wine and suggest we retire to the living room where I plan to attack the "elephant in the room."

CHAPTER 11

We get comfortable, me in the recliner and Tom on the sofa bed.

"It's obvious neither of us is dreaming," I begin.

Tom concurs with a mere chuckle.

"By the way, that box on the wall in the kitchen is called a television. There's another behind those louvered doors," I say pointing across the room. "I have no understanding of how sound and pictures are transported from around the world into my living room, but we can talk about that later; and all the other things that are sure to blow your mind; let me rephrase that," I add before he thinks that his head exploding might be possible in the modern world, "surprise you."

He chuckles into a coughing spasm. I wait for it to pass.

"There have always been purports of supernatural phenomenon, but, to my knowledge, nothing verifiable." Tom nods. "I've tried every which way to rationalize what's happening; to fit it into known reality, but . . ." When he offers no comment, I venture on. "There's a whole genre in modern literature and novels called sci-fi. Tom cocks his head and raises a brow. "Science fiction," I edit. "We speak in abbreviations and acronyms these days." I explain. "There are hundreds of tales and variations on "time travel". My mind is still rebelling, but . . ."

Tom takes the helm of the conversation. "Ah, Ah am familiah with the works of Mr. Jules Verne," he starts. "The poor man's delusions even took him tah the moon."

When my expression conveys that the author's imagination has become reality, Tom is genuinely unnerved. "Indeed", he comments. I shrug. "From my current perspective, Ah cannot deny this . . ." he raises his palms, "whatevah this is that we are experiencin'; but the moon?" I nod. "How cosmopolitan." He pauses and shakes his head. "In any event, Ah find the whole business fascinatin' an' in need of furthah exploration. Are yah up tah anothah—"

"You mean going back out *there* tonight . . . right now? I mean . . . aren't you tired?" I interrupt.

"That is what Ah was suggestin'," he says dryly. "Ah am rested an' have a powerful curiosity that will prevent sleep if it is not satisfied." He rises and stretches.

"You bet!" Before he can change his mind, I am up and heading toward the mudroom for a jacket.

"Ah *will* need mah clothes, Dahlin'," he says with arms out wide, as if modeling the nightclothes he is wearing.

"Oh my," I say and make an abrupt U-turn. I throw open the door to the cellar and bound down the steps.

"Do watch yor step, Dahlin'" he calls down.

I return a minute later with the freshly laundered garments and wait, not so patiently, while he changes in the bathroom. I have to force myself not to run out the door and through the walkway, but I wait and keep to his pace. Once in place, I stand behind him as he reaches to touch the wall. The magic is repeated. In a moment of confusion, I look back at the windows then outside, into the darkness. I check my watch; a few minutes after eight. I turn back to the early morning vision before me, an early morning sky. This time, Tom positions the pry bar; then offers a hand. I take it without hesitation and together we venture into the past. To our right we can see Jefferson looking up the path on the hill. He fires another shot and waits before turning back and walking toward the house apparently satisfied that he has discouraged any danger. A tethered horse snorts as he disappears into the house. The first thing we do is walk beyond where we know the mountain of rock ends. When we turn back, sure enough, there it is, but no barrier to us. How do I wrap my mind around that? Ah, though, I must remember that my return passage through it depends on a physical connection to Tom. As we embark on our exploration, Tom is on the alert leaving me free to study the lay of the land and comparing it to my memory of the photos in the old album.

"See that Mary does the rest of her chores and practices her letters," the voice booms not more than thirty feet away, prompting us to dash back within the rock. We watch as Jefferson abruptly emerges into view. He grabs the reins from the rail just outside the front door and mounts his horse. "I'll be back before supper, and no more mollycoddling, ya hear? See that the child does all her chores," he adds even louder in the wake of spurring his horse into a gallop down the drive toward the road.

"Who's he talkin' tah?" asks Tom.

My heart skips a beat at the idea that I will be meeting Sarah. "Not Mary," I say. "He is talking *about* Mary to someone else. It's got to be her mother! We have to knock on the door and find out," I almost beg.

Tom pats my arm. "All in good time, Dahlin'. Let's be shor Jefferson is . . ." As if psychic, he is interrupted by the sound of returning hoof beats. My great, great, great grandfather is galloping back up the road. He pulls up the reins just short of the barn, mud flying in his wake. A minute later, he swings something over the front of his saddle and gallops away again. I feel Tom's pat on my hand and nod. Duly cautioned, I do not press Tom to satisfy my curiosity. Instead, I pull him towards the back of the barn past the open portal to explore the area on the other side. Beyond the corral outside the barn, there is barbed wire fencing surrounding pasture that seems to stretch forever. I can hear the sounds of cattle in the distance. We continue in the same direction until we come upon a substantial herd.

"How many do you think there are?" I ask.

"Ah'd venchah to guess nine-hundred tah a thousand within sight, that is. Yor granddaddy appears to be a wealthy man." It sounds strange to be speaking of Jefferson in the present. "Ah think it's safe now . . . tah go back an' knock on the door."

I am beyond excited until it dawns on me. "You'll have to go alone," I say spreading my arms as I look down at my outfit.

"Ah, yes," says Tom.

"There's also the fact that I am a clone of my great, great, great grandmother." Tom squints. "That'd be 'spittin' image' in your lingo," I correct. He nods.

"Ah see how that could be a problem," he acknowledges. I wait behind the curtain of rock and watch as Tom makes his way to the front of the house. I regret that the front door is hidden from my vantage point, but I do not want to be caught in the wrong place in the wrong time. Tom is just about out of sight when I hear the gleeful excitement of a child. He steps back and into sight once again, as Mary collides head on into him. "Whoa there, Lil' Dahlin'," he says scooping her up in his arms. Her startled expression quickly dissipates as he sets her down unharmed. "May Ah speak with yor mothah?" he asks. I hold my breath, close my eyes, and cross my fingers.

"A bad man took Momma away when I was little," my great, great, grandmother answers in a sad tone. I feel my heart sink and remember that Tom says this is 1882, three years after Sarah's death. "My auntie came to live with my Pa and me; she's in the house." Mary turns and yells, "Auntie Liz, we have company!" Her intonation tells me that visitors are probably rare.

"Hello," I hear the caution in the woman's voice.

"Don't shoot him, Auntie Liz!" What the . . .

"What can I do for you, Mister?" While Tom and Mary are within sight, Auntie Liz is just out of my view, but I can make out the barrel end of a shotgun.

"Tom McKey," answers Tom raising his hands. "Ah assure yah there's no need for the weapon, Ma'am. Mary, here, was just tellin' me the sad news about Sarah."

"I'm Elizabeth Higgins. You knew my sister?"

I gasp, wondering how he will answer; but he does not

miss a beat. "A mutual acquaintance in The Springs mentioned she had married; that she an' her husband were livin' in these mountains and that Ah should pay my respects if Ah was evah in the area. Is the man of the house at home?"

"Pa went to town for supplies and the mail," little Mary pipes up.'

"I'm afraid Jefferson won't be back till later this afternoon," adds Elizabeth. "You're welcome to come in, Mr. McKey," she offers. "Got fresh coffee on the stove and you are more than welcome to join us for dinner later; there is more than plenty. Sorry about the shotgun, but a body can't be too careful out here."

"Ah undahstand perfectly, Ma'am," he says. "An' I wish I could oblige myself of your generous hospitality, but I'd best stay ahead of the weathah; supposed tah be anothah storm arrivin' anytime now," he replies.

Mary takes one of his hands in both of hers. Little as she is, she is able to pull the off-guard Tom forward a step. "Oh, please, please stay," she begs. It had not taken long for him to charm the little girl.

Tom smiles. "Tell yah what, Lil' One, Ah'll stop again on mah way back," he promises. "An' Ah might jus' have somethin' a young lady bout yor age might enjoy." The man has *me* melting into my boots.

Mary is jumping up and down. "Settle down now; mind your manners, Young Lady." The child responds immediately.

Abruptly she runs in my direction after the barking puppy that has suddenly appeared. I jump back as the paws come toward me. I laugh silently as they appear to hang in mid-air as the little dog sniffs the hillside and emits a funny little growl.

"There's nothing there, Blackie," says Mary as she scoops him up into her arms and turns. He wriggles out of her grasp easily. Together they chase and bounce between house and barn. Mary tosses a ball toward the hillside. It stops a few inches from my feet. The puppy bounds over to retrieve it but stops short. Again, he sniffs at my boots, or rather, the rock in front of him. I hold my breath, fascinated by the physics. "Get it, Blackie; get it," squeals Mary. Blackie takes a few more sniffs before picking up the ball and racing back to his young mistress.

"Mary, come back and say goodbye to Mr. McKey." Mary runs to Tom's side, Blackie on her heels. He gives Tom the once over before obediently sitting at Mary's feet. "Yes, Ma'am; then strikes an adult pose and offers her hand to Tom. "Glad to meet you, Sir," She enunciates perfectly. "I look forward to seeing you again, soon."

Tom smiles and tips his hat. "The pleasure has been all mine, I Ah assure yah, Miss Fielding," he says bending down to plant a kiss across her fingers.

"Oh, Oh!" is all she can say as she jumps up and down before she and the puppy are off again.

"Again, Ah am sorrah tah hear about yor sister," he directs to Elizabeth.

"Thank you, Mr. McKey. Where did you say you were heading?"

"Off tah Denvah," he answers without missing a beat.

"You have a safe trip, Mr. McKey, was it?"

Tom nods and tips his hat again, "An' good day tah yah, Ma'am."

Mary! You come back inside and finish your chores. You heard what your father said."

Tom starts to walk straight along the front of the barn, no doubt covering himself lest the child see him disappearing into the rock. I meet him around the corner on the far side of the barn, already making plans to be with him on his return, appropriately dressed, of course. I must come up with some way to disguise my face.

"You are good," I say complimenting his quick thinking. "A perfect stranger and you had them eating out of your hand in no time."

"She is a charmah, that, great, great, grandmothah of yors.

"She's quite taken with you, as well. Tell me about Elizabeth. I heard the conversation, but couldn't see her."

"It's verah sad," he begins slowly with a look that is

asking me if he should go on.

"What kind of sad?" I ask and swallow.

"It appears that she has been in a terrible accident at some point, a fire, probably as a child, Ah would guess. One side of her face is severely disfigured. She's bent to one side a bit an' walks with a limp, probably the result of scarrin' aftah the burn," he says and sighs. "Yah didn't know about it?"

"I didn't know about *her*," I admit. If only I had read a bit further in Mary's diary . . . We continue to explore the outlying property until the sun is directly overhead. "It must be about noon," I glance at my wrist. To top off everything else, *my* watch has stopped working. I shrug, trying to recall the last time I had replaced the battery.

"This is extraordinary!"

I look and see that Tom has his pocket watch out, a natural reflex, I suppose even though it was not working the last time he checked.

"What?"

"Look at this," he says motioning me closer. When I do, I see that the second hand is back at work.

"That's good," I say. "You were probably so tired when you looked—"

"How long would yah say we have been out here?" he interrupts.

"I don't know for sure; dawn to . . . I'm guessing it's close to noon or thereabouts."

"Ah would agree. Now look at the time on mah watch."

"Five after twelve. So?"

"Unless mah instincts are off . . . Look, I remembah lookin' at my watch as I approached yor barn when Ah first arrived. It was around four in the mornin'."

"Okay . . ."

"Then we came out here earlier today for about an hour, right?"

"I don't get it."

"It was when Ah looked at my watch sometime laytah, I determined that it must have stopped about an hour aftah Ah got here." He is looking to me for an acknowledgement. I throw up my hands.

"Donchah see, not only is it workin' again, it's right on time."

I feel my eyes grow and see the light bulb in Tom's expression. We bolt for the portal and toss aside the pry bar. Safely back in the barn, I look down at my wrist as Tom clutches his chest trying to catch his breath. The second hand has resumed its steady movement. Tom is nodding as he looks down at his own watch. "It's stopped again." I show him my watch and point to the clock in the wall; a few minutes after eight, reading the same as my watch. I look back at Tom, afraid to give voice to the facts.

He is not. "Ain't that a daisy; it would appear that time stops in mah world when Ah am here. We left here and returned at the same time by your timepieces. The same holds true while yah are in mine." We let the awe settle in as we make our way back to the house. Jumping from noon to eight in the evening is quite unsettling.

CHAPTER 12

Over coffee, the two of us spend an hour at the kitchen table attempting to come to terms with the relevance of the day's discovery. It appears that it is as simple as Tom initially observed; that time stops in our respective worlds during our absences. After initial acceptance, it is, we agree, a natural progression in this most unnatural phenomenon. Yesterday, I would never have accepted the things I am now eager to pursue in depth. We are brainstorming the possibilities when Tom begins to fade noticeably. He excuses himself while I tidy up the kitchen. When I enter the living room, he is just coming out of the bathroom in his nightclothes, clearly exhausted and quite pale. I help him settle in and bid him goodnight, but instead of going upstairs, deflect into the study where I begin to comb through the journals I had organized weeks ago. It takes a few minutes to confirm there are no journals attributed to Elizabeth, but I locate what must be Mary's first diary penned in the year 1882. I open the fragile book and lay it flat on the table. The printing is neat and painfully accurate for one so young.

My name is Mary Jane Fielding. I was born on August 26, 1876 on the family ranch in Florissant, Colorado, U.S.A. My father's name is Jefferson Fielding. He is a good man and very strong. My mother's name is Sarah. She went away with a bad man when I was three. Daddy said she didn't love him and me anymore. Then her sister, Elizabeth came to live with us to take care of me and the house and cook. I call her Auntie Liz. She was in a bad fire when she was little like me. She has big scars and can't stand up straight; but she is nice to me and we have a lot of fun. She is teaching me reading and my numbers at home because there is no school near the ranch. Daddy gave me this journal at Christmas and says he will help me write in it every night before I go to bed, just like he does. He says it is important for people to write down the history of their life for their children and their children's children.

I carefully turn each page. Subsequent entries leave no doubt as to her parent's influence. Mary has constant praise for her father, the references unnatural somehow. References to her Aunt, while kindly, ever so subtly expose shortcomings and her father's concern for his daughter's welfare under Auntie Liz's care when he is away for lengthy periods, nuances a young child would fail to recognize. Over the months, Elizabeth Collins is painted as an inept housekeeper, and, at best, a passable cook. Jefferson is portrayed as the long-suffering brother-in-law who is at the mercy of his estranged wife's sister; that the post-abandonment arrangement was more of a favor on his part to his in-laws, taking their disabled daughter off their hands. I come to June 21st.

Today Daddy went to town. When he got home I told him about the nice man who came to the house. He got angry and told me the man was bad like the one Mommy went away with and told me never to speak to a stranger again. He was mad at Auntie Liz for letting me talk to the man. He told her she would have to go if she didn't start taking better care of me. My Daddy loves me very much.

The printing belongs to the child, the words and thoughts to her father.

I sit back in my chair, seething with anger. The man was a master at manipulating the facts. I read on. During the next month, there are increasing hints at Auntie Liz's ineptitude and/or deliberate undermining of the household. The July twelfth entry is as follows:

Today was a very sad day. Auntie Liz was feeding the chickens. She must have slipped and died when she hit her head on a rock. Daddy and me are sad, but he said I am a big girl, now, and we will do just fine without her.

The following days tell of the preparation for the trip to Colorado Springs for the funeral.

July 15th

Today we buried Auntie Liz in Colorado Springs. Grandpa and Grandma Collins are so sad. They told Daddy I could come to live with them, but he said no. When we got home, Daddy said I was the woman of the house, now. I know how to clean and wash clothes and I can cook, too. I have a stool to stand on so I can reach the sink and stove.

The rest of the year's entries detail her daily routine and the progress in her education. They are littered with daily admirations for Dear Old Dad. The child even records the times he takes her outside for a "switching", acknowledging the deservedness of his actions and vowing to do better in the future so she can grow up to be a proper young lady. I have to restrain myself from flinging the little book across the room. Jefferson Fielding was a clever man. After my temper cools, I turn back to reread the account of Elizabeth's accident. An accident my ass, I think.

I leave the journal open and return to the living room. I am bursting to tell Tom the news, but see that he is fast asleep. Instead of waking him, I touch the back of my fingers to his forehead and ascertain his temperature to be at least a hundred and two. I think better of heading upstairs and instead decide to bed down in the recliner beside the houseguest who has just become a serious patient. Knowing sleep will, once again, be elusive, I break protocol and wash a couple of sleeping aids down with yet another glass of wine.

CHAPTER 13

The coughing spasm that rouses me does not seem to disturb its source. My watch, working perfectly now; reads five twenty. I rise and tread softly to the kitchen where I set coffee to brewing. Rain is falling steadily, as predicted. I make my way down to the basement where I start a load of whites. I notice the basket with the contents of Tom's pockets that I had forgotten to bring back upstairs with his clothing and snatch it up, as well.

Back in the kitchen, I pour a cup of coffee and take a seat at the table. Last night's self-medication has left me slightly groggy, but the sound sleep was worth a little post sedative fog. I turn on the morning news, and as I listen, find myself mindlessly fingering the coins from Tom's pockets. The three large ones are twenty-dollar gold pieces. I am no authority, but know they must be worth many times their face value in today's market. Then, again, they went a lot farther in the nineteenth century. The wad of bills is a mixture of gold and silver certificates, mostly in larger denominations. It fits. A quick appraisal tells me Tom McKey is carrying a few thousand dollars on his journey, quite a stash in the 1880's. I wonder what he does for a living. Two envelopes are addressed to a J. H. Holliday, in care of general delivery, Denver, Colorado. One is from a Robert A. Holliday in Georgia; that explains the accent. The other has traveled from Gunnison, Colorado and the name W.B.S. Earp. The one-cent stamps evoke a chuckle. I had stocked up on the "forever" denomination when they first appeared, hoping to avoid future increases. I set the letters aside and turn my attention to the weather report.

The rain continues to fall and more of the same is forecast for the next several days. Being marooned doesn't bother me except for the sick person in the next room. What if he needs immediate medical attention? As much as I want to get back to see Mary and Elizabeth, I make a conscious decision to concentrate on the man's recovery, before suggesting a return to the past. After all, nothing is moving out there while Tom is here.

Once the weathercast concludes, I listen with interest to the sports. My Rockies are having a rough time this season, but I have become a diehard fan. Troy Tulowitski has garnered my favor, not only for his playing ability, but also for his unwavering loyalty and positive attitude in the face of heart-breaking defeat. My attention wanes when the president's face fills the screen. I mute the sound and begin to think about breakfast. Sausage, eggs, and pancakes sound good. That decided, I click to an old movie channel while I prepare the pancake batter. I am in mid-stir when it hits me. Why is Tom carrying opened letters addressed to someone else? I drop the spoon, turn back to the table, and pick up the envelopes. A normally resolute respecter of privacy, it goes against my nature to snoop, but I can't resist. The letter from Robert is full of concern over John's health and the expectation of his return to start their partnership. He makes reference to several family members and the latest developments in their lives; then sends special greetings from Mattie and Sophie. It is signed, your cousin, Robert. Who are these people, and what is their connection to Tom McKey? I open the one from Gunnison.

Doc, All is well here. Plans are in motion with Bat coordinating efforts with Wells Fargo and the army. Hooker is on board. I know you are hell bent on being a part of it, and I won't risk insulting you with an attempt to dissuade. I trust your health is improving and we will see you soon. Yours, Wyatt.

My mind is becoming so familiar with the bizarre that it is more than willing to accept anything; yet this . . . I enter the living room where Tom still rests soundly. My target is the saddlebags in the corner. Without taking in the details at the time, I remember initials were branded into the leather. Kneeling down in the semi-darkness, I feel for the markings. A chill runs up my spine as my finger trace the letters; J H H. Is he a thief after all? Quietly, but swiftly as possible, I make for the study and boot up my laptop. I type Tom McKey in the search engine, hoping he is notable enough to have warranted a place in history. The fourth hit displays a number of photos, one of which is the man sleeping in the next room. I click on it and my world that has already been turned topsy-turvy begins to spin like a top. In a very few minutes I uncover the story; Tom McKey was used as an alias by the notorious John Henry (Doc) Holliday. Apparently, McKey was a surname on his mother's side. He resorted to it periodically for obvious reasons. The pieces fall into place all too neatly. I try to shake off the tingle that is working its way up my spine. My stomach begins to churn as I try to sort through these facts and correlate them with what I have come to surmise from my brief association with Tom McKey. The man in the next room is purported to be an infamous gunfighter, but aside from staring down the barrel of his forty-five, he has been a perfect gentleman. The fact that he is going by an alias, although suspicious, is not criminal. I too, use a name from *my* mother's family to protect myself from echoes of scandal. There are legitimate reasons to change one's name, yet . . . Ping pong balls are bouncing around inside my head. I search my data bank for what I know about the notorious Doc Holliday. Sadly, it is limited to movies, the most recently recollected, *Tombstone* of the nineties. I remember Val Kilmer portraying Doc as the dentist friend of Wyatt Earp, slash charming dentist/gambler/killer. A memory flashes of him drawing against Johnny Ringo. It immediately meshes with that first encounter in the bunkhouse. The cough . . . It all fits. Whoa! The man in my living room has TB. I quickly rack my brain for what I know about the disease. The first word that comes to mind is contagious; the second, fatal. I am wallowing in this new data when I hear a faint knock.   "Mornin', Cassie. Yah haven't been up all night, have yah?"

Oh, shit! I close the laptop and attempt to disguise the guilt I feel. "Nope, just woke up early," I stumble over my words. "Just checking my email." I mentally kick myself for the unnecessary explanation that might raise a red flag of deceit.

He points to the computer and shakes his head in confusion. "Is this somethin' like that pitchah box in the kitchen?"

In spite of my trepidation, I manage a poor excuse for a laugh. "Yeah, I'll explain it later," I say, trying to appear normal. "I'm making sausage, eggs, and pancakes," I say as I rise. "How are you feeling this morning?"

"It appears Ah have been granted anothah day," he says light-heartedly

"You were running a pretty high temperature last night."

"It comes an' goes," he says nonchalantly.

I nod. "And I don't like your pallor. Have you been to a doctor about that cough?" He shrugs. I pretend not to take note and am suddenly desperate for time alone to think. "I'm going to take care of the animals and then I'll make breakfast."

"Ah'll get dressed an' go with yah," he offers genuinely.

"You will not." My tone leaves no room for argument. "There's coffee in the kitchen. It won't take me long, just feeding this morning. Won't be letting anyone out in this downpour," I add. As I head toward the barn, I begin to assimilate the adjusted facts. Not only did that man in my study walk in from 1882, he is Doc Holliday, and for all intents and purposes, dying. "Not in my home, he isn't. Do you hear me?" I say aloud, as I hold Buck's face in both of my hands. "I've got a notorious gunfighter in the house. Don't you guys communicate out here?" I look down the row of stalls, as if I had really expected Buck and the girls to have ferreted out and discussed this information with their equine guest. "You could have warned me." The goats and chickens get an earful, as well. By the time the chores are done, I am calm and have a plan.

When I enter the kitchen, Tom, or rather Doc, is seated at the table pouring the last drops in the flask into his coffee mug. His personal effects remain splayed on the table where I had left them. "Let me refill that for you," in hopes of avoiding a confrontation. He allows me to take the flask; watches as I retrieve a bottle of Jack Daniels from a cupboard and fill the flask. I hand it back to him.

"Well, now," he says looking at his belongings.

The jig is up. So much for best-laid plans, blah, blah, blah . . . Maybe . . . I take a stab. "What? Oh that, I brought your things up from the cellar; had to empty your pockets before I laundered your clothes. I wasn't stealing, if that's what you think." I feel the guilt leaking through my pores.

"Pokah's not yor game, Dahlin'," he says as if disappointed. He points at the letters. Why hadn't I returned them to their envelopes and put them back into the basket with his other things?

Best defense is an offense, right? What do I have to lose? Despite the dangerous reputation of my houseguest, I strike the indignant hands-on-hips pose. "What else have you kept from me?" I ask as I fill my mug and join him at the table.

"It would appear that yah have the advantage of knowin' everythin' Ah do before Ah do it; with yor history books, an' all."

"Funny thing about that; according to the little I was able to glean this morning, there seem to be few things in your past about which historians agree. It's not that uncommon, I suppose. There are new discoveries or more than likely, a new theory that worms its way into past accounts and erodes previously accepted facts. After a while, the past is changed, history reads differently."

"Indeed."

"My personal take is that rewriting history allows politicians to adjust the thinking of their constituents." I roll my eyes in contempt.

"An *what*, pray tell, do history books say about—" A particularly violent coughing spasm prevents him from finishing the sentence. When it subsides, he sips his coffee.

"Doc Holliday? I have to admit, I don't know *that* much, yet. From what I have seen on the "pitchah box", as you call it, you could be a bloodthirsty killer. At best, you are painted as a southern gentleman done wrong by nature who is cramming every bit of life he can into the time he has left." I bite my tongue, wishing my mouth had not gotten ahead of my brain. "I'm sorry; that was thoughtless. It must be awful to be so ill." I pause before going on. "It appears that Wyatt Earp liked you well enough. Of course, there are those who don't think much of him either. By the way, how is Kate these days?" I throw out again wishing I could reign in my tongue.

"History. She an' Ah parted company back in Arizona," he coughs out. "Ah'm afraid she became jus' too much tah bear, if yah get my meanin'." His humor tells me I might have been forgiven for my misdeed or perhaps he accepts some gift for his deceit, and I feel the tension dissipate.

We sip our coffee in silence for the next minute or two. I try to view the scene objectively. Without warning, I am seized by uncontrollable giggling. Tom . . . I mean Doc raises a brow but refrains from comment, as if the outburst is a normal female thing. His deadpan expression fuels the chuckle into rib-racking laughter. I am holding my sides as tears are pouring from my eyes. The sensation is exhilarating and I let it engulf me. I fear I am getting much too good at letting my emotions lead me. It takes several minutes to wind down naturally. Breathlessness is the only thing that keeps me from erupting again in the wake of Doc's poker face, one that has been honed to perfection, given his occupation.

"It's just that . . ." I grab for a napkin, blow my nose, and dab at my eyes. Finally composed, I attempt to explain. "I mean . . . I am sitting in my kitchen in the year 2016 having coffee with *the* Doc Holliday!"

He smiles weakly. "An' Ah am sittin' here in the twenty-first century sharin' coffee with Miss Cassie Collins."

"I can assure you, the prestige attached is not quite the same. Oh, as long as we're coming clean, as it were. *My* real name is Cassie Blakely. I, too, use an alias. Like yourself, the anonymity shades me from scandal, although, in my case, not my own." My new wave of laughter is contagious. Unfortunately, it triggers another severe choking spasm in Doc. "Why don't you lie back down until breakfast is ready," I say after the attack subsides. Holding a napkin to his lips, he shakes his head in agreement. I follow him into the living room, pull back the shutters hiding the big screen and turn on CNN. I desperately needed some time to think about this new revelation, and it is time this man gets a concentrated dose of the modern world. "Relax and watch," I say as I turn on the news. "I'll answer questions later."

CHAPTER 14

We breakfast with minimal conversation. It is all Doc can do to get his meal down between choking spasms. Hunger satisfied, he retreats to the living room with a refill of coffee. I make quick work of the kitchen duties, before retreating to the study and my laptop. While Doc is being inundated with the modern world, good and bad, complements of <u>Live with Kelly and Michael</u>, my fingers are dancing through the super highway of information. While presented as fact on one website, a piece of data is downgraded to unsubstantiated legend or challenged as the theory of a biased source on another. The more I take in, the more flummoxed I become. While this confirms what Doc and I discussed earlier about rewriting history as time goes on, it is annoying me to all end, on this subject. The data is rampant with contradictions. While I care not about the exact particulars of Tom McKey, I am desperate to know the accurate details of the man who sits in my living room. Just how dangerous is the infamous Doc Holliday? Am I in over my head?

Around noon, I pass through the living room. I find him still glued to the miracle of the talking machine. I set up TV trays. He is shaking his head at the emotionally charged conversation amongst a panel of professed political authorities. In the kitchen, I prepare soup and sandwiches, concentrating on the most nourishing ingredients. John Henry Holliday of 1882 is a very sick man, just five years short of a premature death. The thought depresses me. A fanciful notion hopscotches through my mind. What if . . . I discredit the idea as preposterous, but then, this whole scenario is outrageous. Yet Doc Holliday is sitting in my living room; I have been through the portal and seen the past for myself. Where do the options end? I add the salt and peppershakers to the serving tray.

"What do you think of what the human race has done with the last hundred and thirty years?" I ask as I set our lunch plates on the TV trays.

Doc chuckles and takes a sip of soup before answering. "One has tah admire the progress that has been made with electricity, an' machinery, an' whatevah yah call all these . . ."

"The modern term is technology," I finish for him.

He sits back on the sofa and folds his arms across his chest. "Knowledge in all areas seems tah have galloped beyond any proportions that Ah evah imagined . . . Howevah . . ." He takes a bite of sandwich, chews carefully, and swallows.

"The things people have done with the information . . . From mah viewpoint, which is impaired tah say the least . . . It's jus' that Ah can't help but think that legitimate ignorance has given way to the wildly irresponsible. Ah would have expected the human race tah have made life easier, safer for itself. Ah can see the easy, but . . . Yah see, Ah am yustah havin' tah watch' my back. Oh, Ah admit Ah have brought it on myself, what with mah sullied reputation. But in this age, it seems that peril is at every turn for even the most innocent of folk engaged in everyday activities. Yor poorly-termed accidents on the roads, for instance; not tah mention . . ." I wait, but he waves a hand as if adding to the list of his observances would be too tiring. The assessment is, so accurate and so free of any political agenda, the honest appraisal of an unbiased spectator. I conjure up the image of him sitting among the commentators. What commences as a giggle ignites unrestrained laughter, tears and all.

"Indeed."

"Oh, I am sorry. I wasn't making fun of you, I . . ." Trying to hold a straight face only triggers another fit. I opt to let it play out before dabbing my eyes.

"Yah quite finished?" I sit very erect, clear my throat and nod; but fear if I pick up my explanation, it might set me off again, and opt instead for him to continue. "Ah appreciate that my perspective is woefully outdated, but yah did ask mah opinion," he says, arms outstretched in his own defense. I feel another titter knocking at the door of my throat; then suddenly, I realize that I may have offended the man. "The verah least yah could do is tah respect mah humble opinions; maybe try tah hide yor derision."

"No . . . No . . ." I grope for the words that will undo the damage. "Your perspective is something that is desperately needed today. You are right; the world has gone stupid, for want of a better word . . . no . . . stupid's the word. The more you watch, the more that evaluation will be solidified. For me, it is just so . . . so . . . rejuvenating to hear it so ingenuously put into words."

"Then why . . ."

"I was imagining you sitting on that panel offering your commentary. People would be falling off their chairs."

"Ah beg to diffah. From what Ah can discern it would seem that a majority might take tah formin' a lynch mob." Doc looks back at the TV where a discussion of gun control is heating up. His smile is confident as he gestures to the screen. "Ah rest my case." We finish eating in silence as I ponder how this world would change if common sense were to suddenly become politically correct.

"Ah don't know how much more of this Ah can bear," he says as he dabs his mouth with a napkin. I can tell he is serious.

"Pretty sad, state of affairs, isn't it?" I acknowledge. It then occurs to me that I can learn much about this man by listening to his observations on today's society. With that in mind, I aim the remote and begin to shuffle through the guide until I come up to movie that will expose him to modern film content. One of the things that historians do agree on is Doc's relationship with Big Nose Kate. He was no tea-totaling prude by any stretch, but I sense an inner integrity that might well be offended by the amorality of the twenty-first century.

In the kitchen, I take my time cleaning up after lunch. I do not have to wait long before I hear a half gasp/half laugh evolve into another coughing fit. "You okay?" I almost feel guilty as I try to maintain an innocent expression, while he labors to catch his breath, while pointing at the TV.

"Something the matter?"

He sits back and waits for the spasms to recede. "Don't get me wrong, Ah can see the advantage of many of these machines," he says with a sweep of his hand. "But, as Ah mentioned before, they have not come without consequences that seriously put in question their value. But this," he says extending an arm toward the TV. On the screen, is a couple in the throes of wild lovemaking. "Tell me that viewin' this hasn't become substitute for . . ."

"Oh my, no," I say quickly; then realize how this must look from his chronologically challenged perspective.

"So people still . . ."

"Oh yes; of course," I feel myself coloring. While my answer is based on common knowledge, my experience nixes any claim I have as an authority on the subject. After all, how many twenty-six year-old virgins are there in the country? I wonder how things would be different had I been reared in a liberal household sans the handicap of disfigurement.

"Well, that is a relief," he says as I take a seat. "For a minute, I thought perhaps, the human race had invented an alternative method of . . . ah . . . reproducin' itself. That would be a shame, indeed, as the accepted method has such pleasant side effects."

Again, I am taken aback by Doc's naïve insight. Up to this point, his worldliness, circa the 1880's, has put him at an intellectual advantage. I silently reprimand myself for finding this turn of the tables somehow wickedly satisfying and focus my attention on the actors who have moved from passion to bank robbery. "As a matter of fact . . ." When I pause for effect, I watch his expression of incredulity and shock blossom in the reflection of the TV screen. "Medical science has developed what they call in vitro fertilization."

He turns to me. "People have children without . . ."

"Relax; the world hasn't lost all sanity. The procedure and many other treatments continue to be developed for couples who cannot seem to conceive via traditional means."

"How cosmopolitan."

"Believe me, sex has become a preoccupation, if nothing else, that and drugs" I add with some derision in my tone. I cannot ignore the twinge of jealousy. Am I truly disgusted with the sexual revolution or envious of others who are enjoying a satisfying sex life? Somewhere in the middle, I silently conclude. Drugs hold no attraction for me. I find life mind-altering enough.

"Ah am relieved, tah say the least," he says putting a hand to his chest. "Imagine a world without . . ." Unlike most people in his position of ignorance, he does not continue to drill me for details, but seems content to assimilate data piecemeal before moving forward with more questions; or perhaps further exploration of the subject holds no interest for him. In his place, I think I would be holding an inquisition.

As he settles back to soak up more of the visual media, I hand him the remote and educate him as to its basic functions, before sequestering myself in the study.

Occasionally, I am aware of the change of channels, but after an hour or so, snoring drowns out all other sound. Around three, my own edification has been sated and I move on to email. By four, I have overcome the quandary that had seized me earlier. I log off and begin dinner preparation, homemade pizza. While I have never attempted twirling it, I have perfected a decent dough and a palatable sauce. After arranging the slices of sausage, I load up the crust with a myriad of vegetables, pop it in the preheated oven and head back to waken my guest. Not necessary. I hesitate in the doorway. He is engrossed in the images of a multi-vehicle accident on the twenty-five while tippling from his flask. His ghostly pallor remains and beads of sweat trickle toward his brow.

"Hungry?"

He smiles. "Ravenous." I take this a complement of my

cooking. He turns his attention back to the TV. "Horses an' wagons could never compete with such speed, nor with such chaos," he says as he starts to rise.

"Stay where you are," I say. He sits back down without argument.

"Do you like pizza?" I ask.

"Ah don't believe . . ."

"Of course, you've never had it. I think you'll like it." I return from the kitchen with the sliced pie in one hand; two glasses and a bottle of merlot in the other. On the next trip I bring plates and napkins, and find him uncorking the bottle. Before he has time to question protocol of dealing with this new food, I slip one hand under a slice, take a bite and then plop it on my plate. He hands me a glass of wine and then mimics my actions, struggling a bit at first to control the floppy wedge, but soon gets the hang of it.

"Verah tasty."

"It's practically a national icon. We have restaurants dedicated to pizza. In fact, folks who live closer to town can phone in their orders and have the variety of their choice delivered piping hot to the front door in thirty minutes"

Doc just nods in acceptance; then sips his wine. "This is quality fruit of the vine," he says raising his glass to examine its contents. It is obvious that Doc's reputation for enjoying the good life has not been exaggerated, and I am silently complimented. I wonder what he would think of pop tarts or hotdogs. His pallet has yet to be compromised with the empty nutrition of our modern junk food. It's amazing how good it tastes when it is your steady diet, but how dissatisfying it becomes when your routine fare is homemade.

An episode of Everybody Loves Raymond is down to the credits as I come back from tidying the kitchen. "Had enough?" I ask retrieving the remote.

"Duly sated," he says. "Besides, Ah much prefer yor conversation.

"As I do yours," I reply as I take my seat. Several seconds go by before I broach the subject. "Listen, I've been doing some research and some thinking."

"In regard tah?"

"Your health."

"It's pointless," he says without hesitation. "Ah've been livin' on borrowed time for the bettah part of mah years," he says with a sweep of an arm. "The family had hoped a change in climate . . . but I've had tah face the facts, lungers are doomed, Dahlin'."

"That may be true in 1882, but TB, or consumption, as you know it, is quite treatable today." When his expression is unaffected and he offers no comment, I add. "There's no need for you to die of this disease. I have a friend—"

"No!" is his adamant reply.

"But—"

"Ah don't have time for that. Ah've got tah get tah Gunnison in the next few days tah meet—"

"But don't you see," I say. "There is no hurry, now. Remember our watches? Time is standing still in your world while you're here." An expression of guarded fascination etches its way into his face. "You have all the time in the world." When I beckon him to contradict, he tilts his head, as if considering the information. I go into the bathroom and come back with his watch. "See," I say shoving it under his nose. "It's stopped again while mine is running fine. If we were to go through the portal right now, I guarantee that yours would begin ticking and mine would stop. We would see Mary playing with her dog. Don't you see what it means? Whatever you need to do in Gunnison, wouldn't you rather be strong and healthy when you get there. Heck, you might not even make it in your present condition." He remains silent and pensive. "Besides," I go on, "I've already contacted a doctor."

"Yah what?" His attempt to rise off the sofa is aborted by lack of strength, and for the first time, I hear alarm in his tone. "It's one thin' for *yah* tah know who Ah am. That is watah undah the bridge, but . . ." That awful cough takes hold of him and he is forced to flop back onto the sofa hugging his sides.

"Give me some credit," I say letting my offense show. "I didn't make the arrangements until I thought it all through," I begin slowly. "We do have complications in the twenty-first century. It's called "red tape". Unlike your generation, where you can freely assume another identity at will and disappear into the woodwork, the present-day population in this country, at least, is highly regulated. Everybody has a government-assigned designation known as a social security number. There are numbers for driver's licenses and for about anything you can think, not to mention fingerprinting and DNA." I ignore his lost expression. "It's hard to get around that, but there is one loophole we can take advantage of, however."

"Am ah about tah become a numbah?"

"With the advent of organized crime. . ." I stop to explain when I see the query in his eyes. "Sort of like the cowboys in your era, a band of criminals that might resort to protecting themselves from prosecution by, to delicately put it, eliminating potential witnesses." When he nods his understanding, I continue. "We have what we call a witness protection program. In exchange for testimony, the government protects, then reinvents the witness's identity; assigns new numbers, relocates them, and so forth."

"An' pray tell, what would that do foh me?"

"My friend, Jack, is a doctor. He trusts me. I will simply tell him that you are a family friend, that years ago, you were absorbed into the program with your parents and siblings; that your cover has been compromised and that you came here to hide until you deem it safe to contact the authorities and be reassigned. The TB will be harder to explain, as it is rare these days, but we can say that you were forced to go on the run in less than favorable conditions for a long time. Money is no object. My parents left me more than I could ever use. I can't think of a better investment than your health."

The poker face seems to come naturally. "Let me think about it."

"Are you crazy? What is there to think about? Let's see," I say making the motion of playing with a slinky with my hands, "Living, dying, hum; what shall I decide? Besides, I told you; I've already put things in motion. In fact, I need to check my email," I turn and say in a tone that invites no discussion. When I return from the study, I have no news. The flu is sweeping the area and I assume that Jack is busier than normal. "He'll get back to me as soon as he can," I say. "It will be a while before travel will be possible anyway. In the meantime, you need rest."

"Yah are what, in yor early twenties?"

"Twenty-six," I admit.

"An' yor parents are deceased?"

I am instantly unsettled but answer, "Yes."

"What happened?"

I do not want to discuss this but somehow feel it's only fair to endure some mental discomfort in exchange for Doc's.

"I see," says Doc after he listens to the whole, ugly story. "I am sorrah for yor loss."

CHAPTER 15

"Jack will be here as soon as the rain stops and the roads are passable," is my greeting to Doc the next morning. He was already asleep after I checked my email one last time before heading upstairs the night before. I expect at least a minor protest. When I approach the sofa, I see that Doc is completely hidden under the bundle of bedding. "Come on, Sleepyhead," I tease as I tug at the top of the lump. To my horror, I find myself the victim of one the oldest tricks in the book. The throw pillows I had tossed in the corner of the room have been arranged beneath the blankets to mimic a human form. I make a beeline for the door to the causeway praying that I am in time. Once in the barn, a look to my left compounds my initial fear. Doc's saddle is gone. I run past the stalls of the other horses to the one I had assigned to Doc's mount, and am greeted by the equine's rear. Breathing hard, I swing open the stall door to find Doc and saddle crumpled to the side amid the straw, his horse nuzzling him about the head.

"Easy boy," I say patting the concerned gelding. Doc is wet with sweat and burning with fever. I move his horse to another free stall and take the opportunity to feed everybody. What will it hurt to leave the stubborn man on his straw bed for another few minutes while I tend to the animals? Goats and chickens first. The rain is light this morning, but the mud is thicker than ever. My slippers are a lost cause; my robe and pajamas spattered with gooey muck. When I get back into the barn, I set the basket of eggs aside, remove my soggy footwear, and decide how I will get a six-foot, albeit, undernourished man back into the house unassisted. To my surprise, he rouses easily and is more than cooperative as we make our way back along the causeway. After literally dumping him onto the sofa bed, I follow the trail of straw back through the entry into the barn to retrieve my doomed footwear and the eggs. Once back inside, I lock and remove the keys from the deadbolts on both doors. A slight twinge pricks my conscience as I realize I am probably breaking the law by locking Doc in, but doubt that he is going to turn me in to the authorities. Besides, it is for his own good and the phones are out of order. Before heading upstairs to shower and change, I take a detour to flip the switch on the coffee pot.

I shower and dress in record time; forget about drying my hair, and take the stairs two at a time. I need not have knocked myself out, as my patient hasn't stirred. "Poor soul"; the escape attempt was, borrowing a phrase from Doc, "jus' too much for him tah bear."

The coffee is good, the TV weather report promising. There will be a reprieve from the storm systems by tomorrow morning and fair skies are predicted for several days thereafter. After satisfying myself that the world has not come to an end overnight, I begin to a prepare breakfast of omelets, potatoes, and toast; am pouring the juice as Doc comes through the door. To my amazement, he is back in his nightclothes, his expression one of surrender.

"Ah am sorrah," he says helping himself to a glass of juice.

"What were you thinking?"

"That Ah would be on mah way, troublin' yah no furthah."

"Thanks!" is my indignant reply. I cannot resist the sarcasm. "I didn't realize I was making you feel like a burden. I do apologize, Dr. Holliday."

"That is not what Ah intended." His manner is contrite. "Yah have been a gracious hostess, but Ah am used tah fendin' for myself; an independent cuss, Ah'm afraid. Ah do appreciate everythin' yah have been doin' on mah behalf. Ah will admit tah bein' uneasy about bringin' anothah "modern" into the pitchah, but in mah present infirm condition, it is apparent, even tah me, that mah choices are limited. Ah pride myself in bein' an intelligent man; not that Ah entertain any real hope of bein' cured, mind yah. Aside from that, Ah am afraid mah actions of this mornin' were not worthy of me. Ah realize, too, even had Ah escaped into mah world, mah abrupt exit without notice, would have been ill mannered an' caused yah concern. That is unforgiveable for one who deems himself a gentleman. Ah sincerely apologize for mah thoughtlessness, Cassie. It would follow that Ah am at yor mercy for the moment, Dahlin." A coughing fit is right on the heels of his eloquent oration. His ashen complexion cries out for medical attention and soon. Thankfully, he seems to have an appetite; either that or he is forcing himself, for my benefit, to take in the nutrition his body so desperately requires.

Satisfied that his contrition is sincere, my frustration begins to melt away. "As I said, my friend should be here as soon as the roads are cleared. The rain is supposed to stop before tomorrow, and in view of how long travel has been impaired, I'm sure the crews will be right on it." Doc nods as he continues to eat. "And believe me, Jack can be trusted." He says nothing. "You must find it very frustrating to be so ill, for so long, in what should be the prime of your life."

"It isn't always this bad. It comes 'n goes," he says with a shrug. "Ah'm used tah it. When Ah'm feelin' okay, Ah am even able tah crowd my impendin' journey tah an early grave out of mah thoughts completely. Speakin' of the inevitable, have yah forgotten that, in yor world, mah fate was long ago decided an' recorded in yor history books, but please tell me Ah dah not meet mah end in a sickbed."

I do not know what to say.

"Well?" he persists.

"I don't know that history matters at this point."

"Maybe not tah yah, but Ah am alreadah history."

"Really," I counter, "aside from your rough edges, you look very alive to me. What if seeing a doctor can alter your fate? What if you are able to get well while you are here? Medical science has made great strides since your time. Many conditions deemed fatal back then are curable or at least controllable treatable now. You've got to admit, it would be foolish not to at least investigate the possibility."

The look on his face tells me he has not contemplated the option of a cure in several years; that he long ago accepted his premature demise. He does not answer and I detect in his eyes the slightest spark of renewed hope that he might actually escape his fate. He watches me clear the table and load the dishwasher. It is full now, so I add the soap, turn the dial, and push it in. Doc shakes his head as he hears the water flooding into the metal box.

A few minutes later, we settle in the living room. I peruse the array of DVDs in the long cupboard below the TV. I place my selection in the player and we are transported to Tombstone in the late 1870s. Doc leans forward in rapt attention as Val Kilmer makes his first appearance. During the next couple of hours, I watch as he intermittently chuckles and scoffs, at what I imagine are stretches of the truth or downright inaccuracies. He lets loose with full-on laughter during the tin cup scene with Ringo. Doc's mood is pensive throughout the conflicts with the cowboys. His brows knit together and I think I catch him wincing during the famous shootout. Out of the corner of my eye, I see a tear or two escape as Morgan bleeds out on the pool table in Hatch's saloon. His fists ball up as Wyatt rages in the street in the aftermath of the killing and he nods his approval as he watches "Wyatt and his Immortals" dispense unrestrained vengeance on the murderers. There is something I can't quite read in his expression when he watches himself confront Ringo in Wyatt's stead. The vein in Doc's neck reveals his apprehension during the scene where Wyatt sits at his portrayer's bedside in Glenwood Springs. I strain to comprehend what must be going through his mind, watching himself fade away on his deathbed. It is too much and my own tears come. It helps when the story takes a turn for the positive with a quick round up of Wyatt and Josie's subsequent years of happiness.

"Well then," Doc says when the credits start to roll. He slaps his palms to his knees then pushes himself to his feet. "Ah feel the need of a drink tah wash down all that melahdramah." He puts the flask to his lips, tipping it straight up. I can see he is less than satisfied at the result.

"Let me replenish your supply," I say, taking it from him. I question the wisdom of his reckless imbibing, but am desperate for an opportunity to regain my composure in private. Once through the swinging doors, I lunge for the sink board and drop my head, and try to shake off the emotional turmoil. It is one thing to watch gunplay in a movie. It is quite another to watch a participant vicariously relive the terror and heartache, trying to imagine what it must be like for him. The mental wounds must still be fresh; for Doc's world, much of this is very recent. It takes several minutes for me to come to terms and I think that Doc must be appreciating a few minutes of solitude. I make the decision not to edit the portrayal of his last visit with his dear friend. In my research, I had come across the facts of Doc's last days. Per a poignant description attributed to Josie Earp, Doc, when he knew the end was near, became aware of her and Wyatt's presence in Denver. It was Doc who made the effort to travel there to say goodbye to his friend in the lobby of the Windsor Hotel. I find no benefit in belaboring the point. If my plan works, this chronicle of Doc Holliday will more than likely become meaningless. It was interrupted the second he entered my barn. Jack Johnson is an excellent physician and has the latest in treatment at his disposal. Contemplation realigns my thinking, as I refill the flask and pour three fingers for myself. After taking a healthy swig, I manage to paste on a happy face before rejoining my charge. I nurse my drink and focus on the positive. Doc interrupts my musings.

"A little more than five years," he says and sighs. "Longer than Ah expected, actually, an' much longer than mah physicians gave me." His elbows rest on parted knees, his head bowed low.

"The jury is still out," I insist. "Have you heard a word I have said?" He smiles, albeit weakly. Why do I feel he is humoring me? "Who knows; with the proper medication, you just might outlive Wyatt; that is if you can keep that caustic wit under control."

He tightens his lips. "But, Dahlin', what would Ah be without my caustic wit, as yah call it?"

I cock my head and smile as if I know what I am talking about. "The decent man I'm betting you are trying so hard to conceal. In the last day or so, I have read a lot about the big, bad Doc Holliday. Wyatt, known for being a man of few words, had only good ones for you. The man was not stupid; could not have been ignorant of your faults, but apparently did not feel the need to belabor them, accounted them very normal. The picture he paints is of a loyal friend with high standards; quick with a gun when warranted. Of course, there are avid dissenters to his portrayal, mostly cowboys; but I am guessing their opinions are highly prejudiced. I also have personal observation to draw from. After considering all the facts, I have formed my own opinion," I say examining my need for a manicure.

"Oh? Don't forget; Ah am a man not at mah best; mah nature has been considerably subdued."

I ignore his counterargument. "What do you think of Mr. Kilmer's depiction of John Henry Holliday?"

Doc scratches his head and puts his index finger under his lower lip. "Ah have tah plead ignorance durin' mah more inebriated moments; of which there have been many of late. I must say, it is quite disconcertin' tah view my activities objectively. It's like Ah am steppin' outtah mahself an' . . ." He pauses, as if reconsidering. "Though, Ah *can* see the advantage in being able tah view one's futchah actions so they could be amended tah produce the desired outcome." He sighs.

"Exactly," I say, somewhat startled by my deduction. "I mean you *know* what will happen if you don't, at least attempt to change it. I am convinced that through some strange twist of fortune, you have been afforded the opportunity to alter your destiny."

Doc seems to consider the possibility, but his words retreat to the original question. "Ah am flattered by Mr.

Kilmer's portrayal of mah more serious moments. While the details have been skewed an' the timin' is a bit off, Ah would, say the production, all in all, conveys a fairly accurate pitchah of things as they are, pardon me, were."

"Hollywood takes what they call 'poetic' license."

"That anothah term for twistin' the facts?"

"For want of a better phrase," I say setting my glass down. "The industry caters to what they think their audience wants to see. Can't blame them; it's how they earn their living. There are far less accurate interpretations of the story, but, in this case, I think the inaccuracies are less corruptive. In the movie, the cowboys shooting up the Birdcage Theatre predates the shootout. In my readings, according to the dates that theatre did not open until several weeks later. I also read that Virgil was not expected to live from his injuries and was bedridden for several weeks after he was shot that night."

"That's true," he nods. "It was touch an' go; very unsettlin'."

I continue. "And things didn't happen all in one night like the movie suggests, but modern audiences are impatient and crave action without letup. Movies usually run about two, two and a half hours and the people who make them want to include every bit of action they can, so they fudge a little on timing and details here and there. Makes it even more exciting."

"Fools have no idea what it was like. Every day after we shot it out with Clanton and the McLaurys was a challenge; the trial, the threats, the attack on Virgil, and finally, the murdah of Morgan . . ."

I hear the pain in his words, the break in his voice. I venture on. "Warren and James are not even depicted, but I understand both were part of the story. I think the producers of <u>Tombstone</u> did a pretty good job, though."

"Ah concur," he says and I cringe a bit as I watch him take another long swig. Consumption seems to be a dual problem.

But, hey; I am dying to know, did that scene with the tin cup . . . did you really . . ."

"Ah wish," he says. A mischievous grin starts to spread. "Then, again, looks to be onnah my more intoxicated moments. Perhaps . . ."

On that note, I decide lunch is in order. While I surmise that pre-noon drinking might be the norm for my guest, I am not used to imbibing quite this early. The food is diluting the alcohol, but after setting the trays aside, I am down for the count for almost two hours.

CHAPTER 16

I awake to the ringing of the phone, a bit startled, as it has been over a week since I have heard the alert. It is Jack promising to come up tomorrow, late morning. "You have no idea how much I appreciate this. I know it is above and beyond," I say thinking of how he is must be jumping through hoops to accommodate the unusual circumstances. He listens to my explanation of John Hawkin's (the name I have given Doc) precarious situation without pressing me beyond the limited explanation I offer.

"Think nothing of it," Jack insists. "I'm happy to help." He pauses before asking me to recount Doc's symptoms. He offers the current flu as a preliminary diagnosis, tells me to keep him warm and hydrated; and not to worry.

"I will," I say, then add. "I owe you one."

"You do," he says, "and I plan to collect just as soon as your friend is well and resettled," he laughs and I do, too.

"See you tomorrow," I say and hang up. Jack had become *my* doctor shortly after my arrival in Teller County. Turns out, I was suffering from altitude sickness, a common malady when climbing from sea level in the morning to nine thousand feet in the same day. He prescribed lots of water and rest and even made the trip up to the ranch twice during the next week to check on my progress. The second visit came with an offer I could not refuse, dinner with him and his folks in Woodland Park. He came and picked me up, insisting that the mountain roads could be treacherous to a newcomer. After dinner, his mother and father joined us on a walking tour of Woodland Park; stopping at the shops along the way, introducing me to the owners. We returned to the house for dessert before he drove me home. Blessed with good health, my only visits since have been to stop by the office for a few minutes when I am in town to say hello.

"We need to prepare for Jack's visit," I tell Doc as I fill our dinner plates. "You know, get our stories straight to preclude any possibility that he might become suspicious."

"Yah think he might suspect that Ah have entered through a . . . what is it yah called it . . . ah yes, a portal from the past, that he might be treatin' the infamous Doc Holliday?"

"Of course not, but I don't think we can take any chances," I insist and then tread lightly into Doc's personal territory. "For instance, it might be a good idea to shave off your mustache and that chin hair." One hand goes to the growth. I can see that he is attached to the look. "I know It's been over a hundred years but people have not forgotten Doc Holliday. Hollywood has kept you and the Earps alive. Depending on his or her interest and depth of knowledge, someone might recognize that mug of yours. True, they would probably conclude that you're trying to live off the legend; but remember; you are supposed to be laying low in the witness protection program; trying to blend in, not drawing attention to yourself. We'll need to do something with your hair, too." I ignore his apprehension. "Clothes aren't a problem at the moment; you'll be in pajamas when you meet Jack. During your recovery period, you'll no doubt be meeting other friends of mine, so we'll need to see to a more contemporary wardrobe." I sense that I have encroached a bit much, so quickly amend. "Nothing drastic, just an upgrade. Western is always in." He relaxes a bit.

After dinner, I watch as he shaves and I feel a twinge of guilt as the whiskey drip disappears under the blade. It was a good look for him. I trim his hair ever so slightly, and adjust the part a bit. His expression is dubious as he turns his head from side to side in front of the mirror, touching the small scar on his upper lip. He sighs and gives a nod of assent, if not approval. This must be so hard for him. I rest easy, however, confident that something very positive is in the offing.

CHAPTER 17

I hear the shower running as I pass the bathroom on the way to the barn. The animals are thrilled with the sunshine and freedom. Doc enters the kitchen just as I am spooning up the oatmeal. "Sleep well?" I ask trying to get used to his naked face. It was the right thing to do. No one will associate recollections of Doc Holliday with the man sitting across the table.

"Indeed," he replies.

"It's just that I heard you coughing quite a bit."

"Ah am sorrah if Ah disturbed yah."

"I'm sure Jack will be able to give you something for that."

Doc does not say much during the meal; is quite pensive, and I wonder if he is planning a last minute getaway. Jack is a lifesaver. I doubt another doctor would be making this house call, and I know Doc is far from ready to agree with an office visit. Over coffee, we reinforce our cover story with some agreed-on childhood memories. For the time being, John Henry Holliday is set aside and John Hawkins is born. The Witness Protection Program explains the lack of detail and invites cooperation.

Jack pulls up in the drive just before eleven. I introduce John Hawkins, having briefed Jack that it is an alias with no connection whatsoever to his patient. At least *that* is not a lie. I am about to leave them alone when Doc requests that I remain in the room. Jack says nothing, but I can see questions behind his eyes. At the same time, I am picking up on something odd in Doc's inflection, but dismiss it as my imagination. I would be nervous, too, in his position. I sit quietly as Jack goes through the motions of a normal examination. In short order, he takes and records vitals and spends several minutes listening to the sounds in Doc's chest. As expected, he is troubled by what he is hearing. I play along. "It is just the flu, right?" I ask as Jack slowly refolds his stethoscope and replaces it in his bag.

Concern etches into his expression; his answer slow in coming. "I don't want to alarm you, but I think we need to run some tests; tests that can only be conducted in a hospital. I suggest we admit you right away, Mr. Hawkins." Doc shakes his head making no effort to hide his unqualified rejection of the idea. I ignore it.

"What is it, Jack?" I feign the ignorance, but not the concern.

"I don't like to diagnose without corroboration, so, mind you, this is just an educated guess; can't be sure without the tests. It's just that it's so rare today; but with your symptoms and the less than healthy lifestyle, you've obviously been enduring; and mind you, this is just speculation; but I'm afraid it might be TB. If so, you need immediate and aggressive treatment, and Cassie, you need to take precautions to prevent becoming infected, yourself."

"You go ahead. We'll be right behind you," I whisper to Jack without hesitation. Jack packs up the rest of his things and washes his hands thoroughly before leaving.

While presenting as cool as ever, Doc is not prepared for this turn of events. "That's the end of it, then," he says. "Ah am not goin' intah any hospital."

"It will be fine," I say. "I simply will not let you turn your back on this second chance at life."

"Yah will not allow—"

"Look, Jack is fully aware of your need to fly under the radar and . . ."

"Ah beg yor pardon?"

"It means 'laying low', keeping secrets. That's beside the point. I trusted you by stepping into the past; it's your turn to return the favor. You've got to trust me." Sensing he is a god-fearing man, "Think about it, who but God could be arranging this? You're tough, I know, but not tougher than God. Think how He would view your dismissal of His gift." This comment elicits a look of resignation. "I promise, that, if at any time, I sense that your freedom to return to the past is threatened, I'll pull back." Compromised as he is, he lacks the strength to dress for the occasion, let alone back up his protest. I find one of my grandfather's overcoats, a wool scarf to accent the nighttime ensemble.

Doc inhales deeply as we exit the house, clearly at odds with the decision, this further encroachment on his freewill. I veer to the right but realize that instead of following me, Doc is looking toward the barn. Is he expecting that we will make our journey in a horse and buggy? "This way," I say with a devilish grin as I crook my finger. We are on a serious mission, but I cannot help anticipating the amusement in watching the reaction to his first ride in an automobile. He stands to my side as I aim the small remote on my keychain at the garage door. Ever in control, he does not blink an eye as a portion of the garage wall begins to roll upward and out of sight. We enter and I motion him to the left as I open the driver's side of the Wrangler. He fumbles with the handle, but soon gets the idea and takes his place in the passenger seat. I draw my seat belt nodding to Doc to mimic my actions. When he has difficulty, I reach across him and then fasten it in place. Doc is amazingly tolerant. He is clearly used to being in the "driver's seat" of his own life, but observes without comment as I insert the key in the ignition. He does raise a brow as the engine stirs to life and music pours from the radio. I admire his forbearance and kill the noise. I reach for the remote on my visor as we pull out of the garage. Doc just shakes his head and folds his hands in his lap as he turns back to watch the door reappear and secure the garage. Soon, his attention is claimed by the scenery as we wind our way around curves of the freshly graded road. He takes note when it gives way to pavement and when I increase the speed accordingly, takes advantage of the handle to the right of his head to steady himself. "It's a little different than riding a horse," I say, but you'll get used to it and will appreciate the reduction in travel time."

"Indeed," is all he says until we reach the highway.

"Towns haven't changed all that much," he remarks off-handedly as I announce our approach to Florissant. I get the feeling he is trying to convince himself that things are not all that different in the modern world, after all. I am about to remind him of the images he has seen in the last few days on the TV, but decide to let reality speak for itself. He will soon see that Florissant is far from representative of modern cities.

We turn left onto twenty-four and seconds later, he is gripping the armrests and bracing his feet against the floorboard. Traveling at fifty miles an hour sans control of the reins must be unnerving, to say the least; not to mention the threat of oncoming traffic. He's ridden trains, but it's not the same. There is no oncoming traffic. I feel his eyes on me, and after a minute or two, his posture relaxes, I assume, taking a cue from my unconcerned attitude. Casually, I identify highlights as we make our way through the pass toward Divide. He listens in silence, and once or twice, turns to look behind us. His lower lip pushes upward as we come to a stop at the junction of the sixty-seven. His attention turns to the traffic lights. "How sensible." His attention is then drawn to the cars and trucks at the filling station on the left.

"Automobiles need fuel to power the engines. Gas stations are placed strategically along the roads. You *don't* want to run out. You might be able to coax a horse a few hundred yards more with the promise of water and hay, but once your vehicle runs out of gas, there is nothing to do but get out and push. Of course, there's always Triple A." Out of the corner of my eye, I can see he is trying to decipher. He does not ask and I decide to leave it for later. The light at the edge of town turns yellow and I ease onto the brake. An unheeding semi driver just behind and to the left speeds up and passes us by. A cacophony of horns and screaming brakes erupts, but thankfully, the clashing of metal is avoided. I did not think it possible for the man to become paler. Chin up, he handles it well. "How cosmopolitan."

"Unfortunately," I offer in explanation, "People don't always obey the traffic laws. Sometimes, actually more often than not, there are collisions, serious injuries, and deaths. You've seen it on the TV."

"Ah believe that they refer tah these acts of lethal stupidity, as accidents," he says dryly. "Again, Ah don't see the advantage of the speed if it comes with such risk."

"You're a fine one to talk about risk. Besides, do you know how long this trip would take on horseback?"

"Ah do."

The next few miles to the hospital are uneventful. I am pleased to note that the parking lot is nearly empty. Jack is waiting for us when we enter the lobby. He discreetly escorts us down the hallway to an office he has borrowed from an off-duty resident. He explains that the paperwork has been expedited, and in no way, will compromise John's identity; then chaperones us to an examining room where, again, Doc insists I remain. I turn my back as he sheds his pajamas and dons the hospital gown. Jack joins us with a clipboard and begins the first of a battery of tests he can perform in this room. After explaining to Doc that there are some places I cannot accompany him, he whisks him away in a wheelchair and suggests I wait in the examining room for over an hour. This must be awful for him.

Fully expecting Doc to be admitted, I am more than surprised when the two return. "Cassie, why don't you settle with the front desk while John gets dressed," he says laying a light hand on Doc's shoulder.

"I'm taking him home?"

"I think that would be best." His tone infers that this is clearly not his choice.

I am just finishing the transaction when the two come through the swinging doors. Doc looks relieved, Jack concerned.

"I've called several prescriptions into the City Market Pharmacy," Jack says as Doc leads the way toward the entrance. "I've explained everything to John and also wrote it down for you." He hands me a typed set of notes that includes websites to educate me on Doc's condition. "Make sure he takes the meds religiously, that he gets a variety of fresh fruits and vegetables, drinks plenty of water, and of course, gets sufficient rest. No booze, and follow the strict sanitary precautions. It's all here," he says handing me a stack of papers and a couple of booklets. "And see if you can fatten him up while you're at it," he says stopping just short of patting Doc's midsection. "I'll stop by to check on him in a few days, but call me if you are concerned about anything in the meantime; and watch for possible side effects. They'll be listed on the paperwork you get with the medications."

"Then he does have . . ."

Jack increases his volume enough for the waiting room occupants to hear. "Yes, it's the flu, all right." His interruption is accompanied by a light twitch in the direction of the elderly couple sitting on the far side of the waiting room. "County's full of it. Get him at home and in bed, lots of TLC, and he'll be just fine."

"Thank you for everything, Jack." I hug him tightly before leaving. Doc is standing outside, eyes closed, head turned up to the warm rays of the sun. Thank God, it's a beautiful day.

"Well?" I ask as we turn onto the highway. Doc stares out the passenger window as we exit the parking lot. "I can ask Jack, but . . .," He continues silent until I pull into a parking space in front of the market.

"Yor Doctah Johnson confirmed the diagnosis but seems confident of an excellent prognosis, even a full recovery if. . ."

"If?"

"He was less than pleased when Ah refused tah stay in the hospital an. . . ." His tone is flat, unemotional, his words halted in mid-thought. I feel like I have come upon the edge of a cliff and am teetering, barely able to keep myself from falling headlong over the precipice.

I hold my breath. "Go on."

"Accordin' tah the good doctah, my recovery hinges on my strict compliance with his ordahs."

An abbreviated laugh escapes along with the lungsful of

air. I slap a hand to my chest. "You had me worried for a minute."

"An' indeed, yah should be," he says. "Ah am not noted for followin' anyone's ordahs," he warns as we pull into Gold Hills Square and park.

"It won't be *you* who's doing the obeying," I assure him. "Okay," I say as I snatch up my purse and reach for the door handle. "I'll be as quick as possible. Can I trust you not to run off?" He nods and I add, "The worst is over, you know."

The bloodshot eyes dance with mischief for a second or two. "Go ahead. Ah assure yah that Ah am not given tah paradin' 'roun' in public in my nightclothes."

"I mean it, Doc." I muster up a look that I hope conveys no-nonsense.

"Git on with yah, now" he says.

"Thank you, George," I say to my favorite pharmacist as he hands me several little white bags. This is the most amount of money I have spent in one day since I paid cash for the Jeep; and the best spent, I have a feeling. Armed with the medication, I head across the store for the produce section and begin to fill the shopping cart. Dairy is next. Along with my usual fare, I reach for extra rich milk and sour cream, yogurt, and rich whipping cream; envisioning Doc's lean frame filling out a little more with each meal. I pick up a variety of cheeses. The cellar is stocked with meats and staples, so I head back to pick up the healthiest ice cream I can find. I'll have to think about an ice cream maker. I remember reading somewhere that ice cream was big in the west; and who does not like ice cream? Besides, Doc will need something to replace his here-to-for self-medication of choice. I pass on the rest. Everything else will be cooked and baked in my own kitchen.

"Expecting company, Cassie?" asks Susie as she checks through the mound of produce.

"As a matter of fact, I have a friend staying with me," I answer. "He's been ill.

"A 'he' friend, huh?"

"Yes, Susie," I counter. "A friend of the family since we were kids," I reinforce the lie. "He's not well, but is in Dr. Johnson's care now." I answer holding up the bag of prescriptions.

"Two hundred eleven dollars and three cents," announces Susie. I swipe my card and punch in the appropriate code. "I hope your friend gets well soon," says Susie as she's circling my current gas points and extending the lengthy receipt. "Maybe I'll get to meet him before he leaves?"

"More than likely," I say, meaning it. I would hate for Doc to leave this world without meeting my friends, a chance to see that there are a few sane people in the modern world.

After passing on the bagger's help out to my vehicle, I exit the store and am halfway across the driveway before I realize that the Cherokee is not where I left it. Panic swells in my throat. I am chiding myself for gullibility when I hear the short bleep of the Jeep's horn off to my left. A few cars down from its original location is the vehicle with Doc sitting in the driver's seat, hands on the steering wheel sporting an expression of exaggerated pride. I heave the heavy cart and proceed to confront my wayward charge; but the door is locked. I bang on the window. Doc feigns an abrupt recoil and fearful expression. I refuse to play along. I smile sweetly and mime instructions to lower the window and strain to maintain patience as he pretends to fumble with the controls. Before the window begins to lower, I hear the hood unlatch, the windshield wipers battling at top speed, and the emergency lights are flashing. As soon as there is room for my hand, I reach in and unlock the door. "Move over," I growl as I throw open the door. Doc, donning a sheepish grin, gingerly hoists his body over the center console as I snatch the keys from the ignition. Seething, I take my time loading the parcels into the back before re-entering the vehicle. Out of the corner of my eye, I can see Doc staring out the passenger window and calmly tapping the fingers of his left hand on the center console. I am about to let loose with a barrage of scolding when I am disarmed by the jiggling shoulders. Try as I may, I cannot maintain my exasperation. I put a fist to my mouth in an effort to hide my amusement.

"Very funny," I finally say as sternly as I can muster. "You may not realize it, but your stunt could have ended *very* badly. You are not licensed to drive, as required in this modern age, not to mention, you've never operated a vehicle before . . ."

"Ah concede, Dahlin'," he says as he raises his hands and lets the laughter go. Of course, it leads into a pathetic coughing fit that reminds me of his fragile condition.

I look down at my lap. "Don't you dahlin' me. Do not *ever* do this . . . or anything *like* this again. You have no idea how complicated things can get if you were to get into any kind of trouble or altercation. This is not the old west where you can jump over a horse's rear and elude a posse in the hills. God, Doc, if you'd have hit another car, or God forbid, a pedestrian . . . Within minutes, a swarm of police cars would surround you. My car might be impounded, and you could be carted off to jail. You might . . . God, Doc, you might end up in a mental hospital with the explanation you'd give." The words come fast and furiously before they are out-distanced by uncontrollable sobbing.

Instantly, Doc reaches across the console and awkwardly pulls me into his arms. "Ah am sorrah; Ah was curious. Ah intended tah put it back where Ah found it, but anothah, uh, vehicle had taken the spot." he says. His hand is rubbing up and down my back. "Ah thought it would be funneh. Ah didn't think . . . It was a stupid gestah on mah part an' I apologize." He allows me to pull back and grab a tissue from the console. I wipe my eyes and blow my nose.

"Let's forget about it," I say. "I'm overreacting, I know. It's just that this time warp thing is so . . ." I say trying to regain composure. "No harm done, I guess. . . Is there?" He shakes his head. The woman in the next vehicle is pretending to ignore our little scene a she stows her groceries. "I know you're not used to asking permission, but in *my* world, there are rules for everything; lawsuits are the order of the day. You can drive the Jeep all over my property if you like, but you cannot drive on public roads. My God, it's a good thing we're not at an airport." The statement seems lost on him. The thought of Doc innocently, or not, climbing into a cockpit of a 767 and taking a spin around the city is enough to arrest my agitation and trigger my funny bone. A minute later the incident has been laughed away, anxiety forgotten; and we are exiting the parking lot. At the last minute, I turn right. It's late afternoon and the day has been emotionally draining. "Have you ever had Chinese food?" I ask.

"I believe the Chinese predate both of our times, Dahlin'," he reminds facetiously.

"You know what I mean!" I roll my eyes.

"Tombstone has a verah fine Chinese eatin' establishment. Quong Kee is an excellent chef. Ah've eaten there often, an' regret that Ah will not have the opportunity again."

"I think the Fortune Dragon might just ease that regret." I pull into the left lane as we approach Boundary and then make the left into the tiny parking lot.

"Ah don't think Ah'm dressed—"

"Relax; I'm getting it 'take-out." I hesitate before exiting.

"Ah promise," says Doc laying a hand on his chest. If nothing else, he seems to lack the energy to act up further. As insurance, I take the keys and resist the urge to keep checking out the window as I wait for the order. What do I think he might do, hotwire the damn thing? I need not have been concerned as the opening of the door startles him awake. "Ah do believe it smells almost as good in here as in the Can Can's dinin' room," he comments as the tantalizing aromas waft through the interior of the Jeep.

Doc resumes his nap a few minutes into the drive back to the ranch. I suffer alone; my mouth watering all the way home. He wakens at the sound of the garage opening, and ever the gentleman, begins arguing about transporting the groceries. I hand him the large take-out bag; and assure him I intend to reap compensation for all my efforts in due time. The entire load of groceries fits into the wooden cart I have designated just for that chore. I wheel it into the mudroom, park it, and redirect my efforts to the hungry animals.

I return to the mudroom to find the cart empty and Doc standing poker-faced, at attention, his jacket over his pajamas, a tea towel draped over one arm. "Ah wasn't sure about these," Doc says gesturing to several items on the kitchen counter, and, indeed, he has managed to stow the bulk of the groceries. His prescription bottles have been opened and are perched on a shelf near the door to the living room. The dining table is set; serving utensils protrude from the cartons of Chinese, and the wine is breathing. My waiter comes around to the side of the table and pulls out my chair. "Dinnah is served". I struggle to maintain the ambience that he has staged as I sit, then give ridiculous attention to unfolding and smoothing the napkin in my lap. "Ah am truly sorrah, for earlier," he offers; his tone sincere.

"All is forgiven," I assure him.

"Ah trust all is well with the livestock, mah ride, as well?" he asks as he fills my glass. I nod. He moves on to his.

"I don't think so," I say reaching to lay my palm over his glass. "If I remember correctly, Dr. Johnson said no alcohol."

He gently but firmly removes my hand, but before pouring, expounds, "I do believe the good doctor meant tah rule out *hard* liquor, with which instruction Ah am in full agreement, an' will comply. Wine, in moderation, is good for what ails a body; Ah believe the Good Book is quite clear on the subject, an' Ah can attest tah its enhancement of the appetite. I promise to observe all other instructions." His serious expression and tone lets me know he has been pushed to his limit. I give in good-naturedly and without much concern.

He begins to fade again during dinner and gives no resistance when I order him to retire to the living room. After clearing the dishes and taking care of the leftovers, I study the medications and make note of the dosage and timing. Doc seems to have handled the first doses by himself. I have a good feeling about this, I think as I enter the study.

Armed with my laptop, I retire to my seat in the living room. Doc is dozing and I take the time to email major "thank yous" to Jack. A few minutes later, he counters with "de nadas" and asks if Sunday around eleven would be convenient for Doc's first follow-up. I confirm and set the computer aside as Doc is rousing.

"How are you feeling?" I ask feeling my face filled with

hope, yet knowing that any sign of improvement is a ways down the road.

"Jus' capital. Ah do believe Ah am cured," he teases, but the mental relief in his expression is evident. His earlier trepidation has progressed into guarded optimism. Dare we hope?

"What exactly did Jack say while you were taking the tests?"

"He asked me about the last several years; where I'd been, what I'd been doin'. Ah went along with the plan, feedin' him the tidbits yah had come up with that might explain the diagnosis. It was more like he was makin' conversation rather than fishin'. He was careful not tah press; very respectful of the need for privacy." He pauses. "Mostly, he talked about yah."

"What?" I could feel the color rushing to my cheeks.

"Ah may have prompted him just a bit. It didn't take much. He likes talkin' about yah. He seemed concerned about the nature of our relationship," he says defensively.

"What relationship?" My mind spins in several directions at once.

"He somehow got the impression that we had a close relationship years ago an' that Ah came here in hopes of . . ."

"Oh my God!" I say rising to stand over him. He remains unfazed by my concern. "What would make him think that?" I demand.

"Ah don't rightly know. He was askin' leadin' questions in that direction an', when Ah wasn't quick tah respond, Ah guess he assumed a few inaccuracies." Throughout this little dissertation, Doc projects the epitome of innocence.

"What inaccuracies?" He covers his mouth as if about to be assaulted by a coughing fit. "Nice try," I say. "That cough suppressant Jack prescribed is the most potent stuff on the market," I bluff and amazingly, it works.

"Ah might not have denied a childhood infatuation." My eyes slowly begin to swell as he continues. "When he suggested we might have been high school sweethearts . . . Ah . . . uh . . . an' he may have been led tah think that we might have been promised tah marry at some point; yah know, before all the trouble tragically tore us apart."

My eyes have realigned in their sockets, but the gape in my mouth is beginning to hurt. "How could you?"

"Yah must concede that Ah was undah a lot a stress, Dahlin'."

"I'll show you stress," I say, balling my fists.

For the first time, Doc is laughing heartily with no immediate side effects. "Ah may have exaggerated the scenario somewhat. Kept the conversation with the good doctor focused on yah instead of me. What else could Ah do?" His ridiculous admission deflates my anger and I sink back into the recliner.

"How does it feel tah have someone else take ovah yor life?" he says with the raise of a brow. "Come on now, Dahlin, the only possible consequence is that Ah might jus' have spiced up yor love life."

"My relationship with Jack Johnson is none of your business," I say as blandly as I can, directing my attention to the TV; but I cannot ignore him for long. "Seriously," I say. "It's wonderful that the prognosis is so positive. Did Jack give you a time frame?"

"He did mention that if thins progress as he hopes, Ah should be a new man by this time next year."

"How does that feel?"

"Much too long."

"Are you kidding? Most people would be thrilled with that news. You are going to get well. You should be rethinking your future."

"Ah think Ah shall reserve comment for the time bein'," he says. "Ah'm not one tah count my chickens before they hatch. Foxes can wreak havoc in a hen house."

I turn off the TV and we spend the next hour or so picking each other's brains bouncing back and forth between our respective centuries. Doc asks about the particulars of Wyatt and Josie's future. Unfortunately, my knowledge is limited to what we saw in the movie. I promise to show him how to use a computer to search for more definitive answers. I make a mental note to adjust my settings to prevent him from, in an effort to make sport or by accident, compromise my data.

Doc is able to fill me in as to my queries centering around his recent exploits in Tombstone and the people involved. He is unforgiving in his biographies, especially of Curley Bill Brocious and the others directly involved in Virgil's maiming and Morgan's murder. His disgust is so pronounced that he can barely spit out the names of Ike Clanton and Sheriff John Behan, who he holds more than responsible for orchestrating the attacks on the Earps.

"John Ringo," he says, "is anothah wretched soul."

With that recollection, his spirits seem to deteriorate. I change direction and ask him about his childhood, of which I am virtually ignorant. At first, I fear I have made things worse. His eyes glisten with threatening tears as he remembers his mother. "I was born with a deformity that, left untended, would have precluded any normal life, any life for that mattah." He touches the tiny scar on his upper lip and swallows. "She moved heaven an' earth tah have it corrected an' relentlessly coached mah vocal trainin'."

"I would never have guessed."

He clears his throat. "A combination of mah uncle's surgical talent an' a mothah bear of indomitable will. Nevah underestimate the power of a determined woman, especially in regahd for her offspring." The description of his Georgia home before the Civil War betrays a strong love for the life he' had been forced to leave behind. Doc paints a detailed picture of the destruction and waste, his family's loss and relocation; and the interminable resolve to rebuild the family fortune when the holocaust was over. His future appeared bright after his graduation from dental school; then, shortly thereafter, he was pronounced seriously ill, and sent off by family decree to recuperate in the dry warmth of Dallas.

"Your father?"

"We no longah communicate." His tone is dripping with disapproval.

"But I thought . . ."

"He is an accomplished man . . ."

"But?"

Doc seems exasperated. "Instead of mournin' the passin'

of his faithful wife . . ." Doc swallows again. "He promptly replaced her with a youngah woman and went on as if mah mothah had nevah existed."

"Your mother died?"

His voice is cracking. "Of consumption, when Ah was fifteen. Ah am sorrah, but Ah find Ah am quite tired. Ah don't feel like talkin' anymore. Ah am sure yah undahstand," he whispers; his head bowed.

Fighting back my own tears, I rise. Placing my hand on his shoulder, I bend down and kiss the top of his head before scurrying upstairs ahead of the good cry in which I am about to indulge.

CHAPTER 18

After chores and breakfast, I announce an amendment to the living arrangements. Doc will be moving into a spare bedroom upstairs and will have sole use of the upstairs bathroom to, per Jack, maximize protection of my own health and any visitors that might use the downstairs bath. It takes most of the morning to rearrange things; after which, I begin a shopping list.

It does not take long for Doc and me to adapt to the new guidelines and boundaries. At first, I think the stairs might not be such a good idea; then see it as needed exercise, especially during inclement weather. During this first week, Doc initiates taking on more responsibilities, as well. He keeps his personal territory immaculate and takes it upon himself to make coffee and clean the kitchen after meals. I think better about protesting. He takes his time and I know I would feel like pitching in if I were in his shoes. He still coughs, but with less force and frequency. He eats what is put before him and is faithful in taking his medication. When Jack stops in on Sunday, he is more than pleased at his patient's initial response to the combination of powerful drugs. Not only that, but the scale indicates that Doc has gained a couple of pounds.

CHAPTER 19

"It's a beautiful day," I say at breakfast. "What do you say we get out and explore?" I leave out the part about shopping for his new wardrobe. "Want to see Colorado Springs as it is today . . . I mean if you feel up to it?"

"Ah would enjoy that," he replies with anticipation in his expression.

Doc exhibits no tension on this second journey down the pass. I take this as a compliment from one averse to putting himself in the hands of another, especially a member of what his generation refers to as the "weaker" sex. Hah! What about the brave females who crossed the country in covered wagons and fought the elements and Indians alongside their men. In any event, his adaption to the modern world amazes me.

Our first stop is the Cowhand in Woodland Park, a western themed shop with an impressive selection of clothing, accessories, jewelry, and a wide variety of décor items.

We browse separately for a while.

"What do you think of this?" I ask approaching with a shirt that has caught my eye.

"Nice," he says and I return to the rack to pick out a couple more and a pair of black jeans.

"There's a dressing room over there," I say pointing to the curtained cubicle across the room.

"These will do," he insists quietly referring to the seasoned outfit, part of my reclamation from my grandfather's attic stash.

I think about how to deal with his resistance. "I agree they are serviceable, but ill-fitting, and hardly go with the southern gentleman persona." I whisper now. "I can't imagine Doc Holliday being comfortable with such a presentation."

Doc smiles and sighs.

While Doc auditions several articles of clothing, I find a pair of silver earrings I cannot live without and a couple of decorative pieces for the living room. I settle the bill and we continue through town, stopping at Walmart where I stock up on toiletries and other sundries and pick up some extra flannel bed linens. Doc seems overwhelmed by the huge store. His eyes become saucers as he watches the checkout process.

He is quiet as we continue on our way to The Springs. As we emerge from the pass, Doc leans forward. "It's grown some," he understates. Once downtown, he strains against the seat belt looking up at the tall buildings downtown. Of course, he has seen cities larger than this on TV, but it's not quite the same. Colorado Springs is familiar to Doc. In his sphere of thinking, he was here or, actually, there, not long ago. It must be quite unsettling to see such a drastic transformation. Along our way, I pull over near the airport where Doc is mesmerized by the take-offs and landings of the jets. Commercial flights are out of the question for a non-person in our society, but Jack has a pilot friend with his own plane. Maybe . . .

We stop in at a couple more Western clothing stores where we round out his wardrobe. Doc is a discriminating shopper and expresses his surprise at the inferior quality of the cheaper pieces, and quickly moves on to make his choices from those made of natural fibers. I am passing the time looking through some old fashioned dresses when he is suddenly behind me. "This one," he says handing me an emerald green Victorian number. "Ah want to see yah in this one."

"But I wouldn't have anywhere to wear it."

"They wouldn't have them if women didn't buy them. Ah imagine the ladies who purchase them do so with the intent of wearing them." Though intrigued, I continue to hesitate. "Indulge me," he says giving me a gentle push in the direction of the women's dressing room. I know better than to argue with the man of whom I have asked so much.

A few minutes later, there is a knock at the door. "The gentleman thought you might need some help with the buttons."

"Yes, please." I unlock the door for the sales clerk who deftly manipulates the myriad of pearls up the back of the dress. The fit could not be better. "The color is perfect with your hair and complexion," she says. "Now let's stun that handsome man of yours." I let her assumption pass and indulge myself in feeling like a princess. Doc rises immediately. "Ah knew it," he says triumphantly. "Yor a vision, Dahlin'. Now let's try this," he says handing the hat to the clerk who takes great care in arranging my hair to the best advantage. "We'll take those, as well," he says pointing to the pile of satins and lace carelessly tossed on a table off to the side.

"Wait a minute!"

"Yah'll wear them for me," he leans in to whisper as the salesperson makes haste toward the register. "It will ease mah homesickness," he offers with a mischievous smile. I give him a hard stare to which he answers. "You said yah have more money than yah can spend. Ah'm afraid Ah'm gonnah have tah insist'. Ah'm sure yah undahstand about havin' tah insist at times, donchah, Darlin?" I did. The shoe, or maybe the boot in this case, is on the other foot. The man has a sense of humor and I owe it to him to indulge his whims. Walking around at home in satin and lace is another thing.

We settle up and head back via the Freeway. We are stopped at the light at the end of the off-ramp to turn on Cimarron Street. Doc leans forward to look beyond me at the shabbily clothed man. The sign he holds reads, "Out of work, please help." I purposely look away.

"Should we—"

"Absolutely not!" I snap. Doc jolts back like he's been slapped.

"I'm sorry," I say. To reinforce my contrition I reach over to pat his knee. "I know you mean well, but there is a high probability that the man begging for money makes a better living than most working folk. If he is *legitimately* in need, he should be seeking assistance through one or more agencies set up for the indigent. There's no reason for him to be on the street. He's engaging in what we call today a scam. I'm sure you know people who will do anything but work for a living and who trick others into giving up their hard-earned cash."

"Indeed; they are known as cowboys," he says. "Ah'll be damned," he adds taking a final look at the man. I refrain from engaging him in conversation and concentrate on the windy highway.

"A penny for your thoughts?" I ask as we enter the city limits of Woodland Park.

"Ah feel like celebratin'", he announces.

"Excellent idea," I say and turn left into the parking lot of one of the more upscale restaurants in the area.

"Order anything you want in harmony with the diet that Jack laid out, of course," I say after our waiter introduces himself and leaves us to our selections. I watch Doc's eyes widen as he opens the menu. "It's called inflation," I add realizing it is the right side of the menu that's sparked the I-can't-believe-this expression. He must not have noticed the price tags on the clothing. "Don't worry; people don't work for a few dollars a day anymore, either. This is one of the nicest places in Woodland Park and the food is first rate. From what I gather, you are used to the finer things in life."

"Ah enjoy the comforts, when available," he acknowledges. "Were yah born intah money?"

"Yes and no," I begin. "My parents had money; I had no idea how much; I never thought about it. I lived with all the comforts until I 'rebelled' and Dad showed me the door; cut me off without a cent or any hopes of future income. Living frugally was a good experience. Contrary to my father's intent, mother saw to it that I inherited his fortune. I'm rollin' in dough, as it were, with no one telling me how to spend it, having my cake and eating it, too. In spite of their wealth, my parents were never wasteful and instilled that in me, along with an appreciation for quality. Hence, I no longer dine at McDonald's". I pause to answer to the question in his expression. "Fast food; you know, junk food." The nonplussed expression remains. "Of course, you don't." He is probably thinking hard tack and beans. "I'll explain later; but trust me, this is better," I say spreading my arms, "in quality *and* atmosphere.

Doc reaches into a pocket; then discretely washes down his pre-meal meds with water. I am impressed that he, unlike myself, had the foresight to remember to bring the dose. Our waiter approaches. A couple of minutes after we order we are feasting on crisp greens, garnished with freshly grated parmesan.

Doc dabs at his mouth with a napkin. He sighs and I know that he is about to broach a sensitive subject. "Ah hope you know that Ah am not used tah bein' kept. This financial state of affairs is unacceptable, but I will concede necessary for the moment. "At the earliest opportunity—"

"Tell you what," I interrupt him. "You were carrying quite a roll with you—"

"Yes, but Ah take it my currency is a little out of date."

"In a manner of speaking," I say. He cocks his head in a question. "Those twenty dollar gold pieces have escalated in value far beyond your wildest imaginings. The gold and silver certificates are worth a bundle, too." I do not want his money, but reason to refuse compensation would be an insult.

He brightens considerably. "Well then," he says. "We will take care of our financial mattahs back at the ranch."

"As you wish."

The steaks are grilled to our requests and the rest of the meal, perfection as well. For a lark, we share an order of bananas foster. The alcohol burns off, I reason. "That was capital," says Doc as he swallows the last bite. "Ah am not sure how long those new trousers are going tah fit," he says patting his midsection.

"I thought of that," I say, "Had the salespeople include extra pairs in the next two sizes up."

"You're a daisy; but what will yah do with the othahs?"

"I'll take them to GOODWILL, where someone less fortunate can buy quality at a bargain."

"Goodwill? Sounds nice."

"There are several organizations that accept clothing and other goods for which people have no further use and resell them at a considerable discount. We have one in Woodland Park across from the market we stopped at the other day."

He smiles in approval. "Then there are some good things about the futchah, Ah see."

"Getting tired?" I ask when he leans back and closes his eyes.

"Ah believe I have had enough for one day." And with that, we head back home, where true to his word, he dispenses a considerable sum from his stash into my palm.

Having second thoughts, I suggest we stop at a dealer on our next jaunt to The Springs, where Doc can handle the transaction himself after which we can square up more accurately.

CHAPTER 20

October brings the first snowfall. In the intervening weeks, we have progressed to long walks and rides during the nicer days. On inclement days, Doc has taken to spending considerable time on the computer on which he has become quite adept, and he requests regular trips to the Woodland Park Library. My card has never seen so much activity and I'm guessing the library has never made so many inter-branch transfers. Meals are often accompanied by lively discussions of history pre and post 1882.

Dining out again tonight, we are examining the evolution of law and order. Doc questions the outrageous rise in crime with all the advancement humanity has made. He speaks of the orderliness in pre-war Griffin and how that contrasted with the western towns he frequented. "We have witnessed steady erosion in standards an' integrity of individuals, especially with the events in Tombstone. The cowboys are, without question, rustlahs, thieves, and murderahs. Everybody knows it, yet the lawbreakers proceed with little if any consequence. Instead, fine men like the Earps are branded as miscreants. There is a particularly dangerous characteristic that has been responsible for all the ills plaguing mankind; avarice. Some people nevah have enough and, at the same time, do not want tah put forth the personal effort to achieve more than they have earned. Their alternative is tah take from othahs an' murdah them if they protest. Many businessmen and town folk complain about the violence but refuse tah take the appropriate action because the cowboys are responsible for much of the revenue pumped intah their coffahs. They have been able tah buy off law enforcement and managed tah gain control of the local news now that the Epitaph has also fallen into the hands of their supportahs. Even President Arthah's edicts have been ignored by the compromised local authorities. This Mallen fellow has bribed and lied his way intah tryin' tah arrest Wyatt and me. If it weren't for Wyatt and Bat, Ah . . ."

"Can I get you folks anything else?"

"Coffee, please," requests Doc and I nod.

"Bat *Masterson*?"

"Ah see the man has claimed a memorable place in history." Doc smiles. "Mr. Masterson is a good friend of Wyatt's. He takes exception tah me, but out of our mutual regard for Wyatt, he tolerates me. He has been a great help in thwartin' Mallen's efforts tah haul me back tah Tombstone where Ah would most certainly be killed in route. He's in Gunnison with Wyatt at present. That's where Ah was headin' when ah, uh, faltered into yor world."

"I'm glad you chose my place. I wouldn't have missed this for the world. Who is Mallen and why is he after you.

"Perry Mallon is an opportunist tryin' tah ingratiate himself with my enemies. Turned up in Denvah with counterfeit arrest documents. That's when Masterson stepped in."

We concentrate on finishing our meal. The coffee arrives and we resume our commentary on the ills of man.

"Is this Mallen still after you?"

"Ah heard that he fell intah disrepute while still in Denvah; swindled a man into payin' expenses for anothah spurious manhunt in Kansas. He ended up abandonin' the fellah and takin' off with the money. Ah do not know where the cur is now. Trouble is, there are an awful lot of newspapers dispensin' his propaganda. Much of the public is under the impression that the Earps and Ah are still wanted for murdah and many are more than willin' to turn us in dead or alive for the rewards offered. Their prospective benefactors, of course, would prefer us dead. Colorado seems tah be the safest haven for now and the dry climate is kind tah mah condition. But Ah surely thought by now, the west would have been tamed."

"You'd think." I agree. "If it's any consolation, history reflects favorably on you and the Earps for the most part. Tombstone is what they call a tourist attraction. Then, again, it has been dubbed the 'town too tough to die.'" The eyebrows rise again. "The town has been preserved and embellished. Actors stage reenactments of the shootout at the O K Corral." Doc winces. "There are guided tours and signs on the streets and in buildings marking important events. The town is still torn and I hear there are still some diehard supporters of the Clantons in town to this day."

"Interestin'."

"You can judge for yourself," I say. "As soon as you're well enough for longer jaunts, we'll head out that way."

"Nevah thought Ah'd evah see that town again." His expression turns wistful.

"And this time you won't have to look over your shoulder."

At first, these interactions are random, but Doc soon settles into an organized chronological study of the future he now hopes to enjoy. Although I earned good grades in school, I learn more during these dialogues than I ever did in history class. We now limit TV viewing to news and the history channels. As he researches his future, I delve into my family's past. In addition, weather permitting and as Doc gets stronger, we begin to venture out more. He meets several of my friends, but we have yet to engage formal social events. I tell them just enough, to discourage close contact with my sick friend. We take in Garden of the Gods, Cave of the Winds, and several other local high points.

Doc has let his facial hair grow back. I see no problem. Come Halloween, I don one of the dresses Doc picked out and the two of us head down to Woodland Park for the festivities as Doc and Kate. Comments are favorable sans any suspicion and I find the experience wildly entertaining.

CHAPTER 21

Mid-November, we plan a day at Cripple Creek. We have not seen the ground for a few weeks, but the sun is out and the temperature mild. Doc recognizes the scenery on the way as unchanged except for the buildings we pass. We spend the morning exploring Bennet Ave, ducking into Bronco Billy's for breakfast. When I ask Doc if anything looks familiar, he points out that the town of Cripple Creek is not yet a part of his world and we learn during our excursion that it came to life during the Colorado gold rush of the 1890's. We tour the jail, the courthouse, and take the train to see mines outside of town. Our day would not be complete without a visit to The Homestead, the high-class brothel, once operated by the infamous Pearl Devere. Our guides are a couple of older women; one takes the lower floor, the other guides us through the upstairs, explaining in detail the life of a "soiled dove". My midsection aches at the description of the mandatory corsets. The tour is quite informative and our hostesses are not above elbow jabbing and winking at the male members of our tour party, all of whom, including Doc, actively engage in the slightly suggestive banter. Doc leans his head close to mine. "This, Ah am goin' tah remembah," he whispers tapping a finger to the side of his head, "for my newly acquired futchah. Thank you, kindly, Dahlin'." I laugh, but, somewhere inside, am profoundly disturbed at the image of Doc and Pearl making the trek up the staircase arm in arm. Then again, he is a man, I reason with myself, one who until recently was cohabiting with a prostitute. My mental war must show in my expression.

"Somethin' wrong, Cassie?" Putting a hand to my brow, another to my midsection, I attempt to hide the heat that is rushing into my face.

"Just hungry," I lie in absence of a better excuse.

"Then we'd best put the museum off till aftah lunch," he says before turning his attention back to our entertaining hostess. Greatly relieved that he has not picked up on my blindsiding flicker of jealousy, I refocus my concentration on the history being dispensed. We join the rest of the group in thanking the dear ladies for a wonderful half hour, before heading back to Bennet Ave, where most of the action is.

"What about there?" he says pointing across the street at the Wild Horse Casino, "for lunch?" I had since forgotten about my "hunger".

"Never eaten there but hear it is excellent," I answer.

"Mah, mah!" Doc is duly impressed with opulence that demands attention as we enter. The huge main room sparkles. Random shouts of victory punctuate the continuous din of the machines that eagerly snatch bills from the fingers of the eternally optimistic who are convinced they will be among the few who beat the odds. Others stand at tables where dealers quickly dispense cards; then rake in chips. Doc's eyes glisten with anticipation as we make our way to the food court at the far end, though I suspect it has little to do with the food. After finishing our meal, I leave Doc at the table to wait for the change from a hundred dollar bill and add brief instructions about modern tipping.

When I return a few minutes later, the table is being cleared. Not again! It takes several minutes of searching before finding him seated at a blackjack table. While I am not surprised, I could kick myself for not thinking of the probability of this gambler being lured to the tables. From the stack of chips in front of him, he has already turned the change from lunch into a nice profit. I am furious at his non-compliance; then realize that I had not *specifically* told him to wait for me to return to the table and I had not *forbidden* him to play. I watch from a distance, as the cards are dealt and discarded; each time it is Doc raking in the chips. Over the next twenty minutes, several players come and go, they and the dealer falling victim to what I hope is Doc's expertise rather than sleight of hand. When the dealer squints in suspicion, I approach. "The babysitter just called, Hon. Brenda is on her way to the hospital. Tiffany fell and she thinks her arm is broken. We need to leave now!"

Doc looks up in surprise. "My God, how could the girl let that happen?" Without skipping a beat, he has joined the ruse. "We will have tah see about a new sittah; the verah idea." Doc grabs up his winnings. After cashing them in, we make a quick exit.

"Cassie, what is all the fuss about? That game is so simple an' Ah have an excellent memory for . . ."

"I can't believe you!" I scold in muted tones once we are outside. I make a beeline for the parking lot with Doc huffing and puffing to keep up.

"Whatevah do yah mean, Cassie?" He manages to sound innocent. "Why on earth are yah so upset? Gamblin' is my profession, aftah all, and Ah owe yah so much. Ah made us a lottah money back there."

"And, while yah were at it, probably managed to piss off a lottah people," I say in a sarcastic mimic of his accent. "The dealer was watching you; probably thought you were counting cards," I spit out as I pick up speed after we cross the street.

"Of course Ah was keepin' track of the cards."

"That's illegal!" I whisper loudly.

"Surely yah jest."

"Keep your voice down!" I say aiming the remote as the Jeep comes in view. Doc holds his tongue until we are buckled up. I throw my hands at the wheel and let my head come to rest on them.

"So, yor tellin' me that in yor modern world it is unlawful to use one's talents and intellect to ply one's trade?"

"In essence, yes," I look over at him. "Look, I don't know the exact reasoning behind it but I do know they get suspicious when a person is on a winning streak. Counting cards is considered an unfair advantage." Doc throws up his arms in annoyance. "In another minute, you might have been tossed out of the place or arrested." I add and start the Jeep.

"Look, let's go back. Ah'll behave." He rests a hand on my shoulder. "Ah have yet tah see the museum."

"That's impossible now," I say. He draws his head back and raises his brow. "This is a small town, a tourist attraction." His expression deepens. "After that little scene in the casino, we cannot be seen in town. People wander about all day and those who witnessed our little scene in the casino think we have a child at the hospital with a broken arm. I just pray no one recognized me."

"Oh, yes" he says nodding, "our daughter, Tiffany," He chuckles. "Tell me, Dahlin'," he quizzes. "Do we have othah children? How long have we been husband and wife?"

Once again, his straight-man act dares me to hang on to my irritation. In spite of these heart-stopping capers, I am helpless but to savor the adventure of it all. I shake my head, and head back down Teller 1; thoughts and emotions are hopelessly jumbled. I opt to keep them to myself until I can sort them into some kind of sense. While I might be secretly enjoying these little episodes, I know each one is eroding the low profile we must maintain; but am at a loss at how to impress the importance of this on Doc. His inborn recklessness could ruin both of us. Why, with his new lease on life, is he so hell-bent on tempting fate? Apparently indifferent to the risk, the man naps during the drive.

We arrive home, I do not object when he, without comment, heads out to take care of the animals. I make for the kitchen. While my hands prepare dinner, my mind hits on the solution to the dilemma and I plan my appeal. In the past few months, I have discerned where Doc's love and loyalty lie; that there is one person he will not allow himself to disappoint.

I pop my head into the living room where he retreated after coming in from the barn. "Soup's on."

Several minutes of silence elapse before either of us attempts dinner conversation. Doc leans back and reaches into a pocket. "We made a killin', Dahlin'," he announces as he slaps his take from the Wild Horse center table. "We turned forty-three dollahs into three hundred an' nine." When I shake my head, he persists. "At this rate, Ah figure Ah can repay everythin' Ah owe yah in a month or so."

"You'll do no such thing. Your gambling days in my world are over," I say adamantly and with a dash of sarcasm, "Make yourself useful and pour the wine." With no hint of offense, he fills our glasses.

He lets his sip of wine settle on his tongue. "Don't tell me yor still angry, Dahlin?"

"Oh, Doc, I'm not angry." My defenses are down and I make no attempt to hold back my frustration. "What I am is scared. You have no idea the serious trouble you can get into when you pull these stunts."

"It's not goin' tah happen," he says with a toss of his hand.

Inwardly I seethe at his nonchalant attitude, and it takes effort to continue in a civil tone. "Look, there's no question that you have been used to holding all the cards in your world," I start. "What can I say that will make you see that despite your obvious talents you are out of your league in mine?." His silence and non-expression tells me the words are bouncing off that thick skull of his. "If you keep this up," I say as firmly as I can, "you will never get back to yours; you won't be able to help Wyatt with whatever it is he needs you for and . . ."

One brow arches. He swallows his food and washes it down with a generous swig of wine. "Dahlin'," he says confidently, "yor forgettin' history has already been written." He cuts another piece of steak.

"Dahlin'," I mimic the sweet Georgian accent again, "yah are forgettin' that we have already *changed* history. Don't you get it? When you go back, Doc Holliday will not be dying of consumption; but if you get into trouble here and wind up in prison or worse, Doc Holliday will have disappeared on his way from Denver to Gunnison; never to be heard of again. His friend, Wyatt, will be left on his own. You can't have it both ways." I could say more, but I know this is the place to stop. I let the words hang in the air, echoing in the silence.

"But, Dahlin, time is standin' still out there, remembah?"

"Great, who knows how that works? If you don't eventually get back, time will stop in 1882 and I won't exist," I say knowin' this is a preposterous theory. Then it hits me. "You know what I think? I believe that there is definitely a purpose in your visit here. I believe you are being given a second chance. You can use it for your own good and that of others or not. I'm not sure how long you are being given, but if you refuse to appreciate it, God can pull the plug and life will go on without John Henry Holliday."

Doc sets down his knife and fork and sits back in his chair. His eyes narrow. His expression tells me he has not considered his rash actions harming his friend. I see the etching of concern work into way into his expression.

He dabs his mouth. "Yor right, of course," he says barely above a whisper. "Ah seem tah have forgotten my mission. Ah need tah leave . . . now." With exaggerated care, folds his napkin and rises. Hands on the back of the chair, he adds. "Ah want tah thank yah, Cassie, for everythin'. If there is any way possible, Ah shall return an' repay yah . . ."

For the first time, I see real pain in those eyes. "Please sit down," I say softly. He hesitates and I persist. "A few more minutes isn't going to make any difference." He flexes his hands; then pulls out the chair. He sits but pushes his plate aside.

"Doc, you're not doing anything that wrong. It's just that a lot of things in this country have been turned upside down since your time. I think most of it has to do with the erosion of morals. Things were black and white back then. For the most part, in the end, good was rewarded and evil punished. Today, there are so many shades of gray. Victims of crime are more often than not, left without compensation while the perpetrators are slapped on the wrist. Essentially crime in the twenty-first century *does* pay. In the old west, you probably did not have many long-term offenders. If they did not end up swinging from a rope, someone put a bullet in them. Let's face it; longevity wasn't common among criminals. On the other hand, seemingly small offenses, like your little jaunt in the parking lot and counting cards, can make one's life a nightmare." He nods without editing. "The way I see it, through some unfathomable cosmic deviation, the ugly hand you were originally dealt has dissipated with the upending of the laws of time. Since you walked through that portal, each card you turn over now is adding to what could be a royal flush. Do you think God would intervene in the normal operation of the universe without a purpose? Do you really want to muck this up?" I feel the sting of tears in my eyes. "Don't you see? You are *meant* to get well," I insist, my voice starting to crack. "Why? Who knows; maybe God felt bad that a nice guy like you was given such a raw deal; maybe he wants to see what you will do with a new lease on life." I see recognition in his eyes and add. "Look at the good you've done already."

"Ah beg yor pardon."

"Without you, I'd never have seen my family; and you will take me out there again; you will won't you?" I dab at my eyes and nose. "You have got to see this through, Doc. Why do you think time is standing still while you are recuperating? I won't let you blow this; I won't!" I hold my breath, praying that logic will prevail.

Again, maddening silence. Apprehension evolves into fear as the void persists. He cannot go back, not yet. I close my eyes wishing I could turn back the clock to when Doc and I had settled into a comfortable arrangement in which he concentrated on getting well. I have crossed over to another time; it should be possible to turn back the clock; but then, I don't make the time travel rules. Fear that all the headway is unraveling, may have been for not casts its shadow, and is sapping my will.

I feel the gentle pressure on my shoulders. "Ah am not goin' anywhere, jus' yet," Doc says. Strong fingers tenderly knead at the knots. "I am afraid my reaction tah this new lease on life, as yah call it, has been woefully unappreciated on my part. An' yah are right. Internally Ah railed against my maker when the consumption was discovahed. Ah watched mah mothah withah away long before her time and have been livin' fast and loose in rebellion ever since I realized I was doomed tah the same pitiful demise. It is the only way ah can make mah peace with it. Ah could face a premature departure from this life, but am not sure how tah act without that death sentence hangin' over my head. Ah had not planned for a lengthy futchah, but I know Ah should be grateful. And yah, Cassie, yah have been blind-sided as much as I have by this, for want of a bettah description, othah-worldly experience, and yet, without hesitation, yah have embraced it and taken on the care of someone tah whom yah have no obligation . . ."

"Stop; stop," I say standing up and turning to face him. "Everyone is obligated to help another in need; yah know: the golden rule. Yeah," I say. "Your supernatural visit is . . . is . . . I don't know what it is . . . and never expect to fully understand what is transpiring here, but I can't deny it. Now that the shock has worn off, I feel privileged to help. I mean . . . what an opportunity. I just . . ."

"What yah need, or rathah what yah do not deserve, is any more disruption in yor young life. On mah honah," he says putting a hand over his heart. "I promise tah refrain from all disorderly behavyah in the futchah."

My heart is melting at his concession and I regain my sense of humor. "Well, after all, you *are* a southern gentleman. I expect you to behave like one. I will try to think of the possibilities and warn you ahead of time and you will please ask me before you jump into something."

We both laugh and I feel all tension dissipating. Sans regard for propriety, I let myself fall against his chest in abject relief. "I think what we both deserve is anothah glass of that superb wine," he says taking hold of my upper arms. I read quiet disturbance in his eyes as he gently moves me away from his chest. He turns his back to me. "Yah pour the wine an' take it out tah the livin' room, as yah call it. I will clean up in here an' join yah in a minute. Perhaps there is somethin' *light-hearted* on that pitchah box of yors." A few minutes later, all is back to normal, or what has come to pass for normal at present.

CHAPTER 22

The break of day finds me refreshed and in the highest of spirits. "How are you doing today, Doc?" I ask as we breakfast on veggie omelets.

"Ah am rollin', Dahlin'," he says as he drains his coffee cup. "Ah have forgiven yah."

"What?" I regret the demand the instant it leaves my lips

"And yah; have yah forgiven me?"

I sigh in relief at his forbearance. "It's all water under the bridge, as they say. I was thinking that maybe, if you think you might be feeling up to it, we could take another short journey into the past. I'd like to learn as much as I can about my family, not just from old newspapers and their diaries, but firsthand . . . that is, if you think you're up to it?"

"A capital idea!" he agrees without hesitation. I abandon him to the kitchen cleanup and race upstairs to change into something more nineteenth century.

"Cassie?" he says in surprise, when I appear at the top of the stairs. Doc is waiting, decked out in his original outfit. After rummaging through the attic trunks I have transformed myself into what could pass for a young ranch hand, hair tucked up under a hat that had belonged to my grandfather or perhaps to an earlier patriarch.

"I figured I should look the part. There are some old dresses up there, but I thought we could explore on horseback, first; and I refuse to ride sidesaddle. How women put up with the potential danger in the name of some false sense of decency, I'll never know. I have enough trouble staying on astride. Thank God for Annie Oakley and Calamity Jane. I'll bet even Kate . . ."

Doc laughs and nods his approval. "Ah don't know the other ladies yah mentioned, but yes, Kate often forgoes the conventions of the bustle along with othah proprieties."

"Another thing; you've seen the picture of Sarah. Aside from the coloring, we could be twins. I thought it best to disguise the resemblance as much as possible, in view of the circumstances." A devilish thought crosses my mind. "Although, can you imagine if I were to darken my hair and put on one of Sarah's dresses . . . I could knock on the door after Jefferson returns. It would probably scare the—"

"Ah think not . . . in view of the circumstances."

The portal has lost its mystery. Within the hour, we are heading up the hill behind the house where we hope to gain a good view of the surrounding area. The sun is out, the spring temperatures mild; the Peak is still covered in snow. Doc pulls out his watch and announces it to be two twenty-five, as expected; the hands on mine have stopped at a few minutes after eleven. We estimate that we have been riding almost two hours. Buck is as cooperative as ever, but he hesitates often, and I can tell he senses that all is not as it should be. From our vantage point, we are looking down on the entire ranch and two large herds of cattle within sturdy fencing. We can see the house, barn, and a cylindrical tower I am guessing is a grain silo; also, a former chicken housing. "Yor granddaddy is a smart man; ah'll give the rascal that," says Doc. "It is easy to see where yah get yor foresight. The man leaves nothin' tah chance. It would be next to impossible tah get feed up here in the wintah."

We press through the trees another fifty yards or so until we are around the backside of the hill and dismount. Another herd of equal size is watering at a small lake in a meadow below. I soak up the scene for several minutes while Doc checks our cinches after the long climb. The horses prick up their ears and Doc turns on his heels looking toward a neighboring hill to the north.

"What is it?" I ask, unable to make out anything through the dense forest.

"Shh," he cautions; then motions me to remount. Silently, he leads our way down through the trees the way we came, stopping periodically to listen. We are within view of the barn again when I hear approaching riders. Doc detours us off to the west where we settle behind an enormous, fortuitously situated rock. A minute later, I hear horses making their way through the brush and trees. Some twenty or so yards to the east, I can just make out two riders leading two other heavily laden horses. After dismounting, Doc hands me the reins of his horse; again bids me to remain silent and to stay put. He draws and cocks his revolver before disappearing around the side of the rock. My heartbeat pounds in my ears. When he returns, he looks relieved. "A couple a Utes haulin' game back tah camp," he says. "Thought it might be Mallon." He might be relieved, but Indians? What next?

Danger averted, we continue to explore until the sun begins to sink behind the house in the west, and by the time we are approaching the portal, it is dark.

Our trek has given me a good sense of the property in 1882. Because of the altitude and terrain, the modern world has not been as intrusive here. I look toward the house and see a lone light flickering and the shadow of a figure through the curtain of the study window. We lead the horses inside where Buck snorts in surprise of the bright sunlight coming in through the windows on the opposite side of the barn. While Lightning and Baby Girl are contentedly romping with the goats in the pasture, Buck and Doc's horse have been on the trail for hours. After leading them into their stalls, I throw them the extra meal they have earned before turning them out with the others. In my world it is only eleven in the morning, but in the actual passage of time, Doc and I have missed lunch and dinner, as well. We head into the kitchen where I prepare an extra hearty meal. Assuaged hunger and keen anticipation are superseding my fatigue, but Doc must be exhausted. I decide I cannot in good conscience, ask him to go back until he has had a decent rest. As I close the dishwasher, my excitement overrides selfless resolve. "How are you holding up?"

"Amazin'ly well," he is quick to respond after swallowing down his medication. He dabs at his mouth with the napkin. "And yah? Up for a bit more? Ah was thinkin' we could give the house a once-over at night. Ah'm not sure what—"

I suppress the surge of energy flooding through my veins; Doc has to be pushing his limit. "But you must be . . ."

"Ah assure yah, ah am quite fit. All that fresh air did me good," he insists. "Besides, we will not be out there verah long. Yah cannot tell me yah are not dyin' tah take a peek through that windah? Ah know sure as hell Ah am." It did not take much convincing. I am replete with joy. Without thinking, I drop to the side of his chair and hug him tightly.

On the other side of the portal, we stay in the cover of the hillside until we reach the house; then tread lightly as we make our way along the side of the house. As we approach the window, Doc motions for me to stop while he proceeds to the far side. He steals a peek; then nods. Peering through a break in the curtain, I can see Jefferson sitting at the familiar table. Pencil in hand, he is wearing circular spectacles and is hunched over what appears to be some sort of record book. I watch as his hand makes its way across the page several times. He squints and grabs his chin before he closes the book, rises, and walks to the far corner of the room. He kneels behind the door and pulls up a floorboard. In the shadows, I cannot see his movements, but after replacing the strip of wood, he rises empty-handed. As if he has sensed our presence, he turns abruptly and walks toward the window. I duck and hold my breath. The movement in the shadow on the ground beside me tells me Jefferson is pulling the curtain aside to investigate. A minute passes. Apparently satisfied that all is in order, he lets the burlap hang; light and shadow fade. In another minute, the light is gone and I hear what must be the closing of the study door. Doc takes my hand. Quietly, he leads me toward the front of the house. It is not much after eight, but the entire household has turned in for the day. Ranch folk then truly did go to bed with the chickens.

I am not disappointed that there is nothing more to be

learned today. We continue across the front of the house and around the other side to the rear. Within the protection of the hillside, I bolt for the portal. In less than a minute, I am on my knees in the corner of the study frantically testing for loose boards. Doc, having taken a more leisurely pace, appears moments later. Seeing my frustration, he kneels down beside me and indicates that I leave the chore to him. Leaning an ear close to the floor, he begins to tap with his knuckles. He rises abruptly and reaches into a pocket for his knife, and begins to probe gingerly. The two foot by six-inch floorboard groans at Doc's gradual but firm prying. I leave to retrieve a flashlight. By the time I return, two boards are set aside on the floor along with a rusted metal box about the size of the opening. "Ah don't suppose yah have the key?" he asks lifting the large padlock and letting it clang back against the box.

"No." I sit back on my heels. Disappointment washes over me but a second later, it vanishes. "But I do have bolt cutters." My excitement is running high and so am I. The trip to and from the barn takes less than two minutes. Sinking to my knees beside Doc, I align the tool on its target and give it all I have, but fail to put a dent in the thick metal. Doc takes over, and in one snap, the lock clatters to the floor. I grab to pull up the lid, but again, lack the strength to budge the metal fused by time.

"I have an idea," I say. I leave and return a minute later with a towel. I spread it on the table. Doc is on board and lifts the rusty container onto it. In the end, it takes a hammer, a pry bar, and Doc's strength to wrest free the contents of Jefferson Fielding's secret logs. A musty smell escapes as the lid pops loose. Inside are several ledgers each labeled with the year. Expecting them to be fragile, I gently lift the first labeled 1899 and place it on the table. I take a deep breath and look over at Doc who has taken the seat next to mine. Leaning to one side, he props his head on one fist. The top cover threatens to part company with the rest as I open to the first page. Columns are neatly labeled in print, the first allocated to the date, followed by credits, debits, description, and finally balance. Below numerical entries are diary-like comments written across the full width of the page.

More snow today. Lost several more head. Will sell what's left of the herd come spring.

As I carefully turn each page, I see that that the notations are not daily or even weekly, but random. I assume that if nothing of note happened that day, nothing was recorded. The last entry is dated April 23. According to the family Bible, Jefferson passed away six days later just shy of his seventy-fourth birthday in 1899. Apparently, Mary inherited a ranch on its last legs. I set the book aside. Doc and I, with delicate hands, commence examining the remaining ledgers until we locate the two of note, 1879 and 1882. Doc sits back to watch as I begin to read Jefferson's rendition of that fateful spring and summer when he carried out his plan to kill his wife. I find it endearing that my companion respects my privacy, but I am impatient to find the whole truth, and motion to him to start on the other, more recent ledger that should contain the account of Elizabeth's accident.

For the next half hour, with the help of extra lighting and magnifying glasses, Doc and I pour over the brittle pages. It is clear that Jefferson's account was spawned of frustration from the ravages of a lengthy and near-fatal illness. When he had recovered sufficiently to hold a pencil, he scrawled, in far more detail than would have been possible from the limited perspective of his sickbed, an obviously embellished tale of betrayal; a torrid love affair between an ungrateful wife and a sleazy opportunist. He claims to have heard their lovemaking through the walls and seeing evidence of infidelity on her person; not to mention the guilt he imagines she hides underneath her guise of loving care. It is a story invented by the imaginings of a mind distorted by fever. By the time he was recovering, the false memories had been burned into his memory. Not only does he admit locking Sarah and her belongings in the cellar room, he proudly announces the heretofore-unsuspected murder of Frank Brady earlier the same day. That night he wrote:

The whore and her lover are gone. Brady didn't see it coming; didn't know I had him digging his own grave. Don't know if that whack from the shovel killed him or not but I'm sure he didn't last long under six feet of dirt. He won't be missed and his body will never be found. I don't know how long the bitch will suffer, but she deserves every minute. One thing for sure, it will many be a year before her corpse is found, if ever. No one crosses Jefferson Fielding.

I am shaking as I carefully unfold the fragile piece of loose newsprint. Jefferson had left no stone unturned. It was an article decrying the adulterous behavior of Sarah Fielding. *LOCAL WOMAN DESERTS AILING HUSBAND AND YOUNG CHILD*

Sadly, it has been reported that Mr. Jefferson Fielding's wife of four years has recently deserted him and their three-year old daughter, Mary. Mr. Fielding is a prominent cattle rancher in Florissant. Apparently, Mrs. Fielding, who enjoyed the "better" years of the union, became disillusioned when the "worse" came along in the form of the lengthy illness of her much older husband. In Fielding's own words, "She walked out of the house, bag in hand and climbed aboard Frank Brady's buckboard." Frank Brady had been hired by the misses to work the ranch while her husband was incapacitated. An illicit relationship is said to have gone on for some months and things came to a head when Sarah Fielding announced to her husband that she was with child, Brady's. Fielding is taking it in stride, acknowledging that he should have known better. Against his initial misgivings, he married a city girl and had been enduring her dissatisfaction for some time, in hopes she would mature. Mrs. Fielding's parents, John and Mildred Higgins are said to be devastated by their daughter's behavior. Neighbors in The Springs remember Sarah as their late-in-life blessing, some twenty years younger than her only sibling, Elizabeth who has been engaged by her brother-in-law to keep his house and care for her niece in her sister's stead.

Now, I know exactly what happened and why. Jefferson's mind had betrayed him. Try as I might to hate him, I can see only victims in this saga. A thought flits through my mind about my father. Was there something in his past . . . I think of my mother and why she had not deserted my father. Had she, at last, given up all hope for his deliverance from his demons? While still repulsed by her actions, I endeavor to understand the workings of a mind facing death and desperately wanting to leave this world righting a wrong. My father had not been responsible for any deaths . . . as had Jefferson. If fate had favored them and mother differently . . . I set the ledger aside, confused as ever, fearing I might have inherited the potential to react to injustice with bloodshed of an innocent. A shudder travels the length of my spine.

"Ah take it it's not a pretty pitchah?"

"I think Jefferson was at the mercy of fever that stimulated an overactive imagination; that he really believed his wife was having an affair."

"Do yah think that justifies killin' her? Why didn't he just turn her out?"

"I see your point, but if he was not in his right mind . . . The newspaper article said he hoped she would come around. He must have snapped when he imagined her eventual departure. And once he had gone too far, he felt his only recourse was to cover up his evil deed. Perhaps he was thinking of Mary." The more I spin this yarn of explanation, the more ridiculous I feel. "I guess I just don't want to think that my ancestor was a cold-blooded killer."

Doc says nothing but sets before me another frayed yellow newspaper clipping that had been tucked between the pages in the 1882 ledger. It recorded the incident this way.

Front Range Woman Dies in Freak Accident

Elizabeth Higgins, forty-three, died after a fall during a severe thunderstorm last week. She was discovered by her seven-year-old niece, Mary Fielding, who went looking for her when she failed to return from seeing to the animals. It appears that her aunt lost her footing and struck her head on a rock. The young child ran over a mile for help, but Miss Higgins was dead by the time she had recruited a neighbor. As a young girl, Elizabeth had been badly burned in a kitchen fire that left her disfigured and partially crippled. For the last three years, she has been nanny and housekeeper for her brother-in-law, Jefferson Fielding, who was in Colorado Springs buying provisions when the accident occurred. Elizabeth is survived by her parents, John and

Mildred Higgins of Colorado City, her niece, brother-in-law, and presumably her wayward sister, Sarah, whereabouts unknown. Services will be held at the Methodist church in Colorado City this Saturday at noon.

"What a tragedy," I say thinking of everyone involved, but especially Great, Great, Grandmother Mary. She loses her mother, is left with a parent who was not emotionally in tune to being a father, and then her loving aunt.

"Jefferson assessed it a bit differently," Doc adds. "Listen tah this." He pauses before proceeding to read. "You'd bettah prepare yourself, Dahlin'."

"She was just like her sister, always bucking my authority when it came to Mary. I told her I'll be damned before I let that child be coddled. Now, I may well be damned as I sent her to join her slut of a sibling today. May they burn in hell together. I made sure Mary saw me leave early knowing she would eventually look for her aunt when she did not return to the house. The neighbor and sheriff were here when I returned. As expected, the law saw no need of an inquest. Mary will cry for a few days, but will be stronger for the experience and she has the chores and studies to keep her busy. Elizabeth did teach the child to cook and clean. Mary can read, write, and do her sums. When I get to town, I aim to purchase some texts to further her education. The two of us will get on just fine without the interference of busy bodies and nere-do-wells."

My stomach turns as Doc continues to read my great, great, great grandfather's diatribe. Subsequent entries record his recollection of the trip to The Springs to bring Elizabeth's body to her parents for burial. He tells of the Higgins' plea to allow them to raise their granddaughter.

I masked my disdain for the idea with a tearful forced smile and told them that neither Mary or I could bear another loss. This whole family is pathetic and we are well rid of them.

Doc observes. "He condemns himself in words he is confident will never be read, at least in his lifetime. The cur was so full of himself ah do believe he imagined this verah scenario; a futchah resident unearthin' this muck and makin' him famous, pahdon me, infamous." Doc lets the book drop onto the table.

I pick up the ledger and turn a couple pages back to read Jefferson's plot to rid himself of the sister-in-law who had served her purpose and outworn her welcome at Fielding Ranch. His words purge from my heart any empathy I may have conjured up for my forefather. I was ready to forgive his chauvinist ways, accepted as the norm in his day. I had believed that his illness might have distorted his perception to the point of paranoia; I stepped across the line when I accepted his solution as defensible. The nausea is getting worse and must show on my face.

Doc reaches over to close the book. "Enough for now," he says.

It is after five; I had not realized how long we'd been at it. "We need tah eat an' get a good night's rest," he says tugging at my chair. I rise. With a hand on my back, he guides me to the kitchen.

"Ah'll see to the animals."

Drained as I am, I do not object. I peruse the contents of the freezer and retrieve a plastic container labeled chili. I leave it to heat in the microwave while I dice onions and grate a block of sharp cheddar. A salad and garlic bread round out the simple but adequate meal with little effort on my part. By the time he returns from feeding and closing up the barn, the food is on the table. I am too emotionally spent to attempt conversation. It will take a while for me to be able to make peace with this last revelation. Doc seems to sense my uncertainty, but the silence must weigh heavily. He turns on the TV to fill the void. He has his faults, but how many people know when to keep quiet? While Doc cleans up, I dish up chocolate ice cream and drizzle on the chocolate sauce; when the going gets tough, pull out the chocolate. We proceed to the living room where we continue the mindless electronic diversion. Doc returns empty bowls to the kitchen. I hear the rattle of the dishes and utensils, then some unrecognizable sounds. When he reenters, it is with a shot glass and a bottle of Jack. Really? I have no strength to object, and I am not his babysitter. My already vertically challenged spirits plummet as I watch him pour, but rally when he hands the solitary drink to me.

"Yah need this," he says as I accept the glass. "Why Dahlin', Ah do believe you are surprised?" he adds as he sits on the sofa. I take a generous sip and nod.

"Frequent tipplin' eased the effects of the consumption; the pills are controllin' them, now, without dullin' my faculties. Not that Ah won't continue tah enjoy a good swig from time tah time, but Ah am no longer dependent on it tah control the discomfort."

Doc is complicated but I am getting a good feel for the man. The more I learn; the more I come to appreciate him for the man he is inside, the one he masks by the "bad-boy" persona he so expertly projects. I study his profile as he turns his attention back to the TV, now spewing out the mostly dreadful news of the day. He is no longer noticeably gaunt. I am guessing he has put on a good ten pounds. Today's lengthy excursion testifies to a measurable improvement in his stamina. Jack has been out weekly and is more than pleased with Doc's progress. Next on the medical agenda is a follow-up x-ray to confirm his optimism.

Warmth is invading my veins and I let myself slump down in the chair, semi-anesthetized. As the disquietude fades, my mind begins to filter the latest chapter of family history objectively. An hour later, we say our goodnights and head for our respective rooms. Knowing he would object, I wait to tiptoe downstairs to smuggle up another ledger.

In bed, under the lamplight, I open the 1875 ledger. Between the lines, Jefferson's account exposes him as an unsavory character residing in Texas, where, with full pockets and under the cloud of suspicion, Daniel Baxter fled, abandoning a wife and two little girls (an unfaithful bitch and her bastards). As Paul Jorgensen in Taos, New Mexico, he quickly triples his capital. He attributes his success to skillful outmaneuvering and misdirection of any competitors, but it does not take a genius to understand that he was nothing but a skilled criminal and proud of it. I get the feeling that he considered their lack of intuition as an invitation to move in on their property and assets.

I refuse to take responsibility for their failure to protect their own interests.

My ancestor did not believe in being there for his fellow man. His stay was short-lived as a new

crop of jealous, "self-righteous" coveters trumped up unjust accusations.

His choice to settle on Colorado's Front Range under yet another alias was not without purpose. The population was sparse, as his entrance predated the gold rush in the area. Its rugged terrain and harsh climate convinced him that neighbors would be few, distant, and far too busy attending to the demands of their own spreads to invade his privacy. He, without consideration for his marital status, admits to cleverly manipulating a healthy, well-trained young woman to keep his house and bear his sons. I sicken again at his disappointment at the birth of yet another daughter is duly registered. Entries are replete with financial successes, some from competent ranching, several, he proudly attributes to extra-curricular activities out of town under fictitious identities. Victor Farnsworth of Abilene, Kansas, for instance, robbed a bank in Cheyenne. His unmerited pride extended to boasting of his sexual prowess in brothels along his journeys. My disgust builds with every sentence. Entry after terse entry, reveal an ambitious man without scruples, sans any influence of sickness, at least the physical variety. To him women are sources of labor and/or objects of lust subject to their physical appeal or lack thereof. Fellow men are inferiors who exist only to serve Jefferson's interests. His seared conscience permits even murder when his expectations require it; all this sans the influence of fever and illness. As if to justify his superiority, he points to the fact, that, on the Front Range, he is a respected rancher who has the sympathy of his neighbors, believing he has been, without cause, deserted by a philandering wife. He also racks up points for taking in his disabled sister-in-law, then, single-handedly raising is young daughter.

I run my hands up and down my arms, loathe to think of the tainted blood pulsing through my veins. Deep down, I know we are not doomed by heredity, but having monsters on both sides of the family does not sit well, and I know that henceforth, every angry thought will be accompanied by an ugly vision of one or the other of these men.

I set the ledger aside and curl up under the covers. When I close my eyes, my mind dabbles with the idea of restoring Sarah Fielding's reputation.

CHAPTER 23

I awake in the same position, a bit stiff, but fully rested. Somewhere in my dreams, I have written an award-winning expose in answer to the newspaper article of so long ago and am anxious to get Doc's opinion. I rise. Downstairs is quiet. I flip the switch on the coffeepot and head for the animals. At seven, when I return, Doc has still not appeared. I mix up a breakfast casserole and set it to baking before heading upstairs to roust him from bed. When there is no response to my rap, I knock again a little harder, then once more, with even more force. Fear overcomes convention and I let myself in slowly. I am holding my breath as I walk across to the bed. Unlike the encounter of several weeks back, Doc is indeed the lump beneath the bedding. He is sleeping so soundly I take my leave without disturbing him.

I stop in at the study on my way back to the kitchen to pick up my laptop. The article pouring through my fingers onto the screen is nearly finished as Doc makes his appearance, fully dressed but moving slowly. Yesterday has taken its toll. Guilt washes over me. I pray that the regression is not permanent and mentally vow not to let this happen again.

"We overdid yesterday."

"Nonsense; Ah am quite well, really; just a bit tired; laid awake thinkin'," he insists as he pours himself a cup of coffee. "What have we here?" he asks pausing to list over my shoulder.

Thank God, I was just about to explode. "I," I say proudly, "am writing a rebuttal to that scandalous article about Sarah. I know it's silly at this late date; that no one who really counts can read it, but I'll feel better. I'm sure the Courier will find it a great human interest story."

"Ah do not doubt that," he acknowledges, but there is something . . . I cannot put my finger on it . . . almost disobliging in his tone.

"You don't think it's a good idea." I ask as my fingers fly to finish the final sentence.

"It is yor family, yor decision, Dahlin'; surely, not mine. Ah am jus' wondering if yah thought it through." Doc's question impairs my typing.

"What do you mean?"

"If ah understood yah correctly, yah changed yor name when yah moved here in an effort tah avoid family scandal. Ah could be wrong, but Ah would wagah that few here are aware of Sarah's purported infidelity."

"And your point is?"

"If yah succeed in gettin' this intah print, an' there is no doubt that yah will, have yah considered the publicity it will generate? From what Ah have been able tah observe of yor modern news content, reporters have ultimate access intah personal mattahs. The modern public seems tah delight in the misdoin's in one's past, that could turn yor human interest piece intah an embarrassin' expose of yor own life. The truth about Sarah will come out, but might not yor recent family tragedy become fodder for the insatiable press, shinin' a lamp on yor private life?" In one minute, Doc has managed to extinguish my fiery enthusiasm with two questions. "Ah believe yah told me that you took great pains tah see that the discovery of Sarah's body wasn't leaked to the press."

It was true; I was terrified that the story would be splashed on the front page of the local paper; that I would be hounded by an eager reporter who might in pursuit of additional copy, delve into my personal life.

Doc continues. "True, everyone will come tah know that yor great, great, great grandmothah did not really run off an' desert her family, but also, that yor great, great, great grandfathah murdahed her an' her lover; that he was guilty of innumerable othah crimes that might suggest that yor estate was financed with ill-gotten gains; not to mention that someone was murdahed in yor home. Yah might become the talk of the county, maybe even the state. The authorities will no doubt return with yor modern excavation equipment an' tear up half yor ranch in an effort to find the grave of Frank Brady."

"Enough already!" Reality sets in. My mind plays through the anguish I felt when I first found Sarah. No part of me could rationalize resealing the room and forgetting about her; yet, as Doc so aptly reminded me, I was filled with dread at the thought of publicity. Bob had seen to it that the story never saw press coverage. In publically righting this wrong, I would be ceding my privacy and exposing the ranch to possibly months of disarray; and for what? If I were Frank Brady, I do not know that I would be all that thrilled about being dug up and dissected, or whatever forensic science called for at this stage. But what about possible modern-day relatives, who, like myself, have lived with a rotten apple in their family tree. Frank Brady was not a home-wrecker. Then again, it is possible that he might have been guilty of worse crimes. Most likely, he had no children. Would distant cousins even care? I just found out I was not the descendent of an adulteress, an unfit mother. Oh no, I shared the blood of a thief and murderer. Am I happier for that knowledge? I press delete and empty the recycle bin. The file is now beyond recovery as are my ancestors good and bad. Immediately, I regret my rashness. If I thought about it long enough, I might well talk myself into an obligation to Mr. Brady's family. I can always write another article.

"Well, at least I know the truth," I say aloud as I fold up the computer and take it to the study. "It was quite therapeutic just writing it all down."

"There might be anothah way tah clear Sarah's name," Doc says as I reenter the kitchen.

I stare dumbly.

"It would be quite easy, Ah believe," he adds, "given our

present relative control of time and history."

I stand perplexed.

"Are yah forgettin', Dahlin', we have access to yor family in 1882?" Though not comprehending where this is heading, I am all ears. "*We* could," he continues, "expose Sarah's body."

"Oh my God, Doc; you're right!" I jump out of my chair, grab Doc by the arms, and machine gun the next sentences as I pace around like a nervous racehorse. "We could sneak into the cellar and move the safe. We would have to make sure that it is *Elizabeth* who finds the body. It would be awful if Mary were to find her mother. Jefferson's claim would be proven a lie and he would be arrested for her murder and . . ."

"Take heed before yah agree," Doc warns. "He'd most likely hang."

I take a minute to contemplate the scenario, including the effect it might have on Mary. As distasteful as it is, it is better than the way things stand. Elizabeth would no doubt protect her niece from the ugly details, and it would be far better for Mary not to continue to be raised by a murderer with a warped idea of the proper station of the female gender. "I can live with that," I decide quickly. "The paper would print its own retraction and expose the whole thing, including Frank Brady's innocence in the affair. His body would be found and given a decent burial; his family at the time, if any, notified. It's perfect! Oh Doc, do you think we really can?"

"Seems logical. If we can't change a piece of yor family's history, what are yah doin' tryin' to cure me?" And with that, I grab Doc and lead him in a clumsy dance around the kitchen.

"Anothah thin', Dahlin'," he says when he is able to arrest my spinning, "Elizabeth might not have that accident," he adds calmly.

"Oh Doc," I say hugging him soundly. "I can't believe I didn't think of that. Little Mary would have such a different life." I let my mind play with the idea and all its repercussions. The positives far outweigh the negatives, hands down. It takes a minute for the full import of that to sink in. I have but one regret. "Oh, why couldn't you have popped in a few years ago, before Jefferson killed Sarah?"

"Sorrah, but the mattah was beyond mah control," he shrugs. "Is that lovely aroma breakfast?"

"Oh dear." I had forgotten about the casserole, but quickly realize the timer has yet to chime. A minute later, it does. "Do you think you'll be feelin—"

"I have pondahed it," he says. "But I am afraid I won't be good for anythin' today."

I cannot deny wanting an instant fix, but make a determined effort to practice my patience. Doc, at least, in this instance, is the possessor of the more level head. Of the two of us, if there is any breaking and entering experience, it would be in his camp. He is in no shape to exert himself for a few days, and my eagerness is quieted with the knowledge that time is standing still on the other side of the portal. Jefferson is a dangerous man, a killer. We would have only one chance; the scheme must be intricately plotted and precisely executed.

I shoo Doc into the living room while I clean up. I find him snoozing upright on the sofa and have to restrain myself from disturbing him. I busy myself with laundry and upstairs cleaning before retiring to the kitchen to bake bread and set a pot of spaghetti sauce to simmering. That Doc does not move from the sofa is a concern. He denies running a fever but I have my doubts, and he is coughing quite a bit. On the other side of the scale, he is eating heartily. He sleeps the afternoon away. When he wakes, he remains quiet. We dine and retire early.

My faith in Doc counteracts any sleep-disturbing anticipation. Doc sleeps late again and remains sluggish throughout the day, but, again, his healthy appetite allays my unease. His recovery is ahead of schedule and setbacks are inevitable. I clean downstairs avoiding the living room until Doc offers to take a walk. Again, we retire early. When it is clear that he intends on spending another day on the sofa, I opt to retrace our ride of a few days before in my world this time. It did not take me long to locate the remains of the silo and other building, which according to the evidence, must have burnt to the ground. As Buck and I make our way around, I cannot help but wonder where Jefferson had disposed of Frank's body. It makes sense that he would have chosen a location at which Frank would not have questioned being asked to dig the hole that would become his grave. I rack my brain, but realize that the distance of time and the vastness of the ranch preclude me from uncovering that mystery. The venture has cleared my head. I direct Buck toward the barn.

I complement our noon sandwiches with macaroni salad. "Nevah had tunah fish before," Doc says before taking his first bite.

"Well?"

"Ah believe I like tunah."

Continuing to concentrate on his health, I make steak and baked potatoes for dinner, hoping a diet high in protein will replenish his strength.

CHAPTER 24

The next morning Doc is waiting for me in the kitchen, sipping coffee and watching TV.

"If it's not too much trouble, might we have yor delightful French toast?" he asks.

"Absolutely!" I say, thrilled to see that he appears to have bounced back. I am anxious to know if he has come up with an exact plan to expose Jefferson and exonerate Sarah, but concentrate on preparing breakfast. Doc leads the conversation, commenting on the news. I sense he knows he is driving me crazy. I refuse to let on and instead, join in light chitchat during the meal.

"Ah'll clean up while yah change," he offers, starting to remove the dishes from the table. "The occasion calls for somethin' black."

"I beg your pardon?"

"We'll be hahdah tah see in dark clothin'."

"We're going now? But we can't. Jefferson is still. . ."

"Jefferson will be gone overnight." Exhaustion must have clouded his memory or maybe the time warp thing has slipped his mind.

"No, No. Don't you remember? He was in the house when we came back last time. We saw the lights go out. I don't think we should risk it. I want to save Sarah's reputation but not at the cost of a load of buckshot in my ass."

"That was last night."

"I understand, but you're forgetting the time thing. How are we going to deal with that?" My inflection conveys my exasperation along with my surprise that he had not considered the obvious.

"Ah am well aware of the time thin'. Why do yah think I've been so tired the last couple a days?" I shake my head and mimic confusion. "While yah slept, Ah spent almost twenty-four hours on the othah side of the portal advancin' the clock and gettin' Jefferson tah leave the propahty. Ah doubt that Elizabeth or Mary will pose any threat. Now, go get intah somethin' black." he beckons with an outward flip of his hands. "Go on now, git."

I dress in record time, black long-sleeved shirt, black jeans, boots, and a charcoal sweater, all the while thinking of Doc's ingeniousness.

"Whoa there, Dahlin'," he says grabbing me by the arm and turning me around in mid-flight to the entry.

"I thought you were ready to go?"

"Ah need a little more information," he answers directing me to the cellar door. It is then I realize that Doc has never been downstairs and seen the infamous room.

Once downstairs, Doc requests that I walk him through the details of my discovery of Sarah's body. I leave to retrieve the photo album. When I return, he is inspecting the bottom of the safe and the furniture movers. I demonstrate how they make the daunting task possible. He tries and is able to move the safe much quicker than I had. I am at a loss to explain how Jefferson accomplished the same thing. "We'll need these," he says and I mentally rebuke myself for not thinking of them before. They may be under the safe now, but they will not be there in 1882. Doc returns to the table. He leans on his hands and studies the photos depicting the cellar of 1875. He looks over at the safe and back again. He inspects the wall between the tomb and the main cellar; then climbs the stairs up to the outside cellar entrance. I wait by the safe, pry bar in hand, as Doc satisfies his curiosity. He kneels down to retrieve the furniture movers as I pry up one corner of the safe.

"We will have need of light, as well," he adds. I walk to a nearby shelf and pick up two heavy-duty flashlights. After instructing Doc in their use, he shakes his head. His lack of comment suggests that while he is impressed by wireless electrical current, he has ceased to be surprised at modern inventions. Tools in hand, Doc pronounces us ready to embark on our quest of justice. True to his word, darkness is just descending on the other side of the portal, but it is almost twenty-four hours later than when we were here together before. I see no moon rising. The fact that it is quite windy is also to our advantage, as it will cover or distort any sound from our activity in the cellar. Doc and I watch from the shelter of the rock as Jefferson is making his departure.

"Why do you have to go at night, Daddy?" Mary is skipping from the barn as her father mounts his horse. "When will you be back?"

"Never you mind, Girl. Get yourself inside and help your aunt with the chores." Obediently, Mary runs to the house and ducks inside the door. No kiss, no hug; just gruff instructions, and Jefferson rides off in a cloud of dust.

"Come on." Doc takes me by the hand and around to the front of the barn. "We need to kill a little more time," he says. "I thought you might like to see the inside of yor barn in 1882." He opens the lockless door slowly and quietly closes it behind us. I switch on my flashlight and hand the other to Doc. I slap a hand over my mouth to stifle a yelp as a cat streaks past, small rodent's legs and tail dangling under its chin. Five horses are housed within the stalls. The last one is empty. As I look around, I recognize the wood as the same, but lighter, having aged over the passage of time. As with the house, I see that the barn has been maintained, rather than remodeled. There is no overhead lighting, only an oil lantern hanging on a hook. There are several more hooks and built-in compartments in my world, along with modern locks, that reflect the need for increased security in the twenty-first century. It was Mary's daughter's generation that installed electricity, in both the house and the barn. I walk toward the wall of the portal. There is no hint of a hidden passage. I wave Doc over and motion for him to perform his magic, but his touch has no affect in this time. It makes sense. I turn right. The room that serves as my office today is lined with bunks. I back out, turn my attention to the familiar built-in ladder and climb it up to the loft where little has changed other than a few added bins. I spend another half hour schmoozing with the horses that are well groomed and healthy. Doc seems to be enjoying my wonderment. Is this how he feels in my world? Unlike his experience into the future, I can connect with the past; have a personal attachment to the surroundings. All too soon, it is time to go. We douse the lights and leave the barn as stealthily as we entered. When we look toward the house one light still flickers in an upstairs window. A few minutes later, it fades away. We wait another ten minutes before skulking our way across the yard to the cellar doors, fighting gusts of wind along the way. I wrap my arms around myself as we continue to be buffeted at our point of entry. Doc let's another few minutes go by before he reaches for the left handle of the cellar flaps. I grab the right. When I tug against a slight resistance, a sharp squeal screams through the wind. If not for Doc's swift reaction the door would have crashed back into place, betraying our presence. Heart pounding, I dig in my heels and take back my side of the door, this time prepared for heft increased by the wind. Once doors lay splayed on the ground, Doc, flashlight beaming ahead, begins a slow descent into the cellar. I watch him sweep the beam across the room before beckoning me to follow.

Two minutes later, I am kneeling next to the safe. I pull the pry bar from my belt and retrieve the movers from the mesh bag tied to my other side. Doc positions the flashlight so that it shines on the base of the safe. We pause to listen before Doc pries up the first corner while I slip the disc underneath. Doc turns his head and clears his throat. The second positioning goes smoothly, as does the third, but then Doc is seized by a coughing jag. I freeze, breathing and all. He regains control and we wait a full minute before nodding in agreement and proceeding to shove the last disc into place. We are putting our shoulders into it when we hear the creak at the top of the stairs and see the faint beam of light. "Who's down there!" demands the voice. Doc, a finger to his lips, reaches down to shut off the flashlight. Again, we freeze in place. Above us, we can hear the wind whipping at the cellar entrance. We should have anticipated this and shut the doors behind us. Elizabeth must be hearing it too, and begins her cumbersome climb down the stairs. Heedless of the noise I am making, I stumble over my own feet in my dash up the steps. Behind me, Doc grabs at his chest, a coughing spasm paralyzing his ascent. I reach back, snatch the hand from his chest and yank him behind me. In a sudden burst of speed, he has passed me and he is tugging me to the top. An explosion ricochets off the walls. In the same instant, fire ignites in my calf. The second shot shatters the step below me and I cannot hold in the scream. At the same time, "Aunt Lizzy, what's wrong?" I turn back at the sound of Little Mary's voice, but Doc tugs me outside. My ankle gives out and I hit the granite face first.

"Get back upstairs, Child!" The shout is accompanied by the distinct sound of ejecting shells. Doc lets the doors slam closed and hauls me, limping along the side of the house to the safety of the hillside. The two of us crumple into a lump, Doc coughing and sputtering, me gasping for air. In the moonlight, we can see Elizabeth tromping around the side of the house coming in our direction waving the reloaded shotgun as she approaches. When I use my still functioning foot to scoot myself back, Doc reminds me that she cannot see us within the rock. Grateful for the reminder, I slump against him and concentrate on catching my breath.

A few minutes later, Doc rises, pulls my arm around his neck, and hauls me to my feet. We leave Elizabeth to stalking her invisible prey and on three legs, hobble along the back of the house toward the barn. The glare of the morning sun blinds us as we enter the portal. I want to rest a minute, but Doc keeps going through causeway into the house and directly to the recliner that he adjusts to have better access to my injury.

Pulling the knife from his pocket, he deftly cuts through the hem of my jeans and clamps the knife in his teeth, before rending the denim to the knee. He leans in to examine the wound. "Not as bad as it could have been." he says letting out a breath. "But it needs to be seen to directly."

"You'll have to do it."

"Ah am not a doctah."

"A gunshot wound has to be reported to the authorities in this world. I couldn't ask Jack to risk his medical license. I'm sure you've had to do this before."

"Ah see yor point; and yes, a time or two, but nevah on a woman."

"Anatomy is the same down there," I assure him. "In the bathroom; the brown bottle under the sink is antiseptic. There is a large bowl, clean cloths, bandages and tape there, as well."

He returns a minute later and expertly begins to clean the wound. His touch is tender but he is thorough. The hydrogen peroxide bubbles and exposes the wound that is a good three inches long and an inch wide.

"Ah'm afraid we'll need somethin' to dig out the buckshot," his tone is reluctant.

"Hmmm." I had not expected that. "Well, better get another bowl from the kitchen. You know where the knives are and you'll find tweezers in the top drawer in the bathroom. There's a small white tube in the cabinet above the sink marked antiseptic ointment," I say.

While Doc rummages for the medical supplies, I brace myself for the "operation".

He pulls a TV tray next to the recliner and spreads out the paraphernalia. He leaves for the kitchen again, for what, I can't imagine as all he will need is here. I take the opportunity to pour a healthy dose of peroxide into the bowl and wince as I toss in the instruments.

"Drink this," he says folding my hands around the whiskey glass. I take a sip. "All of it," he insists. "Ah don't want you squirmin' around while ah have a knife at your flesh." It takes a few swallows but I get the double shot down. "Open," he says. I do in protest and before I know it, Doc has shoved a clean towel between my teeth. I get the message. This is going to be worse than I thought. For the next twenty minutes or so, I study Doc's face as he sets to the task. He works slowly and so gently that the pain I am expecting amounts to a sting here and there. I let the cloth drop. "You're good," I say as he sets his tools aside.

"Stay still," he orders. He picks up my glass and heads toward the kitchen. He returns with another generous drink. "Yor gonna need this," he says handing it to me. "Ah'm afraid at least one of the pellets is a bit deeper than the othahs." I drink as quickly as I can, the liquid burning my throat as it makes its descent. He replaces my gag. I close my eyes. His next probe brings a searing pain, then blackness.

When I wake, I am aware of a dull throbbing. The TV tray is cleared and Doc's eyes are closed, his head resting comfortably on the back of the sofa. I look down at the expert bandaging job and marvel.

"Yor back." I start at the unexpected words.

"Did I pass out?"

"Believe me, it was for the best. How does it feel?" he says examining his handiwork.

"Okay," I say with a nod. "Didn't know I had a doctor in the house." I chuckle but then disillusionment fills me. "I blew our chance, Doc. What are we going to do now?"

"Nothin', he says in a tone that invites no discussion, before adding, "Till that wound heals, anyway." He rises, turns on his heel, and disappears into the kitchen. He returns, a glass of milk in one hand, his meds in the other. He throws his head back and slaps the hand to his mouth, after which he downs the entire glass of milk. He wipes his mouth with the back of his hand. "That was too close," he says. A sly smile teases the edges of his lips. "First time yah been shot, Dahlin?"

"Very funny. Listen, we have to get out there right away. If Elizabeth finds those furniture movers . . . Time stands still for no man, as they say."

"Ah beg to diffah, Dahlin'," he says. "It does stand still for me, remembah? Yor aunt, unbeknownst to her, of course, is still standin' at the hillside. We have all the time in the world."

I throw up my hands, "I can't seem to get used to that, but right now, I am grateful for it. So what's plan B?"

"Ah beg yor pahdon?"

"It means what's next?"

"The way Ah figyah it, the first thing Elizabeth would do is secure that cellah door from the inside. If she does . . ."

"I know; you could concoct diversion before she can do that, while I sneak back in. You're good at that."

"How are yah going tah . . ."

"Move the safe? You saw me do it. It will take me a bit longer than the two of us, but I can do it. Those furniture movers are the berries . . . I guess you would say daisies." All business now, Doc ignores my attempt at humor; sits down and looks straight ahead. I lean back in the chair and close my eyes; my calf has resumed throbbing. "There is a little bottle of pain killers in that same cabinet." Doc springs to his feet. I hear a bit of fumbling, but he soon returns with the right bottle. While I struggle with the child-proof lid, he goes to the kitchen for something to down the tablets.

He barely breaks through the door before he is adding to the plan. "Yah go aroun' the back of the house. Ah'll go 'roun' the barn an' create a disturbance with the livestock. When Elizabeth goes tah check it out, yah head back intah the cellah an' finish the job. Ah'll keep her busy for as long as I can."

I whirl around in the chair and before I remember my bad leg, plant them both solidly on the floor. "Damn . . ." I ease my injury back onto the chair. "I mean it's perfect and foolproof!" I exclaim. "Give me a couple of hours and . . ."

"I'll give yah a couple a weeks," he says firmly. Aware that arguing will accomplish nothing, I bite my tongue and settle back in the recliner. He is right; there is no urgency except in my own mind. Doc turns on the TV. Before long, the painkillers kick in. I awake to the sound of Doc setting lunch on the trays. He gently rights my chair and hands me my plate.

I instruct Doc in the use of the DVD player and we dine on sandwiches viewing the Kevin Costner/Dennis Quaid version of Wyatt Earp. The plate still rests on my lap when I wake, again. My watch reads two fifteen. Doc's head is slumped to one side, his plate on the cushion beside him.

The TV is prompting to hit "play" again. With utmost care, I set my plate. Slowly I swivel and transfer my weight to my feet. Sore, but tolerable. I'm a big believer in circulation to promote rapid healing. I pick up the plates and glasses. The walk to the kitchen is slow but uneventful. Two weeks, my ass!

CHAPTER 25

Despite my rapid healing, our journey is delayed. A visit from Jack nixes any undue exertion for Doc. I wince as he verbally chides us both, in no uncertain terms, for Doc's over-doing, whatever it entailed. Uncharacteristically, Doc takes the discipline with a series of nods, "Ah undahstands", and "thank yahs". As he is leaving, Jack tells us he has scheduled an x-ray for the following week at his office in Woodland Park.

I escort him back to his vehicle, careful to disguise the slight limp. "Say", he says. "You could probably use a rest from all this nursing. John is beyond needing constant attention. "We haven't been out since he came to town." Jack and I had dated several times, all enjoyable encounters spent getting to know each other while he played tour guide in my new home. He is a gentleman with old fashioned values, perfect for a novice dater. Tempted as I am to continue the budding relationship, I decline. "Not just yet, Jack," I start, scrambling for a plausible explanation. "John is still a bit uneasy, you understand; always looking over his shoulder."

"Is that all it is?"

"Excuse me?"

"It's just that I get the feeling that there's more to your relationship than just a history of friendship. Is it possible that

I am facing some competition? I mean, I understand if that's the case."

"Nothing *like* that," I stutter out. I recall Doc's rendition of their private conversation. A part of me wants to ring his neck. I resist the urge to explain further; feel torn between personal pursuits and loyalty. "I just don't feel comfortable leaving him on his own just yet."

"Let me know when you're free." I lean to accept a kiss on my cheek.

"I will," I promise, thankful for being let off the hook so easily.

When I reenter the house, it is with mixed emotions; feelings that I cannot quite resolve. In an effort to divert my thoughts, I spend hours of the next several days in the attic targeting the boxes sent ahead by my mother. I have been through half of them and have yet to uncover any diaries.

I turn my attention back to the older diaries in the library. I am about to go out of my mind in anticipation. Doc has the patience of a saint and loses himself in internet surfing and history books from the library. I know he must be chomping at the bit to get on his way to Gunnison, but also that he is risking his own priorities and health to help me. I vow to mind my Ps and Qs, busying myself with reading Mary's diaries. The more I read, the more I am convinced we are doing the right thing. Mary's entries either praise her father or explain away his questionable actions. In her mid-teen years, she speaks of a neighbor boy she fancies, but is quick to acknowledge his inadequacies as a potential husband. I attribute her assessment to Jefferson Fielding's selfish influence. I am convinced no beau would meet her father's standards and any would threaten his control. True to his word, Jefferson regularly supplies her with educational materials that still rest on the shelves of the study. Her writing reflects a growing knowledge of English, mathematics, history, and proper etiquette. He sees to it that there is no lack of activity to fill her days, much of them spent on her own, as he pursues his own agenda. Who knows what he was doing?

CHAPTER 26

Back in Jack's office, Doc and I are greeted with a positive report on the x-ray, a surprise to him in view of the previous examination. The apparent setback was deceptive and no doubt due to the excess exertion; the treatment is working, and apparently, quite well. We leave in high spirits, but with Jack's caution not to tempt fate. If he only knew.

"I was so worried," I say on the drive home.

"Ah figyahed Ah was jus' a bit tired," He says.

"We're both in good condition, then."

"Yor ankle?"

"Completely healed," I announce confidently. "And I am happy to say, I will have a little scar to remind me of the experience."

Doc chuckles. "Tomorrow mornin' then."

"You mean?"

He nods.

"You're on," I respond without hesitation. We stop at City Market and stock up on fresh fruit and vegetables. Doc is captivated by the frozen food aisle and selects a couple of cartons of ice cream in flavors that surprised him, along with a few candy bars he spies in the checkout line. As luck would have it, it is Susie's lane and she is duly impressed with his bygone southern charm. She inquires as to his health and readily agrees that Jack is the best doctor in the county. After assuring her we will be seeing her again soon, we take our leave.

In spite of the excitement, a feeling of calm settles over me. I drive leisurely and we stop in Florissant to lunch at the Thunderbird. Back at home, after stowing the groceries, I pull out Scrabble. It takes Doc two minutes to get up to speed. He is a formidable opponent, winning three out of four rounds in less than two hours.

Pumped with victory, Doc heads out to feed and quarter the animals. In light of the burgers and fries earlier, I prepare gourmet salads for dinner, and whip up my own bleu cheese dressing, cornbread and honey butter.

Doc opts for a scoop of each of the exotic ice creams he selected at the market. I try the chocolate concoction but pass on the bubblegum variety. We pull out the Scrabble board again and this time, I manage to break even. It is ten when we decide to turn in.

I fall asleep quickly but wake with a start. The clock reads three twenty-two. Something in the back of my mind. . . Struggling to bring it to the fore does no good. Silently, I tiptoe down to the kitchen for a glass of water. Sitting down at the table, I begin to go over the entire scenario from the discovery of Sarah's body to that of the Jefferson's condemnatory ledger. "That's it," I shout loud before I remember that Doc is still sleeping. I head for the study, where I bury myself in the ledgers for the rest of the night.

Doc offers to feed, gather, and muck while I fry the bacon, potatoes, and eggs. Over breakfast, we hone the details of his strategy to carry out our mission. "We'll need to bring this," I say reaching for the ledger I had studied during the night. "It's the only solid proof that Jefferson killed Sarah. Her diary might not be enough. He might try to claim Frank must have done it. In his ledger, he admits the murder of them both. True, it's already in the house, but we can't get to it; and he's obviously the only one in his time who knows it's under those floorboards. We can leave it on the table in the main part of the cellar."

He looks at me almost in awe. "Yah *are* a daisy," he says.

I purposely take my time preparing for the outing. Before I

know it, Doc is opening the portal. The pry bar in place, we cross the threshold. A strange sensation washes over me and I look down to find the hand clutching the ledger empty. I aim the flashlight at my feet and turn several times in an effort to see where I dropped it. "What the . . ." Doc joins in the search momentarily, before returning into the barn where he picks the ledger up off the floor. "I didn't realize I had dropped it," I said disturbed by my clumsiness. "Guess I'm a bit overexcited." Doc tips his head and squints. I reach for it as he extends it through the portal, but it disappears before I can grasp it. He turns back and looks down at the floor between us. I do the same, and am startled at the sight of the ledger that has silently reappeared near his feet.

"It appears that the ledger is refusin' tah accompany us," he says, "and Ah believe Ah know why.

"Would you like to fill me in?"

"On the othah side, it still exists undah the floor of the study. It cannot be in two places at once in the same time." The thought initially staggers, but is logical. We will have to do without it and hope that justice prevails with the weight of the circumstantial evidence.

Realizing we lost this round, Doc joins me on the other side and we quickly go our separate ways. I am watching Elizabeth approach the face of the mountain where we last saw her. Her face is inches from my nose. Even in the dark, I can see the horrible scarring. One hand planted on the rock, she strains to look to the west away from the house, hoping to catch some movement of the retreating intruders she has followed. A gust of wind tickles my nose. Before I can get my arm up to suppress it, I let loose with a horrendous sneeze that jerks my forehead beyond cover of the hillside and right into that of Elizabeth. She screams and knocked off balance, falls onto her backside. The shotgun goes off, blasting a spray of gravel a few feet away. At the same time, there is another shot in the distance and the sound of horses snorting and whinnying. Chickens are clucking their annoyance at the disturbance of their sleep. Even the milk cow is bellowing. With difficulty, Elizabeth scrambles to her feet. Her skirts billow in the wind as she hurries to protect her niece and home from what she must now be perceiving as some ungodly threat. Oh how I wish I could allay her fears. As soon as she disappears around the corner, hell bent in her clumsy gait on the way to investigate the commotion among the animals, I make my way back toward the cellar where the doors remain open.

Within seconds, I am down the stairs. I click on the flashlight and set it to beam on the job at hand. Bracing myself, I put one shoulder against the heavy safe. Inch after inch, I readjust my footing and push as hard as I can. I have done it before, and as before, I am breathing hard by the time I have exposed the door enough for an adult to be able to pass through. Deciding a man would need another few inches, I resume the process. Finally, I am satisfied, and pumped by adrenaline, I pick up the pry bar and one by one ease up the corners of the safe and nudge the movers aside with the toe of my boot. Mission accomplished. Good sense and prudence urge me to get the hell out of there, but curiosity pulls me toward the newly exposed opening and what lies behind. Setting the tools aside, I slowly open the door to Sarah's sepulcher, praying that Doc still has Elizabeth occupied with whatever havoc he has created. The door creaks, not as much as it does over a hundred years hence, but it protests just the same. The odor is overpowering and reflexively, I slap a hand over my nose, but not before gagging on the stench of a more recent death.

"Auntie Liz? What's happening?" Startled, I drop the flashlight. As fate would have it, the thing lands beam-up at my feet. Mary is standing at the base of the stairway rubbing one eye. Her other clutches the rag doll I saw in the small cradle in the attic. I know I should run, but am unable to move. Mary takes a few steps toward me. "Mama!" She drops the doll and covers the distance between us in less than a second.

Instinctively, I drop to my knees. We collide with such force I nearly fall backwards. Our arms wrap each other naturally and fiercely for several seconds before I feel her loosen her grip. She pushes back so that the light is glowing between us. "Where have you been, Mama? I've missed you so much." I had forgotten, I am the spitting image of my ancestor. Mary was three when her mother disappeared but she remembers her. My heart is aching. The child is so young to have lived through the trauma of losing her mother; she will soon learn that her mother is dead; that her father was responsible, and she will lose him, as well. What have I done? She falls back into my arms, hers draped loosely around my shoulders. I caress her hair. "I knew you'd come back; I knew it!"

I am desperate to find words and when I do, pray that they are the right ones. "I love you so much, Mary. I didn't want to leave you, but God called me to heaven."

"You're an angel?" she asks pulling back again, her eyes a mixture of joy and fear.

"Yes, my darling," I answer, wondering all the while if I might end up in hell for the deceit. "God let me come back to tell you that you don't have to worry about me.

"Daddy said you were bad and ran away; that you didn't love me anymore. I knew that wasn't true. I don't think Auntie Liz believes it either. She will be so happy to see you."

"No, Sweetie, God said I could only see you, and only for a   minute."

"No," she whines pitifully.

"Heaven is such a wondrous place and God has given me a lot of work to do up there. He wanted me to ask you a question." I am making this up as I go.

"Okay."

God wants to know if you are okay and if Daddy is taking good care of you."

Mary stiffens and her eyes drop. "He gets mad sometimes," she says with no little reluctance. "And sometimes he's mean to Auntie Liz." Her expression betrays her guilt at the disloyalty and she quickly aborts elaborating on her father's shortcomings. "But Auntie Liz takes real good care of me and she is ever so nice."

"It's okay, Mary," I say knowing I'm treading dangerously now. "God sees everything and knows that Daddy is mean to you and Auntie Liz. He's going to make everything better."

She looks up. The beam from the light is nothing

compared to the light from her eyes. "When?"

"Very soon," I assure her. "It's time for me to go back to heaven and you to go back to bed. Be a good girl and no matter what happens, remember that I love you and will be waiting for you in heaven. Do what Auntie Liz says. God and I will be watching."

"You will?"

"All the time. You have to be a very good girl so that we can be together again."

"Soon?"

"First you have to grow up, get married, and live a long life with a good husband and have a little girl of your own."

"I will?"

"You will; I promise." With that vow, a wave of apprehension passes through me. What if my interference . . . . No; this is the right thing to do. It will save Elizabeth and improve Mary's life immediately.

"Will you come to see me again?"

"I can't, Honey . . . God only gives us one visit." The cherubic mouth droops in disappointment. "But, I will send a friend of mine to check on you from time to time."

"Who?"

"Remember the nice man who visited the other day?"

"Mr. McKey? Oh yes, I like him!" And with that her smile returns. Oh, to have a child's faith.

I feel tears brimming. Placing a kiss on my great, great, grandmother's forehead, I inhale sharply and draw her into a tight embrace; love bridging a chasm of time. I spin her around quickly. "Now, up to bed with you before Auntie Liz catches you," I say patting her little behind.

She scurries off obediently, then turns back, but only to retrieve her doll before disappearing up the stairs. I stand immobile, basking in the miracle. A shotgun blast snatches me into the present reminding me that time is of the essence. I grab the pry bar and movers and douse my light before heading up through the cellar doors, praying that Auntie Liz is not an excellent shot. In the moonlight, I can just make out Elizabeth shooing the last of the chickens back into the hen house. Doc appears out of nowhere. "Come on," he whispers as he grabs my elbow. "What took so long?" His tone is one of aggravation as he yanks me around the side of the house toward the hillside.

Once within its shelter he lets up and we walk the rest of the way along the back of the house through the portal and into the barn. Still can't get used to the instantaneous flip from night to day.

"Oh Doc, the most glorious thing happened," I say as I walk backwards facing Doc through the causeway. "Watch your step, Dahlin," he warns reaching out to right me in mid-trip over the threshold into the mudroom. "Thanks," I put a hand to my chest

"Ah take it, yah accomplished yor mission?"

"Yes, but that's not the half of it," I say flinging myself onto the recliner. "Doc, I spoke to Mary."

"She saw yah? That's not—" He slumps onto the sofa.

"Oh no; it's all right. Remember the photographs I showed you? Mary thought I was her mother."

"But how did yah . . ."

"I played along," I answer and go on to relate the details of the interaction. "I couldn't very well tell her the truth, could I? She heard all the commotion and came looking for Liz. What else could I do?"

He cocks his head and takes a minute. "Ah do believe yah did the right thin'," he says, then rising, "Ah could use some juice, yah?"

"Sure." I swivel out of the chair and follow Doc into the kitchen. "Oh Doc, it was beyond wonderful." Looking perfectly comfortable in the modern world, Doc opens the fridge, reaches for the pitcher and pours two tall glasses of orange juice. When he turns back after replacing the pitcher into the fridge, I throw my arms around his neck. "Thank you so, so much," I say and then impulsively plant a kiss on his cheek. He smiles that wicked little smile of his and I feel myself color. "Uh, Doc?"

"Yes?"

"I sort of promised Mary that you would be stopping by from time to time." I search his face for disapproval and find only tenderness."

"It will be mah pleasure, Dahlin'." he says.

CHAPTER 27

The morning/night's events, while ultimately fulfilling, have left both of us physically exhausted. Every muscle I did not know I had is aquiver and Doc is left winded. We retire to the living room where he stretches out on the sofa. After my body settles a bit, I go for my laptop. "Anothah article?" asks Doc.

"No, you were right about dredging up the past in the present. I've decided to start a diary; after all, it seems to be a family tradition."

"Did yor mothah keep a journal?"

"I don't know." I pause to think. I haven't found any, but then; I haven't been through all her things. After what happened . . . I mean, I wasn't feeling all that friendly toward Mom. Her farewell letter was such a shock, but it did raise questions. If she kept diaries, perhaps they hold the answers. An involuntary shudder passes through me. "I mean I want to know the whole story, need to know it, but a part of me is afraid of what I might uncover. I'm not sure I'm ready to look deeper into that closet." Doc nods. "For now, I think I'll summarize my life in Colorado and deal with my past later. I'll start with today and work backwards. I don't want to forget a minute of what just happened. It will be interesting reading when I'm ninety and senile." Doc chuckles and closes his eyes.

Energized by the project, I type non-stop for over two hours, during which time I manage to chronicle my life in Colorado with all its twists and turns. I type the last words with the feeling that I have spent the time with a very competent therapist.

Over lunch, I catch Doc up on my progress and add, "Maybe I'll write a book. I wonder if it will be the first non-fiction work to be passed off as a novel."

"It will be quite a story, Dahlin; that's for sure. Ah might just write one myself."

This announcement is offered in jest, but I press the issue. "Oh Doc, you have to. You're so educated and articulate. You'd be a great writer." Just think, your adventures in the twenty-first century might be scoffed at by the majority in your time, but think how history would treat it? And . . . and you could tell the truth about Wyatt Earp and the OK Corral . . . and . . . why, you could be another Jules Verne."

"Slow down there, Dahlin'. Ah will take it undah advisement. Show me what *yah* got, though; Ah will be happy to offah mah critique."

"Would you?" My mind whirls in the possibilities.

His nap and my therapy have renewed us both. I remain silent as Doc reads. After lunch, we opt for a walk in the light, unpredicted dusting of snow. We banter back and forth about the particulars and I find that I have missed more than a few significant anecdotes.

My thoughts turn to what is going on in Mary's life since we left. "We have to go back to make sure . . ."

"Ah'm afraid any furthah venchahs into the past are out of the question," Doc says.

"But I have to find out if things turned out for the better," I insist. "I can't bear not knowing if . . ."

"Ah am in sympathy with yor plight, Dahlin, but we'd be advancing time in the past beyond what Ah can afford," he says with sincere empathy. "You're forgettin' that when Ah dropped in, Ah was on a time-sensitive journey. While it is true that time is standin' still while I am here, it advanced a few days durin' our treks; days for journey lost. Besides, it will take a while for yor family's situation tah work itself out. Ah would love tah see it played out, but . . ."

"I understand," I say, embarrassed by my shortsightedness. I am saying the words, knowing they are right, but my heart is torn. As I continue, I know it is me I am trying to convince. "You have been more than generous. I would never have had the opportunity to help my family if it weren't for you, not to mention being able to work out that plan and accomplish it." I hope it has not taken *too* much of your time. The last thing I want is to be responsible for messing things up for *Wyatt Earp*."

Suddenly, Doc's future plans with his friend swell in importance. "I don't know what you've got going, but I'm sure it will make a significant impact in history and history affects us all." That said, I am filled with the prospect of knowing that I might be a part of something really and truly worthwhile, even if no one were ever to know about it except Doc and me. "Besides, at the very least, we will have cleared Sarah's name and very probably prevented Elizabeth's premature death."

Even as I say it, I know I am trying to convince myself, while my mind plays the devil's advocate. What if Jefferson tries to shift the blame to Frank Brady? But then, how would he explain the discovery of the locked room? When would Brady have had the opportunity to lock Sarah in the room? How would Jefferson account for his failure to notice that the safe had been moved in front of the door in the cellar? He couldn't. His only recourse would be to justify killing his wife because of the affair. Sarah's diary would plead her case. But what would it prove? It would be her word against his. In that scenario, might he be let off easy and allowed to return home to raise Mary and do away with Elizabeth? Oh, if only we could have exposed Jefferson's own condemning record in that ledger. I must put this behind me. We did what we could, with an opportunity I would never have had without Doc. I cannot ask him to sacrifice any more than he has already. I must believe Mary's life has been changed for the better. It is time to concentrate on getting Doc well and on his way to Wyatt.

CHAPTER 28

It is the second week of April. The weather along with Doc's health continues to improve. Snow is wetter and more often than not, the skies are dispensing rain or hail. Doc has been adhering to the prescribed dietary and medication regimes. The x-ray, taken yesterday, has given the three of us cause for celebration. Doc's convalescence is progressing ahead of schedule. Jack educates us on the fickleness of TB; that it affects individuals quite differently and thus the response to treatment is personal as well, and in Doc's case, left untreated for years. His system is responding rapidly to the medication. Jack also cautions us that the damage done by the disease can be arrested but not reversed. He announces, however, that other conditions that were exacerbating the TB have cleared up completely, accounting for the improvement.

"I cannot emphasize enough," he says, "the vigilance that must be maintained in controlling the condition." Doc and I nod in agreement.

While I should be dancing for joy, the ensuing thought of his imminent departure leaves me with an emptiness. How silly. After all, it is not as if I had not known all along that the man would be returning to the past, "his" present, but . . .but what? I attempt to sort out the plethora of emotions that are swirling in my core. I need to concentrate on *my* present, settle down to a normal life. It is just that . . . I have gotten used to having him around. I find it quite disconcerting to think not of life alone, but of life without him. Boy, where did that notion come from and how do I get rid of it?

When he fell into my world during that summer storm, the mundane existence I'd laid out for myself was upended for the third time in less than a year; but this time, with a positive effect. No matter the outcome, when the dust settles this time, the pieces will have rearranged themselves into a pleasant configuration beyond any imaginings. While my parents' deaths had left me emotionally battered, thanks to my mother, the heartache has been assuaged by her wise manipulation of things. Throwing myself into the unfamiliar environment and all it entails, I have been able to all but bury my past, both my humdrum existence and the tragedy that tore me from it. I vow to no longer allow perceived failings of my parents to affect my present or cause me concern for my future. Finding my great, great, great grandmother's body was another bombshell, but the Fielding scandal with all its twists and turns, as well, holds no regret for me. Incredibly, both these situations, pale in significance in the light of Doc's appearance. Death is inevitable, but time travel . . . Doc's entrance into my life has irrevocably altered who I am. Aside from the disruption of the laws of physics, I will be forever grateful to the man for his part in vindicating Sarah. His refreshing honesty, intelligence, and clever wit are constant sources of new information and entertainment. While my last days in California greatly affected my outlook on life, interacting with this man has given me added insight. Oh, how I want to shout this story to the world, but that is quite impossible. However, it will forever be an internal ember that must not be allowed to flame. It is what it is, they say. Doc Holliday is here today and will be gone tomorrow. So, what do I do with the time I have left with this amazing man? These are my thoughts as Doc comes in for breakfast after tending to the animals.

"Think it's time to go to Tombstone? You're well enough for extended travel and you're not scheduled to see Jack again for a month." My announcement is abrupt, the inflection such to discourage any discussion.

While one eyebrow is raised, his smile answers, "Capital idea. As long as Ah'm here I might as well get the most out of it."

"You'll have to promise to behave yourself. You may be protected by crossing state lines in your time, but getting into trouble out of state in the twenty-first century can mean a world of difficulty."

"Yah have mah word as a southahn gentleman."

I waste no time. After the meal, I am on the phone making arrangements for the Pruitts to take care of things on the ranch for the next couple of weeks, as during this journey into my world, time will not be standing still. Doc and I spend the rest of the morning packing. We lunch over road atlases, and together, decide on a route that will include places he wants to see.

By one, we are on our way down the pass. Having already explored The Springs on several shopping outings, our first major stop is Pueblo. Then, on to Trinidad, where we spend several hours in the old part of town before dining Mexican and obtaining rooms for the night. I take pictures and videos and make notes as Doc provides commentary on his adventures in these towns as if it were yesterday, which of course, for him, it was. Before retiring in the evening, I get a kick out of his reaction to watching himself in action replaying on the laptop.

Between planned stops and impromptu detours, we take more than three days to reach Tombstone. For the first time in many months, it dawns on me that Doc has reverted completely to his entry look. It turns out that I need not have worried about the recognition factor, as he has confirmed that most photos purported to be of him are of other gentlemen. He's a good thirty pounds heavier. Dressed in jeans and a western shirt, he fits right in. Improved health and color has shaved more than a decade off the age of the man I met those months ago. While he is attired in contemporary clothing, we have packed his original outfit and the extra shirts he had in one of the saddlebags.

CHAPTER 29

It is a little after noon when we arrive in town. I drive straight to Marie's B & B on Fourth near the corner of Safford Street. I chose the motel because it advertised décor of the 1880s. In the office, Doc pulls the money clip from his pocket to pay for our accommodations. My silent protest is met with a firm wave of his hand. "Thin's are on me from here on out," he says without inflexion.

On one of our shopping trips to The Springs, we were able to stop in at an establishment that not only buys precious metals, but also vintage coins and money. Doc had been amazed at the value of his twenty-dollar gold pieces until I reminded him of inflation's effect on the value of the currency he has received in exchange. Paperwork completed, we settle in and freshen up before walking toward Allen Street. There is no decision to be made when we see the sign for Big Nose Kate's. This is where we will lunch. Now a saloon and restaurant, it was originally, the Grand Hotel.

After dining on hearty fare amid the entertainment of a gifted singer, we take the stairs to the lower level, now a gift shop; and walk over to the dark recess behind iron bars, in which rests a crude bed and a few other items. Doc pleads ignorance of the "swamper". Purportedly, the man was a former caretaker while at the Grand. He had dug a hole in the dirt floor and tunneled into a nearby mine where he allegedly helped himself to ore when the miners were not around. The story goes that the passageway was discovered after he disappeared. No one knows if he got away with his stash or was caught and dispatched by angry miners.

Outside again, we continue our excursion of Allen Street. I find it rather like going to Disneyland for the first time. As Doc and I leisurely stroll, he serves as tour guide comparing the present with the past; in his case, that being only months ago. Several tough-looking characters, cowboys and scantily clad females are in the middle of the street outside the Gunfight Palace exchanging nineteenth century western insults. We pause to take in the comedic banter and the recruiting of an audience for a show to start in a few minutes.

"Sounds like fun," I say to Doc.

"Might be, at that," he agrees.

We cross the street and enter the building.

"Two please," Doc requests at the box office. We enter the small theater with several rows of wooden benches to one side and sit midway on the left. Ahead of us is an abbreviated barroom. One of our hosts briefly introduces the skits we are about to see. The action begins, and performed in front of us, are three scenarios portraying life of soiled doves in western towns. Underneath the generous helping of slapstick, the skits are truly tragic. I am sad for the women who felt they had no other choices but to make their living as prostitutes.

Doc is perusing the exterior of the building and surroundings as if tryin' to get his bearings before offering, "Ah do believe this buildin' used tah be the boardin' house that Kate and ah stayed in when we first hit town."

I follow him across the street to a building labeled Watt & Tarbell Undertakers. Doc touches the exterior bricks.

"How are you folks doing today?" asks a kindly woman.

"We are rollin'," answers Doc for both of us.

"We do host paranormal investigations in this building tonight. We use the same equipment you see on the ghost investigating shows on TV. Shows are at six, eight, and ten."

Doc peeks through the entry.

"This was one of three morgues in town in the 1880's,"

she adds.

"Yes," Doc says.

"Are you folks interested in the paranormal?" she asks.

Her question catches me off guard and I am hard pressed for an answer.

"Let's just say we are open-minded," says Doc.

"Yes," I say and add, "You never know, do you?"

"My sister and I are both sensitives. Come back later and find out," she says with a smile. "We still have room in the eight and ten o'clock shows."

"We'll keep that in mind," I say.

"Have you folks been to the museum on Fremont?" she asks as Doc continues to stare inside.

"No, but it sounds like something we shouldn't miss," I say looking to Doc for an opinion. He nods though his attention is elsewhere and everywhere, as if he expects an old nemesis to ambush him at any moment.

"Turn left past the Birdcage and go up one block. It will be on the northwest corner. Tell them Nora sent you," she says offering her hand.

"We will, Nora, thank you. I'm Cassie and this is Doc," I say without thinking as we shake.

"Thank yah kindly, Ma'am," my escort says as he bends to kiss her fingers. I see Doc's lip twitch ever so slightly at the contact. *Her* reaction, while controlled, is far from hidden. His touch is triggering something anomalous, yet, I am guessing, not totally unexpected by the woman; sort of like playing the lottery every week for years and finding all five winning numbers on your ticket. Theoretically, the possibility is there but you never really expect it to happen. In view of her profession, I would swear that she has just glimpsed a breakthrough of sorts. Her smile seems genuine, but I sense a hint at confusion.

"What did you do to that woman?" I whisper the demand as we come to the patio area just ahead on our right.

"Dahlin, Whatevah do yah mean? Whatevah was done, was done tah me. I felt like that woman was lookin' right intah mah soul." A slight shiver ripples down my vertebrae. Without thinking, I reach for his hand. Was this a good idea?

189

A few doors down, a group of tourists are listening to a costumed gentleman in the lobby of the Birdcage Theater describe the evening ghost tour. Doc makes our reservations and then makes the rounds of the room examining what the rest of us view as artifacts.

We leave further exploration for later and proceed down Sixth to Fremont, note the location of the museum on our left before crossing the street and heading west. As we approach Fourth Street, Doc looks up at Schieffelin Hall. "This is a verah nice establishment. The Earps, ah, and our ladies enjoyed the entertainment here often. Anything happenin' here these days?"

"I think I read somewhere that they still do have events here." I notice the small flyer on one window. "How disappointin'," Doc shrugs pointing to the dates the following month.

We cross Fremont at the corner and proceed west, stopping in front of Fly's Photography Studio on our left. Doc looks toward the street. It is here that the infamous shootout took place. Doc pauses for several minutes and I suspect is reliving the thirty seconds that changed his life forever.

"Guess Virgil's house is gone," he says as we head toward Third.

"I believe I read that it burnt down," I say.

"This town did have its fires," he says wistfully.

"Apparently Wyatt's survived," I say pointing across the street.

We turn left, head south past Allen and continue toward Toughnut passing through what Doc says is Hop Town. "When did they build that," he asks as we approach the stately courthouse ahead.

"Let's find out." We end up spending close to two hours inside the building that was erected in 1882, after Doc and the Earps departure, viewing the exhibits from completely different perspectives. "Everythin' looks so old," Doc notices. "Then, again, I guess it is." He pauses by the faro table set up and smiles. "I'll have to find a game later on."

"Let's get some ice cream," I suggest. "I saw a couple of places on Allen Street."

"Let's" he says offering his arm. They offer just a few flavors, old favorites, though. We sit on a bench outside and watch the tourists as we enjoy our cones. It is Doc who suggests that we go into a shop across the street. We don't leave before I have tried on two dresses along with accessories, at Doc's behest.

Parcels in hand, we head back to the hotel and opt to refresh ourselves with a nap before stepping out into the nightlife of Tombstone.

CHAPTER 30

Doc raps at my door just as I am donning my new shawl. I am wearing one of the dresses he purchased earlier. After looking me over, he sits me before the mirror and looks over the make-up and hair accessories strewn on the vanity. During the next ten minutes, I allow him to transform me into what I am guessing must be a woman that would be on the arm of Doc Holliday circa 1882 for a night on the town. He is remarkably skillful, and the result brings attention to my eyes and a new rosiness to my cheeks. Satisfied with my face, he takes my hair in his hands and, with a few quick twists, has anchored it atop my head in a simple, but elegant coif. I turn from side to side. Doc waits while I get used to the new look. It's not me, but it is fun. Now, if I can just hide the self-conscious tingling. I snatch up my drawstring purse as Doc opens the door. "Dahlin'," he says as he bows and sweeps his hand beckoning me outside.

It is then that I am aware of the pistol in the shoulder holster. "Uh, Doc?"

"Yes, Dahlin?"

"It might not be a good idea to carry the gun," I venture carefully suspecting I will be touching a sore spot,

"Whatevah do yah mean, Dahlin?" He squints; his neck pulls his head back. "I see guns on the street everywhere."

"I agree, but did you notice all the signs on establishments that prohibit weapons? You'd have to surrender that forty-five at the door. It would be out of your possession more than in. Are you willing to risk others handling what some will recognize as a collector's item?"

"Ah see what yah mean. Excuse me." He is gone only a minute or so and when he returns it is sans the weapon if not the unease he feels by its absence.

"I'm quite certain you won't need it," I assure him. "

Strangely, my trepidation fades as he offers his arm, his expression beaming with pride. I return the smile and the two of us step back into time.

It is just getting dark when we set out for the Longhorn Restaurant, which had been highly recommended by the innkeeper at Marie's. Our hostess does a double take when she looks up at Doc, now attired in authentic dress. Her surprise quickly melts into a knowing smile. She looks at me and must be thinking, nice try, but Kate was not a blond and had much more of a figure. Still, the attention is fun.

Our waiter is the next to cover a snicker with suppressed cough when he hears Doc's smooth Georgian drawl. We are halfway through our meal when a young couple apologetically approaches my escort for an autograph; no doubt assuming we are re-enactors. I am somewhat relieved, but a little disappointed that my signature holds no interest for them. They have Bob Boze Bell's book on Tombstone turned to the article on Doc Holliday. Doc smiles and signs his name under one of the pictures.

After an excellent dining experience, we cross kitty-corner to the Crystal Palace. Doc scans the room and I wonder if he is expecting to see Wyatt dealing faro or poker in one of the far corners. He leads me to a table and sets his hat on an empty chair. The couple from the Longhorn is seated across the room with two middle-aged women. The young woman so anxious for Doc's autograph pulls the book from her bag and shows it to their companions who immediately look toward our table. Like dominos falling, a message round robins the room and within minutes, the attention of the audience has moved from the entertainment on the stage to our table. Doc leans across to me. "I do believe they think they are seein' Kate come back to life." I am trying to control my laughter as our waitress appears. "What'll it be, Doc?" the barmaid asks without hesitation. He nods and orders a margarita for me and Old Overholt for himself. "Good costume," she says pinching the arm of Doc's coat. He watches in appreciation as she sashays over to the next table.

A minute later the autograph-seeker is back at his side, book in hand. "Excuse me Sir, how do you explain this?" she asks pointing first to where Doc had signed before flipping the page that bears copy of John Henry Holliday's authentic signature.

"I've gotten pretty good at that haven't I?" he answers. I notice the slightest inflexion of discomfort.

"Doc had to practice for years to perfect it," I add.

"Wow, it's perfect," she says before retreating to the others.

"That was unforeseen," he says quietly.

"Relax; who would believe the truth?"

"Of course," he says. "It is sort of funny . . . I mean the way modern people react to persons of notoriety, livin' or dead, it seems."

"I wonder if it crossed her mind that you might really—"

"What a preposterous idea," he interrupts and we both laugh.

"You are getting a kick out of this," I say.

"Life is to be enjoyed, Dahlin'; that is still the case in the twenty-first century?" he asks as he peruses the room, greeting each stare with a nod in true celebrity fashion; causing the gawkers to retreat with nervous smiles. The modern music does not impress Doc and after finishing our drinks, we take our leave in a chorus of applause, to which Doc turns and bows while tipping his hat as we exit. A couple passing us on their way in look up at Doc and quickly assess the situation. "An' I thought I could nevah return to this town without havin' tah defend my life in the street."

We cross the street and turn toward Kate's to have another round. "It's called karaoke," I say when Doc's attention is drawn to the area below a stage where a young woman is doing a rather remarkable vocal imitation of Dolly

Parton singing <u>I Will Always Love You</u>. I explain the concept and the equipment that allows patrons to sing to the music of their favorite artists.

"Very cosmopolitan," he comments.

I gather that most of the clientele this evening are locals and do not find our attire out of place. It feels good to fit in. We are seated at a table near the action and in the next hour or so, are treated to Merle Haggard, Reba, and a great rendition of Garth Brooks', <u>The Dance</u>. When the deejay announces Doc as the next performer, I almost have heart failure. What had he done during my absence in the restroom this time? To my surprise and relief, he does not stir. A gray-cloaked figure passes by our table and takes the microphone from the deejay. He turns to face the audience. Val Kilmer has taken the stage.

Doc leans and whispers in my ear. "I see myself, comin' an' goin' 'aroun' here."

His rendition of <u>Dixie</u> is impressive, moving spectators to hoot and holler in accompaniment. After listening through a half dozen more performances, we agree it's time to move on.

Passing through the double doors, we come upon Doc's clone and the attractive blonde woman on his arm. The two men are face to face for a moment. "Tell me, do yah sing, as well, Mr.?"

"Holliday, John Henry," Doc says void of inflection. "I'm afraid my condition has not permitted the development of that talent." Doc lays a hand over his chest. "But yah Suh, are quite good in all respects."

With equal stoicism, the clone addresses his date while his eyes dance in amusement. "I don't know Dahlin'; yah think I should hate him?"

The woman plays along, strong Hungarian accent and all. "You don't even know him."

"I don't know; there's somethin' about him . . . somethin' around the eyes reminds me of . . . me. What do yah think, Suh, should I hate yah?"

A smile tickles the corners of Doc's mouth. "Life is much too short, Suh, as we both know all too well."

"Is it now?" replies the clone. "In my book, we just go on and on." He smiles and nods; then tips his hat to me. "I have enjoyed the bantah and bid yah both a good evenin', Suh, Ma'am." Doc returns the sendoff in kind and I smile in acknowledgement. The handsome couple walk ahead of us east down Allen before disappearing into Doc Holliday's Saloon in the next block.

The street is quiet save for the music still coming from the Saloons and as we approach Fifth Street we can hear the band at the Dragoon to the right at the end of the street. "In mah time," he announces, "that hillside would be dotted with tiny lights; some minahs working round the clock to pull wealth from the rocks, or at least guahdin' their claims. Dangerous business, minin'," he says with a sigh. "I prefer to work up here in the fresh air, mahself; seein's that we have so little time above ground in the overall scheme of thin's. I feel like walking for a while." And so we do, through the town basked in moonlight.

We turn left at Fifth Street and then left again onto Fremont. The music fades into quiet the further we get from the center of town and the street is deserted except for an occasional diesel truck. Doc slows as we again approach Fly's studio and stops once more at the sight of the bloody battle of that October afternoon. I cannot shake the feeling of being watched, as if ghosts from the past are present and confused by Doc's presence. The base of my spine begins to tingle. What am I thinking? I *am* walking down the street with a ghost; well, not exactly a ghost, yet . . .

A year ago, I would have dismissed this scenario as ludicrous; something to be seen on some psychic network on TV. I feel a pang of guilt for even unspoken judgments of those who have legitimately purported to have had unverified contacts with the dead or similar reality-defying experiences. With that in mind, I work at convincing myself that whatever eeriness I am experiencing is perfectly normal, and that I am far from alone. This revelation is so enlivening, it is all I can do not to muddy Doc's moment with my own impression and the questions it has engendered. This displacement must be far more disturbing and fascinating for him. Under that poker face, is he struggling with the uncanniness of it all? Is he, as I am, wondering why *we* were chosen for this bizarre experience? As I stand there, I feel my mind experiencing cleansing of sorts, evolution of my soul, I think. When it is complete, will I recognize myself? Is John Henry Holliday transforming, as well? I look at my watch. Neither of us has moved for a full twenty minutes. Sans further conversation, Doc takes my hand and leads me to our motel where we retire to our respective rooms.

CHAPTER 31

We breakfast at the OK Café on Allen and Third. It is old and cozy of décor, the service friendly. Doc is in a clean shirt, under his authentic attire. Donned in another of Doc's fashion selections, I have managed to copy his efforts with makeup and hair. Again, the clientele gives us little notice, although our waitress comments, as if speaking as an authority, that my escort is a dead ringer for *the* Doc Holliday. "If I didn't know better, I'd swear he'd come back from the dead. I mean it; you look like the *real* Doc Holliday." If you only knew, floats through my mind as she notices me and chuckles. "You know, if you dyed your hair and put on a few pounds, you might just pass for Kate."

"Don't pay no mind to her, Dahlin'," Doc says when she walks off to tend other customers. "No amount of physical makeover could evah turn yah into that Hungarian devil; and Ah doubt yah have it in yah to act the part; not that Ah would find that appealin', mind you. Yor fine just the way yah are, Dahlin'." Breakfast is delicious and we linger over our coffee.

We find ourselves at the T. Miller's Mercantile on the northeast corner of Allen and Sixth. Doc drapes a lacy black shawl over my shoulders and turns me toward a mirror.

"Hold that pose," he says.

He returns a minute later with a black derby-styled chapeau with netting and a modest plume, plucks my current headgear, and settles this new one in its place. He nods approvingly and we make our way to the register. Why he insists on purchasing all these soon-to-be useless garments, I have no idea. I decline to protest knowing his southern pride will settle for nothing less. Besides, he seems to be enjoying it so, and I, in Victorian garb in the aura of another time, feel my tomboy persona circling the drain. My father's disparagement of females had led me to reject a ladylike presentation in favor of a more self-sufficient image associated with the male gender. My disfigurement enhanced the façade and I successfully evaded unwanted attention from the opposite sex, any attention, for that matter. When I sensed another's unease, I had sought to excuse myself from their immediate presence if at all possible. But now, Doc's chivalry is becoming quite comfortable and I find myself getting in touch with my feminine side.

We continue our exploration of Tombstone dawdling over the offerings in the various shops. On Fourth Street we overhear a cluster of tourists praising the tour they are exiting. We read the information on the door and decide we want to see the famous rose tree in the patio of the inn that bears it name. After making our way through the rooms full of artifacts of the late nineteenth century common to the area, we exit into the courtyard where we are assaulted by the scent of roses. The sight defies description or explanation. In front of us a little to the left is what appears to be the trunk of a very large tree, some six feet in diameter at its base. It disappears into a latticework covering the patio. Miraculously, it has branched out over eight thousand square feet and each spring erupts into myriads of white blossoms. We climb a small bridge-like structure beyond the patio that allows us to see the tree above the arbor. Without this firsthand viewing, I would not have accepted the existence of such a magnificent rosebush. It is, in fact, the world's largest and over a century old. Doc studies the plaque on the sidewall as I continue to walk around the patio marveling at the magnificent floral expanse above.

We are speechless as we exit the building. We veer left toward Toughnut Street and the much advertised mine tour.

Voluntarily descending into the depths of the earth fills me with trepidation, but I tell myself that thousands have toured the "Good Enough" without harm. Doc pats the hand gripping his arm. "It'll be fine, Dahlin'. Just hang on tah me." Doc and I have to don hard hats for our descent. We must present a comical sight, especially me in my period dress and miner's cap. Mongo, our guide, spices his informative delivery with humorous anecdotes that shift my concentration from the depth of our journey. Our trek is less than an hour and I am hard-pressed to imagine spending eight hours at a time under the tons of rock above, not surfacing even for the noon meal. Our tour goes off without a hitch, but still, I am breathing easier as we emerge into the sunlight. We thank Mongo and turn in our hardhats.

"Ah believe, Dahlin', that a reward is in order for yor bravery down there," says Doc pointing across the way to The Dragoon, an open air bar facing the expanse of the mining district south of town.

"We might be a bit overdressed for this place." My comment is ignored. Doc seats me at a table under the awning while he makes for the bar. After what seems to be a longer-than-necessary conversation with the bartender, he returns with a whiskey and a colorful drink accented with fruit. "What on earth?" I say as he sets the exotic concoction in front of me.

"Ah don't rightly remembah what he called it. Ah jus' told the gentleman to make somethin' worthy of yor fairness," he says smiling as he lifts his glass toward mine in invitation of a tribute. "Tah borrowed time," he says. The clink of glass seals the toast. The mixture of flavors has my taste buds dancing, but the first sip lets me know I need to take it slowly. Over the next forty minutes, I nurse my drink while Doc, without apparent impact, enjoys two more shots. The man has amazing tolerance and announced at our arrival that he would be foregoing the doctor's orders in regard to alcohol during our stay.

Completely relaxed, I inhale deeply and test my legs before agreeing to resume excursion down Toughnut westward. "In mah day,' says Doc, "the air was alive with the sounds of minin' machinery an' tools, men shoutin' orders, an' the occasional exclamation announcin' a new strike. Toughnut," he adds with a sweep of his hand, "was one makeshift bar aftah anothah. No one went thirsty on this street."

We come to the train station that now houses the public library. According to Doc, the railroad must have come and gone between our eras. On the left, just beyond the courthouse, we pass the placard that calls our attention to the remains of the pole from which one John Heath was strung up after being given a life sentence for his part in the murder of several people in nearby Bisbee. Apparently, the town folk took umbrage at the misplaced mercy, came down to Tombstone, broke into the courthouse, and carried out the same sentence received by his partners in crime months earlier. It says he writhed for some twenty-two minutes before succumbing. I find my hand around my neck and swallow hard as I imagine the incredible pain and desperation that Heath must have experienced.

"Don't waste yor consideration, Dahlin'." Doc takes my wrist and returns my hand to my side. "Accordin' to the storah, the man was a cold blooded killer who no doubt gloated when the lenient sentence was handed down. Think of his victims," he says squeezing my hand. I nod. Although it must have been awful for him, the man deserved what he got.

Doc and I head back in the direction we came, and as we pass a restaurant across from the rose tree, Doc tells me the story of Nellie Cashman, dubbed the "angel of Tombstone."

"A truly good woman, that one," he says with fondness in his voice. "Many a person in need is fed at her hands. She runs a fine boardin' house and the meals are excellent." he explains. It's still strange to hear him speak of the past as if it is present.

After taking lunch at the Crystal Palace, we walk across the street where Doc purchases tickets for the stage ride.

"Are you a real cowboy?" asks a small boy who sits across from us inside the coach. He is in snappy western attire complete with matching six shooters.

I sense that Doc is taken aback by the innocent insult. In the little guy's mind cowboys are heroes, not the disreputable enemies of Doc's world.

"Oh no," I interject quickly. "This is Doc Holliday. He helped Wyatt Earp take care of the bad guys in town."

"Wow! Mom . . . Mom . . ." he says tugging at the arm of the young woman at his side whose attention is fixated outside the coach on Mr. "Tall, Dark, and Handsome" in the process of booking his own passage. "He's Doc Holliday!" he says excitedly pointing at us.

"Uh huh; that's nice. Don't bother him or he might shoot you," she says flashing a brief obligatory smile, before scooting over to make sure that Mr. "Eye Candy" chooses the seat on her bench. She adopts her son's look of displeasure when the man helps a young woman into the coach. The couple take the bench in the center; his arm around her. The empty seat next to the mother is soon taken by an elderly woman whose husband slides next to me.

Doc scrutinizes the interior of the coach while I listen intently to the spiel of the throaty-voiced driver as we begin to move. Tom relates the highlights of Tombstone history as he takes us by spots made famous by the former residents.

Doc is the last to step down out of the coach and does so to the drawn guns of his young admirer. He is quickly yanked away by his annoyed parent.

"Some persons should not be allowed tah reproduce," Doc says without inflection, then, "Well, what shall we do next?"

"Want to visit Boot Hill?" He looks puzzled causing me to question when the designation was adopted. "The cemetery," I clarify.

"Ah see; well as long as we're jus' stoppin' by," he says dryly.

"Don't worry. According to the information, it was filled a couple of years after your departure. In fact, we should stop by the newer cemetery, as well." I say. It is such a beautiful day we decide to walk what turns out to be about a mile. Doc is both amused and put off by the content of the gift shop we pass through to gain entry. I imagine that from his perspective, many of the humorous signs and knickknacks are in bad taste. Unlike many of the tourists, Doc walks between the graves with reverence, pausing to comment on occupants with whom he was personally acquainted; noting in particular, those who had passed on since he left town. "These markers . . . they . . . I don't know, and I recall the grounds being largah."

"I believe the original headstones are locked away. These are replicas made to look old. The brochure says that they stopped using this location sometime in 1884; that it was neglected for years until someone decided to restore it. It is smaller than it was originally, many of the graves reclaimed by nature's encroachment and buildings."

"Indian Charley," he hisses. "He was one o' the men that murdahed Morgan. We blew him full a more holes than a . . ." He breaks off abruptly when I touch his shoulder and shift my eyes to our nearest fellow tourists. No one seems to have been listening, but . . . He pauses again at Old Man Clanton's marker, whispering this time. "He and his gang nevah saw us comin'." Next to his grave are those of his son and the McLaury brothers. It is hard to read Doc's thoughts as he inspects the epitaph declaring that they were "murdered on the streets of Tombstone."

"Ah wonder what they wouldah put on my markah had thins gone the othah way?" We move down the row until we come to WM Clayborne. "Well, well; ol' Frank gets Billy in the end. Damn fool kid idahlized Ringo." Doc kneels at the grave of Thos. Cowan, age 11 months; diphtheria. "Cute lad; his mama nearly went mad when he passed." As we move along, we pass several markers that bear only the name and year of death. Others cite horrible accidents and there are several suicides. It was a hard life that became too much to bear for not a few.

Doc is again on his knees at Marshall White's grave. "That boy was too trustin' for his own good."

"Boy?"

"Yeah. Oh, I know your pitcha box made him out to be a much oldah man, but Fred was 'roun' mah age an green when it came to marshlin'; no match for the cowboys. It was

203

incidents like this that made the cowboys such a threat to the town; why Virgil couldn't help hisself from steppin' up an' tryin' to stop the madness."

Near the fence lies Mrs. Clum. "Ah didn't know the lady well; she was of fragile health by the time Ah came to town an' only lived a few more months; a good woman; respected by all. She was the wife of John P., owner of the Epitaph an' one-time mayor of Tombstone before the cowboys made him flee for his life; nearly got him, too, on his way outta town; but he was smart enough to elude his would-be assassins; a loyal friend to the Earps and me. Without him an' a few othah honest men in a position of authority, we might well have been strung up aftah the affair with the cowboys."

Doc continues until we reach the resting place of Archie McBride, listed as the owner of the Grand Hotel. He pauses briefly but makes no comment. In row ten, we find the burial sites of several Chinese, including that of Quong Kee.

"He's the one Ah told yah about, the owner of the Can Can. Good man an' wonderful cook. I see his place on Allen Street has been turned into a photographic studio. Rest in peace Quong," Doc whispers. "Son of a gun lived to be almost a hundred," he announces with admiration when he sees that John Slaughter is buried in the next row, although he lived until 1945, long after the official closure of the cemetery. We notice another latecomer, one Emmett Nunnelley who was granted interment here a year later for his efforts in coordinating the town's people to restore the graveyard. We pass the remainder of the graves without pausing. There are over two hundred and fifty resting here. Very few died of natural causes. The newer cemetery, on the way back to town, is far more populated; but has nowhere near reached its capacity. Here, too, Doc recognizes the names of friends and enemies alike, who met their ends after his departure. We take this tour at a less leisurely pace, for the most part, pausing at only the older-looking graves. There are many family plots surrounded by wrought iron fencing. I am saddened by the number of unmarked mounds and eroded markers. Were these persons unidentified; was there no one to remember them; or had their resting places simply been neglected over time? I recall hearing that unknown corpses would be displayed upright in coffins outside of mortuaries in the hopes that they would be identified.

The total distance of our stroll was greater than estimated and it is well into the afternoon when we return to Allen Street, just in time for the last show at the OK Corral.

"A misnomer," corrects Doc. "The shootin' took place behind the corral on Fremont between Fly's an' the house on the cornah; yah know, where we stopped last evenin'." He studies the weathered, hand drawn map under glass in front of the mannequins of the shootout participants. "Wyatt did a fine job," he comments on his friend's depiction of the positions of the participants in the deadly gunfight. "He always did have an organized mind; one for detail." He looks up. "Well, look at me," he says staring at the life-size statue of himself. It must be strange to see yourself immortalized on the site of the most noted event in your life.

We tour the rest of the grounds, the office and the stables that once boarded the horses and mules. There are several old buggies and other rigs, all labeled and defined. Just a few months back these were, for Doc, in prime condition, ready for hire; the area alive with snorting, pawing, and whinnies. We are engrossed in the history when the show is announced.

My eyes are on Doc as he watches the re-enactment unfold a few feet in front of us. A cold-blooded killer would have relished the replay, not wince as the shots rang out, I decide. Clearly, he and the Earps did what had to be done. They found no joy or excitement in killing the others. We take advantage of the invitation at the close of the show to engage with the actors.

"Ah want tah complement yah on yor fairly accurate portrayal of this unfortunate altercation. However, Ah was troubled by the humor; there was nothin' funnah about it."

"Are you an authority?" The question is asked in all seriousness by one of the performers. Doc opens his mouth, then hesitates.

"What can we say; he was there," I say directing my

hands palms up in his direction. That gets a round of laughter after which I tuck my hand under Doc's arm and lead him out into the corral. On our way out, we take in the extraordinary rotating diorama of Tombstone's history. It is a simple presentation narrated by Vincent Price, informative and fascinating. Doc shakes his head when Mr. Price recounts the town's downward turn when the mines began to flood and overwhelm the pumps straining to clear the tunnels.

When we emerge from the theater, our attention is drawn to the breathtaking panorama painted in purples and oranges across the western sky.

"A display of untainted beauty, is it not? One of an unending array of our Father's unrivaled achievements." Doc's remark is yet another confirmation of my assessment of his character. Not only is he a true gentleman of uncommon loyalty, he has respect for The Creator. Oh, his faith may have wavered a time or two, but he knows who's boss; cocky as all get-out, but God-fearing; I'm sure of it. "Where shall we dine tonight, Dahlin'?" he asks after this moment of reverence.

"Pardon me," we hear behind us. We turn to see one of the re-enactors approaching. "Have you ever considered acting?" the young man asks. Doc raises a brow. "You're well aware of your striking resemblance to the real Doc Holliday. Duh," he says with a palm hit to this head, "you two probably are actors . . ." he says. I am flattered to be included. "I mean the way you're dressed and all." Doc smiles politely. I am as anxious to hear what he comes up with for this inquiry. When he is not immediately forthcoming with an answer, the matter is pressed further. "Oh My God, are you, by chance, a relative of the man?"

I see the familiar twinkle in those gray/blue eyes. "Indeed, Suh; it seems John Henry an' Ah do share the same bloodline."

"You're like what . . . a distant cousin?"

"Somethin' like that," Doc replies. "Ah'm not just sure how distant or removed, but the genes appear to have taken a direct path into mah body," he says spreading his arms, "or so Ah'm told. But no, neither Cassie nor myself ah in the profession."

"Would you like to be? We could use you in the re-enactments."

"Ah appreciate yor interest, Suh; but we ah just passin' through yor fine town."

"Too bad," he says in obvious disappointment. "It was nice meeting, you Mr.?" he says offering his hand.

"Jus' call me Doc," he says returning the gesture. "And this is Miss Collins."

The young man laughs. "Sure, Doc. Please to meet you ma'am," he says tipping his hat before turning away to attend to the rest of the audience still waiting to commend his performance and secure autographs.

"You handled that quite well," I say, thinking I have never had so much fun.

We dine at the Longhorn, again, with less fanfare than our last experience. There seem to be far fewer tourists in the dining room and the regulars are used to seeing us around town. Over dinner via several brochures, we make plans to drive to several destinations of interest outside of town. Johnny Ringo's grave is first on Doc's list. After a long day and several miles of walking, we opt to turn in early.

CHAPTER 32

"If Ah didn't know betta, Ah'd think Ah was back in 1882; except for the automobile, of course," comments Doc once we are driving across the desert the next morning. We are attired sensibly for our trek to the more primitive sites of interest. Why he is studying the map, I know not. Surely, he must know exactly where the outlaw has been laid to rest. After all, it hasn't been that long since he helped plant him there. "It should be just up there on the left," he says; and indeed, it is.

I make a U-turn and park alongside the road in front of the simple sign that marks the trail to the final resting place of John Ringo. We read the entire sign requesting respect and any dogs to be on leashes. The grave is on the private property of descendants of the Sanders' family, who lived there when John Ringo died; and I find it very gracious of them to allow respectful interested parties to view this historic site. Doc frowns when I stuff a five-dollar bill into the receptacle for voluntary donations. "It's not for Ringo," I remind him. "After all, if it hadn't been kept up all this time, you wouldn't be able to see it. It was your idea to come here, if I recall."

"Of course," he says, his attention now on the creek under the shadow of ancient oaks near the pile of stones labeled as Ringo's final resting place.

"Is it as you remember it?"

"Huh?" he says and I restate the question. "Oh, um, Ah didn't stick 'roun' for the interment." He seems troubled and I refrain from pressing further. "Johnnah was responsible for murdahrin' my friend an maimin' anothah," he says matter-of-factly. I detect a catch in his voice that he quickly covers with a manufactured cough. "Wyatt an' I were tight, Virgil a friend by association, but it was Morgan an' Ah that had the fun." He bows his head at the remembrance, then looks between the trees below to the gently flowing waters of West Turkey Creek. "It jus' doesn't seem right that this bastard is restin' in such serenity."

"I'm sure Morgan's grave is nice," I offer in sympathy.

"Couldn't be as nice as this." Doc replaces his hat sighing deeply. "Ah'd like to go now." We walk, then, drive in silence until we get to Charleston. Galeyville was on our list, but its ruins are on private property, as well; the owners of which are averse to tourist traffic.

"They got away with murdah, here," Doc says referring to the cowboys as we stroll around what is left of the town that is just five miles out of Tombstone. We park in the lot and head out on the trail that takes us a mile and a quarter and across the San Pedro River.

"It would seem that the cowboy towns did not fare as well as Tombstone," Doc comments as we stroll in and around the overgrowth which engulfs the ruins of what was once the cowboy headquarters. An earthquake set the San Pedro raging against a large portion of the town that was all but abandoned by 1886 when Tombstone's mining industry ground to a halt due to flooding. As we continue to explore I touch the old adobe walls and try to imagine the town bustling with rowdy inhabitants.

"Don't move!" says Doc abruptly.

I freeze. "What? Don't tell me you're hearing cowboys;" I say as a joke, but want to eat my words as Doc ever so slowly draws the gun from his shoulder holster. Instinctively I close my eyes. The sharp retort a second later echoes among the ruins.

"It's okay now, Dahlin'," he says.

209

I open my eyes and on the ground before me see a four-foot rattlesnake minus its head. "Oh my," I say.

"Indeed. Perhaps we have overstayed our welcome," Doc suggests.

"I'm not opposed to leaving," I say weakly and shudder.

We retrace our steps and after snacking on cheese and crackers in the Jeep, we wash them down with bottled water, before resuming our drive.

Back on the road, Doc points to the right. "That line of trees marks the path of the San Pedro," he says. "The Clanton ranch was anothah refuge for the cowboys an' served as a way-station for the stolen cattle. Those bastards were so bold they even rustled ahmy mules." He shakes his head.

On a whim, we backtrack to Iron Springs where "Wyatt Earp and his immortals" put an end to the exploits of Curly Bill Brocious and several others on the "vendetta ride." Doc looks out over the area in silence.

"Ah didn't say it, but wish Ah wouldah thought of it," he says as we stare at the rushing stream.

"What's that?" I ask.

"That movie in that pitchah box a yors, about Wyatt walkin;' on wahtah. That was what it was like. There were bullets flyin' all 'roun', mostah us duckin' for covah and Wyatt marchin' intah the midst of it all, guns blazin'. Ain't nevah seen anythin' like it before or since."

Several minutes into the ride toward town, Doc volunteers the details of the infamous ride through Cochise County executing the cowboys. He doesn't sugar coat the facts. Wyatt and company spilled cowboy blood like there was no tomorrow. In spite of the violence, all I can think of is what a privilege it is to be sitting here listening to an actual participant in such momentous events of the past. Doc's relation is devoid of emotion; a simple recounting of facts; despite the horror of the unrestrained bloodshed dispensed by men fueled with righteous indignation amidst a community that lacked the courage to exact justice. The ride home is quiet. Doc is talked out, and I am trying to imagine being part of the story he has just related.

Returning to town, we stop in at Kate's for a drink before changing for dinner at the Ringo's. "You haven't coughed once since we got here." I purposely ignore the lapse at Ringo's grave.

"I do believe I was healthier here than any othah place once I got sick. Funny, Colorado was supposed to be bettah for my condition; but then again, it has been, hasn't it?"

"Well, soon, you'll be healthy in any climate." We make it another early night. If it weren't for the physical exertion of the day, I doubt I would be able to sleep. I have never been so excited. Doc seems to be taking it all in stride. It makes sense; today's events must be tame compared to his life up to this point.

CHAPTER 33

I awake refreshed and anticipating another adventurous day. Doc is a good sport as we spend much of it taking in every gift and antique shop in town, stopping to enjoy the street shows throughout the day . . . again. In between, we lunch at Kate's and then head for the museum on the corner of Fremont and Sixth that had been suggested by Nora at the Watt and Tarbell's. We are warmly greeted by a nice looking man dressed as a gentleman of the Tombstone era. Something in the showcase below catches Doc's attention right off, so I take the lead. "You must be Robert," I say. "Nora suggested we take in the museum."

"Yes, good to meet you," he says extending his hand.

"Cassie Collins, from Colorado."

"Welcome Cassie, and you, Sir?"

Doc rises from his knees and looks up to return our host's greeting, though a bit hesitantly, I sense. "Holliday, John Henry." Doc reaches across the counter to shake the man's hand, neither of the two breaking eye contact as the physical connection is made.

"How've you been, Doc?"

"Ah'm in my prime. Yah lookin' verah well, Bat. Course yah always did take care of yahself."

Oh, come on! I almost blurt out. I watch the eyes dance back and forth and wish I could read minds. Hell, why not.

"What do you hear from Wyatt?"

"Had a letter recently. Gonnah hook up in a few days. But then, yah know about all that."

"We keep in touch." Robert's tone is tentative, as if he is feeling his way through the conversation. All the while, their eyes never leave each other's. "Been behaving yourself?"

Doc cocks his head and lets out a snicker. "Ah have suh, an' I want to thank yah for yor timely intrahvention on my behalf. Ah know yah did it out of regard for our mutual friend, but jus' the same, Ah appreciate it an have been usin' mah freedom in verah positive pursuits."

Robert's expression is a mixture of disbelief and delight. "It would appear so. I've never seen you looking so well, Doc. What's your secret?"

"A healthy climate an' good nursin'." Doc puts a hand on my shoulder while maintaining eye contact. Robert appears aware of the gesture, but keeps his focus on Doc, as well.

"What brings yah back here?" asks Doc. I hold my breath. Could it be that this is not our personal phenomenon after all? Has Bat Masterson popped through a portal in Tombstone, as well? The thought is both perplexing and comforting.

"A rebirth of sorts; and you?"

"Ah jus' fell into it, so to speak. Wasn't in mah original plan. Ah was on mah way to Gunnison when Ah ran inta some difficulty near Cassie's place."

"Cassie's place?"

"On the front range of Colorado. Ah was takin' an evasive route."

"Good choice." Robert seems a bit confused. "Say, have you folks been to the Oriental?" asks Robert.

"Doc grins. "Who on earth thought that a saloon like that would be bettah off as a ladies dress shop? An' the garments are hardly the latest in Paris fashion. Are yah responsible for such nonsense?"

Robert laughs, then, as if he has caught his bearings goes back to the subject of Doc's travels. "So, when do to you expect to be on your way?"

"As soon as Ah wrap thin's up at Cassie's, Ah'll be hittin'

the trail to Gunnison an' Wyatt an' Ah will finish our business. Wish us success?"

"It was never in doubt." Robert's smile is a confident one.

"Yah seem different somehow, Bat; sort a mellow, for yah, I'd say."

"Time and space can have an amazing effect on a man's perspective," answers Bat; I mean Rob; I mean I don't know who I mean. "People can look back and see the big picture; it can change a man, don't you agree?"

"Quod non est verum." Doc finally turns to me. "Shall we, Dahlin'? We've been takin' up this man's time an' missin' our tour." He offers his arm and we begin to make our way down the first aisle.

"If you have any questions . . .," says Robert. "Then, again, you probably won't."

We spend a good hour in the museum. Our host remains behind the counter. I try to concentrate on the relics before me, but cannot help wondering what just transpired between the two men. In an undisguised effort, Doc tutors me as we go up and down the aisles, and asks me questions about a few things that postdate him. I answer when I am able. When we are ready to leave, Doc makes a point of thanking Robert, who responds, "It really is good to see you again, Doc."

"Likewise, my friend."

One step outside and I am all over it. "Do you think . . ."

"No."

"What do you mean, no. Is that man Bat Masterson. What? Is the whole wild west invading the twenty-first century?"

"Ah knew the man. He couldn't abide me. This man favors Masterson, but it's not him. For one thin, he's oldah; not as old as he should be in 2016, but oldah. Bat was a couple a years youngah than mahself."

"But . . ."

"Oh, there's no doubt somethin' funny is goin' on. His eyes . . ."

"What about his eyes. I noticed you couldn't take yours off them."

"The eyes were definitely Bat's."

"What? If he didn't like you, I can hardly imagine you looking into each other's eyes that often."

"Oh, but we did, Dahlin'. Yah forget we were gamblahs. Yah can read the cards in a gamblahs hand by lookin' in his eyes."

"Okay, if Rob/Bat didn't fall through a portal, what's the explanation?

"Ah can't rightly say."

"And while we're thinking about; he knows Nora and . . .? You and she definitely had some sort of psychic connection and Robert looked like he was having a mental flashback. I think we should go back in there and . . ."

"No!" His answer is swift and final. "Ah can't risk it. Wyatt is countin' on me." Doc offers his arm. "Ah'm hungry."

We have ribs to die for at the Crystal Palace and per previous instructions, make sure we are not intoxicated as we make our way down the street to The Birdcage Theater to await what is billed as a paranormal tour. Prior to Doc's arrival, I would have condemned such attractions as hoaxes preying on a naive public.

When our party is complete and introductions exchanged, our host, a lovely young woman with black hair flowing the length of her back, begins our tour.

She commences with the lobby describing the theater and the events that were held here, along with the names of famous customers; pointing out bullet holes they left behind.

"Any of them compliments of you?" I lean and whisper to Doc.

"Ah was not in the habit of random gunfire. That was the cowboys," he corrects.

We enter the main floor where patrons enjoyed the entertainment. Again, the ceiling bears marks of spent ammo. Noted is the room to the right of the stage where a chair sits in which men would receive haircuts and shaves. Above in the balcony compartments are mannequins. I recognize one depicting Wyatt Earp. From here we proceed up a small flight of stairs to the backstage area. The first thing my eyes fall on is the hearse to the upper right, known as The Black Moriah in which many of those who met their end in Tombstone were transported to their final places of rest. After several minutes of history, we descend the stairs to the lower room where the notorious eight-year poker game was played. Across the room were small cribs where patrons were said to have engaged the services of "soiled doves".

Farther along the tour, our hostess relates several incidents, both historical and more recent that indicate paranormal activity. She is articulate with a dry wit and skillfully weaves a detailed depiction of what a typical evening afforded patrons of the theater. After inviting our queries and answering, she returns us upstairs to the backstage area where there are table and chairs to accommodate our group. A few of our number have brought their own psychic equipment. Our hostess lays out K-2 meters designed to monitor electromagnetic activity and expose it by means of colored lights that flash upon detection. She explains the spirit boxes next; purported to be able, by means of mixed radio frequencies that manifest in static, to pick up voices from beyond. After encouraging attempts to interact with whatever spirits choose to join us, she cautions us to avoid words directly referring to death, explaining that the reference seems to upset those who have passed on. In all seriousness, she warns us against antagonizing the entities in any way, and for safety reasons, we are not to leave our seats during the blackout. Subsequent to securing the group's unanimous agreement to the admonitions, our hostess explains what remnants of lighting we will notice after the main ones are shut off, so as not to mistake a glow off to the side for a spirit trying to make contact. With that, she leaves momentarily to douse the lights.

For several minutes, we sit, scarcely able to hear our own breathing as we wait for our eyes to adjust to the darkness, and for the alleged most haunted building in Tombstone to awaken. Finally, one member of our party breaks the silence with a whisper. "Is this it? We're just going to sit here in the dark for a half hour?"

"Spirits are sensitive," is murmured by another, quickly followed by a hiss of "show some respect," by a third party and muted chuckles by others, who apparently have not perfected the art of deference to the feelings of others whose opinions differ from their own.

"Look . . . over there in the hearse." Sure enough, a faint glow the size of a golf ball appears to hover in behind the glass. As I watch, it grows and dims as if diluting as it spreads, until it is a mere haze filling the chamber. Either my blood pressure or the room temperature is dropping. The group has again grown silent. Then, as if someone were slowly turning up the volume on a TV, I can hear the slightest suggestion of a conversation.

"I think I see something."

"Hush; I'm trying to hear."

"Smoke and mirrors," voices a skeptic.

"What . . . you expected real ghosts?"

The man to my right who is using his own equipment speaks up. "Look, I realize that not everyone here is serious about this, but there are those of us who are here to do legitimate research, and I think the skeptics owe it to us to be respectful."

"I concur," says our hostess.

"Smell that?"

"That's *cigar* smoke."

Doc twitches beside me. I reach over, put my hand on his upper arm, and put my mouth to his ear. "It's probably part of the show."

"No," he says softly but quite deliberately. Doc reaches over and places his other hand atop mine. A spark ignites at the touch; not out of the ordinary with all the static in this desert air, but it doesn't feel like the sharp sting ignited by an electric shock.

"Are yah in or ah yah out?" The voice is faint, but the words are clearly discernable. Doc stiffening triggers the same in me.

"The lights . . . they're flashing," says one of our group, in reference to one of the boxes on the table. Sure enough, a yellow light is flashing.

The electrical discharges from the spirit box seem to pulsate in tune to the voice coming from downstairs.

"Hold yer horses; Ah'm a thinkin'." The flashing accelerates, and in more than one color accompanying more static.

"Don't hurt yersef, Ike; put up or shut up. We ain't got all night."

"Could've fooled me."

Flash. Flash. Static.

I shake my head and blink once or twice to clear my vision, but see nothing. Even the mist from the hearse has disappeared. The sounds continue and are distinguishable as a poker game in full swing in the room directly below us.

"Oh my god, someone really is here," says a woman across the table. "Speak to us," she says. Suddenly there are two separate conversations going on, that of the excited tourists around the table and the one downstairs. Doc is frozen in place and I am confused. If I were not such a wimp, I would shush the others. We have evoked the spirits so why not shut up and listen to what they have to say.

"Yeah, Mr. Lawdog; like yah got any au-tho-ri- ty in this here jur-is-dic-tion."

"Mah, mah; Ike's done got hissef some ed-i-ca-tion."

Doc chuckles uneasily.

"What's so hilarious?" demands one of the men at the table. Doc adjusts in his chair, and our physical contact is broken. The members of our party are discussing the flashing lights, the activity of which is continuing to fast track. The noise from downstairs has ceased altogether, although the spirit box continues to register conversation. I sense that Doc is more than mildly disturbed and I again reach for his hand.

". . . weren't my friend, Bill . . ." The sudden return of conversation startles me. I release Doc's hand. The voice cuts out. The monitors increase their activity and rivet the total attention of our fellow patrons . . . Oh My God. . . My heart jumps into triple time. I reach again for Doc's hand.

". . . not my friend, Ike; now play before I shoot yer ass." A chill invades my core as my mind comes to grips with the fact that while the others in the room are experiencing the reaction of the machines, Doc, and I through touch are in fact hearing the visiting spirits. I have no doubt that a trek downstairs would confirm this; that we would be the only ones to see the activity at the table. Inwardly, I chafe at the restriction to remain in my seat.

"Yer a son of a bitch, Bill," says Ike. The next sound is of chips being shoved across the table, and the sound of a bet being matched.

"Hell, we're all sons o' bitches," adds a new voice, to which Doc reacts.

"Speak for yourself, Johnny. Come over here, Dahlin'. Yah were meant for bigger thin's. That big pile of chips hardly qualifies."

"Whoa, Sheriff, sure that's the play yah want tah make?" A fresh voice. Could this be the infamous Curley Bill Brocious?

"What's he gonnah do, kill me?" The basement gathering chuckles in unison.

A woman's voice with a European inflection drips with sarcasm. "Neither do fancy clothes and a badge; besides Johnny's pile of winnings is not his biggest claim to fame. I'll stay right where I am, thank you." I feel Doc tense again.

"Are you studyin' your hand, Johnny or contemplatin' breakin' the sheriff's face?" Chips collide with others. "Yer play, Frank."

"Hell, Ah'm out." Cards hit the table.

"Not me, Brother," and I hear the pile grow again.

"Billy?" A few seconds of silence pass. While I am finding it impossible to keep the players in this scene straight, I sense that Doc knows all of them and understands exactly what is transpiring among them. I hear the scooting of chips.

"Shit Billy, that's everthin'. Ah'm not . . ."

"Shut up, Big Brother; it's mah money."

"The last time yah went fer broke . . ."

"As I recall, yah ran off." The answer is curt in word and tone. "Pour me anothah whiskey, Kate!"

A bottle is shoved across the table. "I ain't yer waiter, Billy."

"Speakin' of breakin' faces and goin' for broke, anybody seen the Earps lately?"

"A chance in hell, Sheriff. Them Earps ain't nevah showin' they faces in Tombstone again; and that goes for that lunger friend a theirs, too.

"Believe your right, Ike, but do yah think Dr. Holliday is as smart as his friends? "I sortah got the impression he might still be lookin' for a fight. Ah call."

"Ah shit!"

"Those aces from up yer sleeve, Bill?"

"Christ, Almighty!"

"Anothah hand, Boys?"

"Not me."

"Told yah, Billy. Yah done wiped us out."

"Hey, Ah gottah idea. Those folks are at it agin upstairs, tryin' to make contact. Let's rattle 'em a bit."

"Ah say we scare the bejesus outtah 'em."

"Ike may have somethin'."

"Could be fun. Membah that one time; I thought that guy was gonnah shit his pants when Ah blew in his ear."

In spite of the lively chatter on our level, fueled by the flashing lights and crackling of the radio, I am able to follow the cowboy banter. When the steps creak under the boot falls, I involuntarily squeeze Doc's hand and try to monitor my intake of breath. The K-2 meters are going wild now, and the skeptics have thrown aside their misgivings. The cowboy laughter grows louder and to my utter amazement, the mist ascending the stairway begins to divide into shapes that separate and take positions behind those of us seated around the table. To my amazement just short of horror, faces I have only scene in aged photographs take on definition in the glow that surrounds them.

I sense motion at my side, turn to Doc, and see that he has lowered his head and tipped his hat down. I squeeze his hand and he responds in kind. I assume he is okay and that he has adjusted his posture to obscure his identity if that is possible. This should be interesting, indeed.

The one I surmise is Curly Bill quickly takes his place behind our attractive hostess, who is seated at the head of the table with her back to the front of the stage and to the left of the stairway. When he slowly lowers his hands to her shoulders, she lets forth with an involuntary shudder. "I think we might be . . ." Clockwise starting at her left are Kevin and his blonde girlfriend, Jewel, where Behan comes to rest.

"Oh shit," she expels in barely a whisper as I watch him lace her curly locks through his fingers. The lights are no longer flashing; they are solid. Next to her sits Ed, then his wife, Carla, flanked respectively by Frank and Tom McLaury. Our ghost hunters come next and are claimed by Kate. I am to Jeff's left. Doc's nearest neighbor on the other side is Ray, who will be at Ike's mercy. Other than Doc, and myself, our hostess, and "Blondie", there are eight others; a middle-aged couple Ed and Carla, Jeff and David who are ghost-hunting together, a young man of about twenty, Ray, an older woman, Stella, and her teen granddaughter, Kim, have been corralled by Billy Clanton. Ringo continues around the table. His footsteps stop behind me. I feel myself tense and Doc's reassuringly clutching my arm. I take a deep breath. Ringo chuckles.

"Does anyone else feel like we're surrounded?" asks Jeff.

"I've got that creepy feeling like when you know someone is standing behind you before you see them," says Kim evoking a titter from Billy, who bends to kiss the top of her head, sending her reeling into her grandmother.

"I want everyone to remain calm," says our hostess in a very controlled tone. "We have nothing to fear from the spirits. Obviously, we are being treated to an unusually active session. I've never seen the K-2 boxes freeze like that." She pauses before directing her words to our visitors. "We are happy you have chosen to join us this evening. Can you tell us how many of you are with us?" In turn, each of the men knocks once with his fist on the table in front of those they stand behind. Lastly, Kate slaps the table with the palm of her hand. "Eight; is one of you a woman?" I watch as Kate repeats her previous motion. "O . . . kay," whispers Ed. "Just remember, Carla; this was your idea."

"Yeah," says Ike. "You asked for it. Coochi, coochi, coo," he adds.

"Hey!" I hear his chair scrape as Ray reacts to whatever Ike is up to."

All this while Doc remains, head down rubbing the top of my hand with his thumb. Suddenly, I feel a cold pressure on the sides of both arms, a coolness behind my right ear, and then pick up the whiff of cigar breath. With great restraint, I am able to resist reacting. "Losing yer touch, Lovah Boy?" chides Curley Bill. Instantly, the pressure increases, followed by what I know is a kiss on my ear from Ringo's cold lips. I should have expected an answer to Brocious' taunt. It caught me by surprise and I nearly jump out of my chair. Doc is rubbing harder, now; and I know he must be seething inside. "We must be borin' her fellah'. Either that or he's deader than we ah." I feel Ringo nudge Doc. Unbelievably, he does not react. I think everybody here knows that we cannot physically interact with our guests and it would be foolish to try. I guess there are no rules on the other side. We can't antagonize them, but they are free to goad us.

"Well, what next?" asks Tom. I am relieved that they are moving on.

"Ah know," says Brocious. "Let's levitate the table. That always gets 'em." A second later, the men grab the table and slowly begin to lift and tilt for maybe twenty seconds before letting it drop abruptly. The group exhales in unison and our visitors laugh derisively. "Now let's really mess 'em up. Hands off for a while." I relax, but Doc remains tense, as if he questions Curley Bill's motives; or maybe it's in anticipation of what might follow the intermission.

"This is the first time Ah've seen yah in years. Where yah been keepin' yourself, Bill?" asks Ringo."

"Ah'll never tell," is the reply. "Where the hell yah been, Ringo?"

"Ah got me a peaceful spot long side Turkey Creek."

Kate looks across the table. "You two still hanging out together?" she asks Tom and Frank.

"Same little patch o'groun' in the same neck o'the woods with Billy and his old man," Frank answers for both brothers. "What about yah, Kate, where yah been spending yer time."

"Prescott, if it's any business of yours, Ike. What about

you Sheriff?"

"Got me a little spot in Holy Hope."

"Nevah heard of it," Ike pipes up.

"The likes of you nevah will," counters Johnny.

"Well?" Billy looks up at his brother.

"Well, what?"

"Where's yah stayin' these days, Ike."

"Out in Eagle Creek, on Pegleg Wilson's place; real nice. Ah heard the Earps skedaddled to California."

"'Cept for Warren, he planted hisself in Wilcox and somebody told me Virgil's all the way up in Oregon," says Bill. "Wyatt and Josie are still tagethah in Colma, place called Hills of Eternity or some such nonsense.

"Doc went to Colorado," says Kate. "Last I heard he was resting in Glenwood Springs.'

"Yeah, some sort o' resort for lungers," laughs Ike.

"Like yah said, Ike, Doc and them Earps, they ain't coming back here."

"You fellahs better hope not," says Kate. It's impossible not to notice the taunt in her tone. Then, she removes all doubt. "They whipped yer butts pretty good."

The next thing I know, Kate, is hauled behind me. "Why you . . ." she snipes as she sprawls backwards onto the floor between Doc and me.

"Bye," says Curley Bill before erupting in sadistic laughter, echoed by the others.

From her ungainly posture on the floor, she lifts her head and we come eye to eye. "What are you looking at?" she snarls as she reaches for Doc's elbow to pull herself up off the floor. A jagged spark of light erupts, visible to all in the room. They gasp in response. The sound Kate utters is a smothered squeal. She lets loose of Doc and she drops onto the floor. After several seconds, she recovers her wits and slowly returns to her feet under her own power. Doc has not moved. His hand still covers mine on the table between us; his head bowed. Kate looks down at me, then skirts around Doc, so that she is no longer between us, but on his left side. She looks at me again. I guess I am not surprised when she risks another mini lightning bolt. In a swift motion, her left hand comes up under Doc's hat from the back and sends it sprawling onto the center of the table with a tail of light trailing behind. She snatches her hand back as it had been singed by the contact. As one, the group jerks backward in their chairs. Doc slowly lifts his head. Across the table, Curley Bill squints and leans forward. "God Almighty, Ah don't believe it."

The rest of his companions turn their scrutiny to Doc. "Shit," says Billy Clanton.

"It's a goddamn trick," says his brother.

"Ah don't think so," counters Behan. "Ah thought something was off, tonight. Ah think we should leave."

"It's not him," says Frank.

"Can't be," echoes Tom.

"Hey, Lunger!"

The activity is registering on the paranormal equipment and our hostess cautions us to remain calm.

Doc raises and turns his head to look up at Ringo, still at my back. His eyes are cold. The pressure on my shoulders increases and a chill invades the rest of me. I look up at Kate. Her eyes, also fixed on Ringo, are aglow in horror. She lowers her sight . . .

"Doc?" to which he turns to face her. From the reaction of all in the group, her shriek is echoing between the dimensions.

"Enough!" yells Carla.

"For God's sake, get the lights!" insists her husband.

"Everyone stay where you are!" I see a shadow of movement and hear the scrape of a chair as our hostess leaves. A few seconds later, we are blinded by the return of the lights. The women of the group are visibly shaken. "No need to panic," says David.

"To the contrary," adds Jeff. "We have had a rare experience, indeed." He turns to Doc. "You seem to hold some fascination for the visitors tonight."

Doc offers an innocent shrug as he reaches across the table to retrieve his hat. "It would appear so; but in all likelihood it is the resemblance; don't yah think? Anyway, we thank yah for a most intriguin' evenin'. Cassie is quite tired, so we will be takin' our leave," he finishes while rising and offering his hand to me.

"May I?" asks Jeff, motioning toward Doc's hat. Doc shrugs again. Jeff scrutinizes it inside and out. "Do you smell that?" he asks Doc who takes a whiff of the brim in back.

"Ah believe Ah do detect a slight odah," he acknowledges.

"Exactly," says Jeff. "It's been singed a bit right here." He points to a small defect on the brim. "Listen Buddy, we need to talk before you leave town, seriously."

"It will be mah pleasure," says Doc. "But for now, Ah need to get Cassie outtah here."

"Sure," says Jeff. "Have a good evening."

"An' yah as well, Suh."

I am glad for the early retreat. The others remain seated, apparently eager to discuss the evening's extraordinary events. I would love to be privy to the conversation, but know that Doc would no doubt be forced center stage and grilled regarding his apparent psychic prowess. I can just imagine:

"How do you account for being a target of the spirits tonight, Mr. Holliday?"

"It's verah simple really. Ah recently came through a portal and mah presence in yor modern world has obviously disturbed mah old nemeses."

No, we'd best leave the party to speculate amongst themselves.

"Thank you for coming," says our hostess as we pass her. "I would love to talk to you before you leave town and . . ."

"Of course," I say. "Will you be in tomorrow?" I ask letting her take my hand in both of hers.

"Yes, around ten. I look forward to it. As you can imagine, I have a lot of questions." Doc tips his hat. With that, we hurry down the steps to the main area, through the door to the entry, and out into the night.

"What happened back there?" I gasp out with the breath I have been holding, while trying to keep up with Doc's unusual speed.

"Ah know as much as yah do, Dahlin'. It does answer a

few mysteries of the universe, does it not?"

"I guess it does, at that," I say as we relax our pace now that we are out of sight and earshot of the Birdcage and our fellow patrons. Coming down off all the tension, I find myself unable to hold back laughter. "You sure took the starch out of Kate."

"Ah did, didn't Ah," he says chuckling. "I believe she was jealous. We're yah verah scared, Cassie?"

"Not exactly; a bit taken-aback. I don't know quite what I expected, but I never imagined that. It would be sort of inconsistent to be unnerved after what we're experiencing. What about you?"

Doc stops and looks up at the starry skies. "Yor right, of course. The evenin's events are no more mind bendin' than our situation. Still Ah have heretofore thought of the dead disturbin' the livin', not the reverse."

"I think this situation caught them a bit off guard."

"Indeed. Ah don't know about yah, but Ah could use some refreshment of the spirited variety," he says pointing down the street toward the Four Deuces, on the corner of Allen and Fourth. Thankfully, none of our party from the Birdcage has the same idea.

A few minutes later, my nerves are responding to the warmth of the whiskey Doc persuaded was in order after our chilling encounter. We carefully avoid reminiscing about the experience lest our conversation be overheard and stir unwelcome curiosity. Instead, we make small talk about the town in general, our side excursions,, and what else Doc might want to see before we head back to Colorado.

"Aren't we going to go back and. . ."

"Ah think not, Cassie. Those folks might not be up for the whole truth and Ah would be hard pressed to come up with an alternative explanation. No, Ah'm for risin' early and gettin' the hell outtah town."

And so we do.

CHAPTER 34

After bidding farewell to Tombstone just after dawn, I put a call into the Pruitts where it is an hour later and ranchers are up at the crack of dawn. After inquiring if we are enjoying ourselves, Nancy assures me that all is well at home and not to worry about rushing back. That considered, I suggest to Doc that we venture further and head into California where we make several solemn pilgrimages.

Our first stop is in Los Angeles at the former home of Wyatt and Josie until his death in 1929. It is here we learn that John Clum was among Wyatt's pallbearers.

"George Parsons was a verah good friend," notes Doc at seeing him listed as well. "Hunsaker was Wyatt's attorney, anothah fine gentleman." From here, we journey on to Colma to the Eternity cemetery, the final resting place of Wyatt and Josie; then on to Morgan's gravesite in Hermosa Memorial Gardens in Colton, California where I wander among other graves as Doc kneels to mourn his friend. We spend the most time here.

We decide to forgo the visit to Virgil's final resting place in Oregon. Upon his death, his body had been brought there by a daughter he didn't know he had until later in life, the issue of his childhood bride, whom he thought dead.

Coming back into Arizona, we make a detour to the Grand Canyon where Doc again expresses his awe of the

Creator's handiwork. From there we seek and find Kate's grave in Pioneer Home Cemetery in Prescott. Doc is pleased to see that his one-time lady lived just shy of her ninetieth birthday.

"Sorrah about last night, Ol' Gal. Yah can rest easy now. Ah won't be disturbin' yor haunts again anah time soon."

During each of these visits, Doc is fittingly reverential, kneeling to offer silent prayers in behalf of his friends. How his mind must be bending to accept their deaths, while, to him, all but Morgan are still very much alive. He expresses gratitude at their longevity and for the privilege at having the opportunity to see into the future of his friends. "When we get back," he says, "I'd like to read more about their lives after my premature passin'." I assure him that there is no shortage of material, but warn him of the inconsistencies and debates. Might I get him to think about the possibilities of a book based on his knowledgeable amendments?

We take our time and make many other stops along a more northerly route home. I save the last as a surprise, if you can call it that. We arrive in Glenwood Springs in the late afternoon. Ominous clouds are gathering, making it seem much later than it is as I check us in to the hotel. The desk clerk points to the wall of brochures at my inquiry. I opt to bypass dropping off our bags in our rooms in hopes of beating the weather, which is getting more threatening by the minute.

Doc makes no comment when we park at the Pioneer cemetery, though from his readings thus far, he must recognize the name.

"It's this way," I say, thankful for the guide. The terrain is hilly and I hear faint rumblings in the distance. We are halfway to our destination when the wind picks up, forcing us to lean into it as we make our way. Before long, a light rain begins to fall. Well educated in Colorado weather, now, I had the foresight to bring umbrellas, although the wind may force us to close them at any minute. Just shy of our destination, in front of the fenced-in grave, three young women are huddled together. We hang back allowing them to pay their respects in private, distracting ourselves reading markers to either side. The wind is loud enough to prevent conversation at a normal level. Before we realize it, the trio, heads bent down against the wind, are upon us just as the sky explodes with light and an ear-shattering crack of thunder. I shudder at the closeness of the strike. The women, equally startled, have lifted their heads and are inches from Doc. Frozen, they look from his face to mine, and in unison, let out the most blood-curdling scream before dashing through the mud toward the entrance. I think, if we weren't where we are, it might be funny. Of course, if we weren't where we are, the girls wouldn't be screaming in the wake of encountering what they most certainly are convinced is a ghost. Our line of sight now clear, Doc slowly walks toward his own memorial and squats before the marker.

He looks at me and shakes his head. "So this is it," he says in resignation.

"This *was* it," I say firmly. Doc's hair is soaked, as is my own, the rain streaming down our faces. I wonder if it is obscuring *his* tears, as well. Abruptly, he rises "I'm hungry," he says. Before dining, we retreat to our rooms where we thaw in hot showers. We take the desk clerk's recommendation for a restaurant and are not disappointed. Again, Doc's presence, in his native dress, stirs interest among the employees, who, no doubt are used to answering questions about their infamous resident on the hill. Doc counters the questions of our server with the claim that we are enthusiasts visiting places of note. After giving our order, Doc takes a sip of wine. "Ah want to thank yah for all this," he says. "Not only has it been an education, it has been pleasurable beyond anythin' Ah've experienced."

"For me, as well," I say. "Believe me, it wouldn't have been the same without you along."

"Again, Ah am at a loss as how tah repay yah," he says.

"I do." I say quietly, to which he cocks his head. "You're going to take me with you into your world."

"Cassie, Ah'm sorrah. Ah can't possibly . . ."

"It's not negotiable," I say. "It's only fair."

Doc nods. "Yah have a valid point." He seems to be conceding, but also troubled. After a good night's rest, we start out for home. The drive is uneventful, each of us avoiding further discussion of my demand. We stop in Denver for lunch. The growth of the city and the traffic dampens Doc's desire to explore it, so we proceed on to The Springs. It is sleeting on the way up the pass, but we make it home without incident. It is dark and Jim has already dealt with the stock. I call to let him know we have arrived home safe and sound, and to thank him for watching over the ranch. We leave unpacking for the morrow and kick back with glasses of wine to wash down our cheese and crackers while we take in the evening news.

The next few months are spent relatively close to home, exploring more of Colorado's wonders in the immediate area as Doc's health continues to improve.

CHAPTER 35

"Oh please!" I am so excited I could bust. His silence, as he stares at the computer betrays his apprehension. In the months he has been in my world, at my insistence, he has learned the wisdom of remaining anonymous. Now, I am suggesting that he reveal himself to another.

"How do yah know yah can trust him?" He is leaning over my shoulder eyeing the laptop before me on the kitchen table. His question, rather than an adamant refusal, tells me there is a chance.

"Gut feeling," I answer with full conviction.

"But yah don't know the man," he offers in rebuttal.

"But I think you do." My response evokes a skeptical raise of his brow, but there is fascination in his expression.

"He's got your best friends' blood running through his veins," I say as I hit play on the video clip. Before our eyes, an older Wyatt Earp comes to life relating his adventures in Tombstone. Doc watches in rapt attention.

I had run across the website during my research. Wyatt Earp of Phoenix is a descendant of the uncle of the man whose name he bears. His wife, Terry, writes the plays in which they perform around the country.

Without Doc's knowledge, and of course, without giving up the motive, I had earlier placed a call and to my delight, had been able to speak directly to Mr. Earp, subtly trying to obtain his motivations in portraying his famous ancestor. Our brief conversation convinced me, that while it is a nice way to make a living, Mr. Earp is emotionally attached, not only to his namesake, but also to John Henry Holliday. When asked his opinion of the man, he told me that he had the utmost respect for his ancestor's friend.

When the clip ends, I click onto the one about Doc. A few seconds into it, Doc pulls a chair around next to mine and sits. He studies the screen as he is portrayed as being interviewed in the Denver jail.

"Well?" I ask when it ends.

He sits back in his chair. I get up and refresh our coffees. When I return to the table, I stand behind him and tap his shoulders rapidly with my palms. "Come on, Doc!" I plead. "I've got a good feeling about this. You don't want to miss an opportunity to meet this man."

"Ah will not be pawed at, thank yah verah much," he says.

I snatch my hands away and take my seat. Several minutes go by. I so much want to go, but prodding him further will have a negative effect. Of that, I have no doubt. "It's your decision I say," with my fingers crossed behind my back.

"Let's do it!" he says. "Ah trust yor judgment, Cassie, an' Ah must say, Ah am curious."

I reach over, hug him tightly, and plant a kiss on his cheek. "You won't regret it," I say as I jump up and make for the phone. Within the hour, our reservations are set for the two performances and a hotel for the night in between. I am dancing around the kitchen, not quite sure what will come of this, but anxious to find out. Doc just smiles, but I can tell his mind is trying to wrap around the fact that he will be meeting a descendant that Wyatt would never know.

We make our way back to Cripple Creek. The Imperial Hotel that houses the Gold Bar Theater is not hard to find; right off Bennett Ave on Third. "Supposedly, the place is haunted," I say as I pull into the parking space.

"Indeed."

"A father and daughter. Apparently, she was a little 'off'

and he kept her shut away. The story goes that one day she hit him over the head with a pan and he fell down the stairs to his death. It's said that he hits on women in the place; so I'll rely on you for protection."

"A ghost that hits women?"

"No, hits *on* women; you know, makes overtures . . ."

"Ah see."

"Anyway . . . who knows who might show up?"

"Ah yah suggestin' that Wyatt himself will be joinin' us for the show?"

"With what we've seen, can we really deny the possibility?"

"Yah gottah point, Dahlin'."

CHAPTER 36

The lights dim. The curtain opens. As the stage lights brighten, the details of the seated shadowy figure begin to sharpen, and Doc, quite abruptly leans forward in his chair.

I remember the feeling. When I was young, my mother, during one of Father's religious retreats, snuck me off to Disneyland after securing my promise never to allude to the outing. One of the first attractions we took in was Great Moments with Mr. Lincoln. Through the miracle of automatronics, the mannequin before us was transformed into our sixteenth president. Subtle movement in the face and hands added to the realism and after several minutes, I realized that I had completely forgotten that the speech was not being delivered by a real person. I listened intently to Abraham Lincoln.

This Wyatt Earp, distant kin of his namesake, is a dead ringer for the historical photos I have seen. Doc knows Wyatt in his thirties, yet this older version commands his attention, while my own focuses on my companion. Over the course of the performance, I see deep thought and surprise in his expression, subdued laughter and even an escaping tear or two. I wonder what the actor would think if he knew his ancestor's best friend was in the audience. It will not be long now.

Several in the audience have accepted Mr. Earp's invitation to meet him in person and we station ourselves at the very end of the line.

As we inch our way closer, Doc's head is down while mine is taking in the interaction of our host with his admirers. As during the performance, Doc is keeping his thoughts to himself, and I do not prod. Mr. Earp is quite obviously a patient man. These performances must take their toll, yet he remains animated in his conversations without a hint of weariness or annoyance. I don't think I have ever beheld a more genuine smile. Before we know it, we are next in line. He shakes the hand of the departing guest; then turns his attention to us smiling broadly as he sizes Doc up and down. "Doc Holliday, how the hell are yah?" he asks in mimicry of Kurt Russell in Tombstone as he extends his hand, his expression one of utter delight; yet his demeanor bespeaks the quiet dignity so often portrayed of Wyatt Strapp Berry Earp.

"Wyatt, Ah am rollin'," answers Doc. "Wish Ah could say the same for yah. Yah've aged somethin' terrible."

"Oh?" Wyatt looks closer at Doc as if he should recognize the man in costume. "Forgive me; do I know you, Mr.?"

"Holliday," says Doc very deliberately, "John Henry. We have nevah met, but yor cousins are close friends of mine . . . like my own family, in fact. Yah look so much like Wyatt . . . only . . . I must say, it is verah disconcertin', though of late I have experienced much that is" Suddenly he seems at a loss to explain. "Oh pahdon my oversight," he says turning toward me. "Let me introduce Miss Cassie Collins of Florissant, Colorado. She is verah graciously seein' to mah welfare durin' my visit."

"Pleased to meet you, Miss Collins," Mr. Earp says warmly as he takes my hand in both of his. His eyes seem to be looking to me for explanation, but I do not want to break whatever spell this meeting might be evoking.

"Cassie, please," I say.

Wyatt turns his attention back to Doc. "Where do you hail from, Mr. Holliday?"

"Please, call me Doc. Ah'm sure yor cousins would insist upon it," he says quite sincerely. "Originally, from Georgia, born an' raised in Griffin, but yah know that, Wyatt."

Wyatt's grin is tainted with the slightest hint of frustration, now. "Of course," he says as if playing along in some parody. "You'd, no doubt enjoy the show tomorrow night," he says pointing to the poster advertising The Gentleman Doc Holliday to be performed the next evening.

"Yes, we've made arrangements to stay over," I say.

"Good," says Wyatt. "I gather you are somewhat of an aficionado with regard to the man?" he says returning his attention to Doc.

"Yah might say that, aside from the editin' Ah engage in from time to time; a double-edged sword, Ah have found. My illness necessitated a covah, as it were and Ah'm afraid, Ah began allowin' the embellishment a reputation as cold-blooded killer. It discourages othahs who might otherwise trigger my equally exaggerated temper. Ah was in no condition tah protect myself, yah see; but thanks to the determination of Cassie, here, an' the marvels of yor modern medicine, I am well on my way to regainin' my health. Exploits of that character, Ah am regretful tah say, has greatly distressed mah Georgia relations. "

"You are good, quite good," says Wyatt in open appreciation. "Might this be, then, an impromptu audition?" Wyatt releases that friendly smile again. "I'm afraid this is a small operation. My wife, Terry writes our scripts and the two of us do all the performing. I would hate to be in competition with you, though," he says with a good-natured laugh.

"An, I'm afraid, Wyatt, that I have no actin' experience what so evah. My southahn pride will not allow me to pretend to be anythin' but myself; however, like Ah said, Ah do confess to adoptin' an alias here an' again, to protect the family name."

I stand fascinated as I watch Doc lead Wyatt in a two-step to the tune of "I've Got Friends in Your Family Tree".

Neither man averts his gaze as I watch the imaginary wheels turn in their minds. Doc is challenging this skeptic to indulge what must be a deep-seated yearning. I sense Wyatt's intellect must be warring with a discernable desire to cross the expanse of time to his beloved ancestor.

"Tell me, Doc," he proceeds with the ruse, "What do you

hear from Robert?" The question seems to come out of nowhere, but it evokes a sentimental smile from Doc.

"Robert is doin' quite well without me, Ah am happy to say. He wanted to come to mah aid after that unfortunate incident in Breckenridge several years back, but his duties argued otherwise an' he sent our cousin George in his stead. Ah must confess, Ah was nevah so happy to see anothah person in mah life. Ah miss my family. Ah regret lettin' Robert down; but even more, Ah want most deeply for his companionship. If not for *yor* family, Wyatt, Ah would be alone in the world."

"Does Sophie still write?"

"Sophie nevah learned to read an' write," answers Doc. "That just isn't done, but she does send her love through Robert." Then turning to me he explains, "Sophie was the daughter of a family friend. He sent her to live with us in Fayetteville durin' the war."

"She was the nanny," adds Wyatt.

"Your *nanny*?"

"She was nanny to my youngah cousins in the household. You see, the family circled the wagons, as it were, durin' the war. Sophie is mah friend. She might not know her letters, but her skill with a deck o' cards is unmatched."

"She taught him to play poker," says Wyatt.

"Ah beg yor pardon, Wyatt, she taught me skinnin', very similar tah faro, mah game of preference when Ah'm on the othah side of the table. Ah undahstand it has fallen intah disrepute in yor world; a pity," he said wistfully.

Wyatt looks down and shakes his head. I imagine that he is both disconcerted and a bit giddy at having met his match. He appears to be feeling the exhaustion of the evening or maybe the failure of his attempt at blowing Doc's cover with his inspective questions.

"Look, why don't we continue this tomorrow after the performance," I suggest feeling that this interaction might be more advantageous after both Doc and Wyatt have a chance to sleep on it. Doc lends his vote to that and we excuse ourselves. I can feel Wyatt's eyes as we make for the exit.

"Give him some time, Doc," I say. "It took me a while and

I'm still pinching myself."

We return to our rooms in the hotel. After an hour or so, I wonder if Doc is having the same trouble getting to sleep as I am. The evening's encounter keeps replaying in my mind. In desperation, I retrieve the sleep aid in my overnight bag, swallow the recommended dose with a glass of water and turn on the TV for distraction.

The next thing I know, a weatherman is alerting me to carry an umbrella if I will be venturing out into the predicted thunderstorms. After a cup of instant coffee and a shower, I am ready to face the day. Doc and I have planned to do some more exploring in town. We have plenty of time before heading back to the Imperial to watch Wyatt's portrayal of Doc. We breakfast at Maggie's and partake of a late lunch at Baja Billy's, after which we enter the gaming rooms. Doc, with me in tow this time, attacks the poker table. His skill is such that I find it necessary to pull him away once again before he can be a subject of suspicion. He takes cards very seriously. After all, it is his profession.

"Ya needn't have worried, Dahlin'. Ah had no need to apply my unscrupulous talents. My opponents were amateurs." He winks as he stuffs his winnings in my hand. I waste a few dollars on the slots before we head for the museum missed on our last visit. We nap before a steak dinner; then it's back to the Imperial and another shot at Wyatt.

With a makeover and a wardrobe change, Wyatt Earp has become the Doc I met several months ago, looking much older and thinner than he stands today. The real marvel of this metamorphosis is the voice. Wyatt has mastered the mellow Georgian drawl of his character. None of this impresses Doc, though.

"How does he know all this? Wyatt never asked and I nevah volunteered the details of my family history."

"We'll have to ask him," I respond, wondering myself, not only at the information related but also of its heretofore obscurity. The performance is a bit shorter than the previous night's and we again position ourselves at the rear of the line of congratulators.

It is hard to tell if Wyatt is really more at ease or just prepared for Doc's presence the second time around. In any event, he waits for Doc to start the conversation.

"That was a bit unnervin', Suh," begins Doc.

"How is that?" asks Wyatt.

"You have information that I nevah discussed with Wyatt, up to this point, anyway." He takes on a look of surprise as if he had not considered the possibility that he was going to do so in the future. It must be difficult for him to keep the past and the present in chronological order. "Then, again, perhaps I do so in the futchah."

Wyatt considers this for several seconds before responding. "And what point would that be?"

Doc appears confused for a second. "Aah, I see. My last recollection is the twentieth of June, 1882," Doc answers evoking a raise of Wyatt's brow, then again, that understanding smile. "So tell me, Suh, how *do* yah know all these details about mah personal life?"

Wyatt's stare is challenging, but has no effect on Doc, who waits patiently for the answer. Wyatt cocks his head, brings his arms up; then lets them fall in defeat. "Karen Holliday Tanner is the Great Granddaughter of your cousin Robert," he answers as if he has accepted Doc for who he is. "Although kept under wraps by ancestors who were, to put it delicately, uncomfortable with your reported exploits, Robert's wife, through her association with . . ."

"Robert is married?"

Wyatt thinks for a minute. "That would be a couple years from now in 'your world', of course." He pauses, I imagine, expecting a telltale sign of fraud on Doc's part before continuing. "Mary Fulton, a delightful girl, by all descriptions. Sophie ended up in their household and the two became fast friends. Unlike the others, they refused to be embarrassed by the negative feedback. Mary was ahead of her time and applauded your adventurous spirit. Sophie was always on your side, taking special pride in your gambling success." Doc chuckles. "She lived until 1933 and is largely responsible for preserving your memory for future generations." Doc cannot hide his fascination. "In 1988

Karen received a box of memorabilia along with copious notes on your life. No longer bound by the promise prohibiting publication that might embarrass the family, Karen published your biography in 1998. From it and conversations with her, my wife, Terry created the reenactment you saw this evening."

When Doc remains silent, Wyatt offers more. "As you can see, I have the utmost respect for this man who was my ancestors' loyal friend. I have to say that I am uncomfortable becoming party to a hoax that would dishonor his memory. I consider myself a progressive man, holding on to the values of a more rational era. I've never experienced a paranormal encounter; and while I cannot rule out the possibility of such, I remain a skeptic," he says and lets out a long sigh accompanied by a sympathetic smile.

"How do you explain what you've seen and heard, Mr. Earp?" I ask desperately trying to find the key to opening his mind.

"If I had to guess, I think Doc, here, knows all about Karen's work, has studied it in depth, and has made it his own. He might even believe he really is John Henry." It is his turn to laugh. "Hey, who wouldn't want to be Doc Holliday? I admit that I enjoy stepping into my famous cousin's boots every time I take the stage, and into Doc's too; but I still know who I am and am comfortable with that."

Doc wears his disappointment on his sleeve, but bucks up. He clearly likes this Wyatt Earp. He extends his hand in friendship to this cousin of his friend. "Ah am privileged to have made yor acquaintance, Suh. Ah do believe we have taken enough of this man's time, Cassie," he says to me as he turns to leave. When I do not follow, he reaches for my hand. I am torn. Wyatt's stand is a rational one, but he is missing out on the opportunity of a lifetime. I stand my ground and Doc releases his grip and walks toward the exit.

"I can prove it," I say softly, but with all the conviction I feel.

"What's that?" asks Wyatt turning back.

"I have undisputable evidence that this man is, in fact, Doc Holliday. If I didn't, I wouldn't be caught dead with the man. This is my phone number and address," I say as I rapidly scribble the information on a notepad. If you want to see it, you are welcome." I rip the page from the pad and hand it to him. "But only you. Call first, to make sure we are at home. It has been an honor to meet you, Mr. Earp. Give our regards to your wife. Her work is amazing." After shaking his hand, I leave him staring at the scrap of paper that could change his life. Will he come to the ranch and, if he does, will he venture through the portal with us? And after that . . .

CHAPTER 37

"I'm going."

"Ah I think not." Doc's voice is flat and final. I bite my lip and blink against the sting of tears, put down the fork, and shove aside the plate. The argument started two days ago and neither of us had budged.

"But in Glenwood Springs you said . . ."

"Ah remembah distinctly. Ah said yah had a point, an' yah do but Ah nevah agreed that Ah would take yah."

I had to admit he was right. I had heard what I wanted to hear.

Doc lets out an impatient sigh. "Look, Ah undahstand. Hell, if anyone does, Ah do. Ah have been catapulted intah the twenty-first century. It's been unbelievable, an' Ah want to see more. Ah have no trouble imaginin' what it must be like for yah tah want tah see intah mah world." I turn my head aside, refusing to be placated.

"Damnation, Woman!" Doc drops his fork, and with a sweep of his arm, it and the rest of his breakfast crash and skitter across the tile. Shocked by this uncharacteristic outburst, I almost fall to the floor myself, stumbling backwards out of my chair to avoid the splatter of eggs and potatoes. As quickly as it came, Doc's anger quells and he is out of his chair, coming to me. Before I have time to react, his arms gather me in a vise grip that conveys his desire to have his way and my understanding. He continues to hold me until I sigh in resignation.

He relaxes his grip. With one arm still around me, he takes my chin in his free hand. I avert my eyes.

"Cassie." His gentler tone melts my defenses and I meet his gaze. "Ah promised Wyatt an' Ah can't put it off any longa." The protest does not pass my lips before his hand goes up. "Ah know," he says, "Ah have all the time in the world. The clock has not moved out there since the last time we went through that door; but it is passin' in my mind. Ah have an obligation, an' Ah've got tah get on with it." When I raise a brow in question, he is quick to answer. "An' no, Ah cannot divulge the nature of the business. That is between Wyatt an' me."

"You <u>will</u> come back?"

"That is mah plan *an'* mah desire. Ah am not nearly through with the futchah, by any means" he says flashing that wicked smile of his.

"I guess that's it. I made sandwiches for the trip and there are some cookies, too," I say handing him a bag. He looks at the parcel quizzically. "I made enough for two in case you changed your mind," I add.

"Aah," he says lifting his head. "Thank yah Cassie."

"I'm going to ride over to the Pruitts; see if Jimmy and Janet want to go for a ride," I say before turning on my heels and heading for the barn.

I had fed and taken care of the chores earlier. The horses and other stock are contentedly going about their normal morning routine. I am saddling Buck when I hear Doc enter the barn, his saddlebags in tow. He is dressed in the clothes he wore when I found him in the barn office sans the dust and mud. There is a bulge beneath his coat where he carries the revolver tucked in his shoulder holster. I force a smile.

I turn to him. "You're going to start out in the dark?" I remembered that our last adventure ended late at night.

"Ah went the othah night while yah were asleep an' advanced the clock. It will be dawn in an hour or so," he says laying his bags on the floor.

"Smart," I say. "I wouldn't have thought of that."

I walk over to the next stall and massage the white blaze

of his horse, who throws up his head and emits a friendly snort. I step away as Doc fits the halter and bit, round the corner to the steps leading up to the loft where I wait to bid him goodbye.

Doc walks his horse around and cinches up his saddle.

"Sure you've got everything you need?" I ask.

"Don't need much," he answers. "Ah'm only on horseback tah Coloradah Springs. Ah'll stay the night an' catch the train from there tomorrow mornin', then make a connection tah Gunnison." We let a minute of silence pass. "Look," he finally says. "Ah guess time will pass normally for us both while Ah'm gone. Ah figure, if all goes as planned, Ah could be back inside of a month, possibly less."

"I'll be fine; I was before you came," I say raising my chin. "You have a safe trip. Don't get yourself shot or something stupid like that."

"Yah know, Cassie, Ah will be fine an' of a much bettah nature when Ah return, not havin' this duty hangin' ovah mah head." He smiles, then leans down and plants a gentle kiss on my forehead. I feel a twinge of guilt but push it aside, and hurry up the steps into the loft. I watch from there as he leads his horse out the portal, and at just the right moment, wedge the pry bar into the top far corner of the portal.

It takes me less than five minutes to change into the clothes I have stowed in a corner of the barn and another minute to secure the saddlebags behind Buck's saddle. I am shaking as I slide the rifle into its scabbard and adjust the forty-five in the holster that now encircles my waist, praying that neither will have occasion to be used.

Quietly I lead Buck out into the grayness. In my anticipation, I fail to think about replacing the pry bar that fell from its perch when I pushed the portal wide enough to allow for Buck's girth. The door slams shut and with it, the possibility of my reentry without Doc. A strange fear settles over me, but I refuse to let it take hold. As I heave myself into the saddle, I can make out Doc rounding the first curve of the journey down to The Springs. It will take some doing to follow at a safe distance, which will allow me to remain undetected while not losing sight of my guide. Timing is everything, if I ever expect to return to the twenty-first century.

A few days previously, I had rummaged around further in the trunks of my ancestors for my outfit. With a few alterations, I was able to transform myself. My stature and slight build would not pass for an adult male, to be sure. Hair tucked carefully under my hat, to passersby, if any, I will project the image of a teenage farm boy. I have a hundred dollars in old currency and, dressed as I am, should hardly draw the attention of passers-by.

After a few miles, I settle comfortably in the saddle. It is not as difficult as I thought to stay out of Doc's radar while keeping him in view. I find myself engrossed in the scenery and the unspoiled mountain pass, devoid of the homes and towns yet to come, the roads, mere dirt trails. Doc is unhurried as he traverses the mountain trail. He stops to water his horse along Fountain creek near what is now Green Mountain Falls. Waiting for him to remount and proceed on, I follow suit. After what seems an eternity, I begin to make out the town at the bottom of the pass. I had no idea that The Springs was this large back then.

When we enter town, I am emboldened to close the gap between us. I must see what Doc does about his horse. He heads directly for a stable at the edge of town. Pulling the electronic amplifier from my saddlebag, I insert it in my ear and turn my head toward the direction of the men conversing. I almost feel guilty having the advantage of technological advances, at least as long as the charge lasts. After Doc leaves, saddlebags in hand, I approach the proprietor and make the same arrangements I had overheard Doc make for his mount, handing over a month's fee for Buck's board; after which I ask directions to the train station and appropriate lodging. The saddlebags slung over my shoulder obscure my upper body almost completely. With the blacksmith's directions, I no longer need to follow Doc. Within half an hour, I have purchased my rail ticket south and have procured lodging close to the station.

The modest hotel has a small dining room. I am tempted to explore town, but the day's ride has taken its toll and I opt for a meal and bed. The room contains a bed and a basin, with bath down the hall. I wash up and brush my teeth, still heady with the day's excitement. In spite of the craziness I have embarked upon, I fall asleep quickly and wake refreshed.

I am not hungry in the morning and order only coffee. I make for the station well in advance so that I can see and avoid Doc when he arrives. This maneuver, I find quite easy, as he appears to be preoccupied in thought. I dream that he is regretting leaving me behind. The idea of my following him is obviously not in his considerations. What will I do if he changes his mind and goes back for me? Ah, but that is not in cards. I really didn't think so. After watching him board the train, I follow suit two cars back, and choose a window seat where I can view the scenery as it was a hundred and thirty years ago.

Before I know it, we have pulled into Pueblo. I am alert, once again, to making arrangements for the next leg of the journey, again without detection. I switch on my listening device across the street from where Doc is standing at the depot window. Once the transaction is made, Doc purposely strides toward the main street and a bar, no doubt. I have a couple of hours to reserve my seat on the train for Gunnison. Curious, I decide to follow at a distance. Doc, no surprise to me disappears into a saloon where he will no doubt enjoy himself with drink and games.

There is no place for me here, so I make myself scarce around the back of the depot where I watch from the corner when Doc boards the train to see where he settles. Again, I take a seat two cars behind. A few minutes later, we are on our way to Gunnison. I have not yet figured out when or how I will reveal myself to Doc, but suddenly a shiver washes over me as I anticipate the depth of his displeasure. What's the worst he can do? Another shudder ripples through me. I have lived through more critical situations, I tell myself. But instead of being able to shed all concern, I find myself coming face to face with the gravity of what I have done. This is not a spur-of-the-moment vacation on which I have embarked. I have defied the laws of time and space *and* the wishes of the man I look to protect me in this alien world. There is so much I had not considered. How do I know that I will be able to return? The portal is closed tight and does not respond to my touch. Reality descends, and with it, the fear that rightly accompanies such rashness.

I am finding it hard to sit still; wonder if other passengers are aware of my fidgeting. Stealing a glance around the car, I lock eyes with a bonneted little imp sitting beside an older woman I surmise to be her grandmother. They are seated across the aisle three rows back. The little one smiles coyly, then quickly pushes herself closer into the woman's side; prompting her guardian to search for the cause of the child's action. I fight the urge to turn abruptly and force a smile instead. The woman hugs and whispers to the child who waves with her fingers and giggles. I nod and sigh before continuing my perusal of the car. Two men in business suits of the day sitting ahead of them are engaged in serious conversation, oblivious to anything around them. Another across the aisle from me is absorbed in a newspaper. No one seems to care about the young man traveling alone.

I turn back to the window and for several miles, am content to watch the movie of scenery. However, my ease is short-lived and restlessness reactivates. Impulsively, I gather my belongings and make my way down the aisle rhythmically bouncing off the sides of the aisle seats, nodding "pardon mes" along the way. Maneuvering between cars is a daunting challenge, but I manage. In spite of my crime, two cars ahead, the sight of Doc brings profound relief. He is slouched down in his seat, head back, hat pulled forward over his face. I let out the breath I was not aware I had been holding. There are fewer commuters in this car; none betray any notice of my entrance. I aim to approach casually, but the increased motion from a change in terrain forces me to concentrate on staying on my feet while keeping charge of my possessions. The lurching of the train stirs Doc who pushes his hat back to look out the window. Instinctively I drop my head, my hat obscuring my face. Seemingly satisfied, Doc resumes his nap. Approaching his row, I see that his saddlebags are occupying the aisle seat beside him. Gingerly, I arrange myself and belongings in the row ahead. Knowing he is sitting directly behind me fills me with both comfort and exhilaration. In spite of the uncertainties of this time warp, I find myself unsettled at the thought of ever having to say goodbye to this man.

Whoa! It's as if I have been ambushed physically by my own thoughts, but before I can confront this assault . . . What the . . . Involuntarily I grab to secure my tipping hat with one hand while scrambling to catch the tresses cascading down my back with the other.

"Ah'll be damned." Doc's voice is quiet and cold. My shoulders tense. I had expected to control the time and place of our encounter. I do not turn around. I hear rustling and a second later, he is sitting beside me. For the next twenty minutes he says nothing and I know I'd best follow suit.

"Why Dahlin', it's that delectable scent of yors," he finally says. I had not thought to be betrayed by my toiletries; musk, from shampoo to cologne. How laughable.

"How much trouble am I in?" I say staring at my twiddling digits. The silence that follows echoes louder than any tongue-lashing my father had ever administered.

"It's a hangin' offense, Ah'm afraid," he says with exaggerated firmness before reaching to take my hand in his. "However, Ah am inclined tah grant a pahdon . . ." I reach for and squeeze his hand in excited gratitude and turn to look at him. He is staring straight ahead. "Uh, uh, uh," he adds, "on one unwaverin' condition; that yah strictly obey me in everythin' henceforth."

"I'll do anything you say. I won't be a problem or interfere. I promise."

"Ah mean it," he says sternly before a muted chortle escapes his lips and he turns to meet my gaze. "How on earth . . ."

I cannot hide the self-satisfaction in my tone. "I rigged a block in the portal from the loft."

"Ah applaud yor resourcefulness." I sense he is genuinely impressed.

"But how . . ."

"I followed you down the pass, listened to you negotiate with the blacksmith, and asked directions to the train station and lodging, and . . ." I get out before the need to gulp for air.

Doc's expression is one of amused fascination. He shakes his head. "It would appear that yah planned this verah carefully."

"From the minute you told me you wouldn't take me with you," I admit.

A tsk, tsk follows. "We'll have tah do somethin' about yor wardrobe before yah can meet mah friends."

Doc's words give birth to the most exciting conclusion: I am going to meet Wyatt Earp . . . "When we get tah Gunnison our first stop will be tah outfit yah in some propah ladies' attire." I wince again. I should have packed the dresses he bought.

I squeeze his hand again. The worst is over.

"I'm hungry," I say.

CHAPTER 38

I awake to a touch of a hand on my cheek. "We're here, Dahlin'." I stretch, gather up my belongings, and follow Doc down the aisle, out of the car and touch the ground of Gunnison in 1882. Doc proceeds proudly though the station, as if unaware of the stares we are attracting. What a conundrum; a scruffily dressed woman on the arm of an immaculately groomed gentleman. Doc stops to inquire about clothing shops and lodging.

A few minutes later, our entrance quells several animated conversations in the dress shop Doc has chosen. I fix my eyes on a mannequin as I feel the scrutiny of the other women. They show no signs of welcoming us. Unaffected, Doc leads me across the room to a stately woman arranging a display of hats.

"We would like to purchase an entire wardrobe for the lady." Doc's voice is calm and even but I detect the underlying contempt for the snobs who surround us. Over the past months, I have learned that his sense of justice is absolute and that he has no toleration for prejudice. Doc may present an impeccable appearance, but he would never judge another by his clothing alone.

"I see, of course, Sir. Come this way," the shop owner says leading us to a corner in the rear of the shop when she finally acknowledges that we may be serious customers. I can tell Doc is fighting the urge to slap the woman as he reaches into his inside coat pocket and produces several large bills.

"We need a dozen or so fine dresses, on the ordah of this one here," he says picking up the sleeve of an attractive dress of quality fabric on a nearby rack. I can feel my eyes grow in size. She will need suitable accessories, as well."

The woman is speechless, still staring at the fortune in her hand. "Of, course," she finally sputters out. When I turn back, the other customers, who had been following the encounter, quickly resume attention to their own shopping.

"Ah have othah business in town, Dahlin," he directs to me. "This gracious lady will be takin' care of yor needs." I swallow as if he is leaving me in the lion's den; then remember my promise and nod. Directing his attention back to the stunned woman, he adds, "I trust yah see that my wife is outfitted appropriately?" As if he expected my swoon, Doc quickly clutches me by the shoulders and leans in to kiss my forehead. "Dahlin', spend as much as yah like,"; then to the woman, "There is plenty more where that came from," he says looking down at the money in her hands. "Ah will return for Mrs. Holliday in, say," looking at his watch, "two hours?" The woman nods, and with that, he turns and exits the shop. I watch him walk out the door, too in shock to move.

Her eyebrows rise. For a second, I fear her eyes will bulge out of their sockets, but she recovers quickly; all smiles and sweetness. "Of course, Mr. Holliday."

I feel her hand under my elbow. "Come this way Mrs. Holliday."

"Please," I say, "call me Cassie.".

"My name is Ellie, Ellie Carson. I own this shop, and am proud to say that it is the best in town. Many of the dresses are from Paris." I smile and do not doubt her claim, knowing Doc as I do. He is not a man who settles.

From behind the dressing curtain, I see Doc enter the shop. I feel like a fairy princess when Ellie "presents" me in the blue number Doc had first selected, accented by high-buttoned shoes, gloves, and cape. In addition to outfitting me, she had taken it upon herself to fashion my hair under a stylish hat and added the slightest color to my cheeks and lips. His smile is an approving one. Ellie extends a hand to the stack of parcels set aside.

"I will have the rest delivered. Anything not to your taste can be returned." This butt-kissing is worth her initial snobbery. "Where are you staying, Mr. Holliday?" she asks as she extends the change she owes.

"Ah'm sure everythin' is suitable; and please keep that for yor personal attention," he says, laying on the southern charm. "We are stayin' at the Dawson House," he adds.

"Thank you, Sir." I do not have to be a mind reader to know that the woman is regretting her initial arrogance and is reveling in what is probably the largest tip she has ever received. I doubt she will judge future customers by first impressions. Transaction complete, Doc offers his arm and leads me through the door onto the streets of Gunnison.

.

CHAPTER 39

"Your wife?"

"It's for your own protection, Dahlin'," Doc explains devoid of emotion.

"But . . ."

"Trust me, Cassie'; Ellie Carson will have that gossiped all over town before we can make it to the hotel. No one will dare approach the wife of Doc Holliday inappropriately while Ah am out of town."

"You're leaving me in . . ."

"Ah warned yah about my obligation to Wyatt. It will take me out a town for a week or two, maybe more. Yah will stay with Josie. Ah have a feeling the two of yah will hit it off in grand fashion. She's an independent sort, as well."

As we continue our walk to the Dawson House, I again remind myself of our agreement. "When do I get to meet them?" I ask.

"They'll be joinin' us at the hotel for suppah."

Our hotel is without question, the most elegant in town. The lobby is astir with finely dressed couples. While there are several gentlemen by themselves, there are no unaccompanied women.

"Your room is up the stairs and to the right, Mr. Holliday," says the hotel clerk.

Doc holds my hand as we ascend the staircase and

unlocks the door to our assigned room, singular. The implications flood my thoughts. Doc accesses my unease. "Not to worry, "Mrs. *Holliday*", Ah'll be spendin' in the night in the company of Wyatt an' Warren at the gamin' tables."

"Oh . . . I . . . I mean I didn't mean to . . ." the words tripping over my tongue and bouncing off my lips.

"Yes yah did." Doc's smile projects his amusement. "An' shame on yah for questionin' mah moral uprightness. Ah am a southahn gentleman of the highest ordah," he teases.

"I am sorry. I have no reason to doubt your character. You have been nothing *but* the consummate gentleman," I say hoping to assuage any underlying offense. "My Intrusion on your freedom is unforgiveable and I . . ."

Doc brings his fingers to my lips. "That's history. No actual harm has been done, at least not yet, an' Ah trust implicitly in yor futchah discretion. Let's enjoy this little respite, shall we, Mrs. Holliday?" His smile conveys the sincerity of his words. My shoulders relax, but strangely, I find myself disappointed at this declaration. I am trying to sort out the confusion when there is a knock at the door. A minute later, the floor space has been filled with the boxes from the shop.

I sit on the bed and watch Doc ooh and aah as he disperses the contents into the closet. He has been shopping, himself, and several articles of his clothing are already in place. It is then I notice that he is not attired as he was when we arrived in town. When finished, he looks at his watch and suggests that we take a pre-dinner constitutional before opening our door, bowing and sweeping his arm. I pass ahead of him onto the balcony overlooking the elegant lobby, and accept his arm. I will never forget this feeling.

"Remembah to act the happily married woman," he chuckles as we proceed to the staircase. "This is not the twenty-first century. Othahs will expect yah tah listen attentively and agree with yor husband."

Fifty pairs of eyes watch our descent. As if feeling my apprehension, Doc pats my arm with his spare hand while lifting his chin. I get the message, lift my own, and begin to enjoy the attention we are being afforded. Men nod and ladies offer a slight curtsey that I clumsily manage to mimic as we pass them on our way out into the darkness that has fallen since our arrival this afternoon.

Street lamps are lit. Shop owners are locking up for the evening. As we stroll along, Doc begins a serious dissertation on 1880's western protocol for ladies; when and where in town, it is acceptable for ladies to be seen. "When in doubt, ask Josie," he adds.

"Are you going to tell them . . ."

"Do yah think they would believe us?"

"I guess not." I realize that I must take care in my conversations with Mrs. Earp.

Doc spends the next half hour feeding me "our history" so that our answers individually to the Earps will be in sinc. He had traveled directly to Glenwood Springs when he fled Arizona. His health had improved dramatically by aggressive treatment. I was his nurse. He went on to Denver, and after his difficulties there were cleared up, returned for me before heading here. He includes a variety of details that would withstand any interrogation. I am amazed at his ability to spin such a believable yarn in so short a time. I hope I can remember it all when the time comes.

We have come full circle and are outside the hotel. "Got all that, Dahlin?"

"Yes, my husband," I tease, all the while questioning my confidence.

We pass through the lobby into the elegant dining room. It is filled to capacity with what must be the town's elite engaged in quiet conversation as they dine in style. Heavenly aromas start my mouth to water. A beautiful dark-haired woman is waving discreetly. Doc nods and leads us to her table where two handsome men rise in greeting. Their photographs have not done the trio justice. I have to struggle to maintain casualness as Doc makes the introductions.

"God, Doc," says Wyatt firmly grasping his friend's hand while slinging his other arm around Doc's shoulder and pulling him close. "What the hell happened to you?"

Oh my god, I think to myself. Doc was on his last legs when they parted ways only a couple of months ago. In truth,

Doc had been recuperating for some eight months. There is no rational accounting for his transformation. What if? But of course, they would never suspect the truth. I hope that they will just rejoice in his newfound health.

"Why Wyatt, whatevah do yah mean?"

Wyatt scans his friend up and down. "You look . . ."

"I believe the phrase you are strainin' for is 'in mah prime." Doc says as he and Warren shake hands before jointly helping me into my chair. Doc walks around the table to embrace Josie. "You look lovely, as always, My Dear."

Josie clutches Doc's arms. "You've filled out. Tell us, Doc. Are you 'cured'?"

"Thanks tah the mahvels of modern medicine an' the excellent nursin' of a good woman, Ah am right as rain," he says winking at me, "Reports of mah impending death have been retracted."

"I can't get over it," adds Wyatt. "I'm happy for you; and not only for the improvement in your health. It seems your choice in women has drastically improved, as well," he says looking in my direction. I look down as I feel the color race to my cheeks.

"That's something," Warren chuckles. "Never would have seen Kate blush." His comment evokes the laughter of the others and does much to settle my unease. "This calls for a celebration!"

Wyatt motions for a waiter and orders champagne. When it arrives, he makes a toast to our marriage and Doc's continued well-being.

Doc adds, "Hic ad novum in commodo purus vitae et amoris!" None of us asks.

Josie and Doc take the lead in conversation, catching the group up on the last few months. He spins the fictitious tale of our relationship without faltering. Between his narration and answers to the men, the fairytale has been covered in detail. Josie comments on my dress and asks me about life in Glenwood Springs. I answer briefly, letting her draw out the information. The waiter returns giving me a respite, allowing the wagons in my mind to circle. Doc orders for me. Warren and Doc begin a playful banter. Josie and I laugh intermittently, while Wyatt sits, for the most part, listening, confirming the quiet persona history has attributed to him. What can I say; I am in awe of the man and, as the evening progresses, find myself anxious to be alone with Josie, whom he refers to as Sadie, to engage in girl talk.

The Earps present an easygoing air, and it does not take long to dispel my apprehension, though I do not drop my mental guard. I must remember when and where I am. The meal is excellent. I have never tasted such beef. The pecan pie is to die for. After dessert, the five of us walk to the house on the edge of town that Josie and Wyatt share. Rowdiness echoes from the far side of town and even occasional gunfire. Once they have us safe inside, they bid us adieu and promise to return when they are finished with the business.

"I'll make us some coffee, Cassie," says Josie when we are alone. She declines my offer of help, so I take the time she is in the kitchen to drink in the décor that is tasteful and comfortable. Josie returns and sets down a tray upon which are two china cups with matching saucers and silver coffee service. She sits next to me and pours. "I'll let you add your own cream and sugar," she says handing me my cup.

"Thank you," I say. I cannot help but stare as she doctors her own coffee. Unbelievable; I am sitting in the home of Wyatt Earp, talking with his wife in 1882. It crosses my mind that I have been so transfixed by my experience, that I have no idea of the precise date or even what day of the week this is. From the looks of things in town, people are gearing up to celebrate the Fourth of July.

"I can't imagine what the last couple of years have been like for you," I venture.

"I imagine Doc has filled you in and, of course, the escapades in Tombstone have filled papers across the country." She takes a sip of coffee and sets her cup down. "It's been . . ." She pauses. "I was raised with money, lots of it; in San Francisco, a city that offered anything a girl could want. But I was not satisfied. I always have to see and do things I haven't before. I'd heard and read the romanticized adventures in the Wild West. My parents were not happy about my insistence to see it for myself, but they indulged me and financed my quest. They were pleased when I met Johnny; even financed the house we shared in Tombstone. Of course, they weren't thrilled that we were living in sin, but marriage to him would have been a disaster." I sense that in the far-away look in her eyes she is seeing the faces of her mother and father.

"Why don't you and Wyatt go to San Francisco?"

She comes out of her momentary trance. "Oh, we will; eventually," she says setting her cup on its saucer. "Wyatt still has some loose ends to tie up and it's still dangerous for him to travel through Arizona."

"Yes, I guess it would be." I take another sip of coffee.

She pats my thigh. "I am just so happy that Doc is well and has found a good woman. I don't know what he saw in Kate. She was rude and crude, and headstrong. Of course, I have to admit, I'm somewhat willful myself. They fought constantly; sometimes it came to gunplay. I'm surprised Doc survived the relationship. She never had his best interests at heart; but he wined, dined, and clothed her in style. I guess she saved his butt early in the game, but then, she nearly got him killed later on. Doc finally came to his senses and kicked her out for good."

"Where is she now?"

Josie warms our coffees, picks up her cup, and takes a sip before answering. "Last we heard, she was in Globe." I nod. "Doc would never have married that whore; oh, pardon me." She puts a hand to her mouth. "Although, I think she's passed herself off as his wife."

I reach over and pat her thigh. "Think nothing of it. I'm used to Doc, remember."

"It's a short-coming he and I share; tending to say exactly what we think, decorum be damned. Oops, there I go again."

"Damn," I say and we both lean forward and laugh. I like this woman. We engage in easy conversation after that. I pepper her with questions, first about her life in San Francisco; then return to the events in Tombstone.

"It's hard to believe that Ike Clanton and the McLaury clan are still pressing the issue. Unfortunately, Johnny Behan

seems to be abetting their efforts. The matter has been settled in a court of law, twice. Anyone in town, who wasn't on the take, knew exactly what was going on. After the men were exonerated, the cowboys sent death threats to the judge and several others. John Clum had to leave town and was nearly killed on his way to Benson. When Virgil was shot, Wyatt was beside himself. It was becoming more and more impossible to maintain order in town with Behan backing the cowboys. He never said anything to me, but I know he felt the trouble was goaded on by Johnny out of jealousy. It was touch and go for several weeks. Initially, Virgil wasn't expected to live. And when Morgan was killed . .
. I thought that would be the end of Wyatt and Doc. Doc went on a drunken rampage, and Wyatt was in no condition to control him. Then they left Tombstone to take Virgil and the women to accompany Morgan's body to the train. That procession was the saddest thing I've ever seen. You know what happened after that."

I shake my head and remain silent, in hopes she will continue.

"The next week was the bloodiest. Reports started coming in to town that Warren, Doc, Turkey Creek, and Texas Jack were storming through the county with Wyatt hunting the murderers down. At one point, it was reported that Wyatt had been killed. Johnny was thrilled. I thought I would die. Thank God, the truth quickly followed. They got most of the ringleaders in less than a week before we had to flee out of the state. The honest folk in town applauded the swift and merciless executions, but justice has yet to prevail. We had to leave everything. It's a pity; I really liked it there. If the town folk are not careful, Tombstone will become another Charleston or Galeyville. The cowboys will rule and decent folk will be forced out or die at their hands." She sighs but her voice takes on new strength. "But our men are alive and well. I cannot get over how fit Doc appears. He is really well, isn't he; I mean, you being a nurse and all?"

"Even his doctor is surprised at his recovery. In just a little over . . ." I mock a cough to catch myself before I blunder. I take another sip of coffee. "In just a few months, he's breathing freely and gained back his weight. Of course, he will have to be careful from here on out."

"Back in March we were sure he was knocking on death's door. Still, he insisted on riding with Wyatt against the cowboys. I don't know what Wyatt would have done if something had happened to Doc back then . . ." She smiles weakly. "I doubt that Wyatt will ever be the same, at that. He did what had to be done; the only thing that could be done. His heart was in it, but his mind rebelled. All he wants, now, is to settle down to a quiet life and hang up his guns for good. Something has been troubling him of late, though. Bat was here earlier for several days and they have been communicating almost daily since he went back to Trinidad. Whatever is going on, Doc must be a part of it." With her inflection, the statement seems more of a question. I shrug in equal ignorance and pursue another path.

"Bat Masterson?"

"He and Wyatt have been friends since the Dodge City days. Bat tried to help out in Tombstone. I'm not surprised Doc hasn't mentioned him, though. It's a shame they don't like each other much. I think Doc is a little too wild and crazy for Bat's taste. He is the consummate gentleman; though a little put-on, if you ask me; and he has absolutely no toleration for Doc's antics. That's the difference between Bat and Wyatt; Wyatt accepts Doc as he is; knowing he has the qualities that count in a man. I have known of only one incident that threatened their bond. We were in Albuquerque and Doc was quite drunk, as usual. I don't know the details, but he stepped over the line and offended Wyatt. Thankfully, a little time and a rare apology on Doc's part mended the rift. Bat is cordial when he and Doc meet, for Wyatt's sake. He even bailed him out of that trouble in Denver a while back. I know below the surface, Bat must respect Doc; probably is a bit jealous of him, I think. They are both gentlemen; but Doc is a natural. I think Bat has to work at impressing the ladies. As far as I'm concerned, Doc got a raw deal with the consumption. If I was in his boots I'd be squeezing every lick of fun I could get out of the time I had left." She pauses for a minute and a wistful look comes into her eyes. "Anyway, something is up. I can feel it. Wyatt would never tell me and I imagine Doc protects you the same way?"

I smile and nod; then join Josie in a few minutes of silence. She, like me, is no doubt pondering the secret the men are keeping. It is broken by hearty laughter and foot falls on the porch.

"Good evening, ladies," says Wyatt as he and Warren remove their hats and coats and place them on the rack inside the door. Wyatt walks past me to kiss his wife. There is no question as to how much they mean to each other.

As Doc approaches, I lift my cheek to his warm lips. This role, I am finding, requires no acting on my part; and Doc is a master. Warren smiles at the sight. I have been accepted into this exclusive club without reservation. If they only knew.

"You men take care of your business?" Josie asks.

"Doc cleaned up at the Faro table," says Warren. Wyatt had to call him off before the house went broke." Doc bows before taking a seat beside me on the sofa. Wyatt and Warren take the chairs across from us.

"I'll get more coffee," says Josie.

"None for us," says Doc reaching an arm around my waist. "Cassie and Ah are goin' to call it an evenin'. It was a long trip."

He assists me to my feet. Warren and Wyatt rise. Doc helps me on with my coat and we say our goodnights at the door. I hug Josie tightly and accept pecks from the brothers.

"How was yor evenin', Cassie?" Doc asks as we head back toward the hotel.

"You were right; I like Josie. I like her a lot," I answer readily.

"That's good," he says, "since yah will be stayin' with her for a while." Before I can question the notion, he continues. "Our business is takin' us out a town. I don't want yah stayin' by yorself. Wyatt is informin' Josie, as we speak. Ah'm sure she will be delighted not tah be stayin' alone."

"But . . ."

"Need Ah remind yah of our agreement?"

"Of course not. It will be fun."

"She'll show yah 'roun' town and yah can shop tah yor

heart's content; speakin' of which; open yor purse." I pull the small bag apart and Doc quickly stuffs a wad of bills into it before tugging the drawstrings. My mouth is still agape when he adds, "Ah did indeed, have an auspicious evenin'. It's mah trade, yah remembah." He chuckles at my inability to respond.

Doc opens the door to our room and helps me out of the long velvet cape. "As promised, I will leave yah tah yor rest. There is more business requiring mah attention. Ah bid yah a pleasant goodnight an' Ah will see yah in the mornin', Dahlin'."

Before I can protest, Doc is out the door, sans the peck on the cheek I had come to expect. But alas, there is no audience to play for here.

Left to myself, I plop down on the bed. In the excitement of meeting the Earps, until now, I have not noticed the toll that the day has taken on me. The train trip was a little rough compared to modern day transportation. On top of that, I tried on all those dresses; then again, after altering, to make sure the fitting was correct. Then there was the stress of incurring Doc's wrath, being thrown in amongst the elite ladies in town, and meeting the Earps.

Parts of me are aching that have never given thought to before right now. Where modern women dress for comfort, the female attire of the nineteenth century seems to be designed as a punishment. Unlacing my shoes takes a full five minutes after which I begin at the top of a myriad of buttons that run from my neck to several inches below my waist, in the back, of course. If I am really adept, I figure I will be free of this dress and extensive undergarments within the hour.

Twenty minutes later, however, I have silk sheets next to my skin and an honest-to-goodness down comforter for warmth. I think about what Josie had said. Something of monumental concern is in the offing. It brought Doc here, and it will be taking the men out of town. I pray they aren't going back to Tombstone; but where else would they have unfinished business?

CHAPTER 40

I awake to sunlight streaming in through the lace curtains. I am sure I had drawn the burgundy drapes over them before undressing.

"Doc?" I call louder. "Doc?" I swing my legs from under the bedding and don my new robe while sliding into the matching slippers. My first thought is that it is too bad I cannot stay in these comfortable nightclothes all day. I've never heard of old west women doing such a thing or even thinking of it. When in Rome . . . I stretch and take in a long, deep breath, psyching myself up for the ordeal of dressing. I am sure that Doc is out arranging for our breakfast until I spy the note on the vanity mirror.

Cassie,

As I mentioned last night, you will be staying with Josie for the next few weeks. I have arranged for someone to transfer our things to the Earp residence after you check out at the desk. Josie will meet you for breakfast in the dining room around nine. Uh, uh, uh; remember our agreement. You promised to obey. I will be back as soon as our business is concluded. Be safe and enjoy your stay in Gunnison and your time with Josie.

You're a daisy,

Doc

My nostrils fill with fury and there's nowhere to unleash it.

How dare he up and leave without a proper goodbye, without telling me where he was going? Doesn't he trust me? I got him medical attention, saved his life; if the truth be told, nursed him over the past year and served as his personal tour guide to the twenty-first century. The thoughts thunder in my head. How could he . . .

It all begins to unwind as I recall my own reckless actions, following him secretly after letting him believe I would wait patiently for his return to my world. Well, maybe not patiently. He had forgiven my trespass but had not forgotten my potential for rebellion, and I am in no position to impose any restrictions. I feel my blood pressure returning to normal and prepare to enjoy the day with my new friend, *the* Josephine Earp. I choose a dress I decide is suitable for daywear. The corset is a challenge, but I am getting faster at the buttons and laces; and manage to pin up my hair in a way that suits my hat. In spite of the discomfort, I decide I like playing dress-up. Satisfied I look the part, I make my way down to the lobby and find that Doc, true to his word, has arranged for our checkout and for our luggage, now considerable after our shopping spree, to be delivered to the Earp residence. The grandfather clock tells me I am five minutes late for my meeting with Josie who is already seated in the dining room. "Sorry, I'm late," I say, careful to consider the bustle attached to my rear as I sit.

"I just arrived, myself." I cannot imagine Josie being anything but gracious. "I took the liberty of ordering coffee," she says pointing to my still steaming cup. "And I can recommend the Swedish pancakes." She then leans in to inform me that the cook came to Gunnison directly from the old country where his parents ran a fine restaurant. "They are this thin," she adds pinching her thumb and forefinger just an eighth of an inch apart, "so rich and smothered in blackberry butter." After listening to her description, I set the menu aside and let her order for both of us.

After the waiter takes our order, I go straight for the elephant. "Did they tell you where they were going?"

Josie unfolds her napkin and lets it settle in her lap. "All I know is that Bat sent another wire early this morning. Last I heard, he was still in Trinidad. Honestly, I don't know what's going on. They left on the train heading west. I was hoping maybe Doc told you."

I shake my head. "You don't think . . ."

"That they're going back to Tombstone? God . . . I hope not."

"But why . . ."

"I don't know and think we'd best not dwell on it." We sigh in unison. "Besides, speculating on what that bunch might be up to will interfere with our fun, which the men insisted we have while they're out of town. I'm a big believer in having fun." Her laugh is infectious. "After we're done here, we'll go back to the house and get you settled in the spare room. Then, I thought we'd go for a stroll through town. Everything will be closed tomorrow."

I make a mental note that it is Saturday. "Sounds good. I didn't get to see much of it yesterday."

The pancakes live beyond Josie's build-up and I am glad the up-coming walk to work them off. My new wardrobe won't allow for the slightest weight gain. Once at the house, Josie helps me arrange Doc's and my things in the closets and drawers. By eleven, we are on our way out the door.

Once we reach the town proper, Josie becomes an expert tour guide. Although she and Wyatt moved here only a couple of months ago, she has made the town her own. As we enter each shop, Josie introduces me to the proprietor and, in several cases, most of the customers. It is plain from the effortless exchanges, that the town folk respect the Earps. The eyebrows that rise at the introduction of Mrs. John Henry Holliday knit together just as quickly when they hear my name is not Kate. All in town must know of the liaison between Josie's husband and the infamous Doc Holliday. While mention of the name cannot help but stir a reaction, these people have the ultimate respect for Wyatt Earp; that any friend of his is . . . This they extend to me.

"Mrs. Earp and Mrs. Holliday, how good to see you." We have made our way to the dress shop where I spent several hours the day before. "I trust everything was to your husband's satisfaction, Mrs. Holliday?" Ellie Carson is stepping all over herself to erase yesterday's faux pas.

"He loved it all," I respond as if I had no recall of anything but the pleasantness that followed her etiquette lesson.

"I trust you ladies will be coming to the dance on Tuesday?"

"We'll be in town for the festivities, of course," replies Josie, "but our men are away on business, so we'll skip the dance."

"Nonsense; it will be fun," she says winking at Josie. "And I know you're not one to miss out on fun, Josie. Besides, you two are walking advertisements," she pleads. "The shop will do a land office business on Wednesday when they see my frocks on the dance floor."

"We'll think about it."

"What can I show you, today?"

"Actually, I brought Cassie in to introduce her, but I see you already know each other."

I'm not used to thinking on my feet but surprise myself. "The silliest thing," I start, "my trunk was misplaced when Doc and I changed trains." Josie seems satisfied and I suspect Ellie doesn't know what to think except that it's probably best not to comment on my attire at our first meeting and risk my taking offense. "Doc said not to worry, brought me here, and Mrs. Carson outfitted me with a whole new wardrobe."

"Sounds like Doc. Ooh, I can't wait to see the rest of your new things." The three of us laugh. We take our leave and proceed to cross the street, dodging horses and wagons. Time flies by and Josie suggests we stop to eat. "It hasn't been that long since we had breakfast, but I'm starving," says Josie. We stop in at a modest establishment where many of the locals are dining. "It isn't the Dawson House," she whispers, "but the food is wonderful," she adds as we find a table.

The elderly proprietor greets us immediately. Short, rotund, and jolly as Santa, he suggests the special of the day. "Charley's bison stew is the best and his dinner rolls are without rival." We continue "catching up". Josie starts by relating, from her perspective, the recent saga in

Tombstone, including sidebars that never found their way into the history books. Although it is clear how she is biased, there is a certain candor in her delivery. That, and what I have come to learn of Doc solidify my feelings, not only about Doc, but also of the Earps.

It is one thing to read history; although there are widely diverse accounts of episodes, it is quite another to talk with the people who lived through them; to observe their speech and actions in everyday life. I had doubted Doc's blatant honesty; heck, I doubted his identity. I still expect to wake one morning and discover all this is only my imagination gone wild. In his almost helpless state those first several weeks, he lacked the energy to be creative. While a southern gentleman through and through, openly grateful for the care he was given, our discussions on a variety of subjects revealed he cares not about what others think of his actions and opinions save those of his mother when she was alive. Never has he colored his words to curry my favor, and I find his overt honesty altogether refreshing. His return to health has not altered his freeness of speech and thought; and I, in turn, have basked in the comfortable atmosphere his candid association affords. Around him, I can be myself, and know, that even if we are not agreeing, our right to differ is mutually respected. Our arguments do not threaten our friendship. Granted, I pushed his buttons with my time-travel caper; but I think underneath his disapproval, Doc is secretly pleased. And, when you think about it, what right did he have to bar me from his world; I don't remember him knocking before storming into mine.

The more Josie reveals, the more believable her story becomes. I feel I know the facts as well as the true characters of those involved. Her depictions of the individual cowboys paralleled the performance I was privy to at the Birdcage. Few historians have gotten *all* the facts aligned, but I am being blessed with firsthand accounts.

Charley returns with the steaming bowls and Josie and I halt our conversation while we savor the succulent meat and vegetables accented by a slightly spicy gravy; and slather fresh churned butter on our rolls.

"Charley! Over here!" The command sends a confusing chill down my spine. Josie notices my discomfort and reaches across to lay a hand on mine. "Don't mind him," she says nodding at the large man seated alone across the room. It is then I notice that the other patrons are purposely averting their eyes from the scene. More than a few are discreetly shaking their heads. Silence deafens the room.

The large man is dressed all in black and has a mustache and sculptured beard. Their color matches his neatly trimmed thick mane of salt and pepper hair that just tickles his collar. His appearance is imposing, to say the least, but that is not what is jostling my nerves. It is that deep, stern voice, lacking any hint of empathy; echoing in the same timber as my own father's. I steel a glance as he turns to face Charley, who is scurrying to the man's table with no little trepidation. "This meal is totally unacceptable," he says accusingly. And then I become aware of his eyes, hazel flecked with fiery gold that reflects his annoyance. It was my father's piercing glare. I wince as he continues to berate our kindly host who looks as if he is used to the man's culinary disappointment. As the negative review proceeds, Charley takes the offensive bowl from the table. I notice it is empty. "I am so sorry the stew was not to your liking, Reverend Johnston. Let me get you something else," he says meekly.

"No, as a man of the cloth, I cannot tolerate waste. I'm sated with the slop."

"Then, of course, there will be no charge and please, let me send you home with an apple pie for the family." I wonder if the reverend ever pays for meals.

"That will suffice." The man rises and walks toward the door, recovering his hat and coat off the rack while Charley hurries to the kitchen. The food critic takes the pie from him without a word and ducks as he leaves. I am praying that my shaking is confined within. It was as if I had been left in the wake of one of my father's frequent tongue-lashings only this time, I felt anger. As his target, I felt only fear and humiliation as a child, wondering if and when my father would accelerate to physical abuse. Nothing I did could ever meet his standards, and yet I continued to try until I was nearing legal age, and, alas, was banished as an unrepentant sinner. Deep down, I knew it was his problem and the echo of his constant disappointment gradually faded over the last several years. In times of stress, however, the old insecurities turn up the volume. This glaring display, from an objective stance, however, erased any lingering doubt that my father was a monster. This clone had attacked an innocent man. I had witnessed my father's weekly chastisement of his flock, but it was not the same. Individuals in the congregation, with rare exception, took their discipline as part of the group, confident that none of their fellow parishioners were aware that it was their personal sins that were being condemned, confident that their attendance and monetary offering was clearing their slate for the coming week. But this man, for his own personal gain, had sought to humiliate the restaurateur publically. Not only did he cheat the man out of the price of a meal, but also of dessert for his entire family. It was disgusting, and I decide to reassure Charley of his culinary expertise. I will have to stand in line, as many of my fellow diners are beckoning Charley. I watch in approval, as he goes from table to table accepting their condolences.

"You wonder how he can hold on to a congregation, but he does," comments Josie. "Some of these customers, even the ones who consoled Charley faithfully attend his services. We'll go tomorrow and you can see for yourself."

I cock my head. "But why would . . ."

She shrugs. "There are half a dozen churches in town. He appeals to the more rigid worshippers. Everything that can be enjoyable is an offense against God. Not that I believe for a second that his parishioners believe and practice what he preaches any more than he does. They assume that the attendance proves they do and they can feel smug in their righteousness. The Good Book says that pride goeth before a fall, and Reverend Johnston is in for a big one." How well I know.

"Wyatt does not take kindly to hellfire and damnation intimidation; he's a Methodist; think Doc is too."

I nod. "I think so," I say as we return to our meal.

Something underlying is gnawing at me.

While Josie insists this be her treat, she does allow me to take care of the tip in which I include the price of the reverend's meal. She smiles her endorsement. "I can pretty well guarantee you that every diner in the place with the means is doing the same thing. Charley does not suffer in vain."

"I'm bushed," says Josie as we leave Charley's for home. The strain of remembering who and where I am has taken its toll and I am happy to have my thoughts to myself while Josie takes a nap. My mind wanders to the whereabouts of the men and before long, I too, have slipped into a peaceful slumber in a living room chair.

When we awake, the two of us set out a simple supper, after which Josie tutors me in poker. It is several hands before I get the hang of the game and find it a pleasing way to pass an evening. "Do you expect to hear from Wyatt while they are away?"

"I doubt it," Josie answers. "Hopefully, they won't be gone all that long."

"Doc said maybe a month," I throw out.

"A couple of weeks is what Wyatt told me." I hope that she is right.

In spite of anxiety for Doc, the upsetting experience at Charley's, and considering the possible consequences of this time-travel thing, I fall asleep easily and wake rested to the sounds of Josie stirring in the other bedroom. Dressing quickly, I hope to make it to the kitchen first. Last evening, I had been able to familiarize myself enough to be able to make the coffee and prepare a breakfast; but when I enter the kitchen, I smell the coffee, and see that preparation is well underway for pancakes and bacon. But no Josie. I am able to pick up where Josie left off. A few minutes later, she returns.

"I'm sorry. I'm not feeling very well."

The announcement is troubling, as I am out of my element here. "You just sit; I can take it from here. Should I get a doctor?" I ask as I fill the plates and bring them to the table.

"No, I'm just a little tired," she says taking a sip of coffee.

I touch the back of my hand to her forehead. "You don't seem to have a fever."

"It's my stomach. Must have eaten something . . . Are *you* feeling okay?" she asks in reference to the fact that we ate the same things in the last twenty-four hours.

The question is disturbing after that scene in Charley's. What if the reverend had detected something off in the stew and . . . I stop to assess; nonsense, I'm perfectly fine. "Yeah, I feel fine. Maybe it's the flu of some sort or maybe you're just uneasy about the men."

"Could be. Whatever it is, it'll pass. Thanks for finishing up."

"I won't have you waiting on *me* all the time. I need to feel useful. Let me provide the room service." The phrase slips out before I know it, but it goes unnoticed by Josie. I guess that line in the movie was either speculation or pure invention.

"We are going to get along just fine, Cassie. I like you," she says with a smile as she pours the syrup, pure maple, onto her buttered stack. Instead of forking into it, though, she just stares; then takes another sip of coffee. "Excuse me," she says nearly dropping the cup onto its saucer as she rises, hand to her mouth and dashes out of the kitchen.

I sense her need for privacy and decide to wait for her return.

"I think I'll skip breakfast and just lie down a while longer," she says leaning in the doorway. "No don't get up. Finish your food. I'm fine," she adds as she turns to go back to her room.

I finish my own meal and set on tidying up the kitchen. Pumping water, heating it in the large kettle, and pouring it into the sink full of dishes is a little more involved than pushing a few buttons, but it is somehow quite satisfying. After the dishes are dried and set back in the cupboards, I check on Josie. A book from the small Earp library helps stave off restlessness for an hour or so. I tiptoe into Josie. A light hand to her forehead assures me she is not feverish. I pull the comforter up to her chin, and leave her to her rest;

find pencil and paper in the desk draw in the living room and write a short note, before donning my hat and coat.

The street is quiet. Family groups in their Sunday best are on their way in the opposite direction. As I hesitate on the porch, I hear a familiar voice. "Mrs. Holliday, are you heading for Church?"

"I . . . yes . . . I . . ."

"Is Mrs. Earp coming?"

"Uh, no. She's not feeling well this morning, so I—"

"Well, you just come along with my daughters and me," invites my friendly dressmaker. "Girls, this is Mrs. Holliday, a friend of Mrs. Earp. Cassie, is it?" I nod. "Cassie this is Margaret. She is fifteen and her younger sister, Bethany Ann, is soon to be eleven. Now, mind your manners, girls; say hello to Mrs. Holliday."

Mrs. Carson's daughters curtsy as one. "Hello, Mrs. Holliday," they chorus.

"Good Morning Margaret . . . Bethany Ann," I reply.

We pass up the Catholic Church, The Church of the Good Samaritan, and several other attractive edifices before coming to a small, austere building adorned with a simple white cross. I follow the Carsons down the aisle to a pew in front and watch Ellie nod to those already seated. A woman plays a familiar hymn on a small organ as the seating continues. A few minutes later, the music ceases and the organist takes a seat across the aisle from where I sit with Ellie and her daughters. There are several children in the pew with her ranging from young teenagers, one of which holds a baby of maybe eight months, and assorted grade-schoolers. I am tempted to turn at the sound of footsteps coming up the aisle but they, along with my companions, remain rigidly focused toward the front of the church; almost as if they expected that God himself were coming up the aisle. The suspicion that had begun as a tickle up my spine materializes; *this* is The Reverend Johnston's church.

The man takes his place behind the podium, grips its sides, and looks over his audience for a full minute before he begins to speak. "Let us pray." It is not an invitation so much as a command. I rise with the congregation. As I hear the words, I see my father. The invocation lasts for nearly five minutes. It is filled with agonized pleas for God's mercy on us, the assembled, for lethal misdeeds of the past week. In his incantation, the good reverend inventories individual trespasses of members; although not by name, it is evident that regular attenders cannot help but recognize themselves and others. Among those mentioned is a newcomer who has recognized her precarious position with God. He sums it up with a guilt trip designed to open the pocketbooks of the assembled, who are more than willing to trade their money in hopes of reinstating a favorable position with their creator. The old revulsion awakens; not only is the voice my father's, these are his thoughts, his style of presentation, his sanctimonious tone. We sit at his directive. He proceeds with his sermon, an oration on sin and the fires of hell that await the unrepentant. His tongue becomes a cat-o'-nine-tails inflicting stinging blows for over an hour, after which he orders sinners to come to the altar and repent before the congregation. I watch in horror as parents drag their children along and listen to their tearful renditions. Meanwhile, a fishing net is passed among the parishioners. I had thought that was a more modern adaption meant to embarrass tithers into larger donations than they might be able to afford. Even small children have their dollars ready. Nausea threatens when I hear Mrs. Carson urging her daughters to join the procession, while she, herself, remains seated. Frozen beside her, I wince as I feel her scrutiny, no doubt assured that the wife of the infamous Doc Holliday can hardly be free of sin. It is not that I am determined to stand my ground in the face of this hypocrisy; I honestly cannot move. If I could, I would flee down the aisle in the opposite direction and out the door into God's tabernacle of fresh air and benevolence.

Finally, the reverend calls for another prayer, shorter this time, and a final hymn. After the final note, the chapel becomes awash with conversation. I resist a cringe as the organist approaches, the toddler on her hip. "Hello," she says in a kindly tone. "Welcome to our humble church. I am Mrs. Johnston; you can call me Laura. And this is Joanna."

At the sound of her name, the baby hides her face in her mother's neck.

I swallow and find my voice. "I'm Cassie Holliday," I offer watching for the telltale disgust, but there is none. "Your daughter is beautiful," I add and mean it.

"I'm so glad you joined us, today. Are you a new resident or just visiting?"

"No, I'm staying with a friend while our husbands are out of town on business." I am suddenly struck by the feeling that I know this person. Logic argues that this is impossible; still . . .

"Do I know the family?"

"Wyatt and Josephine Earp," I say still waiting for a shoe to drop.

Laura Johnston remains impervious to the revelation. Either she has surpassing restraint or she secretly does not share her husband's prejudice. "I don't believe I've met them," she says looking around. "Are they with you today?"

"Mr. Earp and my husband are away and Mrs. Earp is not feeling well," I reply wondering how she cannot be aware of the famous lawman in the midst. Then again, maybe she doesn't get out much with that brood of children in her care. Whatever the reason, am thankful for the momentary anonymity. Beyond her, however, I see Mrs. Carson's wagging tongue and the group before her stealing furtive glances in my direction. Apparently, Doc's generous gratuity did not buy her respect for anything but his financial standing. "Are you going to be with us for long, Mrs. Holliday?"

"I'm sorry, what was that? I'm sorry, my mind wandered for a bit." Laura repeats her inquiry. "I'm not sure; it depends on Mr. Holliday's return at this point."

"Well, we hope to see you again next week if you're still in town."

"Yes, thank you," I say. Over my dead body, I think.

Suddenly Ellie Carson is upon us. "Excuse me, Laura, I want to introduce Mrs. Holliday to the reverend. Isn't that one of your son's running around the pews?" Laura excuses herself to tend to her little sinner. Before I can beg off, Ellie is ushering me down the aisle through the front door to join the line of parishioners waiting to praise their leader for his service. It is all I can do to keep from bolting.

As I wait in line, I study the reverend's face; trying to imagine him clean-shaven. It is a foolish contemplation, I know. There is no way . . . then suddenly we are face-to-face, and I am vaguely aware of Ellie's introduction. He is shaking my hand weakly as if I were a carrier of iniquity with which he might become infected. I recall the scene in Tombstone where Doc, when introduced to Sheriff Behan, eloquently evades the handshake of the man he despises. In spite of his slightly disguised revulsion, he continues to hold my hand in his, as if there is some deeper connection.

The preacher's tone is reserved. I had no doubt insulted him by not lining up for absolution. I can almost read his thoughts. Of all in attendance this Sunday, surely the wife of Doc Holliday has the most to be forgiven. It is plain that one must *earn* a place in his favor and few make the grade. His eyes bore into mine and it is all I can do to hold his gaze. Again; the feeling of de je vu. I tell myself that my father was not the only hypocritical preacher in the world, but is it possible . . .

It becomes clear that Ellie feels it necessary to account for my lack of public contrition. "Mrs. Holliday, here, is not familiar with our customs, Reverend. She and her husband are friends of the Earps. Her husband is Doc Holliday." I know full well she had already alerted him to my identity. She has no idea how transparent she is, relishing every minute of this gossip disguised as innocent data. I can just picture her on Facebook. Then, alluding to my earlier faux pas, she adds, "Give her another week or so and she'll feel comfortable with us and the routine."

"Yes, I imagine so," he says finally retrieving his hand. I'll bet he cannot wait to wash it. If only Doc was here; but then, he wouldn't have set foot in this den of duplicity.

The reverend quickly turns his attention to Ellie. "I see you had nothing to confess again this week, Mrs. Carson. I commend you for your self-mastery, but remind you that even the most disciplined among us can never be faultless for long." Yeah, I think, and to whom do you confess?" I take advantage of their interaction to move on; and I can see the reverend is grateful to be rid of me.

"Don't run off, Cassie. We want to see you safely to your door," Ellie says as I trail away before answering the reverend. I stop within earshot as I am dying to know how she answers her spiritual leader.

"I try very hard to resist the devil, Reverend. Of course, a widow like me with children to raise alone, and having to make our living, doesn't get much opportunity to get into trouble; idle hands and all," she titters. "I thank the good Lord for the burden. I try to set a good example for Margaret and Bethany Ann, but as you heard, I am failing in some way, there. You're right, Reverend, I should have confessed to my deficient mothering." Apparently, neither party is familiar with the sin of self-righteousness.

As I linger, several other women introduce themselves, but as soon as they associate the name Holliday with the Earps, bid hasty retreats and shrink away. It is too much and I decide to head back to the house sans the Carson entourage. I am happy to see Josie up and about in the kitchen.

"I'm feeling much better," she offers. "Did you have a nice walk?" When I told her of my experience, she started to laugh. "I'm sorry, If I'd known you were going I would have warned you. I can just imagine what goes on in that church. And that Ellie Carson; she is so proud of her respectability. She's only nice to me because we spend money in her shop. I can just imagine what is said behind my back."

"I'm afraid I've added fuel to the fire." The two of us burst out laughing, long and hard. "You really are feeling better."

"I'm feeling wonderful. I told you it would pass." Josie says as she cuts another slice of bread. "And, see," she adds as she spreads it with butter. "I'm making up for the breakfast I missed."

I spend the afternoon reading while Josie sits mending Wyatt's shirts. We have an early supper of sandwiches and spend the evening playing poker before we take to our beds where my concern for Doc invades my thoughts. Although his coughing spells are mild and rare, now, he is still on medication that he must continue to take until this last prescription runs out, in spite of his remarkable recovery. The doctor made that very clear. How silly of me to think that he will not be conscientious without my nagging.

That dismissed, my mind wanders to my own predicament. There is absolutely nothing to guarantee that I will be able to return to the twenty-first century. What if something happens to Doc on this secret mission? The portal does not respond to my touch. How long has it been there? Would it open to other than Doc? Is it permanent (what a wonderful thought; that we could come and go between our two worlds), or will it disappear? Thankfully, exhaustion takes me.

CHAPTER 41

I wake with a start. When I sit up, I find that my nightgown is wet from perspiration; my heart pounding. I try to recall the disturbing tableau that has prompted the upset, but it is just out of reach. Although I can no longer discount the ability in others, I have never been the least bit intuitive in the paranormal sense. The supernatural developments of the last year have opened my mind to most anything. It now swirls with possibilities. Is the elusive dream a message? Are Doc and I somehow connected telepathically? Has he been hurt or worse? I have no idea where he is. I pull my knees up to my chin and wrap them in my arms. For several minutes, I rock back and forth, trying to view my dilemma objectively, but the more I think about it, the more disturbed I become. Rejecting all thought, I spring out of bed and pour water from the pitcher into the basin. Splashing the wet coldness on my face helps shake my mind's hypothetical wanderings.

Sunshine is pouring into the room through the east window. It is a beautiful day in 1882. Again the unease. What will my life be like if Doc never returns from hi mysterious business with Wyatt? What if I never get back home . . . to Florissant . . . in 2016? How ridiculous. History, as it stands, tells me Doc survives until 1887; that Wyatt and Josie wind up in Los Angeles; that he lives a long life and so does she. Then I remind myself of my interference with the past. Doc's fate will be different now that he is not on the fast track for death by consumption. How will my presence in the lives of Wyatt and Josie affect them? I am decidedly out of my realm and am able to reign in my insecurity by remembering the adage about accepting what cannot be changed. After all, I chose to challenge the laws of physics and agonizing over the consequences at this stage of the game is pointless. It is not the first time my world had turned upside down; and although the initial trigger for the first change had been a tragic loss, my life had improved dramatically on several fronts. I dwell on the interim events. I have yet to learn if Mary's life improves now that Doc and I moved that safe. If fate takes Doc and cannot return to my present, at least I might return to my home and set that concern to rest. With knowledge of the future, I would be able to make a nice life in the past.

Oh, I must dismiss this conjecturing. It is doing nothing to ease my trepidation of my present fix. I force myself with the positives of the here and now. I think of the pleasure of Josie's company and know I would not trade it for my world as I know it. Doc and Wyatt are intelligent, determined men and will return soon. I can feel it.

The house is still quiet. I head for the kitchen, light a fire in the stove, and set the coffee on to brew. I am on my second cup when Josie appears in the doorway. She seems to be pale and I wonder if whatever it is that plagued her yesterday is lingering. "Josie, what is it?"

"I'm just a little tired," she answers. "Didn't sleep too well last night. I guess I'm worried about the men. I think you're right about the stress affecting my stomach," she says crossing the room to pour herself a cup of coffee. "That's better," she says as she takes a sip, then comes to sit across from me. I try to read her face to assess the level of worry.

My need for commiseration overcomes my determination to forego speculation. "I'm worried, too," I sigh out. "Are you sure you don't have some clue as to where they are and what they are doing?"

She shakes her head; her expression is taking her far

away for a time; then refocuses to look at me. "But I'm afraid they went back to Arizona."

"But why? I thought . . ."

"So did I." We drink our coffee in silence, neither wanting to voice the fears we share.

"I'll make us some eggs and toast," I finally say. Josie nods and has another cup of coffee while I pull out the cast iron pan. Josie picks at her food but I am not worried after what I saw her eat yesterday, and she does seem to be feeling better. I realize that our discussion has dampened my appetite as well.

Chores done, we opt to take a walk in another of the residential areas of Gunnison. For a town that was established only three years ago with tents and crude log cabins of gold miners, Gunnison has blossomed rapidly. The lure of gold will do that. Josie points out several homes of prominent citizens and relates their contributions to the town. Italian and French influence can be seen in the architecture of many of their houses. As we return to the business district, Josie explains that Gunnison is host to three schoolhouses, six churches, two banks, and seven hotels. Four newspapers serve the community. We pick up the Gunnison Daily Review to read later.

"We'll have the men take us for some entertainment when they return," she says as we pass the impressive Smith Opera House. Along our route, we pass the Land Office and stop in at the Post Office. "Do you need any stamps?" she asks. "It has been a while since I wrote home. My parents worry ever since Tombstone. Do you have family in Glenwood?" For once, I do not have to lie. I tell her my parents died in a tragic accident about a year and a half ago. She offers belated condolences and thankfully, does not press for details I would be hard pressed to invent.

Tempting aromas call to us from the Vienna Bakery. Josie introduces me to the owner and picks out a couple of pastries to complete our noon meal. "You can find anything you need in this shop," she says as we pass Shilling and Company Dry Goods. Proprietors all along the way are preparing for the big celebration tomorrow. There are banners spanning Main Street and I am anxious to be a part of an old-fashioned Fourth of July.

"What's down there," I ask indicating the far end of the street.

"That's out of bounds for ladies," Josie answers as I strain to see into the distance. With a closer look it is evident that this block is Gunnison's red light district sporting dance halls, brothels, and saloons. "Wyatt deals faro in one of the saloons."

We cross the street and head back to the house where we sit down to dinner, as the noon meal is termed in this world. My mind is on the pastry that will follow and I eat accordingly. Josie, on the other hand is ravenous, and before we finish our dessert, is thinking of our next meal.

"After we clear this away, let's go back to town to the butcher shop and pick out a couple of thick pork chops for supper. We'll catch the vegetable vendor and pick out whatever looks good. There are potatoes in the cellar and apples—"

I am amazed at Josie's resiliency in the face of grief and her enthusiasm is infectious. "I can bake a pie!" I offer. She pops the last bite of bread into her mouth and together we take care of cleaning up. I cannot remember having so much fun with another woman in a kitchen, no mother-daughter time over cookies. We had a cook and a housekeeper while I was growing up. When I started out on my own, I lived mainly on fast food or microwave reheatables. It was only after my sudden windfall and the move to Colorado that I had begun to experiment with the culinary arts.

I meet several more of the town folk on our afternoon expedition and find it easier to stay "in character" while conversing with the curious. Doc's scenario was straight-forward and living in the nineteenth century did not lend itself to a slew of complications that need explanation. The thought crosses my mind that I might make a fair actress, although the spirit is far from willing.

By three, we are back at the house. Josie takes a nap while I busy myself with the apple pie. I do miss the apple peeler I have in my kitchen at home. With that nifty little gadget I would have the apple prep done in ten minutes. It takes me almost an hour with just a knife. This is the first time I have used lard for a crust, and I find the spices in Josie's cupboard more pungent than the ones from modern grocery stores. Under Josie's expert tutelage, I have gotten the hang of getting the woodstove temperature just right, and by five o'clock, I am proud of the pie cooling in the kitchen window. I have just put our potatoes into the oven and am starting to season the pork chops when Josie peeks her head around the corner.

"The aroma of the pie woke me," she says with a yawn. Josie takes the basket of green beans we purchased earlier and begins to snap off the ends. As we work, I question Josie more about her family and life in San Francisco. Her eyes dance as she tells of the gaiety; and yet it is easy to see how an intelligent young woman like herself might get bored and yearn for something different. Sometime during our conversation, I wonder how the Marcus's will fare in the up-coming earthquake; if they are still alive and living there when the San Andreas Fault tears the city apart as it shifts beneath her. I long to tell my new friend so many things, but . . . Maybe Doc . . .

The pork chops are incredible. I think about raising a pig and a steer but question whether I could bear to part with them when it comes time for them to move from pasture to freezer.

"You've done yourself proud with this pie," says Josie as she swallows her first bite. "You and Doc should think about settling down here. I didn't hear either of you mention that you'd put down roots anywhere yet."

"Doc has been concentrating on recovering and then getting back to Wyatt. We haven't had time to make any permanent plans," I say guiltily; knowing full well, I have decided to keep him in the future with me. "Where do you think you and Wyatt will end up?"

"We plan on traveling. I'm afraid I bore easily and there's so much of the world I have yet to see, "she says with a far off look. An idea is born: What if Josie and Wyatt were to come back with us and . . . There is no doubt that Josie would be open to the idea if I could get her past thinking I had lost my mind. Something to ponder.

We are in the throes of a lively poker game when we hear a knock. "I wonder who that could be," says Josie. "We don't usually get many callers, especially this late in the evening. The Earp reputation scares most people off." I watch as she takes a large revolver out of a desk drawer. She cocks and holds it at her side as she approaches the door. Why I am holding my breath, I don't know. Carefully, Josie pulls aside the curtain from its paned window. She looks right and left a second time. "There's no one there," she says as she uncocks the forty-five.

"Maybe it wasn't a knock; just something blowing up against the door? It is pretty windy out there," I suggest, recalling my own encounter with a wooden prowler.

"Probably," she says returning and laying the gun on the table instead of returning it to its place. We resume the game, but in the middle of the hand, Josie gets up. "I'm going to check the back door and make sure all the windows are latched," she says in a voice that is too controlled and higher than normal.

"Is something wrong?" I ask when she returns.

She seems to be debating before she answers. "I'm sure everything's fine, and I'm grateful for your optimism; I think we both know someone knocked." I nod. "It's the first time the men have been out of town overnight, and not everyone in town is . . ."

My lightness of heart takes on weight. "Are you saying you have enemies in town?"

"Wyatt is either a hero or murderer wherever he goes. There's no middle ground and there are still people bent on hauling him back to Tombstone. If they succeed, he'll be dead. Doc must have mentioned Perry Mallon?"

"Uh, yes; that was a close call."

"If it wasn't for Bat, Mallon might have secured the extradition, not only of Doc, but of Wyatt and Warren, as well, if he could have found them or engaged the assistance of those who knew where we were."

"From what Doc says, Mallon is finished."

"That may or may not be true, but he's not the only one," she says with a sigh. "It's not fair; the whole thing should be finished; but I guess as long as the surviving cowboys are protected by John Behan . . ." Josie turns her head; a fist goes to her mouth. I jump to her side and cradle her head under my chin, my arms wrapped tightly around her. It is as much to comfort myself.

"I didn't mean to alarm you, Cassie, and I'm not usually this emotional."

"You've gone through a lot before coming here and, like you said, it's the first time the men have been gone. Maybe it would be a good idea to sleep in the same room until they get home. You wouldn't have another pistol around here would you?"

"As a matter of fact . . ."

A half hour later, we are satisfied that the house is secure and are settled in Josie and Wyatt's room, a forty-five within reach of each of us. An inane thought crosses my mind. I am sleeping in Wyatt Earp's bed. I stop short of mentioning it to Josie. The implication would be lost on her. Despite the proximity of another human, I anticipate a restless night.

CHAPTER 42

I awake to cheerful humming. Not only have I slept uninterrupted, something seems to have erased Josie's unease of the night before. I throw on my robe and shuffle into my slippers. The kitchen is filled with a plethora of aromas.

"Oh," says Josie, noticing my confusion. "I thought I'd fry chicken for a picnic lunch to take to the celebration," she says as she spoons up oatmeal into the bowls. "We have leftover pie and I'm making potato salad and baking bread. I got really ambitious and decided to bake gingerbread for later."

"You must have gotten up before dawn," I say.

"I was a little restless after last night. Oh, I feel a little silly, now. As soon as the sun came up, I opened the front door and look what I found," she says pointing to the large packages on the chair in the living room. "Go ahead; I already opened mine," she says smiling broadly.

I pull on the cloth bow; and open the box. "Wyatt and Doc bought us something for the celebration before they left and arranged for the delivery," she explains as I hold the dress up by the shoulders in front of me and clasp an arm to my midsection. It is red linen trimmed with blue and white ribbons. "Mine is blue with red and white ribbons. Our neighbor across the way was entrusted to deliver them last night, and, according to Wyatt's note, keep an eye on us. I feel so foolish; Wyatt would never have left unless he knew we would be safe."

I breathe a sigh of relief and know that she is right. These are men who take their responsibilities seriously; and although I am not really his charge, Doc has taken it upon himself to see to my well-being. I pray that he is as safe.

"Now, come on and eat your breakfast; you'll need stamina for the full day. Activities are planned from morning till night. There'll be fireworks and everything!"

We are on our way by ten. Main Street is astir. The whole town has turned out.

"My, don't you ladies look festive." The man is just releasing the brake on his wagon as Josie and I are passing.

"Cassie, this is Milt Gregory, our guardian angel while the men are away." The rough looking character blushes.

"Hello, Mr. Gregory," I say extending my hand.

"Nah, nah; none of this Mr. Gregory nonsense; I'm Milt to my friends. And don't you ladies worry about a thing. I've got you covered while your men are away. You can rest easy."

Josie nods. "Thank you, Milt. Join us for a picnic lunch. We made plenty," she says waving the basket.

"I am obliged, Josie, but the Widow Bailey beat you to it," he says with a sheepish grin. "I'm on my way to pick her up now."

"Maybe we'll see you later," says Josie.

"Likely not," says Milt with a wink. Color fills his cheeks again and, no doubt, at the realization of what he is implying, quickly adds, "But I'll be back at the house before dark to watch over things."

"You and the Widow Bailey have a wonderful day, Milt," says Josie.

"Nice to meet you . . . Mr?

His mock frown reminds me. "Milt."

We spend the morning watching children engaging in a number of games apparently organized for the celebration, then gather at the bandstand to listen to the musicians in town give their all to the patriotic tunes. Shortly thereafter, we find a spot under a tree in a large park-like area and spread our blanket. Other families are dotted here and there around us including Mrs. Johnston and the children, but minus the reverend. I am lifting the glass of lemonade to my lips when I feel a forceful blow to the back of my head, sending the glass and its contents spewing all over me and the skirt of Josie's dress. Surprised, but unhurt, we laugh.

"Joshua!" The shout is immediately followed by a piercing wail. We turn to see Mrs. Johnston yanking her young son by the arm heading in our direction.

"I am so sorry, ladies," she says. "My children know they aren't supposed to be playing ball near the picnickers. Joshua, apologize to Mrs. Earp and Mrs. Holliday," she demands sternly.

"It's okay; really it is," says Josie.

"No it isn't. When you have children, I trust you will appreciate the necessity of discipline. Now Joshua!"

"I'm sorry." Joshua must be all of five and shaking in terror. We accept his apology, and not wanting to offend his mother, refrain from further watering down the offense.

"Now go sit down on our blanket and wait for your father," she says firmly.

"Again, I am very sorry, ladies. Send your dresses to me for launder tomorrow."

"That won't be necessary," says Josie and I add my assurance.

"Please sit with us a minute," I say in hopes of getting to know her better. "I admire your ability to handle so many children. They sat so still during the church service the other day."

Mrs. Johnston relaxes and almost smiles. I guess her to be fortyish.

"How many are there?" I ask.

"Three sons and five daughters." As she answers proudly. I am drawn to the locket suspended on a velvet cord on her bodice. Unconsciously reach for my own. It is not there. The chain is there and intact, but the locket is not. I run my fingers along and around the length of the chain. I panic, trying to remember when I last was aware of it. It is one of the few possessions of my father's that I chose to keep. I assumed the picture inside the locket were of the parents of whom he never spoke. No matter my dress, I had worn it constantly over the past year and a half.

"That's a beautiful locket," I say without thinking.

"Thank you. I'm not given to adornment, but my husband had it made for me with our wedding bands," she says opening the locket. "The picture is of us on our wedding day, almost 25 years ago."

I stare in disbelief and clutch at my throat. The picture is identical to the one that should be around own neck. How did she . . . "It's lovely," I finally say working hard to suppress my confusion. I study her face, and see the resemblance under lines of age and a difficult life; and recognize, too, the reverend sans the years and the beard. Just then, a disturbance on the Johnston picnic site has the mother excusing herself.

"Are you all right?" asks Josie.

I am not, but have no idea how I would explain what is troubling me. "I guess it's all the excitement," I say. "I think I need some more lemonade." Josie refills my glass as I make a mental note to check the house and my belongings for the missing locket. In all the mayhem of the last few days, I must have . . . I know I had it on when I left home. At least I think I did. Oh, I have no idea whether it was lost in this world or my own.

But that does not explain the picture. Where did my father get his locket? He always denied knowing his heritage. I can't imagine he would a carry a picture adopted by some agency for general use in vintage lockets? Did my father, who claimed to be raised an orphan, purchase it in some attempt to . . . If that is the case, my locket has no real meaning and is not a great loss. Or was the piece among whatever personal belongings accompanied him to the orphanage? The latter is the scenario I had adopted, as a slender thread to my past.

The rest of the day is filled with music, a lively parade, and patriotic speeches by the town's elite, including Reverend Johnston who manages to bring out a wet blanket, reminding the citizens to restrain themselves; that this is a solemn occasion, not an excuse for revelry. My father could not have said it better himself.

Josie and I are escorted home by Milt, who seeks us out after the fireworks. We opt not to tease him about the Widow Bailey lest we stifle the romance. After saying our goodbyes, Josie and I enter her home and head for separate rooms tonight.

Despite my despair over the missing locket, I fall asleep quickly and sleep soundly.

.

CHAPTER 43

I wake early and examine the chain on my locket. The ring to which the locket was attached is in place so the ring on the locket itself must have weakened and given way at some point. Quietly, I make a search through my own belongings and the house for the elusive locket. When I resign myself to having lost it en route or at home, I am disheartened. I remind myself that things, no matter how precious, are not worth grief. I get busy in the kitchen.

True to her word and heedless to ours, Mrs. Johnston arrives to pick up the soiled dresses. My protestations fall on deaf ears. I relent, gather them up, and hand them to her with hearty thanks. She makes a point to assure me that Joshua was duly punished by his father when they returned home yesterday evening. The vision of the two of them in the proverbial woodshed pains my heart. I am a firm believer in discipline. God knows that the youth of the modern world have run amok amidst widespread permissiveness. "Spare the rod and spoil the child" has been disposed of as abuse, when, in truth, a few whacks on the backside are not out of place when verbal censure fails to correct the problem. On the other hand, there are parents, as Doc mentioned earlier, who should have never been allowed to propagate; who beat and mentally abuse not so much for disobedience as for their personal annoyance. More often than not, they neglect the everyday instruction that would do much to preclude their children's misbehavior. I am sure, however, that this is not the case in the Reverend's domain. Although I was never corporally punished, I remember wishing I would be switched instead of verbally assaulted. Physical pain fades, emotional endures. I fear, however, that the Johnston household doles out both liberally.

Josie and I are becoming closer with each new day. I have to bite my tongue regularly to keep from revealing my unbelievable secret, as, at her hand, I am tutored in a life sans modern amenities. I think about the value of this information. Who knows? There may come a time in the future when, despite all my backup systems, I might have to resort to primitive resources. Josie, despite her self-proclaimed indulgent upbringing, is not averse to the physical labor required of a pioneer wife. She is an excellent cook, housekeeper, and gardener. She educates me in the art of bread making without the convenience of my modern bread-maker. She informs me that her culinary aptitude has been recently acquired.

"I quit acting when Wyatt and I got together and since have concentrated on the domestic arts I would never have had to master in San Francisco where we had servants. I'm learning to knit," she says pointing to a basket in the corner. It contains several balls of yellow yarn, a large pair of needles, and the beginning of a simple project. "I'm afraid I'm not doing too well. Wyatt tells me not to worry about it. He says we'll be much too busy seeing the world."

On the sixth, little Joshua Johnston appears at our door struggling to keep our freshly laundered dresses from touching the ground. He apologizes again. My heart melts and I invite the lad in for cookies and milk. His little face lights up; but then, he declines the invitation. I know he is fearing further reprisals, perhaps for lingering.

"Do you think your parents would mind if you helped us with a chore? You see, our men are gone and . . ." He looks puzzled, but I can see the hope in his eyes. "It's just that Josie and I are a little tired and we need someone to chop and stack some wood. Do you think you could help us?"

"Sure, Mrs. Holliday. I'm supposed to help people

whenever I can." I follow as Josie leads Joshua out to the woodpile. For a young boy, he wields an ax pretty well.

A few minutes later he is at the table with Josie and me; his beaming smile adorned by a milk mustache. I dab it off while Josie writes a quick note to his mother explaining his tardiness.

CHAPTER 44

As the days pass, we fill them with exploring the town, knitting, cooking, and baking, our nights with poker and girl talk. Josie's on-going narration of the Tombstone anecdotes allays my fears for what the men may be dealing with presently. History tells me they survive this time, as well. Of course, I remind myself that this is before I interfered. However, I choose to believe that my well-intentioned meddling will be of little, if any, negative consequence in the larger scheme of things. I think about all the books I've read over the last years and the movies I've seen from Law and Order starring Harey Carey made shortly after Wyatt's death to the most recent films Tombstone and Wyatt Earp; the myriad of different takes on what really happened, what type of men Wyatt and Doc really were. One author, who interviewed Wyatt, believed he was a cold-blooded killer, suave and manipulative, while others depict him as a most honorable man who was pushed into regrettable circumstances that forced his hand.

Doc has been painted as a quick-tempered drunk who loved to kill, although loyal, without question, to Wyatt. In all that I had watched and read in reference to both men during the months Doc was recuperating in my home, veracity has filtered down. While quite capable of acting, my gut feeling tells me he loathes pretense. The multitude of comments from a variety of sources, while widely contradictory, reveal a very basic truth about Wyatt. Those who skirted or flagrantly ignored the law hated the man for interfering with their illegal pursuits; the peaceful, law-abiding factions recognized his dilemma in trying to maintain order in politically charged arenas. As for Doc, I think he behaved as many might have, given the hand he'd been dealt up to the time he fell into my world. Growing up in the midst of the Civil War and the havoc it wrought upon the nation and his own family, he remained a staunch advocate of the essential principles of human decency and emerged into adulthood an educated gentleman with a respectable profession, only to have his efforts nullified by a most unfortunate diagnosis. His dreams of love, vocational prosperity, and longevity were shattered. His transfer to a more favorable environment had proved less than effective. Disappointment evolved into bitterness at the injustice of it all, and he set out to rescue what he could out of the few years he had before him. Robbed of his profession, lest he infect others, he optimized his God-given dexterity and became adept with cards and guns. Notwithstanding his southern gentry breeding and upbringing, he was freed from the compulsion to please at the cost of honesty; and thus, spoke his mind eloquently without reservation, ever-willing to back up his words, if challenged. His turn to alcohol for both mental and physical relief had further loosened his reckless tongue. Although his body weakened and dissipated and his physical presence was less than impressive, he was feared for his quick temper and his prowess with firearms. While his directness often spurred the anger of others, most turned away to postpone a premature trip to the mortuary. In actuality, few men died at his hand, but a bloodthirsty reputation was fueled by those who were envious of him, and idol gossipers loathe to pass on a story without embellishment.

But I . . . I have been privileged to know both these men. Wyatt, at the moment, is troubled by the events of his recent past. He still mourns the loss of Morgan and the maiming of Virgil. While Josie praises his every move as valiant, it is clear from his quietude that he refuses to be gratified by his actions. He is a man living with a heavy burden, determined to avoid future confrontation that might involve bloodshed. Wyatt is resolute, from what I can see, to lead a peaceful life. The conclusion comforts me, as its natural inference is that the current mission is an important, yet peaceful one.

Doc and I have spent much more time together. In sickness and in health, I find his rudimentary nature consistent; and as his health improves, so does his forbearance. Out from under the premature death sentence, Doc's basic temperament evidences his love for life. He is discriminating when it comes to people and requires a standard of deportment that has largely been lost in the modern world. He cannot abide stupidity and is able to distinguish it from ignorance that he will freely remedy, if invited. I find his candor refreshing and admire his ability to weed through people and gather the flowers of humanity into a bouquet, albeit a small one, that enhances his environment. In all our encounters with weeds, I have yet to be embarrassed by his rejection of their company. Not all who take exception to his directness dismiss him easily, and in those cases, a tenuous relationship is sparked; and further interaction leads to friendship.

CHAPTER 45

It is Monday, the tenth. After breakfast this morning, we walk around town, stop for the noon meal at Charley's, and then to purchase a chicken from the butcher. It is my turn to cook. A custard pie is baking in the oven. After picking lettuce and tomatoes from her garden and retrieving potatoes from the cellar, Josie retires for a nap.

As I busy myself preparing the rest of the meal, I am amazed at the vibrant flavors of food in this age before hormones and pesticides. The thought crosses my mind that if I never get back, I may not miss the twenty-first century. Who am I kidding? That reminds me; I have yet to record any of my adventure.

My camera and camcorder are still safely tucked in my saddlebags, now in the trunk that Doc purchased to accommodate my newly acquired wardrobe. Checking to make sure Josie is still asleep, I retrieve them and proceed to film the interior of the Earp home. Confident no one is within sight, I film the outside as well, and with zoom lenses, get views of Gunnison up the road from the house. What I will do with this documentation, the future will tell.

Mission accomplished, I am burying my modern technology when I hear the scream from Josie's room. She is sitting on the edge of the bed holding her mid-section while looking behind her. Rushing to her side, I see the bloodstain. After all, she is about my age, I would guess, maybe a few years older. Certainly . . . "Josie, it's okay. It's just . . ."

"No!" she wails. "Get the doctor!"

Torn between leaving her alone and going for help, I opt to lie her back down and then tear out the front door and turn to run toward the doctor's office that Josie had pointed out on one of our tours.

"Cassie!" It is Milt, on his horse just coming back from the mines.

"Oh, Milt, Josie needs the doctor right away!" The man is off before I finish my plea and I run back to Josie who is now sobbing in earnest.

"This can't be happening," she cries.

It all fits, her tiredness, the queasy stomach. Josie is pregnant; at least she was. It seems somewhere I read that, while she and Wyatt never had any children, she had a series of miscarriages. My heart goes out to my friend. If my invading the past can have any effect, I pray it will change this.

Within several minutes, Dr. Clements arrives. Milt and I sit at the kitchen table. "I had no idea," I say lamely.

"I saw the glow in her eyes a few weeks ago," says Milt. "My Martha never had to tell me. I knew within a few days when the next little Gregory was due to arrive; was there for every birthin'."

"How many children did you and your wife have?" I ask. I have a fierce need to pass the time with positive information.

"Eight altogether; four sons and four daughters. Lucy didn't make it the last time, twin girls born too early to survive. That was twenty-seven years ago." At the reminiscence, a tear rolls down his cheek.

"Your other children?"

"Oh, scattered about. Milt Jr. was killed at Bull Run. Got two sons went to New York where the wife was from. The other lives in Denver. They all got families. The two girls went back east, too; felt the primitive west killed their mom; can't blame 'em." Lucy's buried out behind the house with the twins. I'm here to stay."

We are staring off in that direction when the doctor clears his throat.

"Mrs. Earp will be fine with several days' bed rest," he announces as if it is an accomplishment. Before I can ask, he lowers and shakes his head. "She was about twelve weeks along," he adds solemnly.

I feel my heart breaking. If anyone deserves a good turn, it is Wyatt and Josie. So much loss in so little time. I wonder if Wyatt knew about the pregnancy before he left. What a devastating homecoming.

"It's good that you're here, Mrs. Holliday. She'll need help. I gave her something to sleep. Call me if she needs anything and make sure she stays in bed," says the doctor.

"I'll see myself out," he says when I start to rise.

For a moment, I am frozen; then drop my head into my hands. Sobbing grips me as I felt it should but did not when my parents died. Milt takes me in a gentle headlock and I feel his own tears dripping on my shoulder.

His words are choked out, "At least our Josie is okay," he says squeezing me tightly. "At least Josie is okay." After a few minutes, he straightens up, sniffs and clears his throat. "I'll get the widow Bailey. She's good at a time like this." He grips my shoulder before making for the door, and I give in to a good cry.

I am already curled up asleep in the chair when I hear Kathryn Bailey come through the door. She kisses the top of my head before proceeding to Josie's room. Several minutes later, she tiptoes out and noiselessly shuts the door behind her. "I could use a cup of tea," she says, but I know it is me she is thinking of.

Although it is not cold, I am freezing. I don't think I could move if I tried. It is my standard reaction to a situation such as this. The doctors say my blood pressure drops under stress or shock. It put me in the hospital when my parents died. A cup of hot liquid and some mothering is welcome, indeed. Thank God for people like Milt and the widow Bailey.

"This is always such a sad thing," she says once she has served our tea and seated herself. "I never lost a child, but I can imagine. You love that little person from the moment you know."

"Did Josie know? She never said anything."

"Maybe she was waiting to tell her husband first?"

I had not thought that she might not have been sure before Wyatt left.

"Of course; he should be the first to know." I think about what a sad homecoming this will be for him. The tea is having its effect and I feel I can begin to resume my dutiful role. This is not happening to me; it is not my tragedy. I need to be there for my friend instead of adding to the problem.

"I so appreciate your coming, Mrs. Bailey. Milt speaks so highly of you. I must admit, this has been a shock, but I'm feeling much better now," I say taking another sip of tea. "I've never experienced this myself. What do I need to do for Josie?" I ask.

"No need to thank me; and you can call me Kathryn," she says with a smile.

"Now, mind you, you will need to monitor the bleeding and if it doesn't continue to subside or worsens, call the doctor at once. Doc Clements will check in every day. Make sure she takes nourishment regularly. Don't force her to talk about it, but listen if she does. And whatever you do, don't pass it off as trivial; suggesting there will be other babies; well meaning, perhaps, but cruel, just the same. Mourn with her." I nod and try to imagine myself losing a child and shudder. How would I react and what would I want others to do and say?

"Please stay for supper," I say desperate for the reassuring company. "There will be plenty."

"I wish I could, but I promised my sister-in-law that I would stop by and help with her mother. Woman's heavy and bed-ridden, you know; and Hattie's just a little thing. Me, I'm strong as an ox," she says while helping me bring the tea service to the kitchen. "You'll be alright. I can tell." Her motherly hug is so comforting. Needless to say, my own parents were not big on affection. It feels . . . loving. I walk her to the door and help her with her wrap. She assures me she will be back. I think she must be the "Nellie Cashman" of Gunnison.

"Thank you, again," I say as she waves.

I close the door and head back to the kitchen. Keeping busy is a must if I am not to cave to the overwhelming sadness. I wish the men were back, but it has only been a week and a half. Doc said something about a month; but that was leaving from Florissant. Maybe three weeks at the most from here? This is so hard. A wave of homesickness overtakes. How did I get into this mess? Oh, right, I asked for it. What am I thinking? I know I would do exactly the same thing if I had to do it over again. I have come to love Josie and she needs my help. What would she have done if I had not been here? The picture of her wrapped in a bloody sheet screaming out her door for help slaps me back to reality. Just as I am convinced that Doc's entry into my world was no accident, I feel that I am meant to be here. Whatever sense that does or doesn't make, I am going to make the most of it. That settled, I turn my attention to supper.

By six, the potatoes give to a gentle squeeze and the chicken is tender. I cut up the lettuce and make a buttermilk dressing before going to check on Josie. I find her sitting up in bed.

"I'm okay, really, I am," are her first words. Her cheeks are tear-stained. "It happens. Next time . . ." She lets herself go and I sit down on the bed and hold her until she cries it out. "I'm so glad you're here, Cassie. I don't know what I would have done. . ."

"It's okay, Josie. It's okay," I say and let my own tears come. "I'm sorry, it's not okay, but it will be." We are a sight a few minutes later, noses red and eyes swollen.

"I know. I know." She wipes her tears and smiles. "Doc Clements said it happens more frequently than people think. He says there was no harm done and that I am still able to have children. That's the way to look at things."

"You're a better woman than I," I say admiring this determined female staring grief in the face while mapping out her bright future.

"Is that fried chicken I smell?"

"Are you hungry?"

"Am I!"

"That's good; the doctor and Mrs. Bailey—"

"She's an angel for stopping by," says Josie.

"I'll bring you a tray."

"No; just bring me my robe.

"But the doctor . . ."

"The doctor also said it was good for me to move around when I felt up to it, as long as I am careful and don't overdo. Well, I feel up to it," she says matter-of-factly, then ads in a quieter tone. "You know, Cassie, I didn't tell the doctor, but this isn't the first time. Wyatt doesn't even know about that. I was only a few weeks along." She inhales deeply. "I'd like to get back to normal as soon as possible." It is plain that Josie is not to be challenged in this. I smile at her courage as I help her with her robe and slippers. She acquiesces to leaning on my arm and we take our time making our way to the kitchen.

"This is so good," says Josie as she takes her first bite of the pie.

"Thanks."

"You know, Wyatt was so happy about the baby. He's always wanted children. His first wife was pregnant when she died. I don't know about Mattie . . . if she ever . . . What does that matter now. I feel fortunate that I can still have children; sometimes women can't you know; their insides are damaged permanently; but Doc Clements says I'm okay."

When it seems like she has said her peace, I fill the silence. "You have such a good outlook. You're already looking at the bright side. That's so important. It's all right to grieve, though; let it all out," I say feeling the tears reforming in my own eyes.

"Are you and Doc planning to have children?"

The question catches me by surprise and I fumble for an answer. "I . . . We . . . I mean . . ."

"I'm sorry; I've always been too forward," she says laughing at herself. "You've only been married a short time . . . but in the future, can you imagine a little Doc running around; a little Wyatt; them playing together." It is an amusing vision. Josie starts to giggle; gets me going, but we both end up in tears again.

Over the next few days, Josie lets me take care of the household duties and spends most of her time resting, if not in bed. The doctor stops in daily as do Milt and Mrs. Bailey, who seems to have arranged to have several women from town provide our suppers. Thankfully, there are no complications in Josie's case, and a week after the miscarriage she is beginning to get her normal strength back. She sends me to town to pick up a few things and asks me to check in at the telegraph office. To my surprise, there is a wire from Wyatt. He and Doc will arrive home on tomorrow's train.

CHAPTER 46

"Warren isn't coming with them?" I ask after Josie reads the message.

"I really didn't expect him. He planned to head back to California after their business was finished."

"Listen," I say. "I stopped in at Dawson House and reserved the room for Doc and me starting tomorrow." Josie nods and I know it was the right move. She and Wyatt will need time to themselves. "Someone will call for our things in the morning."

We spend another afternoon playing poker. "You're an apt student," Josie says as she concedes the hand. "You should ask Doc to teach you, you know, but don't let on about our lessons."

"Thanks for the suggestion," I say, anticipating an interesting evening in the near future. We dine on leftovers and turn in early. A profound sense of relief makes for a good night's sleep.

An employee from the Dawson House comes for Doc's and my things while Josie and I are having breakfast. Two hours later, we are on our way to meet the train.

Josie is still ambling gingerly but her color has returned, and I pray that Wyatt will not guess her news. It will be much better delivered in private. Upon arriving at the depot, we learn the train is twenty minutes behind schedule. Josie and I retire to a bench in the shade and try to be patient. This delay must be awful for her. Finally, we hear the whistle and see the smoke in the distance. By the time it sighs to a stop, Josie and I are on the platform awaiting the disembarking passengers. There are only three passengers ahead of Wyatt and Doc. Gunnison, I am guessing, is not so much a destination as a stop along the way.

Josie runs into her husband's arms as his first boot touches the ground. "Whoa there Sadie, I've missed you, too," Wyatt says dropping his carpetbag.

Doc smiles broadly. "Aah, the eternal lovebirds."

"You know how it is, Doc," says Josie. "Now take your wife to the hotel and show her a good time." I feel myself redden. Doc raises a brow and takes my arm.

"It seems, mah love, that we have been dismissed." I have no words as we make our way to Dawson House.

Doc finally breaks the silence. "Yor holdin' on tah me like yah think Ah've been in some sort a peril the last few weeks. Ah assure yah, we were not," he says patting the hand that rests on his arm. I manage to smile through my tears.

I wait until we get back to the room to tell him about the miscarriage. He sits down beside me on the bed. I see tears well up in those blue eyes. His infamous nerves of steel do not hold up to this news. I can imagine a similar faltering when Morgan was killed, although I understand that his grief quickly accelerated into full-blown rage. We spend the next hour sharing the grief in silence.

"It's not fair, what that man has had tah endure," Doc finally spits out. "Look at me. A year ago, Ah didn't expect tah live more than a few months. Ah am not half the man Wyatt is, an' now Ah have a lifetime ahead a me while he loses his brother an' his child in a mattah of a few months. What is God thinkin'?"

"I beg to differ with you, Mr. Holliday. You, indeed, Sir, are a good man. I do not believe that God is responsible for tragedy; but that he is equally outraged at this loss."

Doc looks at me as if seeing me for the first time; then walks over to the basin and throws water on his face before looking at his reflection in the mirror as he towels dry.

"Ah hope yah are right, Dahlin, on all counts." He walks

around, sits on the bed, and removes his boots. "Although quite innocuous, the passage was a bit tirin'. Ah believe a brief respite is in ordah before dinner," he confesses as he lies back. Without thinking, I nestle beside him as if it is a perfectly normal thing to do. He doesn't move. He doesn't comment. In a minute or so, I hear the steady respiration of sleep.

.

CHAPTER 47

Wyatt greets us at the door. The house is festive with candles and flowers. Tempting aromas waft from the kitchen. Josie is aglow with a renewed spirit and Wyatt is emitting a genuine contentment I had not seen at our initial encounter a few weeks ago. In light of their grief, I wonder how this is possible. I choose not to question, but to observe and learn from their mutual faith. I conclude that in this era of uncertain life expectancy, people have developed an urgency to enjoy the moment. Josie is the epitome of this mindset and Wyatt demonstrates an oak-like stance in the face of adversity; a determination to accept what life offers and continue on to the next adventure.

The evening is one of the most pleasant I have known in this era or my own. There is no negative talk, only discussion of future prospects. Josie and Wyatt have plans to travel, see the world, live on room service; I silently add my own commentary. I listen as Doc spins a similar prediction of our imaginary life together; and as he does, an unfamiliar ache develops from within, a longing, but for what, I do not know. "Isn't that right, Dahlin'?" In my musings, I have drifted from the conversation. "It would appear that mah wife has embarked on a journey without me."

I feel myself redden and we all laugh. "I'm sorry, I guess I was lost somewhere; but no, Doc; I wouldn't think of leaving without you," I say. I wonder if he knows how much I mean the words I've just uttered and am suddenly undone by the full import of them myself. Am I prepared to leave all that is familiar; permanently cross the barrier of time, and live in an age primitive to my experience? Would Doc be willing to step into the modern world? I take a cue from my companions and I dismiss the ponderings for a later time.

"Ah for one, would verah much like to see how the Europeans live," says Doc raising his pinky as he sips his coffee, bringing a new round of laughter. "How does an ocean voyage strike yah, Dahlin?"

Suddenly, I am uncomfortable with all these imaginary plans. "I can't swim," I blurt out. When the laughter subsides, a strange silence threatens.

"I know," says Josie. "Why don't we play poker?"

Doc looks over at me ."Ah don't believe Cassie . . ." I catch Josie's subtle wink.

"She's a smart woman. We can teach her," says Josie. "I'll get the deck." She retrieves it from a desk drawer across the room, sits down and begins to shuffle, as the rest of us push our cups aside to accept our hands.

For the next hour or so, I pull off, admirably, I must confess, the "beginners luck" act, clumsy shuffling and all. My innocent performance is abetted by Josie, who is feeding me the cards I need to win. Ignorant of our scheme, Wyatt and Doc are shaking their heads.

"Ah do believe Ah will be forced tah resort tah the underhanded tactics Ah reserve for desperate circumstances, if Ah am tah preserve my reputation," says Doc. At that, our routine falls apart. Josie and I convulse in abject hilarity followed by an admission of our conspiracy.

"I should have known," says Wyatt. "I'll deal with you later, Wife."

"Ah, too, will have tah come up with suitable chastisement," says Doc, his eyes dancing in amusement. "Seriously, ladies; that was an admirable ruse. Now, we play for blood."

"Here, here," Wyatt chimes in, as he nods at the sudden improvement in my shuffling skills.

We play until midnight; Doc and Wyatt dominating the

rest of the hands, sans bottom-of-the-deck dealing or aces up sleeves. The evening is a success. I am convinced of Josie's emotional recovery; know that she and Wyatt will be just fine. Hugs and kisses all around as we bid the unforgettable couple goodnight.

The night is clear, the sky littered with stars as we walk back to the Dawson House. We are comparing our admiration of our friends' ability to deal with their loss positively when gunfire erupts within the immediate vicinity. Without hesitation, Doc abruptly diverts us into the alley and stashes me between two large barrels, while pulling the revolver from his shoulder holster. It's happening so fast; I have no time to think.

"Wha . . ." Doc's finger is at my lips before I can get the word out. He turns away as shouting breaks the silence. Something about a claim. More gunshots. Another boisterous exchange. At least one of the parties is quite intoxicated. I cannot determine the direction of the source, but it appears the violent dispute is occurring a block over, opposite the direction we are heading. That determined, Doc helps me up and gently guides me back onto the walk. The leisureliness in our stride is gone as we continue to our destination.

CHAPTER 48

"I promise to keep to my own side," says Doc after announcing that he desperately requires a good night's rest in a comfortable bed, rather than another round of gambling followed by passing the wee hours of the night in the chair.

"I trust you, Doc," I say, actually thankful for his close proximity. It was true; it never crossed my mind that this man would attempt to take advantage of me or any other woman. From where had that assurance come? I do not know; maybe because he was so ill; but even now, as a healthy, red-blooded male, I have unqualified faith in Doc's respect for me both as a woman and a person. We have become close friends. He is the big brother I never had. Why am I feeling so disappointed?

My mind wanders to what it would be like; what it would take to get his attention? Before he fell into my world, I felt the blossoming of myself as a real woman; for the first time, free of the physical hindrance, that I might be able to experience a relationship with a man. I had been looking forward to dating in spite of my late start. That, of necessity, had been put on hold while Doc was recuperating. Once he was on the mend, could get out and about, I felt compelled to show him how his world had progressed and changed. It was like taking a child to Disneyland for the first time, each town and historic landmark, a thrilling ride. Thinking of that, I wonder what he would think of Disneyland, Knott's Berry Farm or some of the other modern theme parks. Watching and hearing his reactions has been amusing and educational. Does he assess my response to his world similarly?

I try to calculate how my thinking has altered over the past year. I must go back farther, though, to the mental upheaval brought on by the sudden, disconcerting deaths of my parents. That wound had hardly begun to heal when the scab was ripped open by the discovery of my ancestor's body, followed quickly by Doc's appearance that has completely upset my heretofore knowledge of the laws of time and space.

My mind is still processing this data into finished and unfinished business. I have not dwelt on the family tragedy much after leaving LA. Is that due to acceptance of the unchangeable, or simply ignoring it while I throw myself into settling into a foreign environment? Probably a combination. Months of adapting to the altitude, the upkeep of the animals, and upgrading my inheritance had provided the much-needed diversion. I recall the moment when my mind announced that I could relax, when I had become confident that I was prepared for my new life; that the time had come to sit back and enjoy it.

As I had been gazing out the kitchen window at the Peak, I had contemplated the mental journey. I had let the memories flood in, the visit to the morgue and the motivation behind my mother's desperate act, particulars no one else would ever know. I had shuddered and I remember deciding, in that instant, to throw myself into a more pleasant analysis. With that thought, I set out on an in depth exploration of the family home. It would, I was certain, distract me, introduce me to a more distant past, one so removed, it could not distress me; that is, until I found Great, Great, Great Grandmother Sarah tucked away in the corner of the basement, and learned that homicidal tendencies ran in the family genes. I can still feel the wave of doubt that washed over me at the time. Now my brain toys with the idea that there is some sort of family curse in which I am doomed to become a participant. It was in the throes of this mental debate, that Doc suddenly entered the scene and completely pulled the rational rug from under my feet. In the space of a little over a year most of my belief system had been upended, and come crashing down in an unfamiliar arrangement. I had accepted my father for who he was; and although I missed the love that should have been there, I had come to terms with our relationship, or rather, lack there-of. I did not blame myself, did not proverbially beat my head against his immoveable emotional wall. I had accepted his dismissal from his life and the financial consequences. It was my mother's action that lunged at my throat. It was uncharacteristic and implausible in its savagery. She had committed calculated, cold-blooded murder. One could argue that after giving her life over to Father's tyrannical nature, seen to his every whim, only to watch him disown their only child, she did the only thing a loving mother could. I'm sure there are more arguments pro and con; thinking of them now is a futile pursuit. Shouldah, couldah, wouldah . . . If only . . . Hindsight is twenty-twenty. I pull the reigns in; what is, is. Where to go from here? These thoughts now run rampant as I lay in the stillness.

I look over at Doc, his face visible in the moonlight. His gentle snoring is comforting. An unexpected fluttering caresses my heart evoking a startling notion. Is this how love feels? In the course of all the craziness of this time warp thing, concentrating on Doc's health, showing him the modern world, and venturing into his, have I, without realizing it, fallen in love with the man? I am shaken by the possibility, ill prepared for the import of these musings. What about . . . Just as the wheels begin to pick up speed again and I fear I will lie the night awake, Doc fast asleep, shifts to his side, facing me. By the time he is through his unconscious maneuvering, one arm lies across my chest, his chin touching my shoulder. In spite of the ensuing palpitations, my heart soon calms in an unexpected sense of security and sleep overtakes.

I wake to the sound of Doc's morning routine. The first thought to cross my mind is a question. Did he wake with his arm still around me, and if so, what were his thoughts? I feel myself blush, then quickly decide to dispense with the query.

As on previous mornings, we exchange cheery greetings. I catch him just in time to prevent him from sculpting around the beard that has filled most of his lower face during his absence. He does not question, just shrugs and sets the razor aside.

Doc is normally neither talkative nor notably silent like Wyatt. He uses words accurately and refrains from frivolous interactions. This morning, though, I do find him unusually quiet. Is he wondering if I had noticed that he had involuntarily broken his promise to remain on his side of the bed? While assuming it was an unconscious move, I cannot deny that I fancy the idea that it was deliberate or, if not, was guided by powers outside his control. In either case . . . God, where is this going? I push away the awkward thoughts.

"I'll leave yah tah dress an' meet yah downstairs," he says as he dons his hat.

"Doc?" I say once we are settled in the dining room and awaiting our order.

"Hmm?"

"Did you mean it?"

"Did Ah mean what, Dahlin'?"

"You know, at Wyatt's, what you said about traveling, the two us?"

His expression denotes his acceptance of the inevitable. He knew this was coming. He sighs and lays his hands flat on the table between us. The prolonged silence is testing my restraint, but I fight the urge to break it lest I break some sort of spell I hope has been set in force. I remind myself of the adage, "The first one to speak loses."

"Just what did yah have in mind?" he finally asks.

My heart leaps. At least he isn't refusing. "I want to see more of your world, the places you've been." I wait a minute before throwing down the gauntlet. "I want to go to Tombstone and . . ."

"Tombstone!" he says with as much panic as I have ever seen him display. "If Ah go back to that town, it will, indeed, become my final resting place. Yah saved me from an untimely death. Would yah now have me tempt fate by exposin' myself tah an even earlier demise?"

"You know I would never . . .," I say biting my lip in hopes that he knows me better than that. I am determined that he will hear me out. "I have taken that into consideration," I venture.

"Oh, yah have, have yah?" His hands come together under his chin and he interlaces his fingers. "Let's hear this ingenious proposal of yors."

Feeling the heat in my face I clear my throat and relate the plan that I am convinced will incur no threat. I watch Doc's expression and see the initial skepticism begin to erode as I lay out the details. I do not pause to refill my lungs until I see those steely blue eyes frolic with interest. Doc lets go with an infectious laugh that is interrupted only by the waiter returning with our breakfast. Doc arranges his napkin under his chin and picks up his knife and fork. He sends the first bite of ham passing through smiling lips.

"Well?" In spite of the inviting aroma and an appetite, my hands remain in my lap. I cannot possibly take a bite without knowing.

He chuckles as he chews the bite of meat. He stares without wavering as he swallows and takes a sip of coffee before blotting his lips with his napkin. "It appears that yah have given this expedition considerable deliberation."

"I do believe that I have considered all of the possibilities, yes," I say, my voice not quite conveying the affirmation of my words.

"Oh, yah have, indeed," he comments before his next bite. Again, the methodically chewing, swallowing, sipping, and dabbing.

"Well?" I repeat, still with my hands in my lap.

"Not only have yah plotted to counteract the various pitfalls to such an endeavah, but yah have inspired me with the prospects of a personal reckoning of sorts."

My "no" is said a bit too loudly and attracts amused attention from the nearer tables. I lean forward and whisper. "You can't go back to kill the people who have done you wrong."

"Ah agree," he says with another laugh. "The killin' is finished because Wyatt says it is. Those left standin' at this point aren't worth riskin' our necks foh. Howevah, Ah am duly enchanted by the possibility of playin' with the minds, if yah will, of the likes of Ike Clanton an' John Behan." His smile broadens before he weaves in a quite believable British affectation. "Jolly good, your suggestion of the accent. That should complete mah transformation from the thin, sickly, Georgian tah the hale and hearty proper English visitor. An, those, what do yah call them," he says pointing to my eyes.

"Contact lenses," I say. "Mine replace glasses that correct my vision, but the ones I brought for you will merely change your eye color from blue to brown, although I must say, it is a shame to hide your natural color." I feel myself redden again. "We'll also get rid of that grey, temporarily," I add, to which his eyebrows raise. "Hair coloring, it's all the rage in the twenty-first century," I explain and Doc appears speechless.

"So, we're going? You'll take me to Tombstone?" That wicked grin spreads and I know I have a willing conspirator.

"Ah can't think of a better way tah pass some time," he says and I can tell his mind is anticipating the opportunities that such an adventure will afford, and how he will use them to have his passive aggressive way with his unsuspecting enemies.

After our meal, we concentrate on preparation. While my wardrobe is adequate for my role, Doc's requires a bit of attention. We find what he needs rather easily. Gunnison, while relatively young, has been graced with certain European influence, as I had already observed in much of the architecture. Hence, we find several outfits befitting an English gentleman. He frowns at the derby, but agrees that it is so foreign to his established image that it is an acceptable tradeoff for the satisfaction it purports to offer. Our next stop is the railway station where Doc purchases our tickets west. Upon returning to our room in the hotel, I begin his transformation, starting with the bottle of semi-permanent hair color that will wash away the illness gray and restore Doc's once youthful blonde locks.

An hour later, Doc stands before the mirror as Master Thomas Stuart, an impeccably dressed, blond, brown-eyed

Londoner on holiday to explore America's Wild West. I reach into my trunk to retrieve the pair of glasses with plain round lenses and fit them over his ears. He chuckles, as I stand agape at the metamorphosis. I knew he would be unrecognizable, but this is beyond my anticipations.

With perfect British intonation, Doc announces. "I have always taken pride in looking and acting as I am, speaking my mind, just being . . . you know . . . me. However, I am looking forward to this role," he says winking at his reflected image before turning to me. "Dahlin', thank yah foh surprisin' me," he says reverting to his sweet Georgian drawl. "That is not an' easy accomplishment, but one foh which yah seem to have an uncanneh knack."

Without thought, I throw my arms around him; then quickly pull back and, for good measure, pretend to flick lint off his coat here and there.

CHAPTER 49

The train pulls in right on time. Thomas Stuart kisses me on the cheek before boarding. "Remembah what Ah said," he whispers in my ear.

"I do remember and I promise to do everything exactly as you said. You needn't worry," I assure him as he takes the first step up onto the train. "Believe me, I've learned my lesson and I have no inclination to mess this up." He nods, is gone from my sight for a few seconds while entering, then reappears at a window seat. The whistle sounds and the wheels of the locomotive strain to move forward. We exchange waves as the train slowly trudges out of town.

Suddenly, I am excited and lonely at the same time, but remind myself that we will be reunited shortly. I spend the rest of the day packing my trunk and making arrangements for it to be transported to the station for tomorrow's departure. Doc and I had agreed that it was best to leave Wyatt and Josie ignorant of our exact plans. This is easy, for as we anticipated, after their initial hospitality, they would choose to spend some quality time together, sans our company. As far as they knew, we were resuming our honeymoon travels. I do hope, though, that the other evening was not the last I would see of these fine people. Tomorrow is uncertain enough, without the added disadvantage of straddling two worlds separated by more than a century. As expected, I sleep fitfully in anticipation of the adventure, waking hourly, and grateful for the dawn.

CHAPTER 50

I dress quickly and order coffee in the dining room. I am too excited to eat and find myself at the station ridiculously early. I begin to fidget. I rise and walk a ways before discreetly retrieving the camera from the drawstring bag and taking a few more shots of Gunnison in 1882.

Finally, I board the westward bound train and take a window seat. Shortly after we are on our way, a conductor comes through, checks my ticket, and wishes me a comfortable trip. At our first stop, a stately looking woman in her sixties boards and takes the seat next to me.

"Hello," she says friendlier than her appearance would have suggested, "My name is Katherine Bartlett," she offers.

"Glad to make your acquaintance, Ms. Bartlett." Oh my God, I think realizing I had used the modern form for female address. I cough, hoping she will take it for a tickle-induced ellipsis. "My name is Cassie, Cassie Collins."

"I've been visiting my son and his family and am on my way home to San Francisco where I live with my daughter and her children. She lost her husband a few years ago; pneumonia set in while he was recuperating from an accident; terrible thing, just terrible." She sighs and continues in a sing-songy rhythm. "Anyway, we're getting along fine now. I have three lovely grandchildren, two girls and a boy. We have a nice house in the city."

I wait for her to pause. "I'm sorry about your son-in-law."

"Yes." She sighs again, more heavily this time. "The world

is full of tragedy. I lost my own dear Franklin before my children were grown. Life was harder back then, but we made it and things are better now. And you, Cassie, are you married?"

As I was the only boarder from Gunnison, I know that my cover will not be blown. "No, Ma'am," I say.

"You're traveling alone, then?" Her tone implies something between skepticism and disapproval.

"Yes, Ma'am. I have been on my own for some time," I say. I hold up the tablet I purchased earlier in town to complete my costume. "I am an aspiring writer, hoping to capture the west in print for those who are not able to experience it themselves." I say having no clue how this information will strike her.

"You do know that you are venturing into potentially dangerous territory? Neither your journey nor your profession befits a young woman like yourself. Indians and unsavory sorts run rampant between here and the west coast. Where exactly are you heading?" Her concern is genuine.

"I have heard a lot about Tombstone . . ."

She throws up her arms and her voice goes up two octaves. "A young woman like you cannot possibly be thinking of going to that God-forsaken territory. Do you know what has been going on there; all that horrible killing with the Earps and the cowboys; it's . . . it's . . . why you could be killed!" Great, now the whole coach knows my business. I shouldn't have . . . but then again, maybe it's a good thing.

"I appreciate your concern, Ma'am, really, I do; but I'll be alright," I say while regretting my veracity. "I have friends there, so you don't have to worry."

Her skepticism diminishes, and due to the attention she has drawn from the other passengers, I sense she is rethinking her intrusion into another's affairs. "Well, as long as you'll be careful." With that, she seems to have run out of words. After several seconds of rummaging around in the carpetbag at her feet, she pulls out a ball of yarn and what appears to be a sweater in progress. I return to watching the scenery out the window and contemplating my reunion with

Doc.

The journey proceeds without incident. Mrs. Bartlett renews our conversation a few hours later, this time choosing non-controversial topics. By the time we arrive in Benson, I have the complete history of her grandchildren and their life in San Francisco. As I disembark, my traveling companion tops it off with an invitation to visit if I ever find myself in San Francisco. I thank her as genuinely as I am able but am secretly glad to be rid of her company.

As the train pulls away, I spot my Englishman standing near a stagecoach supervising the loading of his trunk. He nods discreetly. "Miss."

Another gentleman in a uniform arrives and after inquiring as to my destination, directs me to the ticket booth, and takes charge of my trunk. A moment later, I am being escorted into the coach reminiscent of the one in which Doc and I took our brief tour of modern-day Tombstone.

"Excuse me," I say as I settle myself in the seat beside a fellow female passenger. She shifts slightly and draws her bag into her lap. Either she is deep in thought, or she has no desire to interact. A man enters the coach just ahead of Doc and the two seat themselves across from us. As premeditated, Doc and I exchange no sign of recognition. Suddenly the stage lurches forward and my seatmate turns her head. Is it my imagination or am I seeing alarm in those brown eyes across from me? I sequester my own reaction and turn to look out the window to contemplate what might have triggered Doc's concern, convincing myself that whatever it was, it was so short-lived that I doubt if anyone else noticed. I force myself to mind the journey until Doc signals otherwise. We are only five minutes out when Doc introduces Thomas Stuart to his seatmate. Jacob Parnell is a rancher, hoping to purchase an available spread on the San Pedro River, now that things seem to be settling down. Doc listens intently and questions the man as if hearing, for the first time, about the seriousness of the recent upheaval in Tombstone. With that invitation, Mr. Parnell begins his rendition of the Cowboys verses the Earps saga.

He has barely begun, when the woman beside me snorts

in exasperation. "You don't know what you're talking about. Mr. Parnell, is it?"

"Is that so?" He is at once surprised and annoyed by the outburst. "And I suppose you do?"

"I was there," she nods. "I saw it all."

"And you are?" He asks.

I notice Doc is smiling and catch a slight wink as if . . .

"Kate Elder, as in the wife of John Henry Holliday. I'm sure you've heard of Doc Holliday."

I feel my eyes grow and turn to the window to regain control. I sneak a peek at Doc who shows no anxiety at the announcement.

"Really?" comments Thomas Stuart, the tone skeptical. "I was led to believe this Big Nose Kate person was a much younger woman." Oh no. The verbal vendetta has commenced.

I keep to my scenic vigilance but can feel the flare of Kate's nostrils. "And I, that Englishmen were gentlemen of the highest order." Her sword, too, is doubled-edged and well-honed.

"Ah, but a true gentleman is never naïve. Integrity prevents denial, no matter the cost. You may be thinking of the French, who will flatter to a fault to improve their positioning with a woman," Mr. Stuart counters.

"Then, it behooves the English to make certain of the facts before misspeaking."

"Indeed, it does. My apologies; my observation is based on physical presentation, alone, not on chronological information." Although I cannot see their faces, I know that a stare-down is in progress. Doc's eyes, I surmise, are void of emotion while Kates are filled with fire at the passive insult. If only I were a mouse within the woman's mind.

"To hell with all that," Mr. Parnell interjects. "I want to hear what the woman has to say, her attractiveness or lack thereof, be hanged." He leans toward Kate. "Just what did you know about the situation?"

"It's all politics," Kate begins. "The cowboys are a bad lot, but they bring major revenue into the town. Crack down on them too hard and Tombstone just might go belly-up. The

Earps were too straight for their own good. It was a train wreck waiting to happen. I warned Doc that his association with them would come to no good. He refused to listen to reason; stuck like glue to those brothers. What did all that lawing get them in the end? They had to leave town with little else save the shirts on their back, their dead and crippled."

Finally, I managed the courage to join the conversation. "How did Mr. Holliday fit into this?"

"And just what is your interest in this?" Kate demands.

"I am hoping to write about the events; possibly publish a book," I respond, my tone purposely dripping with meekness. "I'm Cassie, Cassie Collins, from the East."

Kate threw her head back in uproariously laughter. "A writer, huh?" Her tone is degrading as she gives me the once-over. "I'm surprised a little princess like you made it this far. Just the same, I'll answer your question. Just make sure you quote me accurately and spell my name right." She pauses as if to reorder her thoughts. "I don't know why Doc hung out with those Earps. He was cut from a different cloth altogether; far more educated than that bunch. Had some warped notion of loyalty; so much so, that on Wyatt's word, he kicked me to the street. I'll never forgive that bastard, Earp. Never had it better than with Doc. He knew how to treat a lady. I heard he near went crazy when Morgan was shot; then nearly got himself killed riding with the Earps against the cowboys."

"Where is he now?" I asked.

"Dead, for all I know or care," she spits out, but the look in her eyes reveals she doesn't mean it. "He didn't have long no matter how you measure it. The consumption was eating him up. Me? I tried to make his final years as pleasant as possible, if you get my drift." Kate's smile had an evil twist. Embarrassed, I turn away. "Aren't you gonna write any of this down for your book?" she asked sarcastically.

"Leave the lady alone, Miss Elder," Mr. Stuart says. His tone leaves no room for discussion.

"What's she to you?"

"A fellow human being," he says calmly, "more than I can say for some in this coach."

"Why you sorry excuse for a man," she says poising to hurl herself across at him. I reach across to thwart her efforts. "Please, please, just stop this!" I put as much distressed drama into my voice as I can muster.

"My, my; what do we have here, a romance in bud?" Kate's tone is sarcastic and tinged with jealously as she wrenches her wrist out of my grip. "Stronger than you look, girl. You might just survive after all."

"You know, Mr. Stuart, is it? You remind me of Mr. Holliday," she says.

"Oh," he says off-handedly, "how is that? I favor him in looks?"

"Not at all, but he couldn't hold his tongue either; spoke his mind, even when his words threatened his life. I almost killed him myself a time or two for shooting off his mouth. You'd best watch your tongue, Mister, especially in Tombstone or you'll take up permanent residence in the cemetery." She turns to address me. "He, too, would have come to the aid of a damsel in distress; or a dog that was being beaten."

"As would any true gentleman," I say hoping I give the impression that her slur has been lost on me.

"Pardon me," Kate says. "Have you two been properly introduced?"

Doc takes advantage of the opportunity. "Miss Collins, is it?"

"Please call me Cassie ," I respond.

"Cassie," he acknowledges with a tip of his hat in my direction. "Thomas Stuart, London, England, at your service, and you may call me Thomas."

"Perhaps, Mr. Stuart, I mean, Thomas, we can compare notes on our travels in the West?"

"I should find it a pleasure." And with that we have paved the way for an acceptable casual relationship.

We converse as if we have the coach to ourselves. "I have done extensive research on the infamous shootout between the Earps and the cowboys," I begin with a view of twisting the knife recently inserted in my fellow female passenger. "I have read that the cowboys resented the

Earps coming to town because of their background in law enforcement; that they feared their criminal activities would be threatened by the presence of the lawmen, as, indeed, it was; that they goaded the brothers into the showdown, and when it did not go as expected, decided on extermination."

"I have heard a similar rendition," concurs Mr. Stuart.

"Wyatt didn't help matters with his flirtation with that actress who came to town. Behan has an ego; losing a woman to an Earp was not something he could abide. I wonder where that pair is now, or even, if they're still together," Kate muses. "What people do for love or what they think is love . . ."

"I don't imagine a woman like you could understand a love like that," Doc takes his turn at rotating the blade.

"As if an Englishman would know anything about love and passion. Your lot walk around with damn sticks up your butts."

"I beseech you, Miss Elder. Kindly remember that there is a lady present."

Kate snorts.

"I take it you never been with a Brit?" Doc proceeds.

Kate hesitates before crafting her reply. "Up to this point, I would have considered such dalliance, a waste of my time."

"What has prompted this reevaluation?"

"You have, Sir. You have," she admits with an invitation in her tone. "I detect mixed heritage that is intriguing. Such might account for . . . tell me; is it possible that your mother . . ."

"What a horrible thing to suggest!" I blurt out before Doc can even think of lunging across the coach and strangling his former lover. To my utter amazement, he appears fully in control despite the slur against his beloved mother. I have no doubt that the only thing holding back his concealed rage is the fact that Kate's comment is intended to evoke his temper and he is refusing her the satisfaction.

In its stead he offers, "Unfortunately for you, Miss Elder, there is a Mrs. Stuart waiting for me, thus my parentage can be of no consequence to you," he answers.

It takes great effort to stifle my glee. I concentrate on

absorbing the scenery, and note that in this part of the nation, not much has changed since the time Doc and the Earps were roaming the area. Conversation eludes us for the rest of the journey. Kate's silence, I sense, speaks multitudes, however. I cannot help but think that she has taken Thomas Stuart's disinterest as a challenge.

In spite of the present absence of law and order in the territory, no attempt is made to threaten the stage and we arrive in Tombstone safely.

Per our arrangement, upon arriving in Tombstone, I seek a room at the boarding house of Nellie Cashman on Fifth Street. Thomas Stuart reserves lodging at the Grand, more to the taste of a gentleman of means.

It is noon when I am finally settled in a room. The journey has been tiring and I am ravenous. I rack my mind to put a name to the familiar face that enters Nellie's dining room.

"It's so good to see you, Mr. Parsons." I am thankful to my young waitress, who has diverted her attention from taking my order to greet the entering customer. "Sit wherever you like; I'll be right with you," she says with extra cheeriness than others have been afforded.

After placing my order I ask her, "Is that George Parsons?"

"Why, yes, do you know him?" Is her inflection tainted with jealousy?

"Only by reputation," I say. "I'm a journalist. From what I have heard, you couldn't set your sights on a better man," I offer in hopes of allaying her fears that I might be interested in him personally. "I'd love to interview him. If you could put in a good word for me, I'll return the favor." The love-struck girl's eyes light up and a few minutes later, George Parsons is joining me for dinner.

Mr. Parsons is as well-bred and hard working as I pictured from reading the diaries put into print long after his death. I had picked it up at the courthouse in modern-day Tombstone, figuring that the journal of an average person might reveal more of the truth than the conflicting renditions of recognized historians. I wonder if Mr. Parsons ever dreamed his personal account of everyday life would find its way onto bookshelves of the future. After introducing myself as a journalist, who is heart-set on providing an accurate rendition of the events of the last year, Mr. Parsons reiterates what he experienced along with carefully worded editorial comments. As in his written account, he is painfully vigilant to portray events and the people involved free of bias. He speaks without hesitation or regret, relieved that the ringleaders of the cowboys are dead and sanctions the actions of the Earps in that regard; now looking forward to a more peaceful existence in Tombstone. Little does he know that his town is soon to be all but abandoned with the collapse of the mining industry.

I turn in early. The journey has been long and not that comfortable, but anything but boring. My room is pleasant and I fall asleep in mid-thought.

.

CHAPTER 51

I feel the disapproving stares, as I enter the dining room of The Grand Hotel a little before eight this evening and wait to be seated. My table, as expected is next to the kitchen. The social faux pas is deliberate, hoping that the community will be forgiving of an Eastern visitor unaccustomed to etiquette in the west. When the server appears, she informs me that a gentleman at a window table has invited me to dine with him. I look the direction she indicates.

"Oh, it's the English gentleman from the stage yesterday. Yes," I say, "I would be delighted." This, too, is part of a ruse to curry the town's pity, then favor, for a naïve young woman and the proper foreigner who comes to her rescue.

Thomas Stuart holds out my chair and sees that I am seated comfortably, after which we exchange pleasantries befitting of casual acquaintances for the benefit of the curious straining to overhear. He includes his admonition regarding proper decorum of single ladies in Western towns. Over a hearty breakfast, we review our plans, careful to maintain our pretense of recently introduced traveling companions. When we take our leave, we are confident that our fellow patrons have the impression that we are bonding over our mutual interest in our unfamiliar surroundings, that our shared tour of town will be viewed as inconsequential and attract little attention.

Emerging from the hotel, I am filled with anticipation. "The first thing I want to see is that rosebush," I tell Doc, referring to the visit we made to the Rose Tree Inn in modern Tombstone. We walk toward Fourth Street where we take a right. Mrs. Adamson's boardinghouse down a bit on the left. We are warmly greeted by the owner, but my inquiry about the rosebush is met with confusion. "I am sorry, Miss Collins, I don't know what you mean. There is no rosebush in my courtyard."

"But your friend from Scotland . . . Mrs. Gee . . ."

The lady shakes her head. "You must have me confused with someone else, Miss. I have no acquaintance with anyone by that name," she says with sincere sympathy. Seeing my consternation, Doc quickly takes up the conversation. "Perhaps you were given some erroneous information, Miss Collins." He turns to the lady. "Thank you so much, Mrs. Adamson, and pardon our intrusion."

"Oh, not at all . . . Mr?"

"Stuart . . . Thomas Stuart, London, England, he says bowing slightly. "Here to experience your wild west."

"Ah," she says nodding. "Think it's exciting, do you? Until the Earps got here, it was wild, all right; but there's nothing entertaining about taking your life in your hands just to walk down the streets. When those cowboys are in town, decent folk have to stay inside. It's a shame; just as things were looking up, the cowboys seriously wounded one brother and murdered another. The Earps took down a bunch of them, but the law around here seems to think they were the ones at fault. Don't know what's going to happen now."

"So we've heard," Doc says. "Well, thank you again, Mrs. Adamson and sorry for the inconvenience."

As he guides me back onto the street, I remain non-plussed about the missing rosebush. "I could have sworn . . .," I say looking back.

Keeping his voice down, he explains. "Oh, that's the place, all right. Ah remember distinctly from our visit in yor time."

"Then . . ."

"It's obvious that neither Mrs. Gee nor her rosebush have come tah town, yet. Now that Ah recall, Ah believe Ah read on the plaque that it was planted in '85. This is 1882."

We continue at a leisurely pace, pausing frequently as Doc identifies buildings and their significance to him. Jacob Parnell is just coming out of a land office as we pass. "How are you folks?" he asks, tipping his hat to me.

"Quite, well, Sir," answers Doc for both of us, "and you, Mr. Parnell, is it? Were you able to conclude a satisfactory arrangement on the ranch?"

"On my way to see about it now. You going to be in town long?"

"I'll be here a few more days," Doc says, then looks to me. "I don't know about Miss Collin's plans."

"I'll be staying as long as it takes to get my story," I offer.

"Well, I hope I see you both again. Good luck on your book, Little Lady." With that, the pleasant man is on his way and we continue our tour. Just ahead is the Birdcage Theatre.

"Oh, we've got to go there one evening," I say in an eager tone.

"I don't think so," says Doc. "It's most certainly not the place for a lady like yourself. I would suggest an evening at Schieffelin Hall. It's far more appropriate."

"I see," thinking how easy it would be to get in trouble here without Doc's supervision. As we continue our stroll, Doc points out the houses that Virgil and Wyatt called home when they were in town, and the nearby site where he and the brothers exchanged gunfire with the Clantons and McLaurys. Of course, we saw some of this in modern Tombstone, but it was not the same. The ground is still fresh with the blood of the three fallen cowboys. We take a moment in memory of that awful day that was to be only the beginning of the bloodshed between the cowboys and the Earps. Of course, to Doc, this happened only a few months ago. The gunfire must still echo in his ears. We turn off Fremont on to Third Street.

Distinctive smells and sounds wafting over from our right denote an abrupt change in culture. "Welcome to Hop Town," says Doc, "the home of Tombstone's venerable Chinese population." Sheriff John Behan, one of the proud founders of the Anti-Chinese League in town is coming our way as we approach Allen Street again.

"Miss Collins," he says tipping his hat.

"I don't believe I know you, Sir. How is it that you know my name," I ask salting my tone with unease.

"Forgive me, Miss Collins; I didn't mean to alarm you. It's my job, you see. Permit me to introduce myself; Sheriff John Behan, at your service," he says sweeping off his hat and bowing. "I make it my business to know of all visitors to my town, part of keeping order."

"Then, you must know Mr. Thomas Stuart," I say motioning in Doc's direction. "We met on the stage coming from Benson." I can't help but recall a similar scene in the movie Tombstone, where Kurt Russell is about to introduce the two and Val Kilmer says, "Piss on you, Wyatt."

"Yes," he says trying to cover his annoyance. Doc nods before looking away to abort a handshake that neither seems to favor. Behan, relieved but perplexed, seems happy to turn his attention back to me.

"I understand you are a journalist, Miss Collins, hoping to chronicle the recent unfortunate events in our otherwise fair town. It will be my pleasure to supply you with all the facts, at your convenience, of course; say supper tonight at the Grand around seven?"

While Doc feigns disinterest in the interaction, I accept with enthusiasm. Sheriff Behan is swelling in victory at having won my company for the evening, at, what he no doubt hopes, is the expense of Mr. Stuart who he seems to view as a rival for my attentions.

"Well, then, Miss Collins, I'll call for you at Nellie's a little before seven? And, I'd watch myself around here; Hop Town isn't the safest area. Mind that Miss Collins, here comes to no harm during your excursion, Mr. Stuart," he directs at Doc.

"Please be assured that Miss Collin's safety is a priority, Sheriff."

Doc and I stifle our laughter as we watch Behan swagger away, confident that he is well on his way to another conquest. A few doors down, Kate Elder exits a laundry and we watch the two link arms and head out of Hop Town.

Interesting.

I switch on the listening device, carefully concealed in my hair in my left ear.

"How about you buy me supper tonight?" asks Kate. "We can have *dessert* back at my place."

"Sorry, Kate, supper's taken. Dinner, right now, is open, though; and, I trust, you will still provide dessert?" The two laugh.

"You haven't changed a bit," she says.

"Why should I?" he counters as they disappear around the corner.

"Casanova's got nothing on him," I comment.

"I concur, Miss Collins. Shall we?" Doc says guiding me to the left down Allen Street. We have nearly reached Fourth Street when he opens the door and steers me into the Can Can Restaurant where we are promptly greeted by a Chinese gentleman, hands held together and bowing at the waist.

"Ah, Gentleman and Lady, right this way," he says shuffling ahead to a table with a window view. This is the famous Quong Kee of whom Doc spoke so favorably. I remember, now, the old time photo studio in modern day Tombstone where the article about this man and his restaurant were displayed. Little does he know of his endearment to the town and huge event they will make of his funeral. Quong Kee listens carefully as Doc relays our order; then shuffles though the doors to the kitchen where we hear his exchange with the cooks in their native tongue. He reappears with our tea and continues to attend to the full house of customers. His attentiveness is both gracious and sincere, and is displayed equally at every table. It is clear that the diners, both Chinese and American, are enjoying, not only the fine food, but also their host. As we eat, I take note of a beautiful Chinese woman dining alone. "That exquisite creature is China Mary," Doc explains. "She rules Hop Town, with an iron fist, I'm told; rumored to have Tong affiliation." I don't know much about Chinese history, but I think the Tong might be the equivalent of the Italian Mafia.

"That was the most delicious Oriental meal I have ever

had," I say as we are leaving." Doc nods and I notice a sadness. "I do believe you would have liked to say hello to your friend?"

"Yes," he admits. "Quong Kee is an honorable man respected by all except the bigots." He spits out the word denoting his abhorrence of unwarranted prejudice. "They are good enough to build our railways and take care of our dirty laundry, but not to be accepted in our social circles."

Doc and I continue our circuit of town. He whispers the names of persons we encounter as we pass. None reveal the least hint of recognition of my famous escort. Making our way back to Nellie's doorstep, we publically express our mutual thanks for the company of one another on a tour of the town. I retire to my room to prepare for my evening with Sheriff Behan, while Doc plots an encounter with the available Miss Elder. It should prove to be an interesting evening.

John Behan is twenty minutes late, stating pressing business for the delay. Nice try, Sheriff, but Nellie greeted me ten minutes ago upon her return, and mentioned seeing you on Allen Street, engaged in light-hearted conversation with a group of fawning female admirers. Nellie's comment and my earlier encounter with the sheriff confirm Doc's assessment of the man. John Behan is a womanizer; his tardiness, a ruse to impress upon me, his importance. I keep my true thoughts to myself and instead, tell him I had just made it downstairs myself. His wince confirms my suspicions. This man has to be in control; and, indeed, I plan to let him think he is, except for little jabs here and there. Doc had taken time to school me in his weaknesses over our earlier meal.

Upon arrival at the Grand, the sheriff and I are shown to a prominent table, and find Kate and Mr. Stuart seated across the room, for all appearances, enjoying their meals and each other's company. If all goes as planned, however, these two will be on the road to exasperation before the night is over.

"I see our Mr. Stuart has found another dining companion for the evening. I didn't get the idea that those two got along," he says. His tone expresses disinterest, but I know he is digging.

"Oh, that's Miss Elder, isn't it." I try to sound casual. "She was on the stage from Benson, too. I did witness a rather unfriendly exchange, but I don't think it was serious. If anything, their little tete-a-tete seems to have stimulated their interest in one another, although I do believe, Mr. Stuart mentioned that he was a married man."

"Really?" He glances their way briefly before continuing. "That's Doc and Kate all over again."

"Excuse me?" I say innocently.

"Kate, there, was the infamous Doc Holliday's woman, if you will. They had an unconventional relationship off and on and rather volatile at times."

I put on my best look of surprise.

"Now, don't get me wrong; I am not one to spread gossip; but you can't keep a secret like that with ruckuses they were raising. Folks could hear Kate yelling and screaming, dishes and whatnot crashing against the walls or flying from behind out into the street as Doc exited their room. That wild Hungarian even took a shot at him once or twice. They'd break up and the next thing you know, they'd be walkin' down Allen Street arm and arm, lovey-dovey as you please. She was too much of a woman for the likes of that broken down dentist." He smiles and shakes his head.

Our waiter arrives and the sheriff, without consultation, orders for us. He notices my confusion. "Oh, you're new in town," he says stumbling over his words, "and I happen to know that the pork is fresh today. The wine is their best," he says.

I nod in approval. "You would know better than, I." I notice that it does not take much to get this man swelling with pride. If he puffs his chest out any farther, he'll float out of his chair.

"I assure you I have been well-schooled in how to treat a lady."

I'm thinking, gag-me-with-a-spoon, but offer, "That's a rare quality in this part of the country, from what I have seen thus far."

"It is unfortunate that most of the town folk have little in the way of education in the finer things in life," he sighs. "That will come as the town grows and attracts a higher caliber of people." Just then, the waiter arrives with the wine. Behan makes a show of inspecting the label and tasting. "Ah, perfect," he says gesturing the go-ahead to the waiter, who with equal flair, fills our glasses. It is excellent and I say so, prompting another expansion of the sheriff's chest.

"Mr. Stuart might be a good influence in that regard. I wonder if he and his wife plan to move out here." My suggestion sparks a momentary expression of alarm in his face.

The slightest of sneers pulls at the left side of the sheriff's mouth. He quickly absorbs it in a broad smile. "The English do have culture, but I find their stoic approach to life a bit stuffy. People out here want to have fun without being judged at every turn."

"Oh, I don't find Mr. Stuart stuffy in the least. Why, he possesses a refreshing honesty and a dry, but charming sense of humor." Behan's lip twitches again and I suggest, "Perhaps the ways of the English are less of a culture shock to us Easterners." I bet he'd like to slap me about now, but ignores my comment.

"Getting back to what I was saying before, Miss Collins, most of the men in town are involved in mining. There are very few gentlemen like myself. I'm going to make it a priority to see that your stay here is without incident and that you are shielded from the less than genteel goings-on of our society." I nod as if thankful while my mental image projects a finger heading down my throat.

Our food arrives and, at first bite, I acknowledge its excellence; then for the next hour, I listen to the self-aggrandizing sheriff narrate his heroic exploits. To hear him tell it, he single-handedly quelled the violence brought on by the hatred between the cowboys and the Earps.

"Before those brothers came to town, things were pretty peaceful here in Tombstone, not perfect, mind you, but I had things under control. Wyatt came here with his big reputation and fancy ideas; pissing people off left and right; stirring up trouble where there wasn't any, really. Then Virgil sticks his nose into law enforcement, takes guns away in town, and gets the cowboys all riled up."

He takes a sip of wine, giving me an opportunity to interject. "I heard that it wasn't safe for women and children to be on the streets when the cowboys would come into town; that they were robbing stages and rustling cattle. Someone said that they were stirring up trouble across the border and with the Indians."

"My Dear Miss Collins," he says shaking his head as if disappointed. "I know you're intelligent enough to know that you can't believe everything you read and hear. Why, the former editor of the Epitaph had to sell out and leave town because of the partisan propaganda he printed as news. I trust *your* report on our fair town will not be colored by any political agenda."

"Of course not," I say slapping a hand to my heart, as if I am aghast at the thought. "I thought Mr. Clum and a number of other important men in town had been threatened by the cowboys after the Earps were exonerated in the shootout, including the judge."

"More gossip." His exasperation is beginning to show. "Those important men, as you call them, were bribed by the Earps, for all we know. And don't take this the wrong way, but this is one of those areas that's best left to men. I mean, I have no problem with you chronicling the events for posterity, as long as you record the facts; and I understand that an unmarried woman like yourself is forced to make her own way until she finds a man to take care of her, but there are more reliable, less controversial professions. You would make a great schoolteacher, for instance. You know, if you get too independent, you might discourage eligible bachelors." I do not miss the nervousness beneath his condescending chuckle. "Anyway," he says, as if eager to sum up the discussion and move on to other things, "those street fights were blown all out of proportion and twisted by the press; and, it's all in the past. I've been able to turn things around. Tombstone has become a respectable town, a safe community where decent people can prosper; where a lady like yourself can find a good man, settle down, and raise a passel of kids." He leans across the table and runs a finger every so lightly across the top of my hand. "Besides, you and I having dinner is all that's truly important at the moment, don't you think . . ."

The urge to laugh is mercifully stifled by an explosion somewhere outside. Behan leaps up, his napkin drifting to the floor. I expect him to rush for the entrance, but instead, he hesitantly walks in that direction. A few seconds of silence is again broken by several louder explosions, which I recognize as gunfire that is getting closer, followed by angry shouts of obviously drunken men and a woman screaming. I follow the example of my fellow patrons and duck under our table. Doc, unarmed, as far as I know, is pushing past Sheriff Behan who has not yet ventured outside to see about the fray. A minute later, Doc reenters the Grand with two women.

"Get under a table in the back," he orders, managing to keep in character. I motion them to join me and notice then, that Doc is holding a gun.

"You better send those whores out here!" we hear from outside.

"Yeah," comes from second man. "I ain't got my money's worth yet." Another gunshot.

"Get yourself home, Judd," retorts Behan, "or the marshal will have no choice but to lock you up. Where is that damn marshal, anyway? This is his responsibility."

"I do believe that these men should be taken into custody, immediately," says Doc, "before this pistol play injures innocent bystanders."

Peeking out from my vantage point, I catch the glare Behan sends Doc's way. Before he can comment, I hear other voices. It is the marshal and a deputy demanding that the guns of the offenders be handed over.

"We ain't the guilty parties, Marshal," one of the drunks slurs out. "It's them damn whores holdin' out on us. Mr. Fancy Pants took 'em inside. Send 'em out and we'll go peaceful. We got no beef with anybody else."

I look at the women huddled beside me. One is holding up the front of her dress where it was torn off her left breast, and the other is bleeding from the side of her mouth; both are shaking.

"That true, girls?" asks Behan turning back and kneeling to make eye contact.

"It's rather obvious," says Doc, "that these women are being abused."

Behan rises and spins toward Doc.

"Since when is this any of *your* business? You aren't even a citizen of this country." he demands, his face only inches from Doc's.

"I believe, Sir, that a lady's honor is *always* a gentleman's business," he retorts in a perfectly controlled tone.

"That would suffice, I suppose, if those two *were* ladies," Behan quips, cocking his head in our direction.

"I beg your pardon, Sir," says Doc with a perfunctory bow of his head. "I can see I was wrong," he adds as he walks away, tucking his gun in the shoulder holster I had not noticed earlier.

Behan seems taken aback at the sudden concession. "About what?"

"I was under the impression," says Doc, "that you were one of the few gentlemen in town."

Behan looks as if he is about to bust a gut, anger taking command of every muscle.

"Ah, Marshal, let my boys alone. They just havin' a little fun. Them whores shouldn't be flautin' their wares if'n they ain't ready to put out," says another voice from the street.

"You stay outtah this Ike, or you'll be joinin' your boys."

There are a few seconds of muffled grumbling and then all is quiet outside. Behan turns to face the patrons. "Okay folks. You can get up and finish your supper. Everything's under control," he announces as if he has just saved the world. The three of us girls help each other from under the table.

"I'm Cassie," I say offering my hand.

"Lita," says the brunette, who looks surprised at the overture but shakes anyway. "And this here's Joanie."

After our handshake, I take my napkin and start to dab at the blood on Joanie's face. The girls look to be no more than fifteen or sixteen. "We *is* whores, yah know; that's true," whispers Lita, and in the way of explanation, "but those two ain't bathed in a month and they was slappin' us around. We don't have tah take on just anybody."

"I'm sorry you have to be doing this, at all," I say. "Perhaps . . ."

"That won't be necessary," Behan interrupts while snatching the napkin from my hand. He motions to the waiter for a fresh one, before grabbing Lita and Joanie by their elbows, and roughly escorting them out the door. "Stay on your own side of town," he warns as he gives them a shove out the doors. "You know better than to show yourselves in the Grand." He straightens his coat and tie as he returns to the table.

"I'm sorry you had to witness that," he says lifting the wine glass to his lips. "As you can see, we still have occasional lapses in the peace. Those women are a regretful necessity," shaking his head, "but some of them don't know their place and have to be reminded once in a while."

"But they didn't . . ."

"That foreigner should not have interfered; and even so, those whores shouldn't have set foot in this place. They know better," he says; his tone is one of exasperation. I reach for my wine to ease the uncomfortableness of the silence that follows.

Behan drums his fingers, then sighs. "After all, Cassie, they *chose* the world's oldest profession; no one *forced* them to sell their bodies. They could have just as easily done what you're doing," he says in an effort to justify his attitude. He is failing miserably and knows it. "They knew what they were getting into. Of course, those men should have known better than to chase them up to this end of town."

I remain stunned at his crassness, but he, I am sure, attributes my distress to the ugliness of what had transpired.

"And," he chuckles, "there's no denying that those two could use a bath."

"I guess," I say attempting to return to my meal.

"I hate to mention it, and I know you were well-intentioned, but your display of sympathy for those women might be less than appreciated by the ladies in town," he says glancing around. "I'm sure, however," he continues, "that they will overlook this instance since you are new in town and unfamiliar with the ways of the west; but I strongly urge you to avoid such action in the future . . . for the sake of your *own* reputation, Miss Collins."

"Of course," I say. "I don't know what I was thinking, but as you say, I am not used to such goings-on."

"An honest mistake, springing from a good heart, I might add," he says lifting his glass in a toast. As I reciprocate, I feel Doc's displeasure from across the room. Look, Buddy, I think, we're both making concessions here. After all, look at your date. The end result will be worth it.

"Is it true . . . I mean . . ."

"What Cassie? Oh, forgive me. May I call you by your Christian name?"

"Oh, of course," I answer. "It's just that I've heard stories . . . that Miss Elder is . . . was . . . I mean . . ."

"Let's just say that Kate is one of a kind. She has, shall we say, taken the profession to a new level, periodically catering to wealthy gentlemen whose reputations are not likely to be challenged, thus shielding hers while she is under their, shall we say, cloak of respectability. She is more of a mistress; besides, she scares the hell out of other women, and most men, as well. Doc was the exception; that fool didn't have sense enough to be afraid of anything. He's lucky he survived the relationship."

"She was on the coach from Benson and she indicated they were married?"

Behan nearly chokes on his wine. After bringing the napkin to his lips, he answers. "That's how she presented herself when they hit town. As far as I know, he didn't outright deny it; but everybody knew. He was no prize, himself, sickly, looking twice his actual age or more, coughin' out every other word."

"I understand Mr. Holliday is quite intelligent, well educated, a gentleman from the South. He's a doctor, isn't he?"

"Humph; if you can call a dentist without a practice, a

doctor. The guy's a lunger."

"I beg your pardon?"

"Consumption; his lungs are being eaten up; it's a wonder he's lasted this long."

"He's still alive, then?"

"As far as I know. Why all this interest in Holliday? Are you thinking of interviewing him?" I think for a minute; then fill my expression with anticipation. "Look," Behan continues, "he may have all the book-learning there is, been raised with all the fancy manners, but he's nothing but a smart-mouth killer, pure and simple. Tombstone's glad to be rid of him. I strongly suggest that you do not pursue the idea of making his acquaintance, or that of the Earps either. "Now." His tone implies he is done with the topic, "Let's talk about more pleasant things, shall we?"

"Of course; I did not mean to bring up bad memories." I adjust my perspective and replay the events of the past several minutes filtering them objectively. I cannot say for sure, but some of my fellow diners seem to be troubled by what they had witnessed earlier. Behan's actions came off nothing short of pompous and uncaring. Of course, the town must be used to this. The English visitor's reaction, on the other hand, showed class and courage; his treatment of the women, humane, qualities alien to the sheriff of Tombstone. Then again, my fellow patrons might agree with the sheriff's assessment; that all is fair when it comes to ladies of the night.

"Would you like to see the town tomorrow? I might be able to find time to escort you, or perhaps a buggy ride in the surrounding area. There are some nice spots to picnic along the San Pedro and it's not far. We could—"

"You bastard!" screeches Kate erupting from her chair; at the same time hurling the contents of her wine glass in her date's direction. How he avoids the resulting splatter is beyond me. I have a feeling he was expecting it. His evasive action, unfortunately, has allowed the scarlet liquid to spray the face and bodice of a lady seated at the table behind him who has turned to witness the commotion. A waiter comes rushing to the astonished woman's aid.

"That's what you get for poking in your nose," Kate yells, her ire further fueled by her thwarted effort. She continues to roar at the Englishman "You're nothing but a pompous ass masquerading as . . . as a . . ." Suddenly, she reaches for Doc's glass, but he beats her to it, steps back as if the scene had been choreographed, and calmly takes a sip. All the while, the waiter is frantically attending to the stain on the woman's dress. Kate's face is crimson with rage, now. Mr. Stuart sidesteps as she upends their table, sending dishes and their contents airborne in the direction of the wine-drenched patron and the waiter. Fueled further, Kate charges toward the Englishman, arm pulled back, open hand poised to strike. Behan is up and catches it from behind before she can follow through, although, I am sure he would have rather have seen the man receive the slap.

"Kate!" he says grabbing her wrist. She struggles to wrench away. "Kate," he hisses, no doubt feeling the ogling of all the eyes in the room. "Get hold of yourself." Restrained, she straightens herself, raises her head and allows him to escort her out of the establishment. She digs in her heels at the door and whispers to Behan who allows her to turn around.

"Of course, I will pay for the damages, Leonard," she directs to the waiter, who nods. "And for the lady's dress," she says to the woman wearing her meal. The woman nods but continues to glare.

Once Leonard has done what he can for the couple, I motion him over. "Please bring the gentleman another meal and seat him with the sheriff and myself," I say slipping him bills to pay for the meal.

He bows politely, but it is clear that he is taken-aback by my gesture. "That will not be necessary," he says. "The meal will be charged to Miss Elder. I'm sorry for this vulgar display. This is not the first time this has happened, but it will be the last, I assure you."

A moment later, Mr. Stuart, still off to the side, sipping his wine; nods to acknowledge the waiter's message. He nods, strides over and bows before sitting. He is unaffected by the stares, and soon the silence begins to be replaced with the normal clinking of dishes and utensils and supper chatter. By the time the sheriff returns, conventional atmosphere has been restored.

"I see we have company," Behan says arriving at the table. It is evident that he is annoyed with this intrusion, but knows protocol demands acceptance. Retrieving his napkin, he settles himself at the table and takes a sip from his wine glass. "That's the last Tombstone will see of that woman." His announcement seems tinged with regret. "Just what did you say to set her off?" His question is more like a challenge.

"I daresay," says Thomas. "The woman is no lady. I invited her to supper to ease the tension between us in the coach," he directs at me. "She had the audacity to proposition me, knowing I am a married man, and was insulted when I declined her advances."

"Is that really true?" I ask in disbelief. Why would she . . . It doesn't take long for me to reassess. Kate's attraction to Thomas Stuart makes sense; his intellect and breeding, while of different origin than her one-time lover, still draws her attention, as Doc knew they would. Obviously, the fact that he was married did not deter her. They were in each other's company for only minutes before the verbal sparring commenced in the stagecoach. According to Doc, he and Kate's relationship vacillated between restorative calms and volatile confrontations culminating in arduous lovemaking. Foreplay, to Kate, started with some frivolous irritation aimed at Doc, who, in turn, feigned disinterest, fueling her anger and her insistence on satisfaction. He would continue to ignore; she would start to throw things, the projectiles increasing in lethalness as her rage escalated, forcing him to restrain her. The physical altercation progressed to hands-on paving the way for passion until they fell into exhaustion and sleep. Restored, the couple would emerge from their lair, the picture of harmony.

The scene made sense. Kate is attracted to Thomas Stuart. At the supper table, she no doubt, resurrected their verbal duel from the coach, and, up to a point, got the desired reaction. Thomas played his part, discounting her ideas, acting out the superior role. How Doc must have relished watching her eyes ignite, hearing the annoyance evolve into a fury that exploded physically. The satisfaction he must feel in her public humiliation when he ignored the cue to sweep her off her feet and carry her up to his room. This is fun, more fun than I could ever have imagined.

"Quite, I assure you," answers Thomas as he leans back to accept his new plate of food. After thanking the waiter, "I did not know the woman was a common whore." He bends his head to his fork and misses the scowl Behan aims his way. "I thought you didn't allow such women in this establishment."

"I wouldn't say that Kate is . . ."

"A common whore?" says Thomas. "Just how would you describe a woman who propositions a gentleman who merely invited her for a meal? We don't see this kind of behavior in England," he says meeting Behan's eyes as if daring the sheriff to contest his assessment. I am reminded of British royalty. In England their fooling around is swept under a thick carpet of discretion. Behan clears his throat and reaches for his wine. He scans the room, searching for a retort, but comes up empty. What is there to say?

"Well, perhaps she was emboldened by the liquor," Thomas offers. "And conceivably, she is not common, but a whore she most certainly is, in stark contrast with our present female company, a lady through and through. Surely you agree, Sheriff Behan?" he concludes rhetorically, as he dabs his mouth with his napkin. "Now," he says rising, "I do thank you for accommodating me at your table, but it's time I take my leave." He takes my hand and bows to kiss it, then nods at Behan who immediately seems to relax as he watches Doc start up the staircase to his room.

"Miss Elder has been asked to leave town and not return. It might be best that Mr. Stuart move on, as well. A man of his background is bound, in all innocence, of course, to create difficulties in a culture in which he is unfamiliar. Tombstone is progressive, but as yet, not cosmopolitan. And mind you, I don't hold Kate fully responsible for the altercation. I am sure Mr. Stuart had a part in it. Just because he restrained himself, does not absolve him of responsibility. I do hope his stay in town will be brief. Has he said anything to you?"

"I hardly know the man, so I don't know that I can agree with you. He did nothing out of place as far as I could see, and according to the waiter, your Miss Elder has a reputation for inciting similar incidents. I saw it for myself on the ride into town."

"True, Kate's always been lively; that's for sure. But that Englishman; there's something about him . . . I don't know what it is, but I'd bet anything, he's not what he appears to be. He reminds me of someone . . . I just can't put my finger on it. I just don't like him."

"Do you think that's fair?"

Our waiter appears with two pieces of pie and coffee. "Consider your evening on the house, Sheriff; in appreciation for handling the disturbances," he says with a bow.

Behan thanks the man and looks at me as if trying to read my thoughts. "Forgive me if I speak out of turn. I thought that a woman of your caliber would be more perceptive."

"Excuse me, Sir, but I have come to expect officers of the law to serve without bias. Certainly because a man who has done nothing out of the way, who simply reminds you of another you happen to dislike . . ."

"Please," he says raising both hands. "I didn't mean to upset you." Then he whispers, "Please keep your voice down."

"Why, do I suddenly remind you of Miss Elder?" I say cocking my head and maintaining my volume. "Afraid I will make a scene, dump my coffee in your lap; maybe send this pie into your face?"

The sheriff is literally squirming in his chair. It takes all my effort to hold my lips together to not burst out laughing at the absurdity of it all. Behan's expression is a combination of bewilderment and fear of what I might say or do next. He can control a wildcat like Kate and is vexed at not having the same power over the seeming waif that he presumes me to be. I don't know how much longer I can hold off. A sip of coffee helps.

Behan pulls out his watch and after a glance announces,

as if caught off guard, "This evening has gone longer than expected and I find I must get back to my duties. May I see you back to Nellie's?" he asks with an expression that conveys his hope that I will decline. Although I would love to continue to push his buttons, I think better than to pursue the torture further at present, lest I betray my motives. Behan bids me a good night in a less than sincere manner, although I do not think, in his confused state, that he notices his social faux pas of not insisting on escorting a lady back to her lodging.

The waiter refreshes my coffee. At almost ten, the dining room is thinning out but I linger a while, thinking about the events since I left my other life, the people I have met; the bizarre twist my life has taken.

"Be careful, Miss," says the waiter who comes to my assistance as I take my coat from the rack in preparation to leave.

"Thank you, I will," I say. "The meal was excellent, by the way."

The street is bustling with activity that seems to bounce in and out of the drinking establishments just beginning to rev up for the night. I mind my steps on the uneven boardwalk but stumble sideways into the street when I take a direct hit from an unsteady cowboy who bursts through the swinging doors on my right. The man, too drunk for rational thought, proceeds to swagger across the street without notice of me.

"Hey, yah goddamn fool," yells another who bends down to help me to my feet. He reeks of whiskey and sweat, but appears somewhat soberer than his cohort. Before I can identify the familiar face, he says, "Howdy, Ma'am, Joseph Isaac Clanton, at your service." He removes his hat and almost trips as he bows.

"Thank you, Mr. Clanton," I say dusting off my clothing. "I appreciate your help. I think I'd best be on my way." I start back in the direction of Nellie's when he takes me by the elbow.

"I'll see yah back tah your room," he says. "Things can get sort a wild aroun' here this time o'night, if yah know what I mean."

Although taken by surprise and somewhat uneasy in his company, I dismiss the urge to bolt from his grasp. After all, how many girls get a chance to meet Ike Clanton? As we walk toward Fifth Street, Ike is talkative.

"I own a ranch on the San Pedro," he says with pride. "Passed down from my daddy. He was an important man in these parts, yah know."

"Oh, he's gone?"

"A couple years ago, murdered by those Earps is what I think. They's a slick bunch. Got caught red-handed murderin' Billy . . . that's my brother. Got off, though; crooked politics and all that used to run thin's aroun' here. Not no more; got rid those big shot lawmen and their highbrow ideas . . . They gonna think twice about showin' they faces aroun' here agin; 'cept . . ."

"Except what, Mr. Clanton," I say, nearly gagging on the dignified label; but I know the address is music to the man's ears and will loosen his tongue further.

"'cept Johnny Ringo."

"Who is Johnny Ringo?"

"Guess a lady like yersef wouldn't know about him."

We are at the boarding house, now, my back against the door; Ike's palm against the door. I fight the urge to shrink away, betraying my disgust, and risking his offense.

"Just one o' the smartest cowboys aroun'. He an' Curly Bill . . . when they was alive . . . the cowboys was strong; ruled the whole county; nobody got in our way back then. Earps and that damned drunken dentist ran aroun' killing cowboys left and right. Got Brocious down by Iron Springs. Don't pass that on though; the rest of us took his body and buried it where it'll never be found and spread the story he high-tailed it to Mexico. God, I miss that ornery cuss. Now, Johnny . . ." For a moment I think the drunken man will cry. He snatches at a tear that escapes before it can run down his cheek.

"What happened to Mr. Ringo?"

"Got hisself shot a couple o' weeks ago near the Chiricahuas. They's sayin' he killed hisself, but I know bettah. Goddamned Earps snuck back from Coloradah and murdered him in col' blood, they did. I know it as sure as I knowed they killed my pa."

A chill travels up and down my spine and I jerk into a shiver. "I'd like to get my hands on 'em," he says dropping his arm and rubbing his hands together in anticipation. "They be sorry if'n I ever set eyes on any of 'em again. You takin' a chill there, Missy. Here, let me . . ."

I just barely evade Ike's embrace, swing around and fumble for the doorknob.

"I'm sorry for your losses Mr. Clanton. I'm awfully tired. Thank you so much for seeing me to Nellie's."

He blocks the door with his boot. "Donchah think I deserve a little reward he says, his breath hot in my ear; his body pressing mine into the door. "Say a little kiss? Who knows, you might like it."

"Please unhand me, Mr. Clanton or I will be forced to scream for help."

He laughs at my threat. When I raise my leg, it forces my hip further into his, momentarily giving him the impression, I realize, that I desire the closeness; that is until the heel of my high-buttoned shoe digs into his shin.

Ike yelps at the contact. "You fuckin' tease," he screams. He reaches down to the source of his pain. In swift succession, I fall backward, am yanked inside as the door slams into Ike's face. He thinks better of storming the entrance with the likes of Nellie Cashman on the other side. Through the window, we watch him slink away, as I breathe a sigh of relief.

"Thank you, Mrs. Cashman. Mr. Clanton helped me home after I was knocked down in the street by a drunk. I guess my gratitude gave him the impression I was interested. I'm so sorry for the trouble."

"You had best stay away from the likes of him, Miss Collins. He hangs with a bad lot. And you shouldn't be walking the streets alone. It just isn't done," she says pulling down the last of the shades. "You get yourself a good night's rest. I will see you in the morning. And call me, Nellie, ya hear?"

"Thank you, Mrs. . . . I mean Nellie; thank you for

everything."

If there was ever a woman to admire, it is Nellie Cashman. It's easy to see why people call her "the angel of Tombstone." Her place, we had agreed earlier, would be the safest place in town for me to stay. He's always right. As we say our goodnights, Nellie reaches to hug me.

"Ow!"

"My, my," says Nellie as she notices the bloody tear in the sleeve of my dress under the elbow. "You've been hurt and your lovely dress is torn. Let's get you up to your room," she says gently guiding me up the stairs. "Charles," she calls down as we proceed. "Go get Dr. Goodfellow and send him up to Miss Collin's room."

"No, I'm sure that's not . . ."

"Nonsense; we can't have you getting an infection. Who knows what's in that street."

Her tone leaves no room for rebuttal. I am tired and the pampering feels good. Nellie tackles all the laces and buttons efficiently and within a few minutes I am in my nightclothes with one sleeve pushed up to accommodate the doctor's inspection. A minute later, a light rap announces his arrival. Dr. George Goodfellow is nice looking, in his early thirties, I would guess. After Nellie's brief introduction, he gets down to business. He has a confident air about him and quickly tends to the scrape; cleaning, disinfecting, and bandaging with skill.

"That should do it, Miss Collins. Leave the bandage on for several days and keep it dry. If any redness develops, send for me or come to my office at once. I trust, in the future, you will not try to maneuver our streets alone after dark." Obviously, my hostess has informed him of the circumstances of my injury.

"Yes, thank you, Doctor. How much do I owe you for your services?"

While people in modern times would gasp at the exorbitant sum charged for such a simple procedure, I almost laugh at the pittance of Dr. Goodfellow's fee.

"Keep it," I say handing him more than double his price. "I am very grateful that you came out this late for such a trivial matter. Perhaps you'll have a less fortunate client. You can apply the difference to their bill." The doctor acquiesces graciously and bids me goodnight, as does Nellie, who follows him out.

True to expectations, it has been an interesting evening. When I left the Grand, I had been sleepy, and the incidents afterward had added to my exhaustion; but I have an itch in my mind that I must scratch. If Ike's hunch is true . . . the timing is right . . . it all fits. To my horror, I realize that Wyatt, Warren, and Doc had left Gunnison a few weeks ago to return to Arizona, and kill Johnny Ringo. Did Josie know, after all? Had she simply been trying to protect me? Have I, by association, become an unwitting accessory to murder?

.

CHAPTER 52

With my mind running as it is, I know I will never get to sleep. Thankfully, I remembered to pack the sleep aid that had seen me through after my parents' deaths.

I slumber hard, awaking without having moved. The drug has left me rested but a bit groggy. Dressing quickly, I head downstairs desperate for the caffeine that will clear my head.

Doc and I had previously arranged to "accidentally" bump into one another outside a dress shop around ten. I think about the confrontation with Ike Clanton and decide I will not mention it to Doc. From what I surmised last night, Ike would not live through the day, not that anyone would mourn the loss. Doc, however, is another story. I must not let him risk his new lease on life avenging my honor. History, as it reads now, does not give Ike that much longer, anyway. He will rob one too many stages and pay with his life when resisting apprehension. Let sleeping dogs lie, I say.

Nellie greets me with coffee and a sealed envelope. It is a note from Sheriff Behan expressing regrets that he cannot honor his invitation for this afternoon. In all the commotion of the night before, I had forgotten about the buggy ride and picnic along the river. It is just as well. I'm not sure how much longer I can string along that infuriating man without exposing Doc and myself. After a second refill, the cobwebs are clearing. It is half past eight. I take my time at breakfast, savoring every bite of a meal untainted by modern additives and artificial ingredients before returning to my room briefly for my notebook.

Nellie is there a second later. I had not noticed, last evening, that my damaged dress had disappeared with her.

"Nellie, you didn't have to do that," I say looking at the masterfully mended sleeve. She must have spent half the night repairing and laundering. I embrace her tightly. "You're an angel," I say, wondering if she has yet to hear the label that will become her legacy.

"It is the least I can do for such a nice guest. Now you be more careful out there today."

I promise her not to repeat my mistake before hugging her again. I decide to spend the extra minutes I have perusing Fremont Street. I stop in at the office of the Epitaph, pick up the current issue, and tuck it under my arm. I arrive at the predetermined shop where I am greeted by name by the proprietress. Word spreads fast in a small town. We exchange pleasantries before I try on three or four hats. The last thing I need is another Victorian hat, but I choose one. She boxes it up and I move to the front of the shop where I pretend to scrutinize the dresses adorning the front window. When I see Doc approaching from across the street, I thank the shop owner and excuse myself.

Our timing is perfect, our pretense of colliding, believable; the lid of the hatbox pops off on impact with the walk and out spills my new red felt trimmed in white roses and ribbons. I make show of being distressed, while Mr. Stuart scrambles to assess and undo the damage. The shop owner runs out and agrees there is no harm done. In her presence, I accept Mr. Stuart's apology and agree to join him for coffee as recompense. Several passersby witness the scene, as well, adding credibility to our ruse of being recent acquaintances.

"What have you got there?" Doc asks when I set the paper on the table.

"Just a local paper," I say. "We can see what has been going on in town just before we arrived," I say noticing the date is July 22. I begin perusing and stop short when I get to the headline on an upper right column announcing the death of John Ringo. The article painted a picture of a rather law-abiding citizen who became depressed to the point of taking his own life. Ike Clanton had questioned the cause of death and I suspected he was right.

Doc orders our coffee while I read. "Anything interesting?" he asks when the waiter leaves. I shove the paper across to him and watch Doc scan the front page. His eyes move swiftly left to right, up and down. If I had not come to know him so well, I might not have noticed the slight hesitation. He quickly opens the paper and peruses its content.

"What are your plans for the day," he asks, refolding the paper as if it holds nothing of interest.

"The sheriff had asked to take me for a buggy ride and picnic, but it seems he can't make it," I answer.

"That's too bad. I'd love to explore a little, myself. I'll tell you what; why don't I rent a buggy and . . . My Good Man . . ."

Our waiter appears momentarily. "Yes, Sir?"

"Could you pack a picnic basket for two? "And could you tell me where I can rent a carriage for the day?"

"That would be the O K corral on Allen and Third," he says. "It is a beautiful day for a ride and a picnic."

"Thank you," he says, then turns to me. "I shan't be long." Doc rises, but hesitates, "Sir, perhaps you would be so kind as to direct us to a nice spot for our picnic."

"Oh yes," he says eager to help. "Take the road out of town to the west. The San Pedro's not far. Look for the trees, but stay away from Charleston," he cautions in a whisper, "A bad lot hangs out there."

"I see," says Doc. "Thank you for the advice." He excuses himself promising to return directly.

Twenty minutes later, Doc pulls up front in a carriage. The waiter carries our basket out and helps me up next to Doc.

"I believe west is that way," I say pointing. A few minutes later, I understand our detour.

"Look straight ahead and pretend we are talking and enjoying ourselves," Doc instructs.

"We *are* talking," I say dryly but manage a smile. Out of

the corner of my eye, through the window, I see Sheriff Behan, slamming his fist on the desk in his office.

We have gone about a mile out of town when we see a man on horseback approaching. Doc slows our pace, as does the rider.

"Well, well, well, if it isn't Miss Uppity, too-good-for-a-cowboy and Mr. Fancy Pants." It was not yet noon and Ike Clanton was already drunk. "Your kind ain't wanted around these parts, yah hear?"

"I beg your pardon, Sir," says Doc bristling at the sight of his enemy. "Do you know this man or what he is talking about, Miss Collins?"

"I am sure, I don't know, Mr. Stuart."

"You lyin' bitch!" screams Ike. Quick as lightening Doc has his gun trained on Ike's head, whose eyes widen in abject fear. "I . . . I . . . I must be mistaken, Mister. Now, put that thin' away before somebody gets hurt." Incredibly, Ike leans toward Doc and offers his hand. When Doc declines the gesture, Ike withdraws it and says, "Nice day for buggy ride, yes Sir, mighty fine day; you folks enjoy yourselves." And with that, he spurs his horse and continues toward Tombstone.

Out of earshot and almost sight, Doc becomes himself. "Yah do know what that was about." It was wishful thinking that Doc wouldn't pursue the matter.

"Mr. Clanton escorted me home last night from the Grand."

Doc squints in confusion. "I could have sworn I left yah in slightly bettah company."

"After you left, the conversation got a little too much for the sheriff. He excused himself. I declined his offer to escort me."

"Ah told you—"

"I know that was unwise," I say before he can scold further. "Anyway, a drunk coming out of a saloon accidentally knocked me down. Ike saw it, helped me up and walked me to Nellie's," I said shrugging it off as inconsequential.

"That's not all there was tah it," he says waiting for further explanation.

"He was drunk."

"An'?" Doc was not going to let it go.

"All right," I say. "He tried to kiss me."

Doc turns the buggy and slaps the reins.

"Stop," I yell louder than I thought possible.

"Whoa." Doc pulls the horse up immediately, genuinely shocked at my outburst. I have his full attention and I take advantage of it.

"You can't go off half-cocked just because some drunk . . ." I begin.

"Correction; Ike is not jus' aneh drunk," Doc says calmly and it appears that he might again signal the horse to action.

Calm be damned. "Think about it. He's not worth the trouble, and he's going to be dead in a couple of years anyway." The words spew forth, drenched with emotion I have been holding back since last night. "You've got a full life ahead of you now; you can't throw it away on the likes of him," I sputter; tears flooding down my face. "I didn't help you get healthy just to watch you get shot down or hung over something as stupid as this. And how would I get back home? Have you thought about that?" Fueled by emotion and inertia, I cannot hold back. "Oh, but you've *already* put yourself in harm's way again, haven't you?" Doc looks puzzled. "Oh, you think I'm that stupid? I should have known; all the secrecy; not even Josie knew what you guys were up to. I can add two and two, Doc. Johnny Ringo was killed while you and your friends left Josie and me in Gunnison. He didn't commit suicide like they reported in the paper, which article you pretended not to notice this morning. Even Ike figured that out," I wail.

"Good."

"Good? Murder is good?"

"Yah are makin' judgments based on limited knowledge on which Ah am not at liberty tah expand. This was the verah reason Ah refused tah take yah with me," he says as I turn away now sobbing and sniffing.

Doc reaches around for my chin and pulls my face so that we are looking eye-to-eye. "If Ah would explain tah anyone, it would be tah yah," he says ever so gently and I sense that he is telling the truth. He pulls out his handkerchief and proceeds to wipe my tears as he continues. "If yah have discerned that much, yah know that this was not *mah* operation; an', in truth, not entirely Wyatt's, as may be yor next presumption; although we were both more than obliged to cooperate. That is all Ah am at liberty tah say. Perhaps, by yor time, it has been figyahed out." He shrugs. "We'll have tah check out the history books when we get back," he says rubbing my knee.

"But . . . "

"Why did I say 'good'?" I nod, a tear still escaping here and there. "Good that Ike knows the truth; because the entities involved, me included, want to send a message to the rest of the cowboys. At first glance, it looks like Johnny took his own life, but when the authorities get through deliberating, they will first question, then, if they have any sense at all, discard that theory. The scene was staged with so much conflicting evidence that they will soon give up trying tah figyah out exactly what happened. Coming up with a prosecutable suspect will be impossible."

"But,"

"But the cowboys, as Ike has already revealed; they will know, beyond a doubt, that Ringo's death was calculated, an' a fearful remindah that their reign of terror is ovah."

"I see." And I do. He needs say no more.

"Ah'm guessing that Ah have fallen from that ridiculous pedestal yah've had me perched atop?" I turn from him, again. Why I think I am hiding my feelings from him, I do not know. "Tell me; what did yah know about that vendetta ride before Ah fell into your world?"

I swivel back to face him and have to stop and think. "I don't know, exactly; I guess what I saw in the movie."

"Tombstone, is it; the one where everythin' seems tah run togethah? Where the four of us shoot it out with the cowboys on Fremont; and it looks like Virgil and Morgan get shot on the same night shortly thereaftah; Wyatt, Warren, an' I, and a couple of othahs go tearin' through the countryside killin' the cowboys? I die and Josie and Wyatt live happily evah aftah?"

"Yeah, I guess," motioning my hand to show I am eager to hear his point.

"It didn't happen exactly that way. Virgil was attacked about two months aftah the shootout; Morgan was killed almost three months aftah that. Once we loaded Virgil and the women on the train with Morg's body, we proceeded on a quest to get rid of the cowboys starting with Frank Stillwell, who was gunnin' for us at the station. We put a sizeable dent in the cowboy population before heading to Colorado when we got word that Behan had a posse aftah us. A couple a months laytah, Ah met yah."

"But Ringo,"

"Ringo survived that ride; somehow, evaded us. An' if yah're wonderin', Ah didn't pull the trigger. Don't get me wrong; Ah would love tah have had the privilege. Morgan and Ah were especially close an' when he was murdahed I . . ." Doc's head drops for a moment. When he resumes, his eyes are moist. "Yes, Wyatt, Warren, an' I returned tah Arizona a few weeks ago specifically tah kill Ringo."

"Oh." I can't think of anything else to say. My emotions are all over the place, and it will take some time to sort through them.

Doc takes a deep breath. "Tell me; now that yah know that Ah was involved with Ringo's death a few weeks back instead of a few months ago, how does that change yor opinion a me?"

Looking into his eyes, my perplexity begins to fade. What he is saying makes perfect sense. *When* Johnny Ringo was killed has nothing to do with the issue. And, like a lot of things we think we know, there is more to this than meets the eye. I respect Doc's loyalty, and will not press him to betray a confidence. I will, however, be checking the history books when we return. How silly of me to rely on Hollywood for historic fact.

"I'm sorry," I say. "I—"

Doc puts his hand to my lips. "Ah undahstand," his voice is dripping with empathy. "This must be awfully confusin' foh yah . . . but . . ."

"I know," I admit. "I asked for it. You didn't want to take me with you. You were protecting me in more ways than one. I guess I sort of feel like an accomplice," I say in way of an explanation.

"Yah, indeed, may be," he says in all seriousness that dissolves as his smile broadens evoking my own.

"But Ike . . ."

"Point taken; that sorrah excuse foh a man is not worth riskin' my now healthy neck."

I sink into Doc and let my head rest on his chest. His even heartbeat and breathing are bringing my own back into normal range. We sit there for a while. Finally, our horse turns to look back.

"I think it best that we fohgo our picnic on the rivah. Ike may gathah friends an' decide to join us. I'm afraid he might take our little encountah as an insult that must be answered."

"I think you're right," although I regret having to move.

"Yeah, we'd best head back tah town," he says giving the reins a slap.

We ride back in silence. I do not know what is going on inside Doc's head, but my mind is busy sorting and filing this latest bit of information and correlating it with my feelings. Doc's actions are over a century removed from what we misguidedly refer to as a more civilized time. In his world, life and death decisions demand instant attention, many times with the exchange of gunfire. Could I get used to life in such a world? For whatever reason, I start to enumerate the pros and cons. On the plus side, I would have knowledge of the future; that would be very handy. The pace of life would be considerably slower; I like that; but would I miss my gadgets; my appliances? Do I want to go down to the river and beat my clothes on a rock? No smog; no car accidents or plane crashes; at least not for a few decades. Oh, but acceptable women's clothing, while attractive, fails miserably in the comfort department. What about medical science and the expected lifespan? Enough; my brain rebels. Where is this going?

"Maybe it would be for the best to head back to Colorado?" I throw out there.

"Ah believe that tah be in both our best interests," Doc agrees. "Ah think we've done all the damage we can here."

"I had so much fun ruining Johnny Behan's evening; and your performance with Kate, Oscar-winning."

"Who's Oscah?"

"It's a . . . not important, believe me. You sure know how to yank Kate's chain." I catch his confusion. "Manipulate her."

"It's not hard with a woman like Kate. Unlike yah, Dahlin, she's so verah predictable."

We bring the buggy back early and leave our lunch for the pleasantly surprised blacksmith. Doc walks me to Nellie's where we grab a quick bite. We agree that Doc will call for me at seven and we will return to the Grand for supper. Meanwhile, I am all for a nap after the stress of the morning.

The first thing that comes to mind when we cross the elegant threshold is that this evening will be another opportunity to annoy Sheriff Behan, who is in the company of a far more adoring companion than that of last evening. I notice a slight wince within his forced smile as he nods in acknowledgement of our presence, but seems to relax when we follow our waiter to a table on the far side of the dining room.

It is without conscience that I switch on the microphone secured within my hair in time to tune in to the sheriff's lowdown on the pompous Englishman and his feminist associate. His companion, a striking woman in her early twenties, is a sponge for his gossip. It appears that our temporary residence has emboldened him to create unflattering fictitious backgrounds for each of us. He claims that Thomas Stuart is traveling under an alias and that he left his own country under a cloak of suspicion. The rumor is that he had been involved in an embezzlement scheme. The sheriff explains that he is powerless to do anything but keep a watchful eye on Stuart and make sure that he does not put down roots in Tombstone.

Doc orders for us so I can continue my audio surveillance under the guise of making notes. According to Behan's sources, my story did not check out, and with my actions of the previous evening with the prostitutes, he could come to no other conclusion than that I escaped from the profession myself, and was trying to remake myself as a writer. While he acknowledges that my efforts are commendable, he questions a "leopard being able to change its spots." When his dinner partner conveys her shock, the sheriff warns her to steer clear of me for the sake of her own reputation, if the "truth" were to become public.

"She's certainly not the type of person we want representing our town in print," he says. "I can only hope that our citizens are not too forthcoming about town business." He tops it all off with the "birds of a feather" cliché that would explain the current liaison between Mr. Stuart and Miss Collins. He cautions his date not to spread unsubstantiated facts, however. He reaches to pat her hand and can't help but see the eagerness in her eyes that I can read from across the room. By mid-morning, the whole town will be talking about its unsavory visitors and we will be blackballed.

I set aside my note pad as another scrumptious meal arrives. His mission accomplished, the sheriff dispenses with "negative" talk and begins his subtle seduction routine. I reach up and turn off my microphone. Anyone around us would think that Mr. Stuart and Miss Collins are comparing notes on their visit. Under our pleasant smiles and nods, I give Doc the blow-by-blow of the conversation across the room. I can tell our laughter is creating even more distress for the envious sheriff. Yes, we are pushing major buttons in Tombstone, and have clearly outworn our welcome. After a superb meal and unsurpassed entertainment, Doc escorts me back to Nellie's, reminding me of our morning departure time for Benson.

CHAPTER 53

"You're not leaving so soon?" queries the sheriff as he notices Doc and me purchasing our stage tickets.

"It seems that Miss Collins, here, has completed her research and is eager to move on. We compared our respective itineraries, found that we have several mutual destinations, and concluded that it might be more pleasant to explore your West together. It would be much safer for Miss Collins and her company will enhance my travels, as well," explains Doc.

"That sounds reasonable," he responds curtly; then to me. "I do hope you will remember our town fondly and pass that on to your readers?"

"Of course. I want to thank you Sheriff, for all your assistance during my stay. Tombstone is a delightful town with so many memorable people."

He swells in pride. "Well, I do take pride in keeping a tight-run town," he says taking my compliment personally. His relief at our departure, though, is evident. Is he perhaps having second thoughts about the seeds he had planted at supper last evening? What *might* he do if his gossip galloped through town while we were still in residence? In his eagerness to get rid of us, had he neglected to think of the possibility of exposure? Then again, he has such influence and confidence he might assume the community as a whole, as is so often the case, unfortunately, would embrace the rumors and simply shun us out of town. In any event, Doc and I have had our fun.

We lay over a night en route so Doc can shed his "costume". It is good to see those beautiful blue eyes again. As soon as we cross the border, he announces his intention to head for the nearest barbershop to rid himself of excess facial hair and encourages me to rest in the room we have taken. After dining, we turn in early, and, the next day we continue our journey back to Gunnison.

Doc wires ahead to Wyatt and Josie, apologizing for our abrupt departure a couple of weeks ago and our upcoming arrival. The two meet us at the station. Josie looks well and Wyatt's countenance reflects the ease of mind that I know descended after the business with Johnny Ringo had been finished. They invite us to supper before we head over to the Dawson House.

I opt for a nap. Doc is no doubt off to find a game. Once again, the thoughts of a permanent crossover for one of us tickle my brain. Doc loves the sporting life, as he calls it. He's good at it. Now that he's well, though, he can practice dentistry again; perhaps set up shop with his cousin Robert; pursue his earlier dreams. No matter how I manipulate the possibilities, I cannot see him content in the twenty-first century.

I am aware of the bed moving before anything else. "How long have I been asleep?"

"Long enough for me to greatly enhance our financial situation," he says. He is sitting on the bed straightening and sorting the pile of cash between us. "Time to get ready for our suppah with the Earps, Dahlin'," he announces as he stashes the neatened stack of bills in the pocket of his coat. He reaches down and caresses my cheek. "I'll be downstairs havin' a drink," he says; "be back foh yah in, say, an hour?"

"I'll be ready," I say reaching up to take his hand, while searching his face for the thought that motivated his tender action. Doc smiles as if nothing is out of the ordinary, gets up off the bed, and leaves the room.

The rest has rejuvenated me and I am anxious to deepen my friendship with Wyatt and Josie. I choose one of my plainer dresses sans the bustle; taking my lead from Josie who was dressed similarly, when they met us at the station. Somehow, I think she values comfort above convention, as well.

Doc appears just as I am smoothing my dress. "Yah look lovely, Cassie," he says and then leans down to kiss me ever so chastely on the cheek. I wonder if my outburst in the wake of our encounter with Ike Clanton might have sparked a change in our relationship. We had become good friends during his convalescence, and it is apparent that our enjoyment of each other's company is mutual. We share similar values. Laughter comes easily when we are together, and more importantly, stretches of silence between us are not uncomfortable. Doc offers his arm, and as we walk toward the Earp house, I review the last several days and realize that since that turbulent exchange in the desert, our bond has deepened; that Doc has become physically affectionate. A new layer of trust has been added to our association; any doubts have been bridged; all subconscious reservations have been permanently quelled. Probing deeper, I discover that for the first time in my twenty-six years, I have a sense of total security; as if I am encased in a protective covering that cannot be breached. I rack my brain for worries and find none. The fact that home exists in another time holds no trepidation for me.

"A penny foh yor thoughts?" Doc squeezes my arm with his free hand and I rest mine atop it.

"Nothing really," I lie. The truth be known, I want to spill these musings and evoke his feelings. Then, again, am I prepared for anything but what I yearn to hear? "I, um . . . I'm just so happy to be seeing Wyatt and Josie again."

"Ah know what yah mean," he says. "Wyatt is the consummate friend and he has chosen his mate wisely. Ah enjoy witnessin' their contentment. If any two people deserve a good life, it is mah friend an' his wife." On that note, we reach the Earp's door.

"It smells so good in here," I say as Wyatt opens the door.

"Josie's got a chicken in the oven and the other aroma is buttermilk pie, if I'm not mistaken."

"You are not," quips Josie waving from the kitchen, as

Doc helps me with my wrap. "Hope you two are hungry," she adds. I rush to join her in the kitchen while Wyatt pours drinks for himself and Doc. Josie puts down the ladle and we exchange a lengthy embrace. "Where on earth have you two been? Shame on you for running off like that." She giggles through the scolding, grabs for both my hands and backs up to the kitchen table where we take our seats.

"First," I insist. "How are you feeling?"

"I feel good and the doctor says I am right as rain." Her countenance matches the analysis. Rosy cheeks and sparkling eyes betray a wellness of body and a joyful spirit. "He is convinced that a little Earp will be running around here in the next year or two."

"Oh, Josie, I'm so glad you're okay; I mean; really okay," I say.

"Whether we are blessed with children or not," she says smiling, "Wyatt and I have each other; but we *are* hopeful."

I mentally applaud her attitude, knowing it will be tested further, and wonder if I would be so accepting. What am I thinking? I am not married and am traditional enough not to bring a child into this world on my own. I agree with Josie, though, that true love should survive a marriage without children. Wyatt and Josie have such an enduring love. This knowing the future thing is great.

The four of us are seated around the table eating and laughing. The couple is unprepared as Doc begins relating our adventures in Tombstone. "You went back to Tombstone?" Wyatt frowns with concern.

Doc puts on his British accent. "Not to worry, Old Chap. Miss Collin's skillful transformation of my physical appearance went completely undetected. The residents of Tombstone were none the wiser when Mr. Thomas Stuart, a traveler from England, and Miss Cassie Collins, a writer from the East, sought to broaden their knowledge of the Wild West." Wyatt smiles and shakes his head while Josie remains agape. Soon they are laughing heartily at the tales of our encounters with Sheriff Behan, Kate, and Ike.

"I would love to have seen them squirm," says Josie.

"Yah ought tah have seen Cassie, here, with her naive

comments an' askin' all the sensitive questions, all cloaked in her innocent demeanor. She turned old Behan inside out," Doc laughs. "Had him runnin' for cover at dinnah an' wigglin' out at that picnic invitation. Poor soul, it was jus' too much of a strain. He was attracted tah her but frustrated to no end that he couldn't manipulate her."

Of course, Doc leaves out the part of my insider information. He, also, does not mention Ringo; but I'm sure he and Wyatt have discussed the success privately over their drinks. It was over. Ringo would do no more harm, they could never be incriminated, and the remaining cowboys got the message. That did not mean our men are free to return to Tombstone. Arizona is forever off limits to Doc and the Earps. I caught the wording of my private thoughts; *our men.*

"What are your plans Doc; thinking of staying awhile?" asks Wyatt.

"Oh, that would be wonderful!" says Josie. "We could see the world together!"

I smile but let Doc handle this one. "Wyatt, yah know I sortah left Bat in a fix coverin' foh me in Pueblo. Folks think Ah'm secured in his custody down there. He's probably bustin' a gut. Nah, Ah gottah git back there and straighten out the legal mattahs before anythin' else. Then, I need tah see the doctor up in Glenwood Springs; check up on the progress of mah recovery. After that, who knows, Cassie an I may verah well catch up with yah and do a little travelin'", he says patting my knee. "In any event, Wyatt, we'll see each othah again befoh too long."

It is almost midnight when the conversation becomes punctuated with frequent yawns. Doc is the first to suggest that we call it an evening; the rest of us concur. He and I relive the evening as we make our way back to Dawson House. Once in the room, I let myself flop onto the bed that has considerably more spring than modern ones. Doc removes his hat, coat, and boots; after which he starts to unlace my shoes. I feel a bit awkward but enjoy the personal attention.

"Oh my," I say when he proceeds to rub my feet. I feel the color rush to my face, because to my way of thinking, this is a very intimate gesture.

"Ah don't see how yah women walk in these thin's all day long," he says with a chuckle.

"This woman doesn't, usually," I say. "I can't wait to get back to my cowboy boots, shirts, and jeans; or even my tennis shoes.

Doc rises and flops back on the bed, his hands behind his head.

"And these corsets . . . God, whose idea were these barrels of torture?" I say wiggling in discomfort. Doc laughs. I pull myself onto my knees behind Doc. I begin to rub his neck and shoulders in a way of repayment.

"Now, Dahlin', this is heaven, he says, twisting a little to get the full benefit for about five minutes. "Thank yah kindly," he says rising. I take the cue; the massage is over. I duck behind the partition to change from my dress to the modest flannel granny gown and robe. By the time I return, Doc is already on his side of the bed. He has removed his vest, shirt, and belt and lies atop the bedding, his eyes already closed. I, as gingerly as possible, slide under the comforter.

Having had a nap, I am not as exhausted as I know Doc must be. In addition, my mind will not be put to rest, but insists on pursuing disturbing avenues of contemplation. I find my heart jumping into the discussion tugging here and there at possibilities and their pros and cons. In a matter of minutes, I come face to face with one undeniable fact; I am in love with John Henry Holliday, a man from another time. I lie here next to him, an intruder into his world. Why did I insist on following him? Things were simpler several weeks ago; or were they? I think back to when he refused to take me with him and remember the feeling. The disappointment was more than just being denied the adventure of it all. I couldn't bear for him to leave; couldn't deal with the possibility that he might not return. Who am I kidding? I was in love with him, even then. Oh, what am I going to do? I blink against the tears stinging my eyes. In my chest, an ache is spreading. Doc is well, now, and he can go back to Georgia, to the life he had originally envisioned. Oh, how did I let this happen? My heart is speeding up. I take several deep, controlled breaths to slow it. After several minutes, I come to terms with the fact that sleep will be next to impossible. Resigning myself is somehow calming, and I decide to try a relaxation technique, concentrating on one part of my body at a time, starting with my toes. I am up to my hips when I feel Doc's hand encompassing mine. At first, I think he must be asleep, until he begins toying with my fingers. I find it pleasurable, but disconcerting. I want to reciprocate, but lie frozen.

"Cassie?"

I try to sound casual. "Umm?"

"We need tah talk, Dahlin," Doc says in a whisper.

"About leaving?" I say hurriedly following up immediately with, "I'm okay with that. I know you have—"

He interjects before I can finish. "Sic patet, quod ordine naturae, elit."

"Excuse me?"

"It appears that we mus' redefine the nature of our association."

"I don't understand," I say, and I don't.

"About the fact that we are in love." He turns on his side; his fingers caress my arm through the fabric of my gown. There is no moon. I can hardly make out the outline of his face, but I can feel those piercing blue eyes. "I love yah, Cassie Collins of the futchah."

"I . . . I . . ."

Before I can find the words, Doc's mouth is on mine. His kiss is sweet and gentle; followed by feathery brushes over my cheeks, eyes, and ears. I don't realize I am holding my breath until my lungs scream for air. He sighs, and I feel his weight lift off the bed and silently rebuke my hesitation. By not responding, I have hurt him. Although tired, he will likely head to the saloon where Wyatt is dealing Faro. Then, I hear the brush of fabric against skin and the sound of clothing being slung over the chair. Doc is shedding the rest of his clothing and a new wave of apprehension seizes me as I realize what is coming. Doc sits back down and swivels to lie beside me. He resumes caressing my arm. I cannot control my trembling.

"Yor afraid a me, Cassie?" he whispers.

"No," I manage weakly. "It's just . . . It's just that I've never . . ." I can't find the words to explain what I have come to regard as somewhat embarrassing. I don't know any other twenty-six year old virgins. My strict religious upbringing forbade sex before marriage but, in my disfigured state, I had never been presented with the temptation to break moral protocol. Before the reconstructive surgery, I had never had a relationship, let alone been approached to consummate it. Once the bandages were off, the scar had been replaced with monstrous swelling and bruising for a time. The surgeon's warning did not prepare me for my reflection. I was aghast and immediately regretted my decision, thought I'd been maimed for life. Dr. Craig assured me that the successful effects of his surgery would be revealed in the near future. In truth, it was a few weeks before the swelling and bruising subsided and I found myself staring at a face I never dreamed possible. It was me, alright, but without the disfiguring scar that had run from eye to nose to mouth; distorting those features. For the first time in my life, I had felt pretty, but in the throes of relocating, had had no opportunity for dating. I yearn for normality, have strong feelings for the man next to me, yet find myself unprepared for the prospect of making love for the first time. It is not that I am uneducated in the process; no one can grow up with the media of the twenty-first century and be ignorant of the mechanics of sex. My father would be rolling in his grave if he knew that my physical transformation had invited the attention of men; that I might respond without a ring on my finger. So here I lie, the man of my dreams professing his love, and me scared to death. There is no question that I am wild about him. I don't have time for mulling.

"Experience is overrated. It's not somethin' yah think about, Cassie. It's all in the feelin'."

There is no question about how I feel. I turn off the thought process and turn control of my body to my heart. In the darkness, I reach out and pull Doc's face to mine. Biting wit and hair-trigger temper set aside, the man embarks on a slow precise journey that awakens my every sense, sets fire to every nerve. Feeling and response come so naturally. Doc is guiding my hand to his own core of gratification, my tentative touch eliciting from him a low guttural moan. I find myself more thrilled by his pleasure than my own, and all heretofore- expected shyness dissolves as I explore his body with my hands and lips. Silver screen lovers could never portray the reality of what it is to couple with one's soul mate. Breathing and heart rate override all control. I feel myself racing toward a precipice, a bit frightened about what lies beyond, but a need to know; no, a need to feel it all. Without warning, I am erupting in gratification. The physical experience is such that I fear this might be my last moment on earth. I feel myself melting into oblivion as the sensations ripple through my body. I barely catch my breath before Doc arches and I feel him explode within me, sending yet another sensuous wave of pleasure through me. He sighs and caresses my face with gentle kisses as he lowers himself into me. All the talk shows with their discussions of orgasms, doctors issuing their take on the solution to the lack thereof; it all fades into obscurity as the two of us express our adoration for the other.

"Lorem ipsum dolor sit mih in hoc mundo," he whispers as he rolls aside and cradles me in his arms. I feel I should say something, but am overcome by tears. Doc's thumb is on my cheek wiping them away, along with the ones dripping from his own eyes. "Sleep, Dahlin'." Deliriously content, I surrender to a deep and restful slumber in Doc's embrace, knowing that wherever he decides our future lies, in his world or mine, is of no consequence to me. Love transcends all, is untouched by doubt. For the first time in my life, I willingly relinquish control, confident that I have nothing to fear.

CHAPTER 54

I feel Doc's gentle caress on my cheek. "We'd best get movin'." I open my eyes to see his face inches away, his lips poised to kiss mine. I reach my arms around his handsome face and pull him close. "That's it for now, My Dahlin'. There's a storm rollin' in from the west. If we don't' head up the pass now, it may become blocked."

"That's not fair," I protest trying to pull him back.

"Ah know," he admits. "One shouldn't saddle up the horse if he's not goin' tah ride." He smiles. "Let it be known, that I'm sufferin' as well. Now get yorself dressed," he says trying to be stern, then adding. "Yah'd best wear yor travelin' clothes."

It's been almost two weeks since Doc and I redefined our relationship. Forgoing any discussion of where and when we would live out the rest of our lives, we have spent each day enjoying the present, the first few, in the company of Wyatt and Josie. After leaving Gunnison, we spent two days in Pueblo, just long enough for Doc to settle his legal affairs with Bat Masterson.

The man falls all over himself to impress me. I find him a bit of a dandy. His tentative tolerance for the man I love precludes friendship on my part. It's a shame that both men are so loyal to Wyatt, yet cannot find a common basis for a similar alliance.

Furtively, I snap as many photos as I can. Our next destination is The Springs, where we spend several days.

Getting to explore it in depth, I find it much larger than I expected it to be at this time in history. I imagine Denver would surprise me, as well. The town is quite modern for the times and Doc wines and dines me in the best the city has to offer. We go to shows and elegant dance halls, where we dance into the nights before returning to our hotel and loving until dawn. My fairy "princesshood" is about to be interrupted, though, as we embark on the final leg of the journey back to the twenty-first century, where we will decide our fate. Cocooned in bliss, the future holds no interest for me save to wrap up my affairs.

An hour later, Doc is settling our debts with the blacksmith where we had boarded the horses several weeks ago. He purchases a serviceable wagon to which he hitches his own horse, then loads our trunks, saddles, and tack. After tying Buck to the rear, we begin our trek up the pass. By the time we reach the spot that will, a few years later, become the City of Woodland Park, ominous clouds are gathering above; the predicted storm is coming to meet us. I snuggle closer and Doc turns to kiss me lightly, his eyes boring into my soul. I begin to ache with need, but realize that stopping now would be folly. We turn off the main road onto what is now County Road 5, in Divide; the expanse above us darkening with every turn of the road.

Just a mile from the ranch, jagged bolts of light begin to knife through the clouds followed by resounding thunder, increasing in proximity and decibels. Doc has to work to control his horse who is not at all happy with the situation. Buck is not helping the issue at the other end. They sense the danger. In another few hundred feet, we encounter the inevitable waterfall. Within a minute, we are soaked through and shivering. Doc adjusts our pace as the terrain quickly changes under the battery of the rain. We are in a catch twenty-two. On one hand, we are in danger of being struck by lightning out in the open; on the other going too fast could result in fatal consequences of a wreck off a slippery slope. I marvel at Doc's adeptness in maneuvering around new crevasses that are expanding in depth and width as the deluge pounds the road. The only thing keeping my nerves under control is seeing the concentration and confidence in Doc's profile. I lock my arm firmly under his and make a determined effort to keep my eyes on the rode while anticipating the next lunge of the wagon that threatens to toss us off our seat.

Finally, I see the barn up ahead along with the hill it abuts. I am apprehensive as we approach, but as before, we magically pass right through the rock and around back where we will gain reentrance into the modern world.

When we come to a halt, Doc secures the reins, then jumps off the side of the buckboard and helps me down. The wind and rain are whipping treacherously. He grabs my hand and pulls me to the back of the wagon where he quickly unties a wildly fidgeting and snorting Buck.

"Yah take yor horse," he says handing me the reins, while he reaches into the wagon and grabs my saddle. It is all I can do to control Buck. Doc hurries ahead of me. The back door to the barn that does not exist in my world, opens wide at the touch of his shoulder. Doc, ever the gentleman, steps aside to let me and Buck enter first, after which, he tosses the saddle to the side before turning to head back into the blinding rain to unhitch his horse and bring in our trunks.

As I lead Buck toward the stalls, I welcome the bright sunlight streaming in through the windows on the opposite side of the barn, and remember it was a beautiful morning when we left all those weeks ago. I have had the most astonishing adventure and fallen in love without missing a second of time. How awesome is that!

The muffled scream of a child followed by that of a woman jars me out of my musings. Dropping Buck's reins, I nearly trip as I make for the portal. With only one step to go, I am blinded by an explosion of light. The simultaneous peal of thunder knocks me off my feet and sends me sprawling. I feel a sharp pain on my right temple before the blackness engulfs me.

.

CHAPTER 55

"Hey, Sleepyhead." The identity of a vaguely familiar female voice eludes me as does the friendly face that slowly emerges as the fog between us dissipates. I get the feeling that I know the woman, but . . . Instantly, I regret shaking my head to bring my thoughts front and center. It is as if my brain has become dislodged and is bouncing off the inner walls of my skull. I reach for the source of the pain. It takes a second before I realize that the mound on the right side of my forehead is partly bandaged.

"You have quite a bump there, Cassie; best to lie perfectly still for a while. You whacked your head a good one on the corner of that stool when you went down. It's a good thing Morgan found you when he did. If he hadn't brought that puppy by, you might have been laying in that barn for a couple of days. I take it John is gone?" I look around the room. The pale aqua walls are calming. Behind the peach curtains I can see that it is dark outside. I try to remember, but thinking hurts.

"Puppy?"

"Thunder? The chocolate lab you . . ." The void must be registering on my face. Instantly, concern floods into hers. "Cassie, do you know who I am? Honey!" Her call of alarm is quickly answered by a man dressed in a white coat appearing in the doorway. This face is familiar but . . . "Morgan?" When he squints and cocks his head to the side, my optimism fades.

"Hi Cassie." His voice is calm but his expression is less than reassuring. "What did you call me?"

When I repeat myself, the distress deepens on the woman's face and infects the man's as well, but he responds before panic can take me.

"Cassie, I'm Dr. *Jack* Johnson, and this is my wife Dorie." He gives the statement time to sink in. "You're in a room in our office . . ." His expression reveals his hope that the information is triggering a memory.

"Cassie's just a little confused," says Dorie stoking the side of my cheek. "That happens sometimes with a blow to the head."

"Yes, it does," he says as he checks my pulse. "Take her vitals," he says to Dorie. "I'll be right back."

"Everything is normal," she says when he reenters the room several minutes later.

"Good, let's see what you do remember. It appears that you had been out riding and that sometime after you came back into the barn you fell and hit your head. Do you remember what happened? Did you faint or perhaps stumble?"

I look from one to the other and try to decide what to say that will keep me from being committed. "Yes . . . that's right. There was a storm, I think."

"That's right," says Dorie, her face lighting up with hope. "We had a doozey; it finally dissipated an hour ago."

How long have I been out? The weather on this side of the portal was peaceful when I entered the barn. Since then a storm has come and gone.

I sigh inwardly and scramble for an explanation that will suffice until I can reclaim my memory. "I was unsaddling Buck; remember the barn lighting up; the clap of thunder . . . hurt my ears, seemed to shake my insides."

"Yes, yes," encourages Dorie, her concern easing. "Morgan said that Buck was haltered and wandering about the barn, his saddle in a lump on the floor; not like you at all, Cassie."

"That's it," I say weakly. "I can't remember anything else."

"But you remember your name and where you live?"

"Oh course, Cassie Bl . . . Collins and I live on my family's ranch in Florissant."

"That's a relief."

"I'd really like to get back there . . . the animals and . . ." Doc I think. Where is Doc?

"Whoa!" says Dr. Jack Johnson. "Not quite yet. I want to keep you overnight. I'm going to give you something to sleep, and by tomorrow, things should be a lot clearer. If I'm satisfied you're back in your right mind, that is." He and Dorian chuckle lightheartedly. "Then, we'll talk about going home. In the meantime, Morgan is taking care of the ranch; said not to worry."

I want to ask him who Morgan is and about the puppy, but fear for the conversation to go on, lest I reveal something that will keep me here any longer than necessary; or worse yet, have me sent somewhere for further testing. No, I'd best play along. "Well, if Morgan is taking care of the animals . . ."

"Believe me, it's his pleasure. Now, I'll be staying in the next room. Dorie will be up at the house with the kids. If you need anything, just push this button," he says tucking the hospital-type buzzer under the bedding within easy reach. Dorie painlessly injects my arm with the sedative. Before I can reclaim those last conscious moments when I entered the barn, it takes effect.

CHAPTER 56

I can hear muffled voices and activity down the hall. Sunlight is streaming into the room. Sometime during the night, the mental haze began lifting. I recall blacking out in the barn, waking in Jack's office, and the confusion. I try to elicit the conversation, but it refuses to return. I do know that things are not right. If time did not move forward while Doc and I were gone, how is it that Jack is married? Dorie seems to know me. Who is Morgan? And where is Doc?

"Well, Young Lady, how are we today?" Jack asks as he takes my wrist in between his thumb and finger.

"Much better," I say. "And I'm sorry about last night. I don't remember what I said, only that it wasn't making much sense." I concentrate on paying attention so I can play along.

Jack smiles approvingly and moves on to checking my blood pressure after poking the thermometer between my lips. "Well, all clear this morning?" I nod and smile. "As expected," he says confidently as he reads my temperature; then adds, "Your vitals are strong. How's the head?"

Reflexively, I reach for the bandage as he retrieves the thermometer. "Sore to the touch, but the headache is gone. May I go home, now, Doctor?"

Jack smiles. "I'll call Morgan. He said he'd pick you up when you were ready."

"Where are my clothes," I ask.

"Morgan said he'd bring those, too. What were you doing in those old things you were wearing? They looked like something your granddad would have worn."

Oops; I'd forgotten that I had changed back into the clothes I'd left in to follow Doc when we started up the pass in the buckboard. "As a matter of fact," I say, thankful for the fact that my wits have returned. "I was rummaging through some old trunks in the attic and wanted to get . . . uh . . . I was just fantasizing, I guess."

Jack laughs. "I understand. It's sort of fun to live in the past every now and then." If you only knew, I muse.

A minute later, Dorie appears with a breakfast tray. "You must be starved," she says.

"I am; thank you so much." I waste no time digging in to the bacon, eggs, hash browns and toast, washing them down alternately with fresh grapefruit juice and coffee. "How are the children?" I ask, hoping to fill in a few more gaps.

"Jack Junior and Molly are fine; just sent them off to school. They left this and said to say 'hi and hope you feel better soon'." I open the handmade card rife with crayoned flowers and get well wishes. I press it to my chest as Dorie begins to fill me in on last night's digression. As she does, I feel that I do know her.

"You, know, I got a little jealous when you thought my Jack was Morgan."

I laugh along with her, but am disturbed at the mix-up. The truth be told, I for the life of me, cannot picture Morgan; but I'm keeping that to myself. I reason he must be a neighbor and good friend. Jack and Dorie seem to find nothing out of the ordinary with his actions. After all, he must be familiar with the ranch or Jim Pruitt would be taking care of the stock; and only a close friend would be bringing me a change of clothes; something more in Nancy's jurisdiction, I would think. Oh well, I would soon find out. His appearance will more than likely unlock more memories.

After cleaning my plate, I ask to take a shower. Fresh clothes are on the bed when I come out of the bathroom, and the door is closed. I take my time dressing, all the while preparing myself to meet Morgan, without betraying the fact that I don't remember him. Morgan who? There are a few more layers of haze I need to peel back, but I am confident everything will come back in time. The one thing set in stone is Doc. The past few weeks have not been a dream. Dorie did ask about John, didn't she? I am slipping into my boot when I hear the slight rap at the door.

"Come in," I say. Thankfully, the man who enters is vaguely recognizable, if not clearly definable. "Morgan," I say without hesitation.

"Hey there, Cassie." I remember the easy smile, the eyes, voice. He walks over and kisses my cheek. I recall that, too, but . . . "You had us worried there for a while."

"I owe you one," then quickly amend, "several, I'm told."

"Just being neighborly," he says. "You ready to meet Thunder? I decided to stay at my brothers until the pups were weaned; didn't want to come back empty-handed. I hear your company's gone?"

There it is again, the reference to Doc. "Yeah, John left a few days ago."

"Will he be coming back?"

The question stabs at my heart. "I don't know," I say, unable to hide the disappointment in my tone.

"I see," he says. I get the impression he is making an effort to resign himself to a possibility with which he is none too happy. "Well, then, let's get back and meet Thunder." He settles me in the passenger seat of his pickup. "Have you eaten?"

"Oh my, yes," I say grateful for the change of subject. "Dorie made a feast this morning . . . but if you . . ."

"No, I'm fine. Hope it's all right, I raided your fridge yesterday, and this morning."

"I'm glad you did." Why can't I remember this person who is so familiar with my life?

"How are the Pruitt's?" I venture a few minutes into the drive..

"Jim and Nancy are fine, and send their well wishes."

"So tell me about Thunder."

"As promised, he's the pick of the litter and cute as a button; gonna make a great ranch dog, same as Buckshot." The name evokes a foggy image of a full-grown chocolate lab, free with his kisses until instructed by Morgan to ease up; at which point he sits in obedience. I remember him riding in the truck between us. I strain to bring up more, but it will not come. "Where is Buckshot?"

"I left him baby-sitting Thunder in your mudroom."

"Of course."

"You're gonna love your little guy, and it will be good to have a dog around the place; especially now that your company is gone. A woman shouldn't be out on that big spread without some protection. Your grandparents always had at least one dog on the place. Old Shep passed away a few days after your Gramma. He was so old and I think he held on until he knew she didn't need him anymore."

A fenced-in graveyard in a clearing a few hundred feet from the barn flashes in my mind. The markers, some almost faded beyond reading, bear the names of a succession of loyal pets. It pulls another memory. Shortly after I moved in, it was Morgan who brought it to my attention, at the same time suggesting that I consider a dog; told me his brother in California raised labs. Since I was still getting familiar with the horses, goats, and chickens, that I'd jumped into adopting, I'd put him off. Now I remember; he emailed me while he was visiting his brother just before Doc showed up, telling me about an up-coming litter, and asking me if I was ready. I had given him the go-ahead. My head is beginning to ache again as memories play hide and seek in my mind. Some are scrambled like those of Jack; those of Morgan and Dorie vague, but on the verge of coming into focus, it seems.

I close my eyes and lean my head back willing my mind to empty and readjust. Thoughts of Doc quickly fill the void. I think of my decision to make a life with him in the past. I wonder how Thunder will adapt to life in the old west?

There are so many things to consider; what to do with the goats and the chickens; the Pruitts, of course. Doc and I will take the horses, and Thunder, too. I think about the ranch. I'll have to arrange . . . God, what will people think when I just up and leave? Will they even know? Time can't possibly stand still forever . . . or . . . Oh well, it won't be hard to concoct a story when the time comes. I'll just tell them that we decided to get married and move. I'll sell the ranch. No one will know that we didn't leave in a conventional manner.

That settled, I doze off.

"We're here," Morgan's announcement wakens me and I am happier than I have ever been to see the ranch. He unlocks the front door and we are enthusiastically greeted by two bouncing masses of fur. "Oh, he's beautiful," I say reaching down to pick up my new pet. Thunder is licking my face and making happy puppy noises. Buckshot bounds from me to Morgan. I don't know if he is just overjoyed to see us or happy to be relieved of his babysitting duties. After a few minutes, the little guy follows Buckshot into the trees to take care of business.

I take advantage of the break to check on my other charges. Buck and the mares, all of whom whinny their happiness to see me. The three gallop and romp around me in the corral obliging me to dodge the flying mud thrown from their hooves. I duck under the rails and head over to greet the goats and chickens. Everyone looks fine and I see that Morgan must have gathered the eggs this morning.

When I return, Morgan and the dogs are in the house. The next hour is spent getting acquainted with Thunder. The conversation revolves around his care and feeding, what to expect, and how to train and effectively discipline a new puppy.

While Morgan takes them outside again, I prepare a simple lunch.

"Gosh, you didn't have to do that," he says when they return.

"Of course, I did," I say as I set the soup and sandwiches on the table. "Besides, I'm not through pumping you for information." I keep hoping, as we continue talking that whatever Morgan and I have experienced will come into focus. It's as if the exact nature our relationship is lurking in the shadows, just out of sight and thus, out of mind. As before, pursuing it pushes it farther away.

We sit down to lunch. Thunder sits quietly in imitation of his mentor except for a couple of times. When he does attempt to wander over to mooch, Buckshot who has been well-trained to let his master eat in peace, is right there to herd him back.

"Maybe I should borrow him for a while," I tease. "Buckshot is a one-dog obedience school.

"You can borrow him anytime you want. But you still gotta remember to follow through or the little fella will take advantage; and before you know it, he'll have the upper hand," Morgan says.

"I hear you." Suddenly, fatigue seizes and my head starts to ache again.

"You okay?" Morgan asks.

"Yeah, just a little tired, I guess."

"Jack said that might happen. Why don't you rest a bit. I'll take care of the kitchen," he says rising and coming around to my chair.

"That's silly; you don't have to . . ."

"Oh, but I insist," he says giving me a hand up. I let him lead me into the living room where he sees that I lie down on the sofa before covering me with the afghan that I had thrown over Doc's shoulders that first day a year ago. "Buckshot, watch," he commands. Both dogs come to lie on the floor next to the sofa. "Good boys," says Morgan, patting their heads, then mine, adding, "Good girl." I wait until he disappears behind the kitchen doors before reaching down to pick up Thunder. He snuggles next to me and we both are down for the count.

I awake to the heavenly aroma of sizzling beef. Thunder is licking my face at the first movement. "I love you, too," I say. Buckshot is still at his post, but rouses to greet me, as well. I set the puppy down and the two bound off towards the front door. I follow and let them out.

A second later, Morgan is behind me. "Feeling better?" he asks as we watch the guys romp toward the edge of the forest, disappear for a few minutes, then come running out, playfully bounding back and forth across the front of the house.

"Yeah, much. Thanks."

"I, uh . . ."

"Took the liberty of making dinner," I finish for him.

"There's nothing like the smell of beef on the fire. I'm starved. Will they be alright outside for a while?"

"They ain't goin' anywhere."

He pulls out my chair and as I sit, I realize that I am no longer confused. Morgan Jamison and I have been friends since the day I moved here. His family and mine have interacted for generations; the ranches bordering one another. I can visualize his house, now, just over the rise to the east. It is a white two story stone structure on a high foundation with pillars lining the front creating a huge covered porch accessed by a dozen steps. In truth, it looks more like a governor's mansion than the house of a rancher high in the Rockies. But then, Morgan isn't a rancher, nor had his forbears been. His family came here with money, built the huge house, enjoying the seclusion of the forest. Morgan is familiar with every inch of the Fielding place and has been indispensable in assisting me to make decisions for improvements. The comprehension hits me harder than the tumble that knocked the memories out of me, yet several things do not compute. For instance, I cannot explain why I had not run to him when I first found Sarah's body. It seemed like the most natural thing to do, but I had called Bob and Kim. It's all so fuzzy. Morgan must have been out of town. By the time he returned, the matter had been dealt with and I was grateful that the authorities had kept it quiet. I don't recall Morgan ever mentioning the old scandal.

Slowly, other memories begin to emerge. We have been out a few times. Feelings had begun to develop on both sides, only to be interrupted by Doc's mysterious appearance. Doc has overshadowed my life for almost a year. Where has Morgan been all that time? He travels a lot. This latest excursion had been to his brother's and lasted three months. That was the reason I had asked Jim Pruitt to watch over the ranch while Doc and I went on our modern excursion. Not once, to my knowledge, has Morgan ever . . . He must have known about my childhood friend visiting, but to the best of my recollection, as feeble as it is at the moment, the two of them never crossed paths. Strange. In time . . . In time.

More memories trickle back along with feelings. Morgan is warm and pleasant. He is quick of wit, honest, and hardworking, mostly in the interests of others. It was from other recipients of his good deeds that I learned that he is independently wealthy, through no effort of his own, rather like myself. Morgan is the ultimate gentleman, respectful of the boundaries set by a novice in the dating department. As I continue to reminisce, it comes to me how much like Doc this young man is. Suddenly, I am sick inside. He is such a nice guy and I know I might have fallen for him as time went on, but I am hopelessly in love with Doc, and as soon as he returns . . . I must be careful not to encourage Morgan. I must not allow him to think our relationship can progress beyond what it has.

"Cassie . . . hello?"

"I'm sorry, Morgan," I say aghast at my rudeness. "I guess I drifted off for a bit."

"I'll say. Anything you want to share?"

"Nothing important. This is delicious, Morgan," I say. "You are such a good friend."

"A bachelor has to learn to cook if he doesn't want to eat out every meal. My mom taught all the kids to cook, boys and girls. I think she had an ulterior motive, though. There were five us to help out in the kitchen. Taught us all to keep house, do laundry, and simple mending, too."

"I'm impressed; where's the cake?"

"I . . ."

"I'm kidding; there's ice cream in the fridge," I offer in apology.

After dessert, I am able to buck up enough to convince him that I am back at the top of my game; in no further need of outside assistance. We sit on the stoop and watch the dogs frolic. I don't know who wore out whom, but soon they lay at our feet fully spent as the daylight sinks into the horizon.

"Thank you so much for everything, Morgan," I say. "Can I call you tomorrow, if I need . . ."

"Of course," he says, rising. "Come on, Buckshot; I guess that's our cue."

"I didn't mean . . ."

"Yes, you did; and may I say, you hinted most eloquently. You're sure you're okay to stay alone?"

"Oh, but thanks to you, I won't be alone," I quip. "Thunder will be keeping an eye on me." I raise and turn the puppy to face me, inviting his kisses.

"You're right, there." Morgan leans to kiss my cheek before heading to his pickup. Buckshot jumps in ahead of him. I wave Thunder's paw as they pull out of the drive.

There is not a cloud in the sky, nor the prediction of another storm for the night. I am disappointed, as I am sure that Doc will return during a storm. The only explanation for his absence must be that the portal closed with the thunderclap that knocked me out. It will take another storm, a severe one to reopen the portal. I am sure of that. Thankfully, these mountains experience them regularly. Too tired for anything else, I take Thunder back into the house and upstairs to bed with me.

CHAPTER 57

Thunder wakes me twice to go out. I didn't much care for the disruption of my sleep, but am thankful for avoiding the alternative. Apparently, Morgan has seen to basic training for the little guy. I will see to doggie doors in the mudroom, one into the main house, the other through the wall facing the yard that is bordered by the house, the causeway, the barn, and the wall of rock.

Thankfully, Thunder falls right back to sleep each time we return. We wake together at six. After dressing, we make our trek to the barn where I introduce him to Buck, Lightning, and Baby Girl. The horses seemed to be mindful of their feet as the puppy romps around the pasture dashing in and out among them. He comes promptly when I call and is eager to meet the pigmy goats who are more his size. They, however, view his presence as an intrusion. He is butted and rolled several times before he decides to exit their territory. When we reach the chicken yard, I command a firm "no" accompanied by the shake of my finger. I am not I worried he may attack a chicken; rather that the rooster might lead an assault on him. As with the potty-training, it seems that Morgan has instilled obedience to several commands. This realization is a relief, as I find I have little energy, at present, to embark on a serious training regimen. After gathering the eggs, we head back to the house.

I measure out Thunder's food, per Morgan's suggestion. "Sit," I say and like magic, my puppy rests obediently on his haunches until I give him the go-ahead. After topping off his water bowl, I pour the coffee and set about making myself an omelet as I listen and catch glimpses of the morning news, waiting particularly for the weather, praying for a major thunderstorm. Although the Front Range is still in its monsoon season, the weathergirl is predicting fair skies for the next couple of days. I console myself with knowledge that the report can change with an unforeseen shift in winds.

Thunder and I spend the rest of the day getting to know each other better. I have never had a dog before and I'm finding his companionship a delight. While not a substitute for Doc, he is good company and takes my mind off my lonely heart. After playing for an hour or so, we both curl up on the sofa. I lunch on soup during the midday news. Still no rain in sight.

"We might as well take advantage of all this sunshine." Thunder cocks his head as if trying to understand. "Come on," I say after stowing the soup bowl and spoon into the dishwasher. Excitedly, Thunder follows me to the door. He aims for the trees. He beams with pride at the praise I give him when he trots back. "What do you want to see, first?" Again with the cocked head. "Go on," I say, clapping my hands. "You lead the way." He seems to understand and starts to walk toward the barn, then past it and alongside the pasture fence; checking back periodically to make sure I am following. I try to enjoy the beautiful day convinced that a storm cannot be too far in the offing and Doc's return with it.

It is then that I start analyzing the circumstances that forced our separation. After seeing Buck and me inside, Doc responded to the cries of Mary and Elizabeth. They were out in the storm. Had one or both of them been injured? Several scenarios present themselves; the most logical, that Doc had run to their rescue and is staying on to take care of whatever needs to be done, or until the next storm comes along to reopen the portal. Too bad I cannot 'google' time travel and scroll down to portals. In any event, I have no doubt that Doc and my great, great, grandmother are having a good time together, along with Auntie Elizabeth.

I picture Doc repairing a fence, helping with the animals,

or stalking a coyote who might be threatening the hen house. Before long, I find that Thunder has led me to the family pet cemetery. He sniffs from grave to grave before coming back to my side. I pick up all ten or twelve pounds of him and walk over to a large boulder just outside the gate.

"Wait till Doc sees you," I say to Thunder. We meander on back and I decide to call Morgan to ask his advice on the doggie doors. He assures me he designed and installed his own and will be happy to do the same for me. After asking about Thunder and me he promises to come by early tomorrow to install the doors.

While I am thinking "puppy" I decide to make a list of things I will need for Thunder. Morgan brought a good supply of food, a collar, complete with tags, and a leash, along with the mat, food bowls, and a bed. Toys, I think; lots of toys; a ball, a Frisbee, and . . . I'll know when I get to that section in Pet Smart. Morgan had also programmed the name and number of his vet into my phones before he left yesterday. He took care of all important stuff; left me in charge of the fun. I can handle that.

Animals bedded down for the night, Thunder and I have our dinner and settle in the living room in front of the TV. The vast wasteland is just that tonight, and I begin to scroll through the available movies for rent. Field of Dreams catches my attention, but just as I am about to commit to the rental, it hits me. I jump up, startling poor Thunder who scrambles to keep up with me on my way to the study. The first thing I do is open Jefferson's box of ledgers and am surprised to find only a few. I look on the shelves, under the table, in the cupboards below; nothing. With my memory as unreliable as it has been since I woke from the accident, I have no idea where I will find the rest of them. I do remember that forcing my memory doesn't work, so I move on to Mary's diaries that are still on the shelf where I last remembered them.

I retrieve the one labeled 1882 and head back to the recliner and pull Thunder up beside me. He plants his sizeable paws on my thigh as I hold my breath and open to the appropriate date.

"Here goes," I say, flipping the pages to the date after Doc and I had moved the safe.

After chores, Auntie Liz and I went to visit Mr. and Mrs. Chandler. I got to play with Nadine and Penelope all day. Then a man came and drove our wagon back to the ranch and Auntie Liz told me Daddy is never coming home. I told her I saw Mama last night and she got very scared. I told her it was all right because Mama is an angel and she said God was going to fix things. Auntie said it was just a nice dream, but I know it was real.

Yes! I set the diary and wipe my tears. Thunder starts to whimper at what he must be sensing as distress. I bring his face to mine where he quickly licks my tears away. "It's okay," I say. "It's really okay. These are tears of joy. I'm happy," I say rubbing my nose back and forth against his. "I just realized something. Let's go check it out." I take him with me to the study, and without thinking, almost set him on the table. I remember Morgan's advice to avoiding undoing any previous or potential training and set Thunder on the chair as I pick the ledgers out of Jefferson's chest. My query is answered, my suspicions confirmed. I had removed the 1879 ledger to plant in the cellar. Where did I put it? Those for the five previous years are here, along with the three years after 1883 and forward have vanished.

I dash through the doors and out to the barn, Thunder on my heels yipping excitedly. I stop short and stare at the barren floor trying to remember what I did when Doc and I returned from moving the safe. We were so excited at our accomplishment, anticipatory of the result. I must have picked up the ledger and . . . I look around the room; open the door to the office. There the ledger lies, on the desk where I had hurriedly discarded it.

There are no entries in this ledger following the date of the exposure of the locked room. And the article reporting Elizabeth's death is gone.

"We did it, Doc! We really did it!" I shout. Thunder barks and I turn my attention to him. "Elizabeth did not die at the hands of Jefferson Fielding. Doc and I changed history for the better!" I slump into the chair beside Thunder's, hands splayed on the ledger before me, then look to the wall on which I had organized the family diaries. How I wished I had read them all before I had tampered with the past. I will never know how the family scandal had originally affected the lives of my ancestors, especially Mary's, now that she had been raised by a loving aunt instead of a homicidal father. Who knows how many persons Jefferson might have killed after Elizabeth? What I know for sure is that Doc and I saved at least one life and gave a little girl a chance at a much better one. And, we cleared Sarah Fielding's name, along with that of Frank Brady. I cannot wait to show this to Doc. But of course, he already knows. I walk over to the journals. It has been a long time since I set them on the shelf in chronological order first by name, then by date. Something is not right . . . Then I see it. Sarah's diaries came first, then Mary's, but now, between these volumes is another set I have never seen. They begin with 1879 and go through 1900. I open the one from 1882. In beautiful script typical of the time when one's penmanship was a source of pride, are these words.

The Diary of Elizabeth June Higgins 1882.

I sit down and, without thinking, start to rifle through the days. Thankfully, I catch myself before I do any real damage to the brittle pages. I recognize the date that follows the night Doc and I moved the safe.

I am not sure that I will ever know what actually happened last night; who broke into the cellar or how the animals got loose. All I know is that a power beyond this world has changed Little Mary's and my life forever by exposing Sarah's body in the cellar room that I never knew existed and Mary was too young to remember. Among my sister's belongings was her diary that revealed the truth about her disappearance. The sheriff said that, after his arrest, Jefferson proudly admitted killing Sarah and the young man that had been working for them, but refused to divulge the location of his grave. I am uneasy about what Mary told me. She said that her mother appeared to her in the cellar last night as an angel and told her that God was going to fix things. I am a God-fearing woman, but cannot explain any of this. Thankfully, she did not see her mother's body. I don't know how to answer Mary, but she is so happy. I see no reason to tell her the details, just that God took her father away like he did her mother. When she is older, I will let her read the facts for herself. The ranch belongs to Mary now and the first order of business is to hire a man to do the heavy work.

How I wish Auntie Liz could have discovered Jefferson's ledgers and learned the whole truth; the why, but they apparently remained hidden until Doc and I unearthed them after seeing Jefferson tucking them away below the floorboards. Elizabeth's subsequent entries over the next few weeks reveal that Jefferson hanged himself in his jail cell before he could be tried for the double murder.

I turn to the date of Doc's and my last return from the past:

Today's storm is the worst ever. Mary is small for her age and was nearly blown away by the high winds when she was coming back from the barn. If not for that nice Mr. McKey who had stopped by the ranch before, I am sure she would not have made her way back to the house. We were able to persuade him to stay for dinner, after which he insisted on helping repair the damage done by the storm.

Elizabeth goes on to relate that Doc stayed though the monsoon season.

Tom has been with us for three weeks now. I can find no fault with the man. He has the manners of a gentleman and in spite of all the manual labor he is doing, I doubt that it is his normal manner of making a living. He is so good with Mary and I fear she is becoming quite attached, though he has made it plain that he must be on his way as soon as the weather is no longer a threat. He has one habit that, although harmless, I find most peculiar. In the most threatening throes of storms, he goes outside to the hill where it meets the corner of the barn and lays his hands on it as if it holds some magical power.

My heart leaps at the revelation. Doc is trying to get back to me. One day, in the near future, we will be reunited. I know it.

Elizabeth's entry of September 10th:

Tom McKey left us early this morning. The thunderstorms are gone as well. I had been so worried about Mary's reaction to her friend's leaving, but needn't have been. Tom had already anticipated the problem and presented her with a puppy he'd gotten from a neighbor's litter, asking her to name and take care of him until he could return. I don't know if we will ever see Tom McKey again, but we will never forget him.

I scan the next few weeks. In quick succession, Elizabeth takes on a John Lenwood as a hired hand on a trial basis and her parents come up from The Springs for a weeklong visit and make plans to return for the holidays. It isn't long before the hard worker becomes a permanent fixture on the ranch. My interest grows with Elizabeth's frequent praises of his abilities, seasoned with her approval of his nature and character. On Christmas Eve, she writes:

My parents arrived midday. Mary eyes nearly popped out of her head when they laid the mountain of gifts beneath the pine that John had cut earlier and placed in the big room. After dinner, we all shared in decorating the tree with strung popped corn and cinnamon scented pinecones while we sang hymns and carols.

Christmas Day, 1882, she writes:

My mother must have spent half the year making dresses for Mary and me. Dad surprised us with several pieces of furniture he'd left covered in their wagon until this morning. The pieces will make that cellar room into comfortable guest quarters. John's refurbishing, Father's furniture, and the curtains and drapes that Mary and I sewed together have all but erased the evil associated with the space. It had been my intention to have John move from the bunk house in the barn into it. With money I supplied on their previous visit, the folks purchased school books along with several of the latest novels I thought Mary might enjoy. Mother and Father also remembered John with new boots and work gloves. Mary and I had sewn three new shirts for him. I had no idea that John had secretly been teaching Mary to whittle. Each of us received an animal out of pine. John gave my parents an elaborate scenic carving. To Mary, he gave a cradle he'd made for her doll. My gift was in a tiny box held back until last. It was accompanied by John's request that Daddy give him my hand in marriage. I didn't know what to say or do. I had never allowed myself to entertain the possibility of becoming someone's wife. What man would want a scarred cripple, especially a handsome, fit man like John. Mother, Father, and Mary had no such quandary. John and I are to be married on New Year's Day while my parents are still here. The preacher, dress, and all other arrangements had already been plotted behind my back by John and my parents several weeks ago. His proposal was merely a formality. I guess the spare room will be for company after all. Thank God for his mercies.

A new flow of tears threatens the delicate parchment.

"Please come back soon, Doc. Please," I whisper. Then to Thunder, "Come on, Boy, let's go see our new guest room. It takes less than a minute for us to make our way down to the cellar. My hand is shaking as I slowly turn the knob, not with fear, but with anticipation. There is no ancient creaking as I push the door. I automatically reach to the wall on my left and flip up the switch that had been installed with the rest of the electrical in the house. Instantly, the transformed room is bathed in light. The original dark walls are hidden behind much lighter paneling. Centered against the far wall is a huge rough-hewn oak bed, swathed in a patchwork down comforter on which several accenting shammed pillows lie against a thick headboard that looks as if it was carved out of a single large log to accommodate a bookshelf and a cubbyhole at each end. Atop it are several vintage photographs, in one of which I recognize my mother as a teenager, standing between her parents. At the foot of the bed is a cedar chest on which lies a yellowed embroidered linen runner. I will have to match them up to the ones in the albums in the study that I have yet to examine in detail. The wall to the right that housed the shelf-like bed where I had found Sarah's body is lined with shelves and cupboards that contain an assortment of stuffed animals, school awards, and sports trophies bearing the name

Elizabeth Jane Collins.

"This was my mother's room," I say to Thunder who is busy sniffing out every nook and cranny of the room. Cupboard after cupboard is comfortably filled with everything from clothing to miscellaneous items normal to a teenage girl's life thirty or so years ago. In the refurbished long cupboard, hang dresses, skirts, blouses, jackets, and coats; on the shelf above, a collection of shoes popular in the 80's. I turn to the opposite wall that houses a roll top desk and a sewing cabinet. A cowboy hat, several ball caps, and a heavy coat adorn the old-fashioned hat rack in one corner. A few feet in front of it is a beautifully carved rocking chair with seat and back pads that match the comforter on the bed. My mother's room, I repeat in my mind. I walk over to the cedar chest and carefully set the runner on the bed. The chest is full of linens, and . . . oh My God, this is what they call a "hope chest". It looks like she left everything behind to run away with my father, even the things she had been saving for her marriage. What was the attraction? In any event, her parents left her room just as it was on the day she went away. Had she been at odds with her mother and father? I wonder if they corresponded. The answers must lie in my grandmother's diaries. There is more than ever to learn about my heritage. I know how I will fill my days until Doc returns. I will have so much to tell him. I shut the cedar lid and replace the runner.

"Come on, Thunder." The puppy obediently follows me to the door, where I turn and scan the room again. I walk across to the sewing cabinet, run my finger across the top, and inspect it. Curious. There is not a speck of dust. Will caring for this room become part of my memory? I shrug and head back upstairs, my shadow at my heels.

After his last outing of the night, Thunder sits watch as I shower. The hot water feels so good and adds to the relaxation that had begun to settle over me with the positive update from the family diaries. I dry off and use a corner of the towel to wipe the steam from the mirror. As I do, a terry loop is caught in my necklace. I lean in toward the mirror to see how to untangle the snag without damage to the towel or the jewelry. I drop my eyes from the mirror to the chain and the locket . . . the locket I thought I'd lost sometime between the morning I followed Doc out the portal and the Fourth of July picnic in Gunnison. In spite of my jumbled memory, I am relatively certain that I have not since found and replaced it . . . at least I think I'm sure. How could I? I didn't do it on the way back home and, after that, I hit my head and was taken to Jack's office; from there, home, and . . . No, it's not possible; then how?

I open the locket. The pictures are as I remember them and as I remember the ones inside the one worn by Reverend Johnston's wife.

In spite of the warmth of the bathroom, I feel a sudden chill. Jefferson's ledger . . . we couldn't take it with us because it was already present in 1882. The implication is staggering. When I went back in time, the locket was in the possession of its original owner. This locket and the one around the neck of the pastor's wife are one and the same. Then, they're . . . the pastor and his wife must be somehow connected to my . . . Oh God . . . the pastor's voice . . . his . . .

Doc and I must go back to Gunnison. I must know. I am much too tired now, but tomorrow I will go online to see if there are any genealogical records connecting the families. I think about the interactions I witnessed there in Gunnison. If this was my father's heritage, it could explain a lot and help me to deal with mine. The prospect is comforting and intimidating at the same time.

I dress for bed. If not for the furry bundle beside me, I doubt that I would sleep.

.

CHAPTER 58

I rush through the morning chores before planting myself in the study in front of my laptop and promptly pay for a month's stint on a popular ancestry search website. My father's name sparks no hits, whereas my mother's records are as I found them in the family Bible. I try the opposite tack and type in the Reverend's information. Aha, the marriage of the Johnston's of Gunnison, Colorado is on record followed by a huge family tree branching out from their nine children. I scroll down through the generations to the year my father was born. There are several listings for boys, none with my father's name, but there is a Daniel Johnston that shares my father's birthday. He had said he was adopted but . . . This definitely warrants further investigation.

A knock at the door aborts my search. Hurriedly, I save the document to my hard drive before going to greet Morgan and Buckshot.

Morgan hands me his toolbox and power saw. Thunder bounds out to romp with his mentor, as Morgan retrieves the completed doggie doors from the bed of his pickup.

In less than two hours, the doors are installed and operational. Morgan calls the guys in and directs Buckshot to demonstrate the doors. Thunder happily trots behind his mentor, is a little wary of the flaps at first, but then adapts. Morgan stays for lunch during which ominous clouds begin to roll in and we hear rumbling in the distance. My heart lurches as I anticipate Doc's return.

"Before you go," I say hinting that he will be going shortly, "I have something to show you in the cellar." The four of us traipse down the cellar stairs. "What do you think?" I say as we step inside mother's room. Morgan's eyes scan from left to right. He cocks his head.

"What am I looking for?" The question sends an electric shock from head to foot. Morgan doesn't see the change . . . because the drastic alteration is only in my mind. My memory of finding Sarah's body is now a false one, debunked when Doc and I moved the safe and exposed Sarah's corpse. I never found Sarah's body. It had been moved long ago. I hug my arms. This is getting creepier by the minute. Another hazy memory floats in and begins to materialize. Morgan was here when I first toured my new home, with all the furniture draped in sheets. He had been here countless times growing up; knew my grandparents well, the house and grounds inside and out. It was he who told me this was my mother's room; pointed out her picture on the headboard; told me about my grandparents' heartbreak when she left with my father. He was too small to remember, but he learned the story from my grandmother who never gave up hope that her daughter would return.

"Well, I'm insulted. I have been dusting and scrubbing and . . ."

Morgan puts his arm around my shoulders. "Duh! You're right, it sparkles, now; looks great; ready for company. Sorry, I guess I'm a typical man, take that sort of thing for granted. But really, it's always looked just fine to me. You're a great housekeeper."

The guilt boomerangs. I must be more careful; must discard my pre-Doc memories of this place, lest they get back to Jack and prompt him to question my mental well-being and order a battery of tests.

But this new revelation prompts a query that demands an immediate answer. I run across the room to the last diary on my mother's headboard.

"Whoa," says Morgan as I dash by him, across the cellar, and up the stairs. He follows me to the study at a more leisurely pace. The poor man must think I am completely mad.

I am aware of his amused observation as I snatch the corresponding diary of my grandmother's from the shelf and begin to compare the women's accounts, two sides of an age-old story of a teenage infatuation questioned by loving parents. In the midst of my musings, I remember that Morgan is standing beside me. I gather my wits and set aside the journals.

The grumblings of thunder are getting louder as Morgan drives away. Soon the flashes of light will be become jagged strikes followed by deafening crashes as the storm moves in directly overhead. I nearly trip over Thunder several times, as I feed more swiftly than usual and lock the animals up in their respective enclosures. If he were a small child, I'm sure he would be hugging my ankle. The barn creaks in the wake of the latest clap. The puppy whimpers and is all-aquiver as I scoop him into my arms. An even sharper crack rocks the causeway as we pass the threshold into the house; the lights dim and black out. Within seconds, the generator kicks in and brings them back to life. I check the phone, dead as expected, but I have no fears there either, as my little pal and I have everything we need, everything except Doc, that is and he will arrive shortly. I can feel it.

Once inside the house, I pour a glass of wine and reach for a box of crackers. I have just retrieved the sharp cheddar from the fridge when I change my mind. Doc would appreciate something far more substantial and our reunion warrants a celebratory meal.

In short order, the potatoes are baking and the steaks are marinating. The salad is ready to toss, and the champagne is cradled in a bucket of ice. I would bake a cake if I thought there was time, but the tempest is in full swing now. Every ten to twenty seconds the entire sky lights up followed by thunderclaps that threaten to wrest the house from its foundation. If not for what this violence forebodes, I would be unnerved. Instead, I welcome it; remember the storm that opened the portal and the one that closed it before Doc was safely inside the barn. There is no doubt that present one matches their intensity in portal-opening potential, but then it crosses my mind, that at present, the weather on the other side might be quite different, stormless. It could be spring for all I know. I think back to when Doc and I were returning. While the storm raged in the past, all was clear here. These ping-ponging thoughts do nothing to ease my mind. How will Doc know the portal is open if . . . Please, it can't be that our reuniting is dependent on the coordination of weather, of all things. Disappointment descends like a heavy drape upon my shoulders. I'm so confused, so weary. Keep busy. I must keep busy.

I take my time and give special attention to the table setting, including fancy napkin-folding. I set out candles ready for lighting. That done and dinner taking care of itself, I take my glass of wine to the living room and turn on the evening news. Thunder, who has stuck close through all the prep, joins me on my lap. His trepidation seems to ease with the close contact of his unconcerned master.

The feature story is the storm, of course, which has robbed the area of power for the time-being; and I am so thankful that I listened to my neighbors and installed the generator that has taken over for IREA. To complete my mood, I turn the TV to dvd mode and put in Tombstone. Knowing so much of the truth, I find myself picking up on all the little inaccuracies. The fact that the Birdcage theater didn't open until two months after the infamous gunfight, that Virgil was maimed later that year, and Morgan was killed the following March; and finally, that Ringo was found dead four months later. The poetic license does not bother me. The depiction of the characters, at least the ones I was privileged to meet, is quite accurate, and that is all that matters.

Somewhere along the line, I drift off and wake to the DVD player's prompt to "play" the movie again. It is after eight. The potatoes would be cremated if not for the timer and warming features of the oven.

Outside, the rain is torrential. Lightning is still visible in the distance but appears in large splashes in the sky; the thunder reduced to muted rumblings. Now that the worst of it has passed, anxiety begins to creep up my spine, but I settle it by inventing plausible reasons for Doc's delay. Maybe

Wyatt called for him again . . . or God forbid, that Mallon fellow caught up with him again. No, please not that, not after all this. Perhaps my family needed . . . After all, life in the 1880s in this isolated terrain, sans all the conveniences I have at my fingertips would be treacherous for a woman and child alone. In addition to all the possible threats, there are animals to be cared for, wood to be cut and . . .

Out of some hidden corner of my mind creeps a distressing possibility. Has my naivety and inexperience allowed me to make more of Doc's and my relationship than he did? Now that he is well and has knowledge of what is to come, has he returned to Kate, or perhaps found another more suitable companion? Oh perhaps, perhaps, perhaps. I can't stand this. My mind spins on and on bringing on a headache.

I catch a glimpse of myself in the bathroom mirror as I retrieve the aspirin. The face staring back at me is gaunt and has no color. The eyes are deeply circled, their sparkle gone. A forced smile only accentuates the pitiable reflection. I drop my head. One thing is for sure, if Doc was to appear now, he would hightail it back through that portal forever. I feel beaten, helpless, so tired. I look back to the mirror and vow to take back my life with or without Doc.

Back in the kitchen, I turn off the oven and store the half-prepared meal in the fridge. I pour myself another glass of wine, wash the aspirin down with the first swallow, and wait for my mind to quiet. No such luck. It continues to toy with options. Given my limited vantage point, there is just no way of predicting when Doc will reappear. I cling to the premise that this miraculous experience has a purpose. This determination has served me well thus far. It has seen to restoring Doc's health, saving Elizabeth, securing a better life for Mary, and introduced me to love. I swallow and choke back tears, chide myself for doubting the powers that be and all the goodness of the last couple of years. Oh, it just can't end like this. It can't.

As the pain subsides and the wine begins to dilute my thoughts, I turn my attention back to my original plan and prepare a plate of crackers and cheese before retreating to the living room where I pull the sofa into a bed. I turn back the bedding and prop the pillows; then swing my legs onto the bed. After arranging the blankets, I grab the tray of snacks off the end table and settle in to watch the evening's TV fare. Weariness descends. Having had too much wine to care about cleaning or even to move, I set the tray aside and sink down into the bedding. When I turn my head, I find the pillow infused with Doc's scent.

CHAPTER 59

Thunder responds to my first stirrings, licking my face to life before jumping off the sofa bed and running for the doggie door. The crick in my neck is painful; the result of sleeping soundly slumped to one side. The morning news is on and the time registered in the corner of the screen says five fifty-two. Remembering the promise to myself the night before, I fight the apprehension that spontaneously begins to build; telling myself that there is good reason that Doc has not yet returned. The weatherman is predicting another storm for mid-day as Thunder bounds back on the sofa. I lavish praise on him for adapting so quickly to the new potty arrangement. Per Morgan, consistent positive reinforcement is imperative. That part comes naturally while I still have a little trouble with necessary scolding.

Together, we head upstairs where I shower and dress, making an effort to mask the damage inflicted by melancholia. Thunder cocks his head from side to side as I talk him through the intense beauty regime. His reaction makes me laugh and I find myself in heightened spirits on this new day.

Outside is bathed in sunshine and mild temperatures. Every hen has produced this morning in spite of the chaotic weather and their happy cackling announces they welcome the stretch of sunshine. The goats are frolicking in their pasture. I hear Buck whinny my arrival to the other horses as

I enter the barn. I feed them outside and watch as they gallop around the pasture. I cringe, as inevitably, they each take a roll or two in the puddles, keeping my distance to avoid the inevitable splatter when they shake off their mud baths. After mucking the stalls and checking on all the water troughs, Thunder and I enjoy a walk around the perimeter of the buildings, inspecting for any damage the storm might have caused. Everything seems to be in order. We cross in front of the house. Approaching its housing, I can hear the steady hum of the generator signaling that power has yet to be restored to the area.

Knowing that exercise works against depression, I opt to take a more extensive trek. Thunder runs circles around me as we head out past the barn where a large herd of cattle grazed. I imagine Sarah, Mary, and Elizabeth as they might have taken this very stroll, think of all the work that went into preserving this beautiful place, and how grateful I am that it was entrusted to me.

"Let's get some breakfast, Boy."

Thunder barks in agreement and leads the way back to the house.

As expected, the morning weathercaster is urging residents to stay put unless necessity warrants travel, as many of the dirt roads are slick with runoff. With more storms in the near future, the terrain will only get worse. I have no worries, I think to myself, except that Doc has not returned. I would trade it for any of a dozen others. A red flag goes up in my mind warning me that I am treading close to another bout of depression. I force my thoughts to take a U-turn toward the day's possibilities. Maybe I'll do some deeper exploration in one of those old trunks in the attic.

In the end, I pass the day doing perfunctory chores, laundry, dusting, vacuuming, until it is time to feed and settle the animals in for the night. I am just locking the barn when the onslaught begins. Per the earlier forecast, the clouds move in swiftly and with them, the lightning and thunder. Through the side window, I see the marble-size hail that is creating the roar on the barn roof. Unconsciously, my feet take me to the back of the barn. I rest one palm on the wall.

Thunder sniffs at the floor. As if following a scent, he noses his way into the office and jumps onto the bunk where Doc spent his first night in my world. I watch as my faithful companion continues to investigate, retracing his steps coming to sit beside me. Suddenly, he moves forward. He paws at the enchanted wall and whines softly. Does he sense Doc on the other side? I hold my breath until it bursts forth involuntarily. Several minutes pass before I sigh myself into acknowledging that my loyal pup is merely mimicking my behavior. How many times has he seen me pause wistfully at this very spot?

"Time to think about dinner, Thunder." And with those words, the spell is broken.

CHAPTER 60

Two weeks have passed with little let-up in the storms. They have varied in intensity and length, several I thought equal to the storm that separated Doc and me, and the one that opened the portal when Doc first arrived. I reason that those explosions of power must have had their full force directed exactly where the barn abutted the mountain, dispelling the theory that lightning never strikes in the same place twice. It could be argued that when that same combination of strength and location unite, the portal will reopen and Doc will be ready and waiting. The thought infuses me with new hope albeit the hope that a gambler has that a one-armed bandit will pay off. What are the chances, rational thinking contends. With that downer, my mind gallops down the path to pessimism. I ransack my memory for a clue to why Doc might have changed his mind. No! No! Our conversation on the ride from The Springs, before it was cut short by the storm, had been full of laughter and anticipation of how we would handle our trans-time relationship. We talked about the pros and cons of living in each other's world and joked about the predicaments that could arise. The increasing loudness of the storm prevented our coming to a conclusion other than that we would be together, wherever that might be.

Looking back on the discussion, there is no doubt in my mind; Doc will return as soon as the weather permits; the reasonable deduction is for me to take up residence in the nineteenth century where one can pop in without suspicion. History has prepared me for what I might face. In fact, my knowledge of what has transpired in between 1882 and the present would be invaluable in so many ways. Would I miss modern technology? Perhaps, for a while, but I would adapt. Saying goodbye to the chaos and uncertainty of the modern world that lives under constant threat of extinction by a global war or the gradual poisoning by pollution of the land, water, and air would hardly be a problem. Even in my personal Eden, where daily frustrations are kept to a minimum by semi-isolation and money, I have not been able to ignore or pass off the suffering that continues to grow worldwide.

Besides, in my world, how would Doc's appearance be explained? I can just imagine his reaction to all the "red tape". How could I ask him to understand and become tolerant of the objectionable behavior that has evolved as acceptable over the decades; to adapt his code of justice to the leniency toward crimes in this modern generation? For that matter, how could I possibly hope to keep him out of jail? I picture some smart aleck yelling from his vehicle and Doc blowing a tire out with his forty-five. Even in the "make my day" state, he would soon be behind bars.

I look around me, grateful for my lot in life, yet willing to leave it all for the man I have come to love unconditionally. I had, if I think about it, made my choice on that stormy journey, but fate has postponed its implementation. Surely, it will not be so cruel as to refuse to rectify the situation. Oh why, didn't I just insist we stay in the past? If I wasn't so damn responsible, I would have done just that. Who am I kidding? Doc would not have permitted it. We were coming back to tie up the loose ends of my life in the present and he would not allow regret to mar our life together.

At the weight of my despair, my heart sags in my chest. One minute I am preparing for his return; the next I am fighting to come to grips with the fact that our personal portal has been forever closed, that its opening was a chance cosmic intersection that will never be repeated. The most

important episode in my life and I have absolutely no control.
I hate that.

CHAPTER 61

The dream is a disorganized montage of the last two years. Back in the morgue, I stare down at my father's distorted face. A tear drips from my cheek onto his. His eyes flip open in accusation. I jump back in horror, colliding into someone behind me. I turn to see, not Detective Paulson, but Doc grinning widely and holding out his arms.

"Yor mah daisy," he says. Relief rushes through me, but when I lean into his embrace, he vanishes and I feel myself falling. Before I land, I am wandering on the streets of Tombstone. It is dark and I can hear the boisterous revelry coming from the bars. I round the corner from Fifth onto Allen Street and head through the doors of the Oriental. Searching the bustling room, I let out the breath I have been holding as I see Doc playing poker at the table in one corner. I have to elbow my way through the rowdy group and when I get to the table, I find Kate is standing at his side, leaning on his shoulder, eyeing his hand. All is silent and I feel the eyes of the crowd boring into me from all directions. Doc looks up.

"Look, Dahlin', it's Cassie, that gal from the futchah." Then to me, "You may go, now." Laughter fills the room. Humiliated, I run for the exit. The doors open to bright sunlight in the twenty-first century. Doc is there to greet me with a nosegay of small white roses. I reach for them, but when I bring them close to inhale their sweetness, I find my hands are filled with small tarantulas. I scream and toss the arachnid bouquet. Doc vanishes and I am running up the road to the ranch, but now have no clue as to the century. Thunder in the distance warns of a storm. I pick up speed and run into the wall of rain. Someone is shouting behind me. The sky lights up as I turn to see Doc laboring to catch up. Coughing, he comes to a stop, drops to his knees and grabs his chest as the heavens continue to rage. I try to run to him, but my dress is becoming heavy with water and the high button shoes are slipping in the mud. After exhausting effort, I am by his side.

"We have to get back to the ranch," I scream as I try to help him to his feet."

He waves a hand, trying to catch his breath, "Ah can't make it," Doc says shaking his head. "Take care of him," he insists with urgency. I look around. The sky explodes and all goes black.

I wake to my heart beating in tandem with the pounding rain. I lie still and take slow deep breaths until it slows and when it does, I find, to my amazement, that I am completely relaxed. As frightening and unsettling as nightmares are, they are said to release one's pent up anxiety, sort of like a tightly wound coil that suddenly springs free. In any event, I am relieved to find that the horror was a product of imagination gone awry. Aside from slight nausea from hunger, I feel much better than when I retired last night. The clock tells me that I've only been asleep an hour, but it feels much longer. My movement wakes Thunder and together we make our way down to the kitchen and listen to the driving rain pummeling against the window as I pour a glass of milk and put some in a bowl for Thunder.

"This is going to be hard," I tell him. "I'm so glad I have you to wait with me."

My stomach settled, I rinse the glass and bowl and set them in the dishwasher before heading back to bed. The steady rain lulls me to sleep.

CHAPTER 62

Rays of sun are warming my face through the glass and I panic when I see lateness of the hour.

"Thunder, we have to get up!" I say in a panic.

At once, the puppy is bouncing around me. I am scrupulous about feeding the horses by six and imagine them snorting and pawing in their stalls. The goats and chickens are no doubt expressing their displeasure at the lousy barnyard service as well. I throw on a shirt, jeans, and boots and hurry down the stairs. As I near the barn, I can hear the chorus of unhappy tenants.

"Sorry, guys," I say as I hurriedly open the door leading out to the horse pen. I quickly toss the hay and alfalfa into the individual troughs before opening the stalls. I am all but ignored as the horses rush past me toward their brunch.

I release the goats next. Thankfully, they are pigmies and do little damage when they butt at the backs of my knees. The cackling from the hen house quiets as the girls clumsily tromp over one another into the sunlight to pick up the scratch I am tossing. I watch them pick at the grain and force myself to count the blessings in my life, picturesque surroundings, good friends, freedom from financial anxiety; a fairytale life, really, not to mention what I decide to file away as a paranormal encounter that few others will have the privilege of experiencing. Hunger stirs me from my

407

daydreams. My flip-flopping emotions are affecting my appetite and my strength. I force myself, for the sake of my adopted family to prepare a hearty meal.

I look at the rancher's breakfast before me and find that my eyes far have exceeded the capacity of my stomach, shrunken after several days of picking at my food. If not for a belt, my jeans would be riding on my hips. I turn on the radio while clearing the dishes.

The monsoon season is winding down. Most of my neighbors will be grateful for the reprieve from the rain and mud, while I am resigning myself to possibly another year without Doc. I am just loading the last of the utensils into the dishwasher when I see the Pruitt's pull into the drive.

"How are you doing with all this rain?" asks Nancy when I greet her and Jim at the door. "Oh my, who's this," she asks as Thunder barks by my side.

I pick up my bodyguard." This is Thunder," I say. "Morgan brought him back from his brother's for me a few weeks ago. And everything's fine," I say as we exchange a hug.

"What a cutie," she says while Jim kneels and begins to caress the fur around Thunder's head. "Say, Jim and I are headed for town. We're all out of perishables and thought you might want to hitch a ride with us, the roads being the way they are and all."

Jumping at the chance to get out of the house with some lively company, I respond quickly.

"That would be great," I say as they step into the mudroom. "Just let me get a jacket and my wallet," I say.

"John not still staying with you?" she asks as I lock up and we head to the truck.

Caught off guard, I find myself swallowing the lump that has instantly formed. "No, he had to leave a few weeks ago," I say and suddenly my stomach turns.

"That's too bad," she says. He seems like such a nice young man and we thought maybe. . ."

I cut her off before her words can rekindle the ache in my heart.

"He's well now and decided it was time to move on," I say, careful not to let the grief creep into my tone. "He said to say 'goodbye' to everyone, though." I quickly jump into another subject. "How are the twins?"

"Can't you hear them?" she laughs pointing to the truck.

"Let's not tell them about my new addition until we get back," I suggest.

"Are you kidding?" Jim says. "If we told them now, we never would get to the market." The three of us laugh.

As we approach the one-ton extra cab, Jimmy and Janet are clapping in excitement as I join them in the back seat. I listen with interest to their lively chatter, thankful for the diversion. They accompany me as I walk the aisles of the market and help me pick out fruit and vegetables.

"You probably need milk," suggests Janet. "We ran out."

"You're right," I say. "And some cheese and sour cream," I add. "Oh, and some butter, yogurt, and cottage cheese."

"I think you better buy some ice cream and cookies," says Jimmy. "You look skinny," he says.

"That's not nice," his sister reprimands.

"He's right, Janet." I say grabbing a belt loop with one thumb and tugging to accentuate the gap. "Let's stock up. We'll get chocolate, vanilla, *and* strawberry. Then we'll need to find the hot fudge, marshmallow and pineapple toppings, bananas, nuts, whipping cream, and cherries. One of you guys know how to make banana splits?" The question gets a unanimous response and I give the cart a shove toward the frozen food aisle; my appetite returning at the anticipation of one of my favorite ice cream concoctions. The twins squeal in stereo as I grab a package of chocolate cookies on the way. It's been a while since I've filled the cookie jar with home-baked.

"I've got the chocolate," says Janet as I reach into the freezer above her for a carton of vanilla.

"I'm too short," says Jimmy straining toward the strawberry on the top shelf of the adjoining column of shelfs. I hand it to him and let him drop it into the cart. Within short order, we find the rest of the fixings.

"There," I say. "I think that'll do it for me. Let's find your folks."

On the drive home, I tell the twins I have a surprise.

Jimmy and Janet take turns guessing anything but a new puppy. By the time each Pruitt grabs a bag, there are no groceries left for me to carry. When I open the door, the surprise comes bounding out. Jimmy drops to his knees, bag and all. Janet sets hers down gently before coming to kneel beside her brother. Thunder bounces from one face to the other giving and accepting kisses. I pick up their bags and we adults leave the three to play out front. Jim and Nancy know better than to turn down my offer of lunch knowing that the kids have been looking forward to dessert. Their perishable groceries are carefully stowed in a huge ice chest they carry in the bed of the truck. Reluctantly, Jimmy and Janet come in for lunch and it's everything they can do to refrain from offering their new friend bites of their sandwiches. After the proper nourishment, they and their dad play with Thunder while Nancy helps me prepare the ice cream treats.

An hour later, my company is gone and I am sitting on the sofa watching the noonday news. The outing with the Pruitts has been therapeutic, but tiring, and I stretch out for a nap.

Darkness is settling in along with the rain when I rouse. I feed and lock up the animals. I find that I am ravenous with no desire to cook. Ice cream, it is; only this time it's a hot fudge sundae.

It is just before nine when the phone rings. Power had come back on a few days ago, but the phone lines had taken a while longer to restore.

It is Morgan.

"You and Thunder doing okay?"

"Doing great; following all your suggestions. He took to the doggie doors right away. Oh, and you'd best be careful the next time you show up. He's showing his guard dog side already," I tease.

"Heard from John?" he asks sending the imaginary knife to my heart.

I feel the onset of tears and clear my throat.

"Not likely," I say. "But I'm sure he's fine," I preface before explaining the "witness protection" thing, or have I done that before?

"I see," he says. "You feeling okay?"

"Humm?"

"You sound tired and like you might have a cold."

"Oh, I had a big morning in town with the Pruitts; hard to keep up with the twins. Other than that, I'm fine," I say hoping my inflection is confirming my stretch of the truth. "Listen," I add to the deceit, "I've got a pot that's about to boil over. Let me call you back?"

Thankfully, he accedes quickly and I am able to hang up while I can still control my voice. So much for my resolve to accept the possibility that Doc may never return and to go ahead with my life. At least word will get around, and that should discourage further questioning. But for now, I feel depression once again descending.

I am not surprised when I see Morgan's name on the caller I D an hour later. I let it ring several times before picking up and feigning a sleepy voice. I apologize for neglecting to return his call, he for waking me. We agree to get together soon. When he calls the next day, I tell him he was right, that I am coming down with a cold. After ascertaining that it is nothing more serious and that I have everything I might need, he agrees to wait a week or so before calling to make plans; insists I call him if I need anything or decide a trip to Dr. Jack is necessary. I am less than pleased when he calls three days later and let the answering machine pick up. "Hope you're feeling better, Cassie. I just called to tell you that I will be out of town for the next two weeks or so; going to New York. My sister had her baby two months early and . . ."

I hear the crack in his voice and pick up the phone. "Sorry," I say. "I was just coming in," I lie. "What happened?"

"She slipped and fell on the steps outside her apartment and it sent her into labor. The baby is not quite three pounds and it's going to be touch and go."

"I'm so sorry, Morgan. I hope she and the baby will be okay."

"Yeah," he says with a sigh, "me, too. You doin' okay?"

"Yeah." I cough and sniff. "You know colds; they have to run their course. Fever's gone, though, and I'm feeling much

411

better."

"Good," he says. "I'm heading out for the airport in a few."

"What about Buckshot?"

"A friend is staying at the house to look after things. I would have asked you, but I knew you weren't feeling well."

Guilt washes over me.

"Have a safe trip and keep me up to date on your sister and the baby."

"Will do. You take care. Talk to you soon."

I hang up and resolve to stop feeling sorry for myself, but weaken before the day is done. Two days later, Morgan calls with better news. His little niece is a fighter and her prognosis has been upgraded to excellent; but he will be staying for a while to keep his brother-in-law company and then to get acquainted with his new niece. I am happy for him, yet grateful that he will be away for the foreseeable future.

Disturbing new memories have awakened since yesterday. I now recollect Morgan as much more than a helpful friend. In essence, he has taken on the part that my memory had previously assigned to Jack Johnson. I remember how bewildered I was when I came to in Jack's clinic, to find him a family man, married to Morgan's sister. Yet now, while I can still recall meeting Jack and his parents when I first came to town, the memories of a budding relationship with Jack have all but faded away. Curious. I rub my head. It's as if . . . oh wow . . . unbelievable. My memories must be slowly adjusting to some change in my personal history, but nothing Doc and I did back then could have changed my life now . . . could it? I strain to comprehend, but nothing will come. Perhaps the family diaries can enlighten me.

I think about Morgan and more of the mental mist dissipates. After initially meeting my neighbor through Jim and Nancy, he had visited the ranch several times to pitch in with muscle and helpful advice. I was secretly thrilled when he asked me to have lunch at the Thunderbird. A few days later, he suggested a tour of Cripple Creek and dinner at wonderful steakhouse. Our dates became more frequent and although, as far as my current recollections reveal, they had not progressed beyond a deepening friendship and chaste goodnight kisses, tender sentiments are tugging at my heart, sensations that I had thought to have experienced first and only with Doc. Will I wake up tomorrow with memories of a deeper relationship. I wish I knew. What must Morgan be thinking? Have I unknowingly initiated a trans-era love triangle? Was I so enthralled with Doc that I disregarded my relationship with Morgan? Oh, why can't I remember?

Morgan must be terribly confused by my lack of response. Then, again, he might be attributing it to the year's hiatus in our relationship. He must have the understanding and patience of a saint. I wonder how much he might have guessed about my relationship with Doc. How could he? He wasn't around, yet . . . I'm afraid, that unconsciously, I have been wearing my heart on my sleeve, as they say. Of course I have. I've been in a funk ever since I woke up in the present without Doc. Funny, I used to be a master at concealing awkward feelings. None of my friends or co-workers ever had reason to question that I had anything but a normal upbringing. They assumed that I was accepting of my personal appearance. Lately, it seems I am losing the battle to control my personal presentation. It's affecting me physically which, in turn, is accelerating the emotional drain. I'm entering a vicious cycle. God, is Morgan seeing all that? Perhaps, now that he knows John Hawkins, as he knows Doc, is out of the picture permanently, he is hoping to rekindle our association. My heart aches in confusion and guilt. My stomach threatens to rebel as my thoughts turn against me.

CHAPTER 63

I'm back to continuing to go through the motions of living. If it were not for the animals, I don't think I would get out of bed some days. Thunder is a constant source of joy but even his playful attention cannot dispel the ominous foreboding that engulfs me. My stomach churns with snowballing misery and the fatigue it imposes. My edited past is becoming clearer, but my time with Doc is clouding, so that in retrospect, I am no longer sure of what is real and what I may have imagined. Could I have dreamt his presence? No, that's not possible, I reason. My past changed because of our association . . . didn't it? That bump on the head, could it have generated the older memories, including finding Sarah's body? No that can't be, either. The proof that she had been murdered and hidden away is recorded in the family diaries and had that always been the case, that she had been discovered by Elizabeth, my father would have had no tale to tell of her infidelity. Finally, something tangible to which to tether my thoughts. This constant reanalysis is torture and I question my ability to endure much more.

I am just coming in from the morning chores when I hear the phone. "Miss Collins?"

"Yes."

"This is Wyatt Earp," says the voice on the other end. A flood of emotion renders me speechless. "Cassie? This is

Wyatt. We met a few months . . ."

"I know who you are." I'm not likely to forget. I know I should be friendly to the man, but I haven't got it in me at the moment. "What can I do for you, Mr. Earp?" I add curtly.

My shirtsleeve indifference does not seem to dampen his congenial nature.

"I will be out your way for a show in a couple weeks, Cripple Creek, to be specific."

"Okay."

"I just thought . . ."

"And you're ready to see the proof," I say unable to filter the sarcasm from the words before they leave my mouth. "Sorry, Mr. Earp, I no longer have anything to show you," I say. "Doc had to get back to help your ancestor; something about some unfinished business in Arizona. He wanted to come back, but it wasn't possible." I pause briefly. "Sorry," I add curtly.

"I see," says Wyatt. I can only imagine what is going through his mind. "Sorry to have bothered you," he says before breaking the connection. Is he mentally kicking himself for not following us back to the ranch after his performance; or is he sighing in relief, confident that I am a less than stable woman who fed him a flight of fancy, or worse, that Doc and I were a couple of scammers that might have caused him harm? I care not what he thinks of me. Well, now you'll never know, I think, and it serves you right. If you had only come when I asked. I could use an ally about now; someone to comfort me in my loss. An hour later, I regret my deplorable behavior and my ugly thoughts. What is happening to me? Am I doomed to become a bitter old woman? I should call him back and apologize, but choose to indulge myself by wallowing in my grief. It is not only that I probably will never see Doc again. I don't know what happened to him. Then, it hits me. Wyatt's call is further proof that Doc's visit was real.

It is when I am dusting in the study that the notion hits me. It is from my family's diaries that I was able to confirm that Doc and I had changed their history. That's it! I abort my housecleaning and head to the study and my laptop.

I take a deep breath and type in "Doc Holliday" and scroll down to "death of." How long did we extend his life? I click on the appropriate listing. This can't be right. The picture that fills the screen is that of his grave in Glenwood Springs. The dates are the same. I click back to the original listings and this time, choose Wikipedia. I scan the article. The end result is the same; John Henry Holliday died in Glenwood Springs of consumption in November of 1887.

"Nooooooooooo!!! I scream so loud I startle Thunder who has been resting on the floor beside my chair. Poor fellow does not know what to do and neither do I. Heartbroken, frustrated, and angry beyond comprehension at the same time, I manage to regain control long enough to let Thunder outside; after which I run down to the cellar; to my grandmother's room and scream off and on as loud as I'm able. "I don't understand," I yell at no one in particular and everyone in general. "It worked with my family; why not with Doc? He was healthy or well on his way to it, when he left. He couldn't have . . ." It's not long before I exhaust myself and slump to the floor beside Mother's hope chest. I lay my head on the runner, adding my tears to the decades of other stains, and sob myself to sleep.

CHAPTER 64

Today is November twenty-ninth, and I am turning twenty-eight; three months since Doc's departure; a few weeks since Morgan's return from New York. I am grateful that the subject of my birthday never came up among the locals. It's not that they wouldn't care; it's that by the time my first birthday in Colorado rolled around, Doc was here and in the throes of illness. I am sitting at the kitchen table when the familiar knock interrupts my thoughts. Morgan has been very attentive since his return from New York. In spite of vigilant effort and adamant denials, I have not been able to hide my depression and its effects. It continues to gnaw at my health and suck up my energy. This new life with all its promise holds little interest for me in light of what could have been with Doc. That, along with learning that none of it mattered in the long run for him, is draining my will to go on. Not that I'm suicidal. Nothing could make me follow in my mother's footsteps, but I just cannot seem to care about anything. Maybe I should just sell this place and go back . . . to what? I don't even have the energy to do that. I am content in my rut, at the same time, ashamed that I am not able to pull myself up by the bootstraps and embark on a new phase of life, as I did after the deaths of my parents. Somehow, this is not the same. Their deaths, while tragic and sad, had sparked positive changes in my life, instant wealth, a physical transformation, along with the relocation to what most people would consider a retirement dream. All helped to ease the hurt. Try as I may, I cannot find the silver lining behind this cloud. Nothing has changed this time aside from the history of my family, and while I am happy that Elizabeth lived and Mary was rescued from under the thumb of her cruel father, I cannot make myself see that as an equal trade for the heartache I am now enduring. Food either holds no interest for me or refuses to stay down much of the time. Maybe I will starve to death. Perhaps people will conclude that I died of a broken heart over my childhood friend, John Hawkins.

I tell myself that I should be thankful for the adventure I had with Doc; that what we had experienced was an inconceivable bonus in both our lives; something known to very few, if any others, at all.

While Morgan may harbor romantic motives, I know he is sincere in his efforts to help as a friend and will continue to do so. It's not fair to him. Even a severe case of the flu only lasts so long, and it will not be long before he surmises the truth; that, at the root of my physical symptoms, is a broken heart. My stomach churns; threatening to expel the French toast I have just eaten. I am about to lie down when I hear the knock. I rise and head for the entry, knowing it will do no good to pretend I am not at home.

"Hello Morgan," I say forcing a smile. "I'm sorry, but I'm not really feeling up to company this morning. I lean against the doorframe, making no motion toward unlatching the screen door despite the frantic urgings of Buckshot and Thunder on either side.

"I'm afraid that I have no control over the situation, this time," he says raising the box he holds in both hands. "This was delivered to my place about an hour ago by special courier with written instructions that I was to bring it to Miss Cassie Collins at this address, on this date; and that the box was to be opened in my presence. This key was in the envelope," he says waiving the small skeleton key between his fingers.

"Nice try," I say, though impressed with his creative persistence.

"Honestly, I have no clue." His shrug is an innocent one.

"Right, and you have no idea that this is my birthday."

"Golly Cassie; I wish I *had* known. Happy birthday." Although I find it hard to believe, I sense he is telling the truth.

"I don't understand," I say. I open the door and lead the way to the kitchen table as Thunder joins his pal out front. I am about to sit down. "Excuse me a minute," I say and head for the bathroom where, indeed, I do lose my toast and coffee. It is almost a relief. I splash water on my face and will myself to "buck up."

"Are you still sick?" Morgan's concern is growing with each visit. I really have to get a grip.

"I'm fine." It's not a lie, really; because, after all, if I can just get my head and heart in order, I know the rest of my body will follow.

"I understand," he says. "You've had quite a couple of years. One thing after another and you haven't really had the time to cope with things in between. Your parents, then your friend coming back into your life and having to disappear again must be hard to take. I don't want to belabor the point, but you really do need to get out and be with people again, aside from your trips to the market," he says wincing and I know he is afraid that under his prodding I might withdraw even further. "The folks around here miss you."

"I apologize for being less than cordial lately and I think you might be right. I never really took the time to grieve. It all just hit me at once, I guess." Yeah right. "I'm letting things get to me and . . ."

"Well," he says tapping on the box. "This ought to divert your attention, momentarily, at least. I'm curious as hell. I mean, why was it sent through me?"

"Who is it from?" I ask as I examine it.

"Haven't a clue," he says. "Neat old box, though." Morgan hands me the antique key. The box and its lock are quite old, but in quite good condition. The key turns easily but there is the groan of hinges as I raise the lid.

Atop the black velvet cloth that covers the contents of the box is a discolored envelope addressed to me; the handwriting distinctive and familiar. I am trembling and struggle with the flap.

"Let me help." Morgan opens the envelope, gently retrieves and hands me the contents. Taking a deep breath, I unfold the several pages and begin to read.

My Beloved Cassie,

If you are reading this, my wishes have withstood the years and uncertainty that, in spite of my explicit instructions and payment, others might not be inclined or able to follow through. In your world it should be 29 November 2015, your birthday; in mine it is my own, in the year 1940. I am about to embark on my 89th year and sense the end is near. I am not ill, but I can feel my body wearing down. I don't leave the house much anymore; my sight is going and I don't hear that well. I am, however, in the caring hands of my granddaughter and her husband and am enjoying the amusement of my great grandsons.

I feel my eyes grow. My mind is racing to catch up with the words. I read them again.

"May I?" Morgan is asking as he motions toward the cloth.

"What? Yeah . . . sure," I say and return to the halting script.

Thanks to you and your Doc Johnson, I have had many healthy years I otherwise would not have had; and once I came to terms with the fact that our worlds had been severed forever, I have had many years of happiness, as well. I tried countless times to find my way back to you, but the door into your world had vanished forever that August afternoon of 1882. I picture you in the barn during subsequent storms, waiting for that wall of rock to dissipate at my touch; but it was never to be.

I wipe the tears that are blurring my vision.

"These are yours, aren't they?" says Morgan holding up my camcorder, camera, and tape recorder. "John must have sent this stuff. That accounts for the way it came, with no return address and all. At least we know he's alright," he says with a smile that he hopes will evoke one from me. "Don't cry. What does he say?"

I shake my head, not yet willing to reveal the secret, and continue to read silently.

Sensing death at the door, I have been sorting through my personal possessions and have come across the trunk of your things that was still on the wagon when we were so cruelly parted. You were no more than safely inside before the thunder spooked my horse and I heard Little Mary and Elizabeth scream. Mary was being swept away by the wind and rain. Elizabeth was frantic that she would be lost in the storm. Thankfully, I was able to get Mary safely to the house and your family was reunited, unhurt. Believing me to be a hero, Elizabeth and Mary begged me to supper. I declined, insisting I had to keep moving. I hadn't noticed until then, that the horse and wagon were at the side of the barn. When I climbed aboard and started back toward the mountain my horse refused to challenge the wall of rock he had just come through. I got down and as I approached the mountainside, found that, I, too, was now barred from passing through as we had done several times before. I failed to grasp the full import at the time and assumed that, when conditions were right, I would be able to reenter your world. It stood to reason that I had to be available when time came, so I took your family up on their offer. They gave me shelter for several weeks thereafter. I helped out on the ranch during the day and bunked in the barn; but after every clap of thunder I would race around to see if the way back to you had reopened. After the storm season passed, and with it, the hopes of our reuniting, I knew it was time to move on. I hated to leave little Mary and I knew she would be sad to have me go as well, so I got her a puppy. It made our parting a pleasant one.

If you haven't discovered it yet, our efforts paid off in full. During our travels, Jefferson had been exposed and the bastard hung himself in jail before the law could. Soon after my departure, Elizabeth's life changed in a way we never expected thanks to a hired hand that took a fancy to her. They married and together raised Mary. Today, your great, great grandmother is living a wonderful life with a good husband. Her daughter, son-in-law, and granddaughter live in Cripple Creek.

There has never been a day when I have not thought about you, Cassie. I might have questioned the reality of our encounter but for the fact that my friends have made mention of you over the years and I have the trunk with your things safely tucked away in the attic. You, I realize, were left with nothing but memories. I recalled the agonizing frustration those first few years. I was alone in my heartache; had no one in whom I could confide. It was maddening. Now, looking back on my life, thinking about what we shared and my indebtedness to you , I realize it is within my power to repay you in a small way by sparing you some of what I went through; to unburden you of any doubt you may be experiencing. The idea in retrospect, was so simple. I don't know why I didn't think of it before, but, then again, it makes no difference, as you will get this letter on your birthday just a few months after our parting no matter when I do this.

It is my fervent hope that what I do today will unburden you of any doubt that you may be experiencing as to your sanity and my well-being. I am arranging with my solicitor to have your personal things returned to you along with this letter.

"But . . ."

"What is it?" asks Morgan as he continues to examine the contents of the box.

I shake my head and read on.

First, let me say that I have been blessed in so many ways by our encounter, not the least of which is my complete recovery from consumption. It facilitated my permanent change of identity. John Henry Holliday died and a whole new life opened up for Tom McKey. Shortly after my stay with your family ended, I had a good run at the poker tables and bought a piece of land adjoining your family's ranch, where I could keep an eye on your great, great grandmother and her aunt. After Elizabeth married John Lenwood, they continued to raise Mary and stayed on the ranch until her marriage. Mary chose a good man in Jonathon Bartlett. I made a point to discourage previous suitors who I deemed unworthy of her, and was honored to give away the bride.

Their daughter Emma married Frank De Long a few years back. Your grandmother, Miriam just turned four and is the cutest thing; calls me Uncle Tom.

As for me, I found love again, as I pray you will do, and married in the spring of 1885. You would have liked Sallie Mae. She was a lot like you. We had nearly 55 happy years together until her passing this past spring. Our son, Morgan Wyatt, died defending his country in the "war to end all wars." As I learned when I was in your world, it will not live up to its name and, again, our country finds itself on the brink of a far worse conflict with weapons that make those of previous conflicts pale in significance. How I would jump at the chance to fill this Hitler fellow full of lead. Alas, my jumping days are over. It was one thing to have read about the horrors of wars that involve so much of the world; it is quite another to live in their wake. I think of the day when the Japanese will all but destroy our navy in Pearl Harbor, and thank God I will not be alive to see it. I thank Him, too, that my daughters, Melanie and Cassie, whose husband survived that first world conflict, have produced only female offspring.

All this may be quite a shock to you if you have checked history since your return and found my death report unchanged. Let me explain. As the date of my original demise approached, I made a decision that would insure me a peaceful life. I made my way back to Glenwood Springs and found a doctor who would, for a healthy sum, purvey the record of John Henry Holliday's death on the appropriate date. We signed an agreement that held dire consequences for us both if confidentiality was ever breached. Ergo, as far as history is concerned, my original legacy remains unchanged.

Thanks to your library and the hours of television, (which, by the way, is just getting off the ground now), I observed during my recovery, a knowledge of the future that has enabled me to invest wisely and become a very wealthy man. Sallie Mae and I have traveled the world. Friends and acquaintances marvel at my good fortune, suggesting I have the "Midas touch". In addition, although not completely unscathed, my family and I have avoided many a potential tragedy.

My wish for you is that you, too, live a full, happy life and that you find love again. I am living proof, make that historical, proof that it is possible. I am forever in his debt for the miracle Dr. Johnson performed in my behalf. Even today, medical science is sorely equipped to treat sufferers of tuberculosis.

I doubt that the contents of this box will be of value other than to assure you of your sanity and comfort you, knowing that I have had a most glorious life. Who knows, perhaps a few years down the road, our travel through time will become part of everyday living, and you will be able to share our experience without fear of being carted off to an asylum. Whatever the case, I have paid handsomely to ensure that this box and its contents will be legally secured through the years in the hands of my solicitors and their successors. Inside you will find your photographic and other electronic equipment. I am hopeful that they will have withstood the deterioration that can come with age; that the evidence of our time together remains intact. I've included other mementos, as well, in hopes of bringing that beautiful smile to your face.

Again, if my directives were followed, this box has been delivered to you through a family representative who will be able to verify through included documents that he or she is the progeny of John Henry (Doc) Holliday. I am hopeful that any blood of mine will take this as welcome news and that you will be instrumental in easing the shock. And remember; there's no normal life, Cassie. It's just life. Get on with it. Love again and love well.

    Forever yor daisy,
    Doc

I reread the last paragraph, then clutch the letter to my chest. I want to laugh, cry, scream, all at the same time.

"Well?" Morgan shrugs. "Ready to tell me what this is all about?" Spread on the table between us are my tape recorder, camera, and camcorder. "What did he have to say? What's this guy trying to pull?" He places a package of what is still discernable as trail mix. No wonder our ecology is threatened, I think. Modern day packaging refuses to decompose. "Look at this," Morgan says as he pulls a contact lens case from the box and tosses it among the other items. "Oh please; give me a break," he says in exasperation, lifting out a lock of ash blonde hair tied with string.

Without thinking, I snatch the tress from him and touch it to my cheek.

Morgan shakes his head. "Do you know where he is?" I nod in acknowledgement. "I guess you'll be going to meet him?" he adds in a tone of resignation.

"One day," I say. Suddenly I am warm inside and find myself smiling through the last of my tears. I look across at Morgan, searching beyond his confusion for a glimmer of resemblance. Maybe the ears?

"What are you going to do? You're obviously in love this character. Although, I swear; I don't know what you see . . . I mean I never met the guy but —"

"I see you," I say much too abruptly.

"What on earth are you talking about, Cassie?" He reaches to touch my brow with the back of his hand. "No fever. I think that bump on your head . . ."

I hand him the letter and then paw through the box for the documents Doc referred to in his letter. Among the other mementos he spoke of is a roll of cash, several coins, and poker chips, dating back to our travels in 1882. There is a small leather pouch containing a broach I remember admiring while shopping in Gunnison with Josie. Clipped into the delicate piece is a note: *Josie handed this to me just before we left and asked me to give it to you on your next birthday.* I smile at her thoughtfulness. There is a deck of well-worn playing cards. Another pouch holds Doc's diamond pinky ring and pocket watch. I close my eyes and bask in the memories, completely forgetting Morgan until he shoots up abruptly sending his chair crashing to the floor and the pages of Doc's letter parachuting from on high.

"Is this some kind of insane joke?" he demands, clearly unaccepting of what he has just read. "This man does not belong in witness protection; he belongs in an asylum for the chronologically insane." I cannot help but chuckle at the label. "What? You have been pining over this lunatic for weeks and you find this funny? What kind of a person creates a fantasy like this at the expense of other's feelings? Are you in on this? Is this your way of completely killing our relationship, making me think you're mentally unbalanced? Fine, you're a nutball?" Coming to my senses, I realize Morgan is serious and deeply annoyed. "I'm outtah, here," he says with disgust as he rights the chair.

"No, Morgan! Wait! I know this must seem crazy, but —"
"But what?"
"There's proof," I say, remembering what I had first been searching for in the box. I scramble through the contents and find it under another layer of velvet. Morgan is still shaking his head in frustration as I empty the envelope onto the table. Quickly, I spread the papers, desperately searching for irrefutable evidence.

"Look," I say, pulling out an old tintype. In it, Doc is seated alongside a woman. Standing behind them is a young boy and girl. Seated on the woman's lap is baby. On the back, in Doc's handwriting is this note: Mr. and Mrs. Tom McKey, Melanie, Cassie, and baby Morgan, 1891. I remember imagining my blood turn green when I met Kate on the stagecoach, but there are no feelings of jealously as I look upon this couple and their family. Morgan takes the photo and sinks back into the chair. Although grainy, the photograph is without question, of the man I passed off as a witness-protected John Hawkins. A marriage license and birth certificates are among other documents before us, as is the agreement made between Doc and the physician who signed his premature death certificate. There are several other photographs of the children and a newspaper article from 1916 with Morgan McKey's obituary. There are pictures of the next generation, and also several of our two families together, many of which Morgan recognizes from old family albums. Included is a newspaper from four years earlier, its bold headline announcing the sinking of the Titanic, with a note scribbled in the margin. *Had one hell of an argument with Sallie Mae when I refused to let us sail back home on this unsinkable ship on her maiden voyage. In a different hand are the words; Glad he won.* I see the spark of recognition in Morgan's eyes. Although he had never seen this clipping, he had been told the story. I listen in wonderment as he relates the tale of his great, great grandparents arguing over taking the Titanic home after touring Europe; how his grandmother had refused to speak with her husband for a whole week; until they got the disastrous news, of course.

"All this proves is that he got into my house while I was gone. How else would your friend get my family's things?" In spite of this evidence, Morgan is not ready to accept the truth. His tone is indignant and demanding.

While he stews and continues to paw through the contents, I retrieve my wallet and pull out the snapshot of Doc and myself that I carry there and hand it over to him. This is Morgan's first glimpse of John Hawkins, the moniker I assigned him, aka Doc Holliday, aka Tom McKey. "This is a picture of my friend," I say. "I passed him off as a childhood friend who had been put into witness protection. It was a story I made up because we couldn't tell anyone the truth; that he was Doc Holliday from another time. Don't you see? He didn't steal these things; they belonged to him."

I can almost see the scales falling from Morgan's eyes. "But this . . . this is . . ."

"I know, impossible," I say softly.

"Why is it that in a year's time, I never met your friend? I was traveling a lot, but it just seems that we would have crossed paths at some point."

I ponder the reasonable query for a minute or two before the equally logical explanation comes to me.

"You didn't exist," I answer cautiously, "until Doc returned to the past a healthy man and was able to have a family." Even as I utter the explanation, I am trying to wrap my mind around it.

Morgan is speechless but returns to right the chair and seat himself. Head in his hands. "You know what you're suggesting is preposterous."

"How else do you explain this?

427

Morgan raises a finger. "Wait a minute," he says as he walks to the phone. "This should be easy to clear up once and for all. Are *you* ready for the truth?" When I nod, he pulls out his cell, then punches in a number on the land line. "Yes, this is Morgan Jamison. I need to speak with Mr. Corrigan. It will only take a minute, and it's urgent." After a brief interlude, "Hello, Mr. Corrigan. Yes, I'm fine, just a little confused . . . But Morgan is cut off by the voice on the other end. He listens for several minutes, his facial expression evolves from confidence into disbelief, and finally resignation. "Thank you Mr. Corrigan. No . . . no problem. Thanks . . . no that's all. Talk to you soon. Yes, you, too; goodbye."

"Who's Mr. Corrigan?"

"He's the family lawyer," he says shaking off what I hope to be the last of his doubts. "Seems he was expecting my call," Morgan says pausing as if to let what he has just heard settle in his mind. I have no trouble empathizing, as I have been there many times in the recent past. He swallows, before going on. "He just confirmed that this box has been passed down from the time of his grandfather who started the firm. The files indicate that it was entrusted into its care in September of 1940 by Tom McKey, my, great, great grandfather. While his instructions made no sense at the time to Mr. Corrigan's grandfather, the $10,000 retainer sealed the agreement. Mr. Corrigan assured me that the box was locked in the safe when he joined the firm almost fifty years ago. He had heard the story of its receipt directly from his grandfather, and was hoping to be the one that would be able to see it to its ultimate destination. He's curious to know . . ."

"You're not going to tell him?" I panic.

"Are you kidding?" he says resuming his seat. He puts his hands palm to palm against his mouth, elbows on the table. I can see the emotions bouncing around behind his eyes. "But how . . ."

"This is not the half of it," I venture.

He looks at me in disbelief. "Lay it on me," he says, throwing his hands up in the air. He continues to stare at the evidence before him and the irrefutable testimony of his lawyer.

"You can't imagine what *I've* been going through; not being about to tell anyone what has been happening around here."

Sensing that Morgan may need a little alone time, I say, "I could use a little fresh air." Heedless of my mental relief, my stomach is still refusing to settle.

"I'm for that," he readily agrees helping me on with my jacket. Guess not. The weather is getting cooler, now, but the day is picture perfect. We sit on the stoop. Buckshot and Thunder seem to sense the seriousness of it all and settle at our feet. Over the next two hours, I relate the tale, starting with finding Doc in the barn and the both of us coming to the realization that we were caught in some kind of supernatural occurrence. "He was in desperate need of medical care, and I made up the only story that I thought would fly to keep him under the radar." I then proceed to fill Morgan in on Doc's and my ventures into the past to save my ancestral aunt from being murdered by Great, great, great grandfather Fielding and to exonerate Sarah. I told him about finding her body in that dank hidden room, and how everything transformed once Doc and I moved the safe. Morgan had heard about our excursions in this century once Doc was on the road to recovery, but our trek into the past is news.

"You mean you met . . ."

"Yep, Warren, Wyatt, and Josie in Gunnison, rode on a stagecoach into Tombstone with Big Nose Kate, dined with Sheriff Johnny Behan, was hit on by Ike Clanton, stayed at Nellie Cashman's boarding house; and was treated by Dr. Charles Goodfellow." Morgan shakes his head and I add, "If they survived the years, the pictures should still be in the cameras. I recorded some interesting conversations on the tape recorder as well." Morgan chuckles and I have the feeling, at this point, I could tell him I had been to Mars and back and he might just consider it.

We head back into the kitchen. Morgan picks up the fallen pages as if they are sacred documents and looks from them to the spread of items on the table.

I feel compelled to include the full extent of the relationship between Doc and me. "You nailed it. I fell for him," I tell Morgan. He says nothing. "I was devastated when that portal closed. I have spent every thunderstorm since checking the back of the barn, waiting for his return." I say after detailing that last day with Doc.

"Do you think . . . I must say, I would love to meet the man, then, again, I don't relish the competition."

"Hey, don't sell yourself short. I was only his girlfriend; you're his . . ."

"Hey, yeah," Morgan lights up. "I've got *Doc Holliday's* blood running through my veins," he says turning his hands palms up. "Too bad we can't tell anybody."

I concur. "Not even your family."

"Never," he agrees, "but at least *we* know it." We laugh in stereo and I am thinking how wonderful that, thanks to Doc's quick thinking, I finally have someone with whom to share this greatest of all secrets. Hand in hand, we make for the study. After replacing the batteries and hooking up my camera to the computer, I pray that the pictures can still be extracted. When prompted, I select the destination of the contents and name the folder. Morgan and I watch as the files are being transferred from one device to the other. I hold my breath as I open the folder that contains over a hundred photos taken during the last few weeks I spent with doc. Morgan is not alone in gasping as the images pop up on the screen. Technically, they are poor from a photographer's standpoint. Forced, on most occasions, to shoot from odd angles so as to keep the camera out of sight, rarely was I able to get clean shots or center my subjects. Doc had learned to operate the equipment and would have made a great spy. Individually, the photos might be disputed but, as a group, they leave no doubt, and the fact that they and the videos have been transferred directly from the camera and camcorder, argues against the possibility of photo-shopping. There are pictures of me with Wyatt and Josie, Warren, Johnny Behan, Big Nose Kate, Bat Masterson, and, of course, the notorious Ike Clanton. In addition, there are many shots of Gunnison and Tombstone as they were in 1882. We snapped pics of Pueblo and Colorado Springs as well. My camcorder is filled with scenery and clips of conversations.

Morgan let's out an overwhelmed sigh.

"Let's save the tape recordings for tomorrow. I say we get out of the house and go down to The Thunderbird for dinner. I need food and space."

.

CHAPTER 65

Over the next week, Morgan and I review the pictures, films, and audio recordings, while I provide commentary. We have information on which historians can only speculate, in many cases erroneously. After sating ourselves on the contents of Doc's box, we turn to my family diaries and delight to read Mary's and Emma's accounts of their interactions with Tom McKey and his family over the years.

At Morgan's house, we begin to pour over his family heirlooms that are scattered about the house. His forebears were not diary keepers, but they didn't throw much away; and a lot of family lore had been passed down verbally through the generations. Morgan has a library of stories in his head and we hope to put together an even clearer understanding of the McKey family, much of which can be explained by the influence of the infamous Doc Holliday. A particular treasure is an old chest full of letters written to the family by friends and family members that had moved away, including several letters from the McKeys to their grown children during their extensive travels.

Today, we move up to the attic. Like my own, Morgan's is chock full of tangible objects attached to memories. I cry as he pulls one of Doc's coats out of an old trunk. I carefully take the gray wool and bring it to my face. I swear I can smell Doc beneath the must and mothballs. Within minutes, I have extracted several recognizable pieces of Doc's clothing. As we continue to maneuver through the relics of the past, we are like kids at Disneyland. Each box reveals something memorable. It is hard to stop for lunch, but I can't go on. Between the stale air and the hunger, I am still feeling a little woozy, but my refreshed emotional state has had a positive effect on my physical health. Once we make our way downstairs, I check on the mutts who are sleeping peacefully inside the screened–in porch. They wake at my appearance and join us in the kitchen.

"I doubt that I would ever have gone through all this stuff if not for . . . I don't quite know how to label what's happening," admits Morgan as he prepares us BLT's.

"And I never thought I would meet another affiliate of the Doc club, let alone a blood carrying member," I laugh.

In spite of our excitement, we take our time with lunch before returning to the attic. We have one last corner to explore. A half dozen boxes are stacked on a large trunk. All are covered in decades of dust. The boxes contain books, old newspapers, greeting cards, baby clothes, and other memorabilia. It will be such fun to examine each piece and find the story behind it. I begin to dust the old trunk. It is faded and its leather straps are shredding with age.

"Oh my God," I gasp. My heart leaps inside my chest as I struggle to loosen the latch.

"Here, let me get that," Morgan says. Eagerness is spreading to every nerve, and I have to fight to remain patient. In the end, Morgan has to go for a screwdriver and hammer to release the rusted hardware. I hold my breath as I strain to lift the lid that creaks and groans under the disturbance.

"My things!" I reach into the trunk for the hat that flew out of its box when Doc and I collided outside the dress shop in Tombstone. It and its trimmings have faded with time. The dresses, wraps, hats, and purses he purchased for me at Ellie Carson's shop in Gunnison; they are all there. Carefully, I position the hat atop my head and take a deep breath.

"Very flattering," says Morgan. He lifts out one of the dresses. I stand, take it from him and hold it up against me, swaying back and forth. "Look here," he says guiding me in front of the proverbial free-standing full length mirror that seems to be stock in trade in old attics. "Hold that pose," he adds. Less than a minute later I see him approaching from behind, clad in Doc's coat and one of the hats we found earlier. He comes to stand next to me.

"I never thought I would see these again," I say, tears forming.

"Hey, Cassie; just think of all the fun we're going to have. You don't think Doc would want us to be sad, do you?"

"I'm not sad . . . I don't know quite how to describe how I'm feeling . . . but, it's definitely not sad. It is funny, because what we learned today confirms Doc is never coming back to this world. When I first suspicioned that, I didn't think that I could go on; but now, ironically, I am strangely at peace with the fact." Morgan doesn't comment, just stands and waits.

"It's as if I have another new chapter opening in my life," I say as I reverently fold the dress and replace it and the hat in the trunk. Suddenly I am too overwhelmed to dig further. The day has been both exhilarating and draining. I look up.

"I'm all in, Morgan." He smiles and crosses the room to return the hat and coat while I close the old trunk. I am pushing on the lid to help myself up when a strange sensation starts to creep up behind my ears and . . .

.

CHAPTER 66

Morgan and I will celebrate my birthday this year as man and wife.

John Henry Holliday Jamison started to crawl last week and is into everything. He is the spittin' image, as they say, of his half-brother by well over a hundred years, Morgan Wyatt McKey. We learned he was on the way when Morgan rushed me to Dr. Jack after my swoon in the attic. After recovering from the unexpected diagnosis, Morgan and I did some fancy verbal footwork in the doctor's office before we left with the congratulations of our confused friend.

"I know I'll never be Doc, but you have to admit that you're not going to get any closer and he did tell you to love again. I think he'd approve." Morgan had said when I was speechless at his proposal on the drive home. "Sleep on it."

I had slept and dreamt on it. Doc stood at my bedside that night, looking a bit perturbed at my indecision. "It's not hard, Dahlin'. When I came tah the understandin' that it was not in the cards for me tah return tah yah mahself, I made sure to send a replacement. Morgan is my gift to yah and little John Henry. Grab that good man an' make him yor own."

EPILOGUE

It has been exactly a year since we first opened Doc's box. We keep it locked away in a fireproof safe along with an album of the photographs we printed. I pull them out every so often to remind myself of my paranormal adventure. Perhaps, one day, the world will come to appreciate the supernatural as not so super; sort of like discovering the world was not flat after all. Morgan and I will be able to tell Little Doc, as we call him, all about his real father, and it will seem the most natural thing in the world. Maybe we will find a way through the portal again and . . . A girl can dream. In the meantime, the three of us, and maybe more, will live as Doc intended.

Little Doc is napping and Morgan, Buckshot and Thunder are on a hay run. The ranches are one now. We live between the two houses; an unusual arrangement, but one that suits us. Neither Morgan nor I can bear to part with Doc's home nor the portal site through which he entered our world for that brief period that was to change our lives and his forever. Twice a year, on the dates of his birth and death we place daisies on the grave within a small natural rock citadel on the McKey ranch. Carved into the interior wall per his wishes in his will, are these words, "Tom McKey: 1851 – 1940: A man who lived on borrowed time."

My musings ignite a sudden compulsion to sort through

Doc's things for the umpteenth time. My hands are shaking as I lift the box from the protection of the safe. Reverently, I place the items on the table before me and reread his words. I turn my attention to the photographs we took while traveling in the past and my heart swells in the memories of my friendship with Josie. I remember the fun Doc had at maneuvering Wyatt and himself into positions where I could snap photos of the two without raising Wyatt's suspicions. As I focus on the image, I am reminded of a loyalty seldom seen these days, even among friends, a loyalty that faced death for another without question. Quickly, but carefully, I return Doc's legacy to the safe. My heart is hammering and I nearly trip on my race to the kitchen phone. Impatiently, I scroll through the directory. It's still there. I hit the speed dial and pray the call is answered.

"Hello," says the cheerful voice on the other end.

"Mr. Earp." I take a deep breath. "This is Cassie Jamison . . . I mean Collins . . . I mean it was Collins when we met . . ."

"Yes, I remember; you, Cassie and that delightful young man who —"

"I have something to show you, now, Mr. Earp."

ABOUT THE AUTHOR

Jacklin Kimkris resides in Tombstone, AZ. <u>On Borrowed Time</u> is her first published novel. Contact her at:

jacklinkimkris317@gmail.com
or
P O Box 632, Tombstone, AZ 85638